WHO DO YOU TRUST?

KIRSTY FERGUSON

Boldwood

First published in Great Britain in 2021 by Boldwood Books Ltd.

Cover Design: Nick Castle Design

Cover Photography: Shutterstock

A CIP catalogue record for this book is available from the British Library.

Paperback ISBN 978-1-83889-899-1

Large Print ISBN 978-1-83889-898-4

Hardback ISBN 978-1-80162-568-5

Ebook ISBN 978-1-83889-901-1

Kindle ISBN 978-1-83889-900-4

Audio CD ISBN 978-1-83889-893-9

MP3 CD ISBN 978-1-83889-894-6

Digital audio download ISBN 978-1-83889-897-7

Boldwood Books Ltd
23 Bowerdean Street
London SW6 3TN
www.boldwoodbooks.com

For my Nan and Pop, Natalie and Ted. Always guiding lights through the darkness.

1

The dark-haired woman sat in the passenger seat of the old station wagon drumming her fingers along the arm rest. Dana was slightly annoyed with her husband, Logan, for making them late. She glanced in the back seat at their four-year-old daughter, Kelsey, who had fallen asleep, mouth open, summer sunlight streaming in on her pretty face. They were driving out to Dana's parents' property on the other side of town and they were running behind schedule. Looking out of the window at the bush bordering either side of the road, the sun glinting off the barbed-wire fences, Dana was reminded of her idyllic childhood. The rolled-down window allowed the sounds of the bush, trees groaning together, birds cawing overhead, the scent of the earth, to permeate the car.

Logan drove down the rutted driveway towards the house, pulling up in a cloud of dust. Dana followed him as he took a still-sleeping Kelsey from the back seat and carried her into the spare bedroom. She watched as her husband laid her on the bed gently. Dana then kissed Kelsey's forehead softly and left the door ajar so she could hear if she called out.

Logan considered his job done and didn't help Dana unpack the car, leaving her to carry in the camp chair, the salads and Kelsey's bag. All Logan cared about was getting his cooler full of beer into the back yard where his brother-in-law, James, was already setting up his chair. He had positioned himself downwind of the BBQ where Dana's father, Robert, was grilling hamburgers, sausages and onions for lunch, while her mother, Mischa, cut and buttered rolls, putting them in a colourful bowl on the wooden table that sat under the shade of the veranda.

'Hi, Mum, Dad,' Dana said as she hurried through the front door, giving them a kiss in turn, then hugging her mum awkwardly with one arm, a potato salad wedged under her other arm.

'Let me take that for you before you drop it,' her mum said, grasping the purple container and putting it on the table. Things were still strained between Dana and her mother, but Dana viewed the BBQ as a chance to repair, to heal the wounds she carried. Logan was supposed to be an emotional support to her today, but it looked as if he was going to be no help as he was already getting drunk with James.

'You're late, love. Lunch is nearly ready. Thought you'd gotten lost,' her mum said, pointedly looking at the table already covered with food.

'Sorry, Mum, someone just *had* to finish watching the game.' She threw her husband an exasperated look. They'd argued for half an hour before they'd even left the house. She knew Logan loved her, Dana had never doubted his love, not one bit, and he was a great father, but sometimes she wanted to wring his neck. Dana had wanted to leave on time to arrive before her mum and dad sat down to eat.

'It's OK, you're here now and that's all that matters. Have you said hello to your sister yet?' her mum asked, striving for casual and failing. She looked at Dana through her lowered lashes, not able to meet her daughter's penetrating gaze. Dana knew how hard this was for her mum, knowing the part she had played in their bitter argument, but Dana was ready to try and work through it with her.

Brushing away a stray hair that had caught between her glossed lips, she replied, 'No, I haven't seen her, must have missed her when I was coming in.' That was a lie. Dana had seen her younger sister, Alesha, but had ducked out of the back door before Alesha had seen her. She was delaying their meeting as long as she could because the last time they had seen each other, three months ago, Alesha had said some very unkind words to her. It had ended in a full-blown fight, where Alesha had unleashed years of pent-up resentment on her. Dana had had no idea her sister felt that way and was still hurt, but they were both here today because their parents had asked them to be. Mum and Dad were trying to stage an intervention on neutral territory, to make the sisters bury the hatchet. Dana could appreciate that having their daughters fighting was hard on them both, but they weren't exactly blameless in this either. But Dana knew that the time had come to mend fences.

The two sisters had never been very close – Dana had the impression that Alesha was a deeply unhappy woman, stuck in a life she didn't want. She believed that was why Alesha's emotional outburst had been so aggressive towards Dana that day. In an attempt to distract herself, Dana looked towards her husband, in his element, acting as though he hadn't seen James for a whole year instead of several months. They were unlikely friends from the outside – James was a lawyer and Logan a plumber – but it worked somehow. Their loud laughter carried across the yard, reaching his still annoyed wife.

Dana's thoughts were interrupted by the back door slamming. She turned slowly and saw Alesha frozen two steps behind her.

'Hey, Dana,' Alesha said quietly, both of them aware that every eye was upon them. Dana felt the hush of the afternoon, the pressure to do something other than stare silently at her sister.

'Hi,' she eventually settled on. Non-committal yet still polite – no one could accuse her of being rude.

Alesha assessed her reply, small frown lines appearing between her light brown eyes. She seemed almost defeated, her shoulders slumped, eyes pleading with her sister. Dana didn't know what to say next and, without warning, Alesha stepped forward and folded her older sister into her arms. Dana stood stiff for a long moment, wanting to punish Alesha for her hurtful behaviour, before eventually putting her arms around Alesha and hugging her back. After what Dana considered an appropriate amount of time, she stepped back, severing the connection, straightening her top. Dana caught her mother's eye; her mother smiled at her and mouthed, *Thank you.*

Of course, it wasn't as easy as that – they weren't just going to hug it out and all would be forgotten. No, those devastating words would always crowd out the space between them, always be remembered, but, for their parents' sake, Dana would let it go, for now. Yet she knew she would never forgive Alesha.

'So, how have you been?' Alesha asked Dana in a stilted and formal voice.

Dana replied, 'I'm OK, we're OK, thanks.' Speaking to Alesha was much harder than she'd thought it would be. How were they supposed to just go back to what they were before? There had been so much said, and so much more left unsaid. None of them could retrieve the words that had been hurled through the air that day three months ago. They would have to find a way to move forward from here on; Dana was at least willing to try to move past the ugliness.

'That's good,' replied Alesha, kicking the ground with her left toe, her brown hair sweeping across her face as she ducked her head down, unable to meet her sister's gaze.

There was an uncomfortable silence, which Dana eventually broke by saying, 'Well, I'd better go see if Dad needs any help.'

'Give her time,' she heard her mum say to Alesha quietly as she walked away.

Time. Was there ever enough of it?

Dana took a deep steadying breath and was heading over towards her dad when she was called over to where Logan sat on his chair.

'What do you want, Logan?' she asked, a little irritated. He could have at least offered to help her bring in their things from the car or asked her dad if he needed a hand grilling.

''Nother beer would be nice,' he said, smiling and shaking his empty beer can at her. James just laughed.

Dana silenced James with a glare. 'And one for James too,' Logan said, turning to grin at his brother-in-law, who looked at Dana sheepishly before his gaze slid away from her frustrated expression.

Wife glared at husband, a silent battle of wills raging between them. 'C'mon, babe, I'm thirsty and I love you.' The two had no connection to each other whatsoever but when he held out his hand, she came within range of him, and he rubbed his thumb over her fingers. They both knew, no matter how he behaved, she was still under his spell, as she had always been.

Nodding, she walked over to the cooler, which, when she opened it, had five or six cans of beer fewer already. Clearly Logan was settling in for a big session with James. Her dad didn't drink, so he wouldn't be joining in. She looked over at her father, tall with grey threaded through his brown hair, tending the grill. Dana sighed and picked up two cans, one in each hand, and walked slowly back to the men, who reached out greedily, popping the tops and taking a gulp each. Logan sighed with contentment, dropping his empty can on the ground by his chair where there was a pile gathering already.

Dana was glad someone was content. She was thirty-two weeks pregnant and really should have been resting up, but here she was, running after Logan. She loved him deeply but sometimes she felt as if he were just another child for her to mother.

Turning, she locked eyes with her sister, who had come back outside and given her a hesitant smile, which Dana returned. Yes, it was time to mend fences. Kelsey appeared at the back door, rubbing sleep from her brown eyes.

'Kels!' Logan boomed, making the little girl jump in fright. 'Come give Daddy a hug.' He was slurring his words slightly and talking way too loudly, laughing at nothing, a sound that carried across the grass and made Dana wince with embarrassment. Sober Logan was considerate, loving and helpful, but when he drank like this, he was basically useless to her. More than useless, he was a burden, one she didn't need right now.

Kelsey looked at her dad, then at Dana, and chose to run to her mother rather than her father. Watching him take another long pull on his beer, Dana worried that Logan's drinking was getting out of control. He was a manual labourer, a plumber by trade, and she understood that part of that job was socialising with the boys after work. But a couple of drinks at the pub often turned into a few more, and then Dana was called to come and pick him up as he was too drunk to drive. She resented being a taxi service at two in the morning, rousing Kelsey from her bed, but it was better than him driving home drunk and killing someone or himself. And at least he was a jovial drunk. He put wet kisses on her face that smelt of beer and grabbed her bum hoping to get lucky. She had to admit that sometimes it worked.

Dana could see her mother waving her over to the table she was setting. She walked slowly over to her, Kelsey at her side tugging on her clothes tearfully. The little girl was getting too big to carry and her weight pushed against the baby bump uncomfortably, but she was usually clingy when she first woke up. Dana's ankles were killing her, threatening to buckle with each step as she carried Kelsey to the table; her back felt as if it were broken in two and sewn back together the wrong way round. This pregnancy was proving more difficult than her first and she couldn't wait to welcome their little one into the world. Kelsey hadn't wanted a brother or sister at first and Dana guessed she might be feeling displaced, so she was doing everything she could to reassure her that the baby would be loved equal to her.

Popping Kelsey onto one of the wooden bench seats, Dana asked, 'You OK, Mum?' Mischa had her beautiful brown hair caught up in a large clip today. She was, as always, made up and beautifully dressed, even for a BBQ in their back yard. Dana looked down at herself, her flowing dress reaching the ground, the most comfortable one she owned. She was a pretty woman, holding her own as she aged. Long glossy black hair, brown eyes, and a slim figure – well, usually, when she wasn't close to giving birth. Dana's figure had bounced back after Kelsey was born and so she hoped it would be the case with this baby. They hadn't found out which sex it was, although Dana was secretly hoping for another little girl while Logan was leaning towards a boy.

When they found out they were pregnant again, they were ecstatic. Dana wanted to emulate the childhood she'd had with her parents and sister, and Logan, well, Logan had had a shitty childhood. His father ran out when he was young and his mother couldn't cope so Logan wanted to break the cycle and give his child the stable home life he never had.

One evening Dana had been at her parents' house and having a heart-to-heart with Alesha about family life. Her sister and James had chosen not to have kids as both of them had very lucrative professional careers that neither of them wanted to give up for a baby, or so Dana had thought. But, while drunk, Alesha had confided to Dana that she was very jealous of her. When Dana had asked why, Alesha had inclined her head and said, 'Because you have everything, and I feel that I have nothing. Just my job and a disinterested husband.'

'Disinterested? How do you mean?'

Alesha had sighed. 'We haven't had sex in over a year and I think he's having an affair with his secretary. How clichéd can you get?' Alesha's laughter had been brittle and bitter. It was the most Alesha had said about her marriage in years.

Dana guessed she was lucky. She had a husband who loved her and who provided well for his family, and then there was Kelsey, the light of her heart. She felt badly for her sister and when she'd tried to broach the subject a couple of weeks later, Alesha had brushed it off, saying she didn't want to talk about it any more. Dana hadn't pushed but had looked at James differently after that. Was he really cheating on Alesha and, if so, what was she going to do about it? Dana wondered what she would do if her husband ever cheated on her, but she couldn't imagine a scenario where that would happen.

Dana looked over at her beautiful little girl as she sat at the table next to her nan. Kelsey was quiet, munching on a bread roll, her nan fussing over her, putting a plate in front of her to catch the crumbs and a napkin over her lap so she didn't ruin her pretty party dress.

'Mum, I just have to make a quick call to Pippa, back in a sec. Can you please watch Kelsey?'

'Of course, love.'

Dana moved to the other end of the veranda, out of earshot, and rang her best friend. 'It's not as bad as I thought,' Dana said when Pippa asked how it was all going. 'We haven't spoken about it and Mum is trying hard to keep the whole day upbeat. Dad has his head in the BBQ and Alesha said hi to me, gave me a hug and everything. It was awkward but at least she's trying.'

'And Logan? Is he supporting you?' Pippa asked, knowing how he could get when he drank.

'Not really. He's drinking with James, seems to be ignoring everything else as usual.' She looked over at her husband, connecting with his hazel eyes before turning her back on him. 'You know how he gets when they're together.'

'Yeah, I remember,' said Pippa. She was part of the family and had spent many afternoons out at Dana's parents' house eating and drinking with them.

'Mummy!' yelled Kelsey. Dana could hear tears in her voice.

'Shit, I've got to go, talk later.' She disconnected the call. 'What is it, sweetheart?' she asked, walking back towards the table.

'Where's Boo Boo?'

Shit, the damn bear. They must have left it in the car. She had asked Logan to pack it – it was the one thing she'd asked of him.

'I don't know, love. Are you sure it's not in the spare room? Maybe he dropped on the floor?' Dana asked, worried that Logan had indeed forgotten it and it wasn't just discarded in the car somewhere.

Kelsey shook her head, little arms crossed, a tearful look on her face. 'How about I check the car?' Dana suggested.

'All right. Mummy, please find him,' Kelsey said in that sweet yet insistent voice, the promise of a tantrum in her tone.

Dana knew if they didn't find him, Kelsey wouldn't settle and would cry and sulk the whole time, becoming more and more upset. Dana grabbed the keys from her bag and went through the house, unlocking the car as she went out of the front door. She checked the boot first as that was where all the stuff had been stored. Then the back seat, hoping that Kelsey had dropped the bear on the floor. He wasn't there either. With a sinking heart she checked the front seat. No Boo Boo. The most important thing after Kelsey was that damn bear and they'd left him at home. How would she tell her daughter they'd forgotten him? Someone, meaning her, would just have to drive home, find him and bring him back to her. Dana trudged back into the house slowly, not wanting to meet the hope-filled eyes of her daughter. She couldn't believe the stupidity of her husband, allowing the one thing that calmed their daughter to be left at home.

Kelsey was sitting with her nan, on the very edge of the bench seat, legs dangling, unable to touch the ground yet. 'Mummy, did you find him?'

'I'm sorry, baby, he must have been left at home by accident.'

2

The bear had belonged to Kelsey since birth, a present from her doting nan and pop, and now all Kelsey wanted was Boo Boo. If she didn't get what she wanted her bottom lip would quiver and her eyes would water before she launched into heart wrenching cries and ear-piercing screams. Kelsey was crying up a storm and it didn't look as if she was going to stop any time soon. When Kelsey cried, everyone knew about it.

'Logan, you forgot to pack Boo Boo,' Dana snapped at her husband as she changed course, walking over to where he sat. 'That was your only job.' Dana was pissed off and Kelsey was working herself up into a fury. Not a good start to the afternoon. It was going to be stressful enough without this on top of it. It made Dana weary just thinking about what was to come.

Logan burped loudly in response, scoring him a fist bump from James, who sat beside him in a matching sky-blue camping chair.

Logan looked up at the squall coming from his daughter but stayed sitting in his chair, content in the knowledge that his capable wife would handle it.

'Darling, can you have one of Nan's toys for today? Boo Boo will be waiting for you when you get home.' She tried to placate her daughter, but she was having none of it.

'I want Boo Boo.' Dana pulled Kelsey close to her, smoothing down her hair, yet the little girl continued to wail and Dana looked at her mother over the top of Kelsey's head.

Alesha came out of the house carrying a Bavarian cheesecake. 'What's all the racket, young lady?' she asked, trying to inject cheerfulness into her voice.

'We forgot to pack Boo Boo. I'm going to have to drive home and grab him now,' Dana said, disentangling herself from Kelsey's strangling hug. 'Honey, I'll be back soon. I'll bring Boo Boo with me, OK?' Kelsey pouted for a moment longer, then smiled. For Dana to see her daughter smile at her like that meant everything.

'How 'bout I watch her while you're gone?' Alesha offered, meeting her eyes. Dana hesitated. She was torn. On one hand, Alesha was a responsible adult, not like her inebriated husband, but on the other, they still weren't on the best of terms. Could she trust her? Dana looked over at Logan, who was onto his sixth or seventh beer, she had lost count, then back at her sister. Alesha loved Kelsey, she would look after her – besides, her mother and father would be there too and home wasn't far away. Surely Alesha could handle Kelsey for half an hour or so. The sooner Dana went home and brought back the bear, the better.

Dana, Logan and Kelsey lived in a small cottage in town, which would be too small when the baby was older. Dana had already begun boxing up some stuff to go to charity for when they eventually moved house. Their current place was quaint, a real fixer-upper. It had old patterned lino flooring in the kitchen, threadbare carpet in the lounge and was stuffed with furniture, pieces Dana had collected over the years. None of it matched, but somehow it worked.

'OK,' Dana said hesitantly. 'Thanks for that.' Alesha was fiddling with the salad bowls, rearranging them. 'Just keep an eye on her,' Dana said, worry in her voice.

'Mmm, I will,' Alesha said quietly.

'Logan!' Dana shouted, walking across the grass to where he sat surrounded by crushed empty cans. 'I have to go back home. Kelsey is upset because you forgot Boo Boo,' she told him, reiterating that he was the one who forgot the bear. Logan was looking at James as if to say, *crazy wife,* but she was having none of it. She didn't care if she embarrassed him in front of his friend. 'You need to keep an eye on her and Alesha. You too, James. Kelsey's an escape artist and she'll run off. Logan,' she said, snapping her fingers in front of his unfocused eyes. God, how much had he had to drink? 'Watch your daughter,' she said before angrily striding off as fast as her body would allow her to move. Grabbing her handbag, the heavily pregnant woman walked through the front door, passing her dad's old dog, Max, who lifted his head as she went by him.

Dana slid awkwardly behind the wheel of the car, stuffing her stomach into position so she could drive. She would have to give up driving shortly, as she was already having trouble. Kelsey only went to nursery once a week and Pippa had offered to drive her until after the baby was born. Dana had a few loose ends to tie up before the baby arrived. The cot had been set up in their bedroom, as Kelsey had the other room and there was no way a cot was fitting in amongst the toys, doll's house, bed and dresser, but she still didn't have bottles, nappies, the little things.

Dana sat in the car for a moment, enjoying the complete silence. She couldn't even hear the birds singing outside as she cranked up the air conditioner to full, the cool air blasting her hot face. She was covered in a light sweat just from walking around in the heat.

Dana put the automatic car into gear and reversed out of the marked parking spot. She was always careful when driving, especially with Kelsey in the car, and since she had got pregnant she'd become even more cautious, worried about both her children. She touched the accelerator a bit too hard then felt the car shake and shudder as it moved backwards. It felt as if she'd hit one of her father's damn rocks. A horrible thought flew into her mind. What if she'd run over Max? Her dad would never forgive her. She put the car into park and got out to see what she'd hit.

Pushing the door open with her swollen foot, Dana heaved herself from the car and walked around the side, bending down as much as she could to check if there was anything under there, but she saw nothing. Hand on the body of the car, steadying herself, hoping she didn't see the dog, she moved towards the back of the car, out of breath just from this small act of walking and bending. She bent forward, bracing herself with her hands on her knees until she saw it. Yes, she'd definitely hit something. Groaning and holding her stomach, she bent further down.

Suddenly she began to scream, so loudly that the birds in the trees above flew from where they were perched high in the branches. Still screaming, Dana put her hands on the boot of the car and started trying to push the heavy old station wagon, but it wouldn't budge; her stomach pulled and cramped, hurting her, but still she struggled, her breath coming out in short pants. Dana dropped to her knees, pebbles digging into her tender flesh, and reached for Kelsey's arm, pulling hard, not caring if she pulled it out of the socket, as long as she could get her out from under the car.

She screamed over and over, her voice cutting through the silent afternoon. Finally, her family heard her cries. Her dad was the first one out at the front, crashing straight through the fly wire door.

'Dana, what's wrong?' he asked, terrified. 'Is it the baby? What are you doing on the ground? Get up, that's no place for a pregnant woman.'

'Kelsey's under there! Help me!' she shrieked as the others ran out of the house, joining the group that stood watching her, unable to comprehend what was happening.

Her father bent down then stood back up; all colour had drained from his face. 'Sweet Jesus. Call an ambulance.' When no one moved he yelled, 'Call a fucking ambulance!' He dropped to his knees, then his stomach, sliding under the car, something that Dana couldn't do. She cried as she watched him assess the situation, his years of paramedic training kicking in. He checked Kelsey's pulse, then wriggled back out from under the car. He squatted beside Dana.

'Sweetheart,' he said quietly, 'she's gone. I'm so sorry.' He put his hand on his daughter's arm to comfort her, but she shook it off.

'No!' she screamed. 'Help me!' She clambered to her feet awkwardly and began trying to push the car again. 'Help me!' she yelled to her shocked family. 'Fucking help me!'

Her father put a hand on her arm again. 'She's gone, Dana. She's gone.' He began to cry, gut-wrenching cries that scared her. Her father didn't cry. There was silence from her family; even Logan stood there, his face slack with shock. Uncomprehending.

Dana looked at her father's face, with all her heart not wanting it to be true, but, deep down inside, knowing it was. 'Daddy,' she cried before falling into his arms, sobbing uncontrollably.

She could hear the sounds around her, the buzzing after the complete silence. She wished she couldn't. She wished she could lie down with Kelsey and never wake up again.

'Oh my God,' cried her sister finally, clinging to James for support. He smoothed down her hair and said soothing words to her. In that moment, Dana hated her. Why was she crying? It wasn't her baby stuck under the car, crumpled like a discarded rag doll.

She turned and locked eyes with Logan, who for a moment stood rooted to the spot before being nudged forward by James. She could tell from his face that his beer buzz was completely gone as he looked at the car, then stared at his pregnant wife. He took two steps forward, reached out and caught her just as she collapsed into his waiting arms.

* * *

Dana was lost in a world of memories. She and Kelsey were having a tea party, just after she found out that she was pregnant. Dana was squashed into the small wooden chair so she could drink imaginary tea and eat imaginary fairy cakes. She was wearing a pair of glittery pink fairy wings, as was Kelsey, and they were having a wonderful time.

'So, Kels, how would you feel about having a baby brother or sister?'

'What for?' her daughter asked in her sweet voice.

'Does that mean you don't want one?'

'I love you, Mummy,' Kelsey said, pouring a cup of imaginary tea for Dana and herself.

'I love you too, honey, but I have to tell you something. You *are* getting a baby brother or sister. Mummy and Daddy are having another baby.'

Dana waited for her delighted reaction, but instead, Kelsey replied, 'I'll hate it.'

'Kelsey,' she said as her little girl jumped up from the table and shot out of the door, crying.

'I'll hate it!'

Rising to her feet, Dana walked down the hallway, peering through doors trying to find her. It took a while but eventually she found the little girl hiding under her parents' bed. Dana bent down, then got onto her knees.

'Honey, why are you so upset? This is a good thing. You'll have someone to play with.'

'I just want to play with you,' Kelsey said, her eyes round and brimming with tears.

'Come on, crawl out from under there.' She did, little bits of fluff clinging to her glittering wings. 'There will be some changes, but I think you're old enough to handle them – you're a big girl now and I'm going to need help from you, OK? And besides, I'll always have time to play with you.' Dana was worried now but she had a while to work on Kels and prepare her for the arrival of the baby.

Dana remembered that a week after that conversation she had bought Kelsey a baby doll that cried, needed to be fed and have her nappies changed. Dana thought it would help Kelsey prepare for what was coming. But Kelsey had left the doll in the corner and piled other toys on top of it so she didn't have to see it. Dana kept pulling it out and placing it on her bed and Kelsey kept hiding it again. One day when Dana had found the doll, its arms had been ripped off.

When she'd shown Logan, he'd just laughed.

'Jesus, Logan, take this seriously! Look. The arms have been ripped off. Aren't you worried about this at all? Kelsey refuses to acknowledge the fact that we're having a baby and won't listen to me when I try to talk to her about it. She even ignores my growing stomach. She treats me like I've got the plague or something.' Logan laughed again. 'This is so not funny. What happens when the baby comes and, God forbid, she hurts it?'

'Oh, so now she's a psychopath who hurts babies?' Logan's eyes had crinkled as he smiled, teasing her.

'Logan, be serious. Maybe you could try talking to her, you know, properly, without me being around to cloud the issue.'

'Fine.' Dana stayed in the bedroom while he stomped down the hallway.

'Kelsey?' she heard him call. 'Where are you, pumpkin?' He was gone for nearly forty-five minutes and when he came back, he looked less cheerful.

'Well?' she asked. 'What did she say?'

'She feels like she's not going to be loved any more, by you.'

'What?'

'Obviously the way you've explained the baby coming home spooked her into thinking that you'd only love the baby. She feels that you'll spend all your time with him or her and won't have time for tea parties and fairy wings. I did my part, it's up to you to convince her now.'

'Well, did you let her know that that isn't the case at all?'

'I told her she could always come to me if she was worried or unhappy about anything.'

'Gee, thanks, make me look like the shitty parent and you the hero.'

'Fuck, Dana, what do you want me to say? I did what you asked, I tried to make her feel better about the baby being born and I'm still copping flak.'

'You're right, I'm sorry. It doesn't matter which one of us she speaks to, as long as she's got someone.' Dana walked over, running her hands through Logan's hair, tilting his head down so she could reach his lips. 'I love you,' she whispered.

'You too.'

It had taken another three months of cold shoulders, lost hugs and *I love yous* before Kelsey started coming around. One day it was as if she had just resigned herself to the fate of having a sibling and broken the stand-off when she hugged her mum and said, 'The baby can come live with us now, Mummy.' Dana was so relieved, she cried.

'Kelsey, I love you and I'll never stop loving you, no matter what, OK?'

3

Dana woke slowly, the sights and sounds coming into focus, bit by bit. Her head ached as if she had the mother of all hangovers but, of course, she hadn't been drinking. She felt the baby kicking behind the skin of her stomach, a constant pummelling, as if trying to enter the world weeks too early. Something was wrong, she could feel it. Behind closed eyelids, she saw the flashing blue and red lights, the strobes of colour making her eyes hurt. With her eyes still closed, she reached out a hand to feel where she was and, rather than in a comfortable bed, where she was lying was hard, unyielding. She was on the ground, but not yet ready to face the world.

'Dana, open your eyes, love,' her mother whispered urgently. Dana could hear screaming, someone, a woman, was screaming. Why? She recognised her sister's voice. Why was Alesha screaming? Had something happened to her? Was she OK?

She felt the hand touching hers shift, replaced by a strong, firm one that gripped her almost painfully. She wanted to say stop, but her tongue was stuck to the roof of her mouth, a lump in her throat, blocking any noise from passing her lips into the warm air. The breeze washed across her face, moving her long black hair over her cheek. Just as fast as it settled, it was brushed away by a loving hand. She felt deep inside that she didn't want to know what was going on and took these last few moments to stay in the nothingness where she knew no one and nothing could hurt her.

She parted her eyes a crack, the light blinding, the red and blue colours blurry, but she recognised that they were from an emergency vehicle. Was someone hurt? She tried to remember but it was as if her mind had been wiped clean of any memories.

'That's it, sweetheart, try to open your eyes.' It was her husband speaking. He was tender, loving and not at all slurring his words. Was it the next day? Had she been asleep for that long? Her eyes felt sewn together, as if she were trying to stretch the stitches that held them fast.

She swallowed the lump in her throat and whispered, 'Logan?' with a voice that was hoarse, her throat sore.

'Oh, thank God. I thought... I thought...' He couldn't finish his sentence and that frightened her. She had never heard him at a loss for words before. But here he was, bent over her, unable to talk.

Dana forced her eyes open wider, the sunlight stinging them. She was indeed on the ground, Logan beside her, grasping her shoulder. She looked up at him; he was crying, quietly, his eyes red raw, his face pale underneath his tan. He looked... despondent... heartbroken.

'What is it, Logan? What happened?' Dana asked. She cleared her throat but the pain remained. Why was it hurting? Logan helped her into a sitting position and she looked around her hesitantly. She was at the side of her parents' house, a fence and a gate sectioning off the back yard from the front yard. Something tugged at her memory. She looked at the faces of the people standing around her. Without exception, all of them were crying. *What had happened?*

'What is it?' she asked again. 'Tell me.'

'They said we should wait,' her mother whispered, as if afraid to break some spell.

'Who is *they*? What are you waiting for?' Dana felt weak as a kitten, unable to hold herself up without Logan's support. Why were her family acting so strangely?

Family.

Kelsey.

Dana scanned their faces, looking for one in particular, one absent from the group. She tried to remember what had happened, but failed.

'Where's Kelsey?' she asked, the seeds of fear beginning to grow.

They all stilled, as if made of stone. No one spoke, no one met her eyes or answered her question.

'Is she asleep again?'

'No, Dana... she...' Logan couldn't finish his sentence. He tried again as she looked up at him, wanting the truth, desperate for it. 'She's gone, honey,' he eventually whispered, tears pouring down his face, his hand swiping across his cheeks to dry the tears.

'Gone where?' She couldn't understand what he meant. Someone had taken her somewhere?

'Dana, the car...'

It came back to her in flashes: the bear, Logan drunk, Alesha, Kelsey, reversing out of the drive, hitting something.

Oh, God! No!

Dana staggered to her feet much quicker than a pregnant woman should be able to, flinging off her husband's hand as he tried to grab her. Her family stood in shock; no one thought to catch her. She burst through the side gate, running as fast as she could, holding onto her stomach with both hands, stumbling but managing to stay upright somehow.

Her car, halfway out of the drive, was stationary, no longer idling. She could see the flashing lights clearly now. They belonged to an ambulance. The back end of her car was covered in a black tarp, pegged to the ground. Logan, running up behind her, grabbed her arm, trying to pull her backwards, away from the car, but he was no match for her as she took a step forward.

'What's underneath the tarp, Logan?' she demanded as she turned to face him, the tears already coursing down her face. *She knew.*

'Dana...'

'What's underneath the tarp? Say it!' she screamed. He jumped a little at the sudden noise as the paramedics looked over at her.

'You know what's under the tarp,' he said softly, trying to take her hand.

She screamed, the sound tearing itself from her raw throat, bursting into the air with the force of a hundred birds flapping their wings in unison. She ran forward. A paramedic tried to restrain her but she pulled free of him and dropped to her knees, crawling under the tarp, flattening her stomach as much as she could, her knees resting painfully on the ground, but she barely noticed. She craned her neck to see her, reaching out her hand to find a smaller version of herself lying still on the ground. So *still*. Kelsey was never still.

Her daughter. Could this be happening? Was this real? She must be stuck in a nightmare, but even as she bit into the flesh of her own lip to wake herself up, she knew it was real.

She began to scream Kelsey's name until her voice broke, just like her heart. Eventually they came for her. Logan and her father. The tarp was pulled back to allow them to pick her up from the dirt.

'Leave me alone,' she whispered furiously, wanting nothing more than to lie beside her little girl, to hold her hand in hers. But they persisted, almost dragging her back inside the house and pushing her unyielding body onto the couch. Her eyes glazed over and she started to zone out. Her mother asked her if she wanted a cup of tea. What a ridiculous fucking question, one she couldn't and wouldn't answer, so her mother wandered away.

She heard a truck coming down the driveway and she stood up, crossing the room to the window. Logan wasn't quick enough to stop her from looking. It was a crane truck – and then it hit her. The truck was coming to raise her car so they could retrieve her daughter's lifeless and crushed body from beneath the wheel.

Her car.

She did this. *She* killed her little girl. The sadness kept on coming. She couldn't catch her breath and began to gasp for air that wouldn't come. She clawed at her throat, leaving deep grooves in her skin, sure that she was choking to death. Would it really be so bad to die? She'd be with Kelsey again. The baby inside her kicked, a reminder that he or she still needed her to live. Logan grabbed Dana's hands and pulled them from her throat. His voice sounded far away, as if he were talking through a windstorm, the words torn from his mouth and thrown away like leaves in the summer breeze.

'Panic attack...' she saw him mouth. *Panic attacks passed; grief never did.* Grief would be her lifelong companion from now until she died.

She heard the car being lifted, metal creaking; it sounded like tortured thunder to her ears. She couldn't watch as they removed the tarp. She did not want her final view of her daughter to be... that. She would remember her with fairy wings, pouring her a cup of imaginary tea. She half smiled at the memory from her dream, before allowing herself to be guided back to the couch where her mum made her a cup of tea, putting it on the coffee table in front of her.

Dana heard the truck reversing and she knew that her car was being hauled away. She didn't know what they'd do with it, but she knew she never wanted to see it again. She hoped they crushed it and turned it into a cube where all her misery could reside. Dana needed to go home. There was nothing for her here any more. She just wanted to sit, alone in Kelsey's bedroom surrounded by her things, and cry. Her shell collection, picked from various beaches where they had camped over the years; her favourite doll, Emma; her pink unicorn that her nan had given her three months ago, one for which she still hadn't settled upon a name so it was just Pinky. Now it would never be named. And, of course, Boo Boo.

'Take me home, Logan,' Dana murmured, standing up so quickly that her head spun. He stood too and she leaned on him for support.

'I'll drive you home soon,' her father announced, and for a moment she couldn't think of why he would be driving them home at all. Then she remembered. Would it be like this forever? A moment of forgetting, only then to be slammed with the truth? It probably would be, and she deserved it.

'Let's go, Dad.'

He looked pained. 'What is it?' she asked wearily, unable to take much more.

'It's just... Kelsey. She's still there, love. They haven't... finished yet.' He looked distraught at having to say the words out loud, his figure hunched, his complexion grey, seemingly years older.

'Oh.' She didn't know what else to say. They were all looking at her as if she would break down but she knew she couldn't, not again, not until she was home and alone, surrounded by the shells, the doll, the unicorn, Boo Boo. Dana sat back down, her head held in her hands, elbows resting on her knees. Boo Boo. This all started because of that damn bear. But she couldn't think about that now or she might start screaming again and not stop this time.

Dana lay down on the couch, her head in Logan's lap. Finally her husband said, 'Let's get you home,' sitting her up and guiding her by the shoulders as he steered her towards the front door. By the time she stepped out onto the veranda, the emergency services were gone, the truck was gone and her daughter was gone. Time seemed to have both stood still and sped up.

Her mother, Alesha and James had come out to see them off. They murmured their goodbyes, kissing her on the cheek, gave her gentle hugs as if she would snap under too much pressure. Her dad slid behind the wheel of the car and Logan folded her into the back seat, buckling her seat belt up for her. She grabbed his hand, stopping him from leaving, and looked up at him desperately. The distraught mother opened her mouth but no words came out.

'I know,' he said. 'I know, sweetheart,' he sighed, closing the door.

4

Logan opened the door of their house and ushered her inside. Her dad held up a hand in farewell, a grim set to his lips as he drove away. The house was quiet, too quiet. It all looked different now. It seemed tiny, suffocating. Her furniture, the eclectic style that she had cultivated, annoying rather than pleasingly quirky. Suddenly she needed everything to match. Order in her now chaotic world. Logan helped her to the kitchen table and she sat automatically. He left her alone and she played with the salt and pepper shakers, smashing them into one another over and over. They were shaped like love hearts.

Smash, smash, smash.

The salt and pepper shakers broke, white grains spilling onto the small wooden table, and pepper scented the air. It took her a while but she realised that Logan hadn't come back in yet. She stood, the world tilting alarmingly for a moment. She righted herself by placing a shaky hand on the table.

'Logan?' Dana called softly. The house wasn't that big, he should have heard her, but he didn't answer. She kicked off her shoes and padded down the hallway. He wasn't in their bedroom, or the bathroom, or the lounge, that just left Kelsey's room.

She pushed open the partially closed door. He was sitting on the bed, Kelsey's bed, holding Emma, her favourite doll.

'What are you doing in here?' she demanded.

He turned, eyes swollen, tears trickling down his cheeks. 'I just wanted to be close to her.'

'You don't belong in here.'

'Dana, I was just—'

'Get out!' she screamed. She saw the stunned and hurt look on his face, but she couldn't seem to make herself stop. 'Get out, get out, get out!' She began tearing at her hair and would have pulled it out had he not grabbed her hands and ripped them from her head. He grasped them tightly between his.

'Calm down!' he yelled in her face. She could tell he wanted to yell some more but he quietened himself, trying to show restraint towards his grieving wife. 'Calm down,' he said again, this time softly. He pulled her into his arms and hugged her.

'This is all a nightmare. Tell me it's a nightmare, Logan, please,' she whimpered.

He kissed her on the forehead. 'I wish I could. All I want in the world is to do this day over. To have Kelsey by our side, where she's meant to be.' He kissed her again. 'I'm sorry.'

Dana nodded, not trusting herself to speak. 'Let me make you some tea,' he said.

'I don't want tea,' she whispered, yet she allowed herself to be taken back into the kitchen. She sat on a wooden chair with a floral cushion on it. Kelsey's chair. The cushion was so the little girl could reach the table to eat with them. Something she would never do again. Logan came back with a cup of tea in his hands, which sat on the table untouched until finally he spoke.

'Do you want to go for a sleep?' he asked, blowing the steam off his cup of tea.

'I don't think I can ever sleep again.'

'OK.' He looked away, unsure of what to say next. She didn't blame him; she didn't know either.

The baby kicked and she spilt her tea in fright. She had actually forgotten that she was pregnant for a moment.

'You all right?' Logan asked.

She gave him a look.

'Stupid question, sorry. You spilt your tea,' he pointed out uselessly.

'Baby kicked,' she murmured.

'Could I feel it?' he asked. She wanted to tell him no, to go to hell. That they'd lost a child today and, no, he couldn't touch their other one, but then she looked at him, really looked at him. His eyes red from crying, he seemed smaller somehow and she felt pity for him.

'Yes,' she said quietly. She turned in her chair and positioned his hand on her belly. She could see the material moving with the baby's feet as they pushed against her skin. Dana and Logan looked at each other, one child lost, one soon to be born. How were they supposed to get through this?

'You look exhausted and this stress can't be good for the baby. Please go lie down, even if you don't sleep, it's better than this... this sitting around waiting for something, anything to happen.' He rubbed a hand over his grief-stricken face.

She tried to smile, but it didn't feel right. It felt as if she were plastering over a gaping wound that would never heal. It fell from her face even as Logan returned her smile. After hesitating, he too stopped smiling. They were just two people who had no fucking clue how to act and how to be around each other any more. Dana began to cry. Logan looked at her before reaching out and awkwardly patting her on the shoulder, as if he was now incapable of touching her with his former ease.

Lovers separated by tragedy.

They should be leaning on each other, but Logan had left the room before his wife had even stopped crying. Dana heard the back door close and the shed door open. He began hammering something, she didn't know what and, right now, she didn't really give a fuck. She wanted to go into Kelsey's room, to touch her things, to be alone. It was all she had of her girl now. As she walked towards Kelsey's room, she passed the framed photos that hung from the walls. Smiling family shots, close-up photos of Kelsey at all ages, professional photos from when she was a baby. Dana's whole life had been about her daughter. She loved being a mother to such a sweet little girl. So caring, so smart, so loving. She wondered if she was still a mother if she'd lost her daughter or would she only become a mother again when the baby was born? She looked down at her swollen stomach and, for a second, she hated the baby within her because it wasn't Kelsey.

How could she think like that? This baby was a miracle, it would save her.

The baby would give her something to live for because, right now, she just wanted to die. To lie on a steel table linking hands with her daughter. Her heart felt hollowed out and she wondered if she was mentally and emotionally capable of being a mother again. The baby kicked. He or she was very active, had been for the past few weeks. It served as yet another reminder that it was there, that it needed to be loved, to be taken care of.

The bedroom door beckoned her. Dana grasped the door-frame tightly, not sure now if she could cross the threshold. She looked around at the room; it was tidy, the bed made and covered with a pink throw that Kelsey's nan had knitted for her. She wondered, if she touched it, if she'd feel Kelsey. With a hesitant step, feeling as if she was crossing the invisible line of life and death, she entered the bedroom.

Logan had thrown Emma onto the bed, not where she belonged, in the little wooden chair ready to drink tea with her friends. How many times had Dana squashed herself into those chairs, drinking imaginary tea and talking about dolls, teddies and playing with the beautifully crafted wooden doll's house that Pop had made her for Christmas? Kelsey had loved it; her eyes had lit up with surprise and joy at the gift. Dana's father had even made a table for it to rest on, painting it green and adding little flowers and trees, and her mother had provided the furniture and the outfits for the little dolls that lived there.

Dana made her way across the room and bent down, looking inside. Some of the furniture was crooked so she put her hand inside to straighten it, hesitated, then pulled it back out, not wanting to disturb anything. Kelsey was the last person to touch just about everything in this room, and it needed to stay the exact same way. So Dana just stood there, looking at each treasured possession in turn. Taking in each carefully selected toy, the curtains she'd made herself, fairy material, the pale pink accent wall, the throw pillows edged in lace. It was a fairy paradise and Kelsey had loved her room, asking if she could have a pink wall when they moved again. They wouldn't be leaving here now. This was where her daughter had lived and died, all the memories of her short life were here.

Dana jumped when someone touched her on the shoulder. So lost in her thoughts, she hadn't heard Logan come up behind her. He stood back, hands held up in front of him. 'Sorry, I thought you heard me coming.' He looked apologetic and for a long beat she stared at him, wondering if she should slap him or not for intruding. 'What are you doing in here?' she demanded, not wanting him inside her sanctuary.

'I called for you, but you didn't answer so I came looking for you,' he explained. It sounded reasonable but she wasn't in a reasonable mood. Logan turned and left the room, Dana trailing behind him. She took one last look at the room and she closed the door.

She followed him back to the kitchen and went and sat down on Kelsey's chair again, making circles with her feet, trying to stretch the tight muscles in her calves. She saw Logan look at her, obviously noticing where she was sitting, but he didn't say anything.

'I was thinking we should get pizza for dinner,' he said quietly.

She looked at him as if he had said, *Let's assassinate someone.*

'What?' Dana asked in shock, unsure that she'd heard him correctly.

'Pizza. Obviously you aren't able to cook and we need to eat. You need to eat; you've had a shock and you need to keep your strength up for the baby.'

There were so many things wrong with that sentence that she didn't know where to start.

'Logan, I didn't have a *shock,* I lost my little girl. She died today. And I don't want to fucking *eat!*' She yelled the last word, wishing the salt and pepper shakers weren't already broken; she would have hurled them at the wall in anger. 'How can you even think of food at a time like this?'

'Everyone grieves in their own way. I lost a daughter today too.'

'Well, you're not acting like it,' she said cruelly. She was beyond angry, desperate to hurt him as she was hurting. She was convinced nothing could compare to a mother's love, and, therefore, a mother's loss. There was just no way he could understand what she was going through.

'You're not acting rationally. If you don't want pizza, then don't eat it, but I'm ordering dinner,' he said, pulling out his phone.

Finally, something else to smash. As quick as she could, which wasn't very quick, she leaned towards him, reaching out her hand to grab the phone. He held it above his head out of her reach. 'What the hell, Dana?' he demanded. He pushed her away, hand on her shoulder. He shoved her harder than he meant to and she fell back into the chair, which wobbled alarmingly. He looked stricken with guilt, his face creased, haggard and lined. 'Dana, I'm so sorry,' he began.

'Save it,' she said quietly, eyes narrowed, her mouth thin and set. Dana stormed off, holding a hand on the top and bottom of her stomach, something not lost on her husband. She could see the remorse on Logan's face, but she didn't care. Their daughter had died, and he'd shoved his pregnant wife? *Charming.*

Kelsey's broken body flashed before her eyes and she stifled a sob. How could she possibly live with herself after what she did? But she was pregnant, she had no choice but to go on living, even if she didn't know what that looked like any more.

Dana headed to the bedroom that she shared with Logan in their cosy two-bedroom home, but it now seemed way too small for the two of them, the space crowded out by their collective grief. She thought about changing her clothes, but she couldn't face it, it was too hard and she felt exhausted just thinking about it, and there was no way she was asking her husband to help her dress. She grabbed her pillow and the spare blanket from the wardrobe then walked into the lounge, throwing her pillow on the end of the couch, followed by the blanket. She flipped back the blanket and clambered under it awkwardly, feeling huge and cumbersome, thrashing about until she found a position that was almost comfortable, on her side, with a cushion under her stomach to hold it in place. It was only six in the evening but as soon as she got herself settled; she felt her eyes drooping. She tried to keep them open; what if she forgot what Kelsey looked like while she was sleeping?

She fell into a deep sleep, waking briefly when the doorbell sounded. *Damn him, he's ordered pizza,* she thought before falling back into such a deep sleep that she might have been unconscious.

* * *

Someone was shaking her shoulder gently. She bolted upright, the baby kicking its disapproval immediately. Logan was squatting beside the couch.

'What is it? Is it Kelsey?' she asked, frightened that there was something terribly wrong. Why was she on the couch? Had Logan been snoring again?

A pained look crossed his face. 'Honey, don't you remember?'

All of a sudden, it came back to her and she tried to suppress a cry. 'It wasn't some horrible nightmare?' she whimpered, wiping at her watering eyes.

'No. It wasn't. Kelsey is gone.' His face was full of compassion and he tried to touch her again, then he registered the look of anger on her face and withdrew his hand. He stood up. 'What is it?' he asked.

'You're dressed for work,' she said in an accusatory tone, eying him up and down.

'Yeah,' he sighed. 'I can't sit around here all day; this house is full of Kelsey. I need to get out and work will take my mind off... things,' he finished weakly.

'I cannot believe you're actually going to work today of all days. We lost our daughter yesterday. You can't go back to work like nothing happened. What will people think?'

'I don't care what other people think.'

'Then what about me? Do you care about me at all?'

Logan rubbed his hand over his greying whiskers. 'Of course, I care about you. I just can't stay here. I've called your mother to come and be with you. She agrees with me that I should go to work. She'll be here in twenty and I'll be home in time for tea.'

'More pizza?' she asked bitterly.

He didn't even bother to answer, just walked into the hallway, grabbing his keys and slamming the front door closed behind him. He hadn't even kissed her goodbye. Was this the way things were now?

Dana threw back the blanket, padding into the kitchen.

She put the kettle on to boil, knowing that her mum would want to make her a cup of tea just to have something to do. The white noise of the kettle almost drowned out her thoughts, but not quite. She rewound yesterday's memories, trying and failing to make sense of what had happened. Everyone at the BBQ knew she was going home so how the hell did Kelsey end up behind her car? She thought of the jolt as the car ran over Kelsey and rushed to the sink, vomit spewing from her. She coughed, her stomach heaving again and again. She had had nothing to eat, so it was just bile, but her stomach kept spasming painfully.

The little girl must have come through the side gate and for some reason stood behind the car while Dana fastened her seat belt, not seeing her. Dana's stomach churned and she gripped the edge of the sink, vomiting again, mouth filling with disgusting-tasting liquid. She spat, clearing her throat and wiping her mouth on her sleeve, then rinsed her mouth. She went into the bathroom and looked at herself in the mirror. She was pale, sweaty, her eyes empty and haunted. Already, the stress and grief were taking their toll on her physically, etching themselves onto her face. She brushed her teeth, her only concession to personal care.

She didn't brush her hair, wash her face or get changed. Her long black hair was a tangled mess; she'd tossed and turned in her sleep, stuck in an endless loop of seeing her daughter wedged under the car. Thank God she hadn't seen her face in real life, but in her dreams she saw it in all its gory detail. She had heard her father use the words *closed coffin* with finality. Could this really be happening?

There was a small and timid knock at the front door, as if her mum was afraid to break the silence in the tomb-like house. Dana opened the door.

Her mother was well dressed as always. She was wearing make-up and fancy shoes with tassels on them that moved jauntily as she stepped inside the door. Dana moved back to allow the immaculately put-together woman to squeeze past her. Dana didn't care that she looked a mess. She didn't give two flying fucks what anyone thought.

Her mother followed Dana into the kitchen before Dana dropped into Kelsey's chair, wanting to feel some sort of connection with her daughter. Her mum immediately said, 'Why don't I make you some tea and a piece of toast?' As if tea and toast were going to solve her problems. But she let her mother do her thing. She seemed to need to keep her hands busy.

'Why are you here?' Dana asked.

'What do you mean?' her mother replied, placing a slice of bread in the toaster, pushing the lever down.

'I mean, why are you here? I don't need a babysitter, you know.'

Her mother's painted lips pursed in a thin line. 'Logan asked me to come over. He wanted to make sure you had company in case you wanted to talk.'

'Talk? Haven't we done enough of that already?' Dana was

being deliberately antagonistic, trying to get a rise from her mother but she wouldn't budge.

Three months ago, Dana had found out a life-changing secret, one that they had kept from her for nearly four decades. And now, losing Kelsey was just one more thing dividing them, and Dana wondered if she and her family would ever reconcile again.

5

That fateful day had been a beautiful summer's afternoon. Dana, Logan and a very happy Kelsey had been invited to spend time with her parents, Alesha and James at their property. Pop had promised Kelsey a ride on the tractor so she had been ecstatic and couldn't wait to go. In fact, she had been pleading with them to go early for an hour, pouting and begging in equal parts. It had got to the point where Logan had said, 'Let's just go, it won't matter to your parents if we're early.'

Kelsey had whooped with joy, her tiny face breaking out into a huge smile. They had loaded the car with everything they needed, including Kelsey's favourite toy, Boo Boo. As they walked into her parents' house, Dana went into the kitchen, bags rustling noisily as she loaded them onto the bench. Logan and Kelsey stayed in the lounge room, so they weren't in the kitchen to overhear the conversation going on outside. After hearing her name, Dana peeked out of the window. Her parents, Alesha and James sat under the veranda in the wooden chairs that looked out onto the large expanse of grass behind the house.

'So, we're definitely going to tell her today? No putting it off any more?' asked her father, looking at no one in particular.

Her mother shook her head, her brown hair dancing in the breeze. 'It has to be done now. She needs to know the truth. Although I am worried how she'll take it. Maybe it's not the right time.'

'Mischa. Don't chicken out, we made the decision together. It's time,' her father said, sounding uncharacteristically harsh with her mother. Her parents had barely said a cross word to each other for as long as Dana could remember.

'Alesha, honey, what do you think?' asked her mother.

Alesha turned to the side, looking at her mum. 'I agree. She'll be upset and shocked, but I think it's time she knew. You know how I feel about her, but... don't you think it's time, James?' she asked her husband, as if his opinion mattered.

James, who clearly didn't care either way, gave a bored, 'Yes.'

She'd heard enough. Dana opened the back door and cleared her throat, stepping out onto the veranda.

There was silence from her family. It took her a moment to place it, but they all wore the same expression – guilt.

'What's going on?' Dana asked. 'Why are you talking about me? What will I be upset about?' She looked at each of her family members in turn, staring them directly in the eye, ending with her mother.

'Mum? Tell me what's going on. Right now,' she demanded, hands clenched by her sides.

'Dana, don't take that tone with Mum,' Alesha said harshly. Dana looked at her in surprise. They hadn't always got along but why was she being so hostile?

'Piss off, Alesha, I wasn't talking to you,' Dana replied, her hackles immediately rising. Why were they talking about her so secretively?

Her mum stood, walking towards her, hands held out in front of her. 'Dana, please just sit and we'll talk.'

'I'm fine where I am.' She crossed her arms. 'What were you talking about? Someone tell me right now.'

'Always such a drama queen,' Alesha attacked again, glaring at Dana. 'No wonder you don't—'

'Alesha!' hissed her father, glaring at his youngest daughter.

'No,' Dana said, 'finish what you were going to say, Alesha. You have never been one to hold back, so tell me what you were going to say.'

'Belong. I was going to say you don't *belong*. Haven't you worked it out yet? You don't look like us, you don't act like us, you're not *one* of us.' Alesha was standing by this time, inching closer to Dana as she spat the hurtful words at her.

'Alesha, don't,' begged her mother, holding up her hand as if she could physically stop the words coming out of Alesha's mouth.

'You're adopted, you fucking idiot,' her sister yelled at her.

Dana felt her whole world tilt. What the actual fuck? 'Dad?' Her father looked away when her gaze fell upon him. He studied his fingernails. 'I'm adopted? I can't be. You and Mum have told me my story plenty of times and none of those stories included adoption. Why am I just finding out now? Why does Alesha know before I do?' Her dad said nothing.

'Well, I can't tell you why Mum and Dad lied, but I found the papers years ago in a box in the study. I read them and I finally understood why you were different, why we never got along. It's so bloody obvious now. We're not sisters.' She seemed to be taking pleasure in the cruel words she was saying.

'You've known for years, Alesha? Years and you didn't tell me?' Dana was so hurt that she felt physically sick. Her stomach was churning, her head thumping with a sudden and blinding headache behind her eyes. Even if they weren't close, why wouldn't Alesha tell her?

'Were you ever going to tell me?'

Her mother met her stare and tried to smile. 'Dana, you're our daughter and we love you, so very much. *I* love you.' She smiled again but it wasn't the same any more. Dana knew the truth now. She really didn't belong, to any of them. 'Please, Dana,' her mother said quietly.

'Don't say my name like that!' Dana screamed, unable to handle it any more. The smug look on her sister's face, the pleading words of her mother, the ignorance of her father, the indifference of her brother-in-law. She had to get out of there; she couldn't process what was happening. Why did her parents adopt her? Was Alesha adopted too? Why had it taken them so long to tell her? So many questions but she couldn't deal with the answers right now. Storming back into the house, she slammed the door. Logan looked up in surprise as she appeared in the lounge.

'Everything OK?' he immediately asked, seeing the look of pure shock on her face, her mouth open and slack, tears in her dark eyes.

'No. We're leaving. Now,' she said. 'Kels, grab Boo Boo, we're going home.'

Logan knew from the look on her face that something serious had happened. She shook her head at him just as her mother came running into the lounge. 'Please don't go, sweetheart, let's talk about this.'

'There's nothing to talk about. I'm leaving and I'm not coming back. Not ever,' she replied emphatically, grabbing Kelsey's hand and all but dragging her out to the car.

As Logan drove home Dana stared silently out of the window, not focusing on the beautiful scenery that passed her by. Instead, she tried to pinpoint where she might have missed the huge secret her family had been keeping from her. But she couldn't. Her parents treated her the same as Alesha. So, where did she come from? Who were her real parents? Did it even matter? Did she owe her loyalty to her adopted parents instead?

Once they arrived at home, Kelsey went off to her room to play and Logan turned to his wife, pulling her into his arms for a hug. 'What happened?' he asked, kissing her hair lightly.

'I just found out that I'm adopted,' she choked out in shock.

'You're what?' He stepped back, still holding her. 'How is that possible?'

'They kept it from me. I overheard them talking about me and I confronted them. Alesha yelled it at me.' Finally Dana broke down with the realisation that they had all lied to her for decades.

'Oh, baby,' Logan whispered as she sobbed. He held her in his arms tenderly until finally her cries tapered off then stopped altogether. She couldn't process the information, the only thing she could focus on was: *you don't belong*. So who *did* she belong to?

* * *

After the stress of finding out about her past, Dana fell into an exhausted sleep. The phone vibrating beside her woke her up. Her mobile was on the coffee table, a sticky note beside it.

Gone to get tea, back soon. Love you.

She looked at the screen through the fog of sleepiness. It was her mother calling. Dana didn't want to pick up, she wasn't ready to talk to her, but she felt rude not answering. The phone stopped ringing. Problem solved. Dana threw the thick blanket off her, touched that Logan had thought to cover her up. He might have his faults, but right now, he was being her rock.

The front door clicked closed quietly and she heard careful footsteps coming down the hallway. 'I'm awake,' she called out.

Logan and Kelsey appeared in the lounge. 'Hi, Mummy, we went and got fish and chips for tea. Daddy said I could have an ice cream after.' This was all very exciting for their daughter; fish and chips drowned in tomato sauce were her favourite.

'You feeling a bit better?' Logan asked as she followed him into the kitchen.

'No. Mum tried calling.'

'Did you pick up?' her husband asked, turning after he put the fish and chips on the bench.

'Of course not. I'm nowhere near ready to talk to her about this.'

'I actually think you're better off doing it now rather than waiting. Use your anger and hurt to get the answers you need. They're at your mercy. You wait long enough and they'll have time to work out answers to any difficult questions you might ask.' He turned back to the bench, bending down and grabbing plates.

Dana thought about what he said. There was truth to it, for sure, but just the thought of hearing her mother's voice had her breaking out into a cold sweat, her heart rate jumping alarmingly. No, she just couldn't right now, if ever. If they weren't her family, then that was it, right? She had her family, Logan, Kelsey, and the baby growing inside her. They were all she needed.

Three months later she still hadn't spoken to any of her family. Life had gone on; it hadn't imploded. She felt free of the shackles that bound her to those... liars. She had stopped speculating as to how they had come to adopt her and why they had taken so long to tell her. It wasn't good for her mind to dwell on things she couldn't change, so she focused on her own little family, making sure that they knew they were loved. Things were good between her and Logan. They were closer than ever, looking forward to the birth of their second child.

Dana found that once she had taken away the stress, despite the unanswered questions she had conveniently pushed to one side, her sexual side took over. She didn't know if it was because she felt as if she needed validation now or if it was purely the baby hormones, but she and Logan were making love at least three times a week, dragging each other's clothes off as soon as Kelsey was asleep. Before, Dana was strictly a bed girl, but now, well, now it was as if a different person had stepped into her blooming body and her husband wasn't about to complain.

He had come home one afternoon, calling for his girls, only to be confronted by a completely naked Dana.

'Hi,' she said quietly, not even a little bit self-conscious about her body.

'Where's Kelsey?' he immediately asked, his eyes darting around the room.

'Relax, Logan, I had Pippa come and get her for a few hours. We'll go pick her up later. But for now, it's just you and me,' she said, walking over to him slowly. He was already kicking off his shoes and pulling his work shirt over his head, casting it to the side. In no time at all he was standing in front of her, as naked as she was. She stared at her husband, her eyes travelling up his body, appreciating the way the muscles in his arms rolled and slightly bulged as he moved. She turned and walked into the lounge, giving him an enticing view of her bum.

Dana bent over the couch, steadying her hands on the edge, waiting. She spread her legs and heard him groan behind her. He wanted this as much as she did. Quite often their love making was hurried, in between whose turn it was to settle Kelsey if she had a nightmare or sleepwalked, early morning work or pregnancy-related sickness. But this time it was all about fucking the way they wanted to, where they wanted to. She was horny and, as Logan was pressed up behind her, she could tell he was too.

He grabbed onto her hips. 'You sure?' he whispered.

'Don't talk, just fuck me.' She could see their reflection in the windows; she had deliberately left the curtains open, adding to the craziness and sexiness of it all.

That was all the encouragement he needed. He reached between her legs, finding her clit, and gently began rubbing it in lazy circles. Dana moaned quietly; he had always known how to turn her on and this was a damn fine start. She moved her hips to match his rhythm, grinding onto his fingers. He pushed his fingers inside her, then pulled them out, rubbing her clit again. She hadn't felt this good, this desired in a long time. She felt the familiar build coming up, like a small wave that continued to swell, but just as she began to reach the point of no return Logan stopped and pushed the head of his cock inside her. She smiled, seeing herself reflected in the window, then he pushed himself all the way in. She gasped with shock, then moaned with pleasure. This was exactly how she'd pictured it. Alone time with her husband, seducing him, although he hadn't needed much seducing.

He began to thrust into her over and over. She knew his patterns: he could be quick or last a long time, it depended on what she did to him, and Dana wanted it down and dirty. She pushed her arse back into him, a sure sign that he should go harder and faster. She gripped the couch as he pumped into her repeatedly, pulling nearly all the way out, only to slam back in. It wasn't polite sex; it was a rough fuck. Exactly what they both needed. She began to feel him swell, she knew his balls would be tight and full as she rocked backwards and forwards, slapping against him. He reached around with one hand and began massaging her breast, but she pushed his hand away, looked at the window, saw him watching and began touching herself instead, pulling at her hard nipples. He groaned into her ear.

'You're so fucking hot!' He slammed even deeper, each stroke bringing him that much closer to a satisfying end for them both. He began playing with her clit again, knowing exactly how she liked it. Within seconds, she was on the verge of releasing.

'I'm gonna come,' he moaned into her ear as he furiously pounded away and rubbed her hard.

'Me too,' she panted back.

Another three strokes and he came, one last slam into her, coming deep inside her. He rubbed her a few moments more until she too came, shuddering against his fingers, her muscles tightening around his cock with pleasure.

He gently pulled out, hugging her from behind. 'Well, aren't you just full of surprises?' he said to her, kissing the damp nape of her neck.

She turned around. 'I aim to please.'

He gently grasped a still hard nipple. 'You succeeded.' He kissed her again. 'Shower?'

Dana nodded and padded her way to the bathroom, now feeling exposed in her nakedness. Her whole body tingled and she felt desirable, loved and safe. When Logan offered to go and pick up Kelsey from Pippa's house, she kissed him. 'You'd do that for me?' He'd really stepped up his game since she had her falling out with her family. Pippa had also been supportive but had been gently encouraging her to talk to her mum at least. Pippa had lost her mum at an early age, so she viewed the mother-daughter relationship as sacred.

Once Logan had gone, Dana allowed some of the traitorous thoughts to creep in. Someone had thrown her away like rubbish.

They must have, otherwise how would she have ended up with her adopted parents? She slid her hand down her belly and touched her curves. She couldn't wait for this baby to be born. A new start for them all, a new baby brother or sister for Kelsey, who'd finally made peace with the fact that she was going to become a big sister shortly.

Dana walked into the bedroom and pulled on a comfy pair of pyjamas. She was tired but wanted to wait up until Kelsey and Logan came home. After forty minutes, she began to get worried. The trip was fifteen minutes there and back, easy, so what was taking him so long? She wanted to call to make sure that he was all right but reasoned that he had his mobile, he'd call if something went wrong. So she waited and, soon enough, he was unlocking the door and closing it with his foot while he held their sleeping child in his arms. Dana trailed along behind him to Kelsey's bedroom where Dana had moved most of the teddies and dolls off the bed, all except two favourites, and Logan laid Kelsey gently down on the bed. Dana pulled up the blanket and bent down to give her daughter a kiss.

Logan closed the door halfway as they walked out, heading towards the lounge.

'I was getting worried about you guys. Pippa's place isn't that far away – you get talking?'

'Yeah, actually we did. She's had her hair done. It looks nice.'

She and Pippa were close, very close. They did lots of things together before Kelsey was born and Pippa had been a great support to her after, even babysitting for the occasional special date night, like tonight. But Pippa was lonely. She had moved to town about six years ago and had never seemed to make any other friends. Dana had found it odd but had never brought it up with her. She was ten years younger than Dana, and looked up to her like a mentor, so Dana tried to guide Pippa through life's trials, especially where men were concerned. She got too serious too fast, every single time. She scared them off with her enthusiasm for starting a life together immediately. She had still to overcome that fatal relationship flaw, something Dana suspected would never happen. She loved Pippa like a sister and Logan thought the world of her too. They got along like a house on fire and Kelsey loved her like an aunt. Since everything had imploded with her family, Pippa was more of a support to her than ever.

6

The distance from her family was good for Dana. It had given her time to take a breath, to figure out what she wanted to do with the knowledge that she was adopted. She had so many unanswered questions. Where did she come from? Who were her people? Because it definitely wasn't her adopted family. They were liars. One night, she was sitting up in bed, her head resting against the headboard, hand on her ever expanding belly. She was lost inside the book she was reading.

Logan rolled over and sat up. 'Hun?' he began before stopping, clearing his throat and continuing, 'Don't you think you've punished them enough?'

She didn't have to ask who *they* were. 'What?' she asked with surprise, putting the book on the bedside table. 'Where did that come from?' He'd supported her decision not to speak to her parents, now here he was, changing his mind?

'Your mother called me. Actually, she's called a lot. I've let it go to voicemail every time although you know I love her, so it's been difficult to ignore her, but then I listened to one of her messages. She sounded so distraught over losing you, she was crying, and I just couldn't handle it. So when she called me again the next day, I picked up. She said... Dana... your dad is sick. I don't know how sick, just, sick. Your mum wants you to call her.' He said it all in a rush, trying to get it all out before Dana shut him down.

She pondered his words. 'What do you mean "sick"?'

'I don't know, love. She didn't say. I think you should call her though.' He looked at her, finally meeting her eyes properly. 'It's time.'

Dana ran a weary hand through her hair. These past few months had been very hard on her. She'd wrestled with her iden-tity, questioning everything she'd thought she knew about her family, herself. But when she had come to terms with it all, her life had become largely worry and stress free thanks to no family ties clouding her judgment. Now here was Logan, knowing what she'd gone through, asking her to go back there, to that place, be OK with it, all because her mother said her dad was sick.

'At least hear her out,' Logan said, starting back up again. 'You can't stay angry at them forever, you know. Of course, I'll support you whatever you decide to do but, remember, it's not just about you. You have a daughter that hasn't seen her nan and pop for months now. Kelsey doesn't understand what's going on but she told me the other day that Boo Boo missed them.'

'You didn't tell me that,' Dana said, eyes flashing with fire.

'I've tried talking to you, but you've just shut me down every time.'

Dana stared at him, throwing back the sheet in frustration. 'Wouldn't you be angry with them? For what they did to you, then lying about it for nearly forty years? How would you feel if it was your family that had hid something so monumental from you? Wouldn't you be angry? Hurt? Betrayed?' It wasn't that she didn't miss aspects of her family, because she did. As she thought about her father's bear hugs, her mother's love and even her sister's competitiveness, she missed them. Was Logan right? Maybe it was time to end the silence. She at least had to know that her father was all right.

'Fine,' Dana finally capitulated. Logan leaned over and kissed her loudly on the cheek.

'Call her tomorrow, please, love.'

'Don't push your luck. I've just agreed to hear her out,' she said, feeling as if she'd just crossed an invisible barrier.

The next day, after she had dropped Kelsey off at nursery, her phone rang as she was hopping back into the car. She quickly looked at the screen then stilled. It was her mother. She had two choices, answer or don't answer, but she had made a promise to Logan to hear her out.

'Hello?' She couldn't bring herself to say, *Hi, Mum.*

'Oh, Dana!' was all her mother could say before she burst into tears. For a moment, Dana felt terrible that she was the cause of such misery to her. Then she remembered what her family had done to her. Dana stayed silent.

'Dana? Are you still there?' her mother managed to choke out once she'd calmed down a bit.

After a long beat Dana said, 'Yeah, I'm here. What do you want?' She might have decided to speak to her but that didn't mean she had to make it easy on her.

'I want, I *need*, to explain. Why we didn't tell you.'

'Well, why didn't you tell me?'

'Not over the phone. I need to do this in person. You need to see how sorry I am when I tell you your story.'

'Oh, so now it's *my* story, something you've kept from me all these years. How could it possibly have been *my* story?'

'Dana, please. Can I come over to the house and see you? We'll get everything out in the open this time.'

Dana sighed, looking at the time on her watch. 'I'll be home in fifteen minutes. I'll wait for five minutes then I'll leave again and I won't pick up the phone a second time.'

'I'll be there,' her mother said breathlessly before abruptly hanging up.

Dana drove home watching the traffic around her carefully. She was busy thinking about how her mum was going to explain away decades of lies and she found her mind wandering, so she wound down the window and refocused. It would do nobody any good for her to get into an accident. She made it home in one piece, went inside and put the kettle on. She was so involved in making the tea that the knock at the front door startled her.

Dana opened it. Her mother stood on the veranda, a step back from the door, her hands clasped, dressed smartly with make-up on. But Dana noticed that the make-up was smudged, the mascara running slightly, and her mother's hair looked mussed, as though she'd just run a hand through it and not fixed it up again. Very unlike her. Her mother began to whimper, putting her hand to her mouth in a futile attempt to stem her cries. She looked down at Dana's belly, covered in a flowing maxi dress. She held out her arms to hug her daughter.

'Come in,' Dana said, turning, not willing to yield yet and offer her comfort. She had told Logan she'd hear her mother out. If she thought she was being lied to, that would be that. 'I've made tea.'

Dana put the cups on the table, then sat down opposite her mother and waited for her to start talking.

'Dana...' she began.

'Why, Mum? Why didn't you tell me?' Dana jumped in, not even giving her a chance to talk.

Her mother sighed. 'There's no easy answer for why we didn't tell you. At the time, it was to protect you, but—'

'Protect me from what?' Dana asked with annoyance in her voice.

Her mum stayed quiet for a moment, as if gathering her thoughts before she spoke. 'When I was young, just fresh out of high school, I met your father. We fell in love. He was a little older than me, just over two years, and was about to move away for work.'

'I know all this already,' Dana said coldly, fiddling with the handle of her cup of tea. 'You and Dad moved away and then found out you were pregnant with me soon after. But that was a lie, wasn't it? You're not my mum.'

'I *am* your mum,' the woman opposite flared up before her shoulders slumped again in defeat and she sniffed back a sob.

'Where are my *biological* parents?'

'Let me tell the story in my own way, Dana. Your dad had this friend at work and he and his girlfriend became close to us. They came around to our house all the time. We weren't rich but those times hold some of the fondest memories for me. Listening to music on the record player and drinking cheap wine from the box.' She seemed to fall into a memory, a look of calm across her face, then a smile.

'Danny, your father's friend, and his girlfriend, Jackie, found out that they were having a baby. We had been talking about starting a family too. We were making money and we both loved kids. We had no family around, just Danny and Jackie, but they were family to us.'

Dana sat, enthralled by the story, these people, her people.

'Danny died in a motorcycle accident right after he found out about the baby. Jackie was distraught. You can imagine. She had nothing and no one any more, except us. Her family had disowned her when she'd taken up with Danny. They viewed him as a loser, but let me be absolutely clear, he was a wonderful man and would have made an amazing father if given the chance. Jackie, she couldn't get over his death, and she began living with us so we could take care of her emotionally and financially. After about three months she woke us up one night, and asked the impossible question: "Will you raise my baby?"'

This time Dana's mother did begin to cry, remembering her friend and her desperate situation. Dana reached out her hand and her mother immediately grabbed it, holding it so tightly it hurt.

'After trying to persuade her to rethink, we said yes in the end, of course we did, what else could we say? When you were born, we were right there, holding Jackie's hands the whole time. Jackie signed the paperwork straight away. She cried like her heart was breaking. Which it was. She kissed your tiny head, saying how much Danny would have loved you. She was going to continue to live with us until she got on her feet, but just two days later when your dad was at work and I was out for a walk with you, she left. Disappeared, just gone. We had no idea where she went to. We rang around her other friends, but no one had seen her for months, not since... Danny.'

By this time, Dana had tears in her eyes too. She wiped at them with her free hand.

'We stayed in town just in case she ever came back. We wanted her to be able to find us. But we never heard from her. Not until she tracked me down a few months ago.'

Dana gasped. 'What? You know where my mother is?' She didn't miss the wince from her mum. She felt bad, but this was monumental. They knew where her real mother was.

'Yes, I know where she is. Now you can see why we struggled with how to tell you that, not only were you adopted, but that your birth mum had contacted us, and she wants to see you.' Her mother stayed silent, letting that sink in.

Her birth mother had found her and wanted to meet her? After months of not knowing where she came from, she would finally find out. Her mother, Jackie. She tested the name, and it sounded right, familiar, home, even though they'd yet to meet. 'What did you say when she contacted you?'

'Well, I explained that we had decided not to tell you about Danny and her. She was... upset, understandably. You knew nothing of them or their story. I think she understood though. I'll arrange a meeting when you're ready...'

'Right away, I'm ready now.' The words tumbled out of her mouth. Dana ran a shaky hand through her hair. This was huge news.

'There's something I need to tell you first, love. The reason why she contacted us, she has cancer and is unlikely to see the next few months. She just wanted to meet you before she passed.'

'Oh, fuck, that's not fair. You can't give her to me then take her away.' Dana held back her tears with great effort.

'Sweetheart, I didn't do either. But that's why we were discussing you that day you overheard us, we were going to tell you, and organise for you to meet her.'

Dana looked at her with trepidation. 'Is she... is she still alive?'

'Yes. I spoke to her yesterday. She's the only other person that knows our secret. We never even told our family, our parents. They wouldn't have understood. They were so angry when they thought you were ours because we were so young, but to be told we'd adopted you? No, it was better this way. Over time, it became harder and harder to think about telling you, so we just didn't talk about it until forced to.'

'Is Alesha yours?'

'Yes. But we love you exactly the same.'

Dana didn't believe that, but she didn't call her mum on it. 'I want to see Jackie. Now.'

'She's at the hospital having chemo treatment, she'll be in town for a while. I'll drive you there myself tomorrow. Logan can take care of Kelsey, and Alesha can watch your father for the day.'

She was afraid to ask but her mum did it for her. 'The stress of all this, of losing you, of Jackie coming back into our lives. It was just all too much for him. He suffered a stroke last week.'

'Oh, God, Mum! Is he OK?' Dana was devastated. She had caused all of this.

'It was a small one, he's all right, just really weak right now, love. He'll be OK but I don't want him by himself, so Alesha can take the day off work and step up. I'll take you, I promise I will,' she said.

Dana walked around the table to her mother, who stayed sitting. She pulled her mum's shoulders forward until her head rested on her large belly. Her mum slipped her arms around her stomach and began to cry; this time she couldn't be stopped and Dana felt her dress clinging to her where her mother's tears soaked through the thin material. Then Dana felt the baby kick; it was as if the baby knew his or her grandmother needed some comfort. Mischa pulled back and began to laugh. Dana smiled too. She had the impression that her mum hadn't been doing much laughing lately and she felt the guilt rushing throughout her entire body.

'Mum, I'm sorry—'

'Stop right there. You have nothing to apologise for, honey. You didn't ask for any of this, OK? We should have told you many years ago. You could handle it, but we couldn't. *We* were weak. We thought that you wouldn't love us as much if you knew you weren't biologically ours. We underestimated you and I'm so sorry for that. Can we start again? No more secrets? No more lies?'

She smiled at her mum. 'I'd like that.'

Her mum wiped her eyes with a tissue that she pulled from her handbag. 'I'll pick you up in the morning, at ten?'

'I'll be waiting.' Dana saw her to the door and gently put her arms around her. 'Mum? I forgive you,' she whispered.

Her mother's voice cracked as she said, 'Thank you.'

7

Dana had a fitful sleep. She dreamt of her father riding his bike, his helmet snug against his head, speeding down the road, minding his own business. The next thing she saw was a truck ploughing into him. The dream haunted her, even after she woke. Dana kept seeing the look in his eyes in that split second when he realised that he was going to die. That he would never see his child be born or grow up.

It was early, the sun barely up, just lightening around the edges of the curtains. Logan snored when she slid from the bed and pulled on one of his jumpers. She was nervous, jumpy and afraid, yet understandably wired to be meeting Jackie. Her mum. Her biological mum. Mischa had explained that Jackie had the same beautiful black hair that Dana did, and brown eyes. Apparently Dana had her father's nose and her mother's lips. Mischa no longer had any photos of Danny, her father, so she hoped Jackie had some. She would like to see the man who, but for a twist of fate, would have been raising her.

Dana was so deep in thought that when Logan touched her

on the shoulder, she let out a squeak of fright and nearly leapt off the chair.

'Shit, Logan!' she whispered loudly. 'You scared me.'

'Sorry. Nervous about today, love?' He stood behind her and began to massage the tension from her neck and shoulders.

'You could say that. I've been imagining what my parents would be like for the past few months, so to finally be able to find out is daunting and, honestly, I'm scared. I really am. What if I'm a disappointment to her?'

'Don't make yourself out to be less than what you are: amazing.' He leaned over and kissed the side of her neck.

She reached up a hand to cup his stubbled cheek. 'Thank you,' she said. 'I needed that.'

'I'll have a shower, then get the little poppet dressed and fed before her nan gets here. We're going to have a play date together today. I'm looking forward to spending some quality time with Kels.'

'I have to go and pick an outfit, then I'll jump in the shower after you.'

'Or you could join me and we could save on our hot water bill.' He gave her a cheeky grin that melted her heart.

'You had me at water bill.' She laughed.

* * *

Her mum arrived promptly at ten.

'Nan!' screamed Kelsey when her nan walked into the lounge. Dana's mum bent down and collected the small figure hurtling towards her. She hugged the little girl fiercely and planted a kiss on her cheek, then wiped the lipstick off.

'Why haven't you come to see me in days?' Kelsey demanded,

little hands on her hips. It had been months, but no one was going to correct her.

'Want a cupcake for morning tea, darling?' she asked Kelsey, who gave a resounding yes, question forgotten. Dana's mum pulled a small cake tin from her calico shopping bag. There were four ornately decorated cupcakes in there. Works of art that it seemed a shame to eat. It was as if Dana's mother had taken the last three months of lost love and had stored it all up for these cupcakes, and they looked amazing. Dana smiled. Her mum was trying, so she would too.

'Should we go, Mum?' Dana was anxious and didn't want to waste any more time before getting to know her real mum.

Logan came over and gave her a firm hug, his hands roaming over her back. 'You'll be fine, babe,' he whispered in her ear. 'Kels, Mummy and Nan have to go now, come say goodbye.'

The light of Dana's life ran up and stuck herself to her baby bump. 'I'm giving her a cuddle goodbye.'

'That's so sweet, baby girl. So you've decided that you're having a sister now?'

'Yes, a dream whispered it to me.' Dana wanted to laugh at the sweetness of it. She dropped a kiss on her head. 'Be good for Daddy. I'll be back later this afternoon.' Dana took one last look at her little family and ushered her mum out of the door. Inside her over-sized handbag, amongst the essentials, she had a stack of photos of her family, including handfuls of Kelsey. She wanted Jackie to know that she had a healthy and happy granddaughter and, if she wanted to, Jackie could meet her one day soon. Maybe she could come for tea. Dana knew that she was getting ahead of herself, but she couldn't help it. She wanted to plan her future with her birth mum in it as well, standing beside her mum and dad, Logan and Kelsey. It would be perfect. Her mind wouldn't let her explore the possibility that this wouldn't work out, that she'd leave the hospital disappointed.

Her mum was quiet on the drive over. After ten minutes of being wrapped up in her own world, Dana finally thought to ask her how she was feeling.

'I'm not sure, love. Ever since you found out about Danny and Jackie, I'm... remembering things about them, mostly good stuff, you know, to tell you when you were ready, but Jackie... I don't know, I guess I'm being silly. I just have this sense that something is going to go wrong. I guess now I'm being a little jealous, wanting to keep you to myself just a little longer.'

'You're always going to be my mum, even if Jackie does want to be in my life, and that's a big *if*. I love you.'

'I love you too, Dana. So very, very much. I'm just glad we could get this sorted. Jackie is of course welcomed into the family if that's what she wants. Kelsey would have two nans to spoil her then. She'd love that.'

Dana was amazed at how well her mum was taking the reappearance of her birth mum. But she still felt guilty; nearly three months hating her parents for a good deed that they had done decades before. Yes, they should have told her when she was young, but they'd thought they were protecting her. It had been an impossible position and Dana didn't know that she would have done anything different.

The turn-off for the hospital loomed ahead of them and Dana looked over at her mum, catching her eye. *This is it.*

As Dana exited the car she couldn't figure out why the voice inside her mind was screaming at her to run. But she needed answers, and the woman in that hospital ward had those very answers she sought. Dana had to go and see her, had to hear her truth. She looked over the roof of the car at her mum. *Mum.* A word that covered so many rights and wrongs. No matter what had happened between them, her parents had done a wonderful and selfless act by agreeing to adopt her. Logically she knew that. How much pain and terror must Jackie have felt being alone and pregnant, then handing over her new-born daughter to someone else, even if she had asked them to take her? Dana couldn't even imagine the heartbreak she went through, what scars Jackie carried. What kind of life had Jackie had after she had given Dana up?

As they walked up the path, which was bordered by colourful pansies, Dana saw a small shudder run through her mum's thin body. She stopped.

'You don't have to do this if you don't want to. If it'll be too hard on you, Mum.'

'I have to admit, I'm scared. Scared that she'll be your mum and not me, but she specifically asked me to be there with you, so I will.' Her mum's lips tried to settle into a smile as she grasped Dana's hand tightly. 'Whatever happens, we face it together.'

Dana squeezed her hand back. 'Right.'

* * *

The hospital hallway had many people along its length, but, despite the traffic, was surprisingly quiet. Even the opening and closing of doors was hushed, the nurses walking on silent rubber shoes that didn't squeak or scuff the floor. Dana guessed it must be in an effort to be considerate to those receiving treatment. A nurse showed them to the cancer treatment room and they stood outside, both seemingly lost in their own thoughts. Dana had lived her whole life without this woman, so why did she need her now?

Because she's your mother. Standing straighter, she nodded to her mum, who knocked on the door and pushed it open.

Dana followed her in, looking around the room, at the large space, the window that looked out onto a garden, the machinery, the two women in the room.

'Jackie,' her mother said quietly, obviously recognising her. Dana looked at the woman now folded into her mother's arms. Jackie was frail, that much was obvious, and her mother released her carefully.

Jackie was gaunt, shockingly so, her bones so sharp they threatened to poke through her pale, thin skin. She was stretched tighter than a drum, but despite all that Dana could see herself in the woman before her. Same hair, same facial features and what she didn't see, she must have inherited from her father. Jackie's pain-filled eyes tracked her as Dana's eyes roamed her body and face.

Finally, breaking the silence, Jackie said, 'Come here.' Her voice was croaky.

Dana walked over to her, standing at the side of the recliner chair. Her mum spoke softly, 'Jackie, I'd like you to meet Danica, Dana, for short. We named her after Danny.'

Jackie's eyes welled up with unshed tears. 'That's lovely.'

'It seemed like the right thing to do. A tribute to a great man and great friend.'

Jackie reached out and Dana knew she wanted to hold her hand. Dana looked over at her mother, who nodded slightly, saying it was OK, that she was coping. Jackie's hand was dry, scaly, the skin paper thin, but Dana clung to it all the same, her tears finally breaking free.

'You look so much like your dad.' Jackie looked over at Dana's mum. 'You've done a great job, she's lovely,' Jackie said, talking about her daughter as if she weren't in the room. 'Tell me. Does she know about your history with her daddy yet?'

Dana looked over at her mum, who paled immediately, the colour leaching from her face. 'I don't know what you mean,' Mischa choked out.

Jackie dropped Dana's hand and Dana stood there, staring between the two women, unsure of what was happening. Jackie glared at her mother, her whole face changing from a sick woman to a woman angered beyond all reason. Her face twisted into a snarl. 'I only found out after he was gone. He died while you went on to have a good life, children, a family,' Jackie said venomously. 'How fitting. Little, innocent Mischa never showing her true colours to anyone except Danny. The way you two were always whispering together in the corners, like you shared secrets. Guess you did. Took me a while to see that though. He loved you.'

Dana's mother just stood still, shocked, silent in the face of the accusations.

Jackie leaned forward in her chair, inching closer to Mischa. 'You know, when I told him I was having his baby, he wasn't even happy. We fought, the worst fight we'd ever had. I yelled at him that he didn't love me and he admitted that his feelings had changed. I asked if there was someone else and he hesitated. I let him walk out that door, upset, not knowing where we stood. When the police came later that night, it was raining. I remember I was by myself, so upset, just waiting on Danny to come back home so we could fix things. But he never did.'

Dana leaned in, needing to know what happened next. She knew the ending but was missing the middle of the story.

'Danny had taken off on his motorcycle, in the rain, he wasn't wearing his helmet when he hit the oncoming truck. The police told me that the distraught driver said he veered into his path. That there was nothing he could do, and I believed that. I knew. I *knew* that telling him I was pregnant had caused him to commit suicide. Death was better than the thought of being stuck with me forever. I found the letters in a box months later, after I had given you the baby. I read every single one of them. I was such an idiot to not see what was going on. But neither of us got him in the end,' she said bitterly.

Finally, Jackie turned her gaze upon Dana. 'Your very existence caused your dad to kill himself.'

Dana cried out, the words cutting deep, and hung onto her mum for support.

'Enough!' roared her mother, all traces of shock now gone from her face. 'How dare you talk to my daughter like this? Danny made his own choice. If what you said is true, then he chose to take his own life after carefully weighing up his options. He was like that. I should know. He asked me to marry him before he died. Hours before he died, actually. Bet your little love letters didn't tell you that.'

Jackie looked crestfallen. 'Get out,' she whispered. Neither of the women moved. 'Get out!' This time, much louder.

'Come on, Dana, there's nothing for us here.' Her mum grabbed her hand, leading her to the door, neither one of them looking back. Dana was in shock, her hands shaking, her breath catching in her throat.

'What... what just happened in there, Mum?' Dana asked shakily, stopping in the middle of the hallway, grabbing her mum's arm. 'You were going to leave Dad for my real father? What the hell? Does dad even know?'

Her mother turned to face her directly. 'You might as well know the full truth. Yes, Danny and I were in love, but it was something that happened gradually. We didn't mean for it to happen. We were friends for ages and it just grew from there. He told me that he was going to tell Jackie about us and that I should tell Robert. He asked me to marry him and I said yes,' she said, tears streaming down her face. She made no effort to wipe them from her cheeks. 'Then he died. I was devastated. In mourning. Jackie gave us a different version of what happened, drunk driver, not Danny's fault. Then she told us that she was pregnant. When your father and I adopted you, all I could think about was having a piece of Danny still in my life. You're so much like him – he was a truly wonderful person. Raising you has been the best and the hardest decision I've ever made, but I've never regretted it, not for one minute. I love you, Dana, just like I loved your father.'

'Which one?' Dana asked, feeling numb from all these revelations.

'Both. I have always loved Robert, but I was willing to leave him for a new life, but then, once we had you, I recommitted to him. I fell deeper in love and we have led a good life. I've been happy raising you and your sister.'

'Except she's not my sister, not really. This explains a lot. Especially her behaviour towards me over the past few years.'

'Dana,' her mother sighed with exasperation, 'ties are ties and love is love. Blood doesn't define you. Alesha is your sister and, whether you fight or not, nothing will ever change that. You need to forgive her too. She's so terribly sorry for blurting everything out like she did. It wasn't her story to tell.' This time it was her mum who grabbed her arm. 'Forgive her. She didn't mean what she said. You *are* one of us and you *do* belong.'

'I'll think about it but it's not that easy. She hurt me. You all did,' Dana said, pulling away from her.

'Darling, why don't we have a BBQ, just us family? Dad will grill, the boys will have fun together, and you know Kelsey is dying to be pulled around by Pop on the tractor. You can talk to your sister and you can mend fences with each other. How does that sound?' Her face was hopeful and Dana found herself wanting to make her happy after the day they'd had.

'OK,' Dana said before she could change her mind.

They both stayed quiet on the way home, each lost in their own thoughts. A couple of times Dana looked over at her mother but she ignored her, so Dana stared out of the window instead, trying to make sense of Jackie's revelations. She needed to talk to Logan, get her feelings sorted out. Right now they were a jumble of wires tying her brain in knots. It had been one hell of a day.

Her mother dropped her off at the front of the cottage, reminding her about the get-together on Saturday.

'I won't forget, Mum.'

'Dana...' She turned to face her. 'About Danny—'

'Don't worry, I won't tell Dad, but I think you should.' She slammed the car door and unlocked the front door, heading inside.

'Mummy! You're home!' squealed Kelsey, running down the hallway as Dana closed the door.

'Hey, baby,' she said, squatting down and wiping her face of the grief and exhaustion she felt. She smiled for her little girl. 'I missed you, poppet. Did you have a good day with Daddy?'

'Yup, and Aunt Pippa's here too.'

'Well, then, I'd better go say hi.' Dana released her daughter with a little tickle; Kelsey laughed then thumped down the short hallway to the lounge. 'Hey, love,' Dana said as she walked in. Logan was sitting on the couch with Pippa next to him, his arm stretched out along the back behind Pippa.

Pippa stood and the two women hugged warmly. 'Love the new haircut,' Dana said, making an effort despite the shit day she'd had. 'Logan's right, it really does suit you.'

Pippa fluffed her hair. 'You really like it?' she asked, looking at Logan as she said it. He nodded and smiled, as did Dana.

'Well, I'd better get going. Logan, Miss Kelsey, thanks for the wonderful day.' She kissed Kelsey on the head and Dana walked her to the front door. 'Thanks for popping by, Pip. I'll see you later?'

'Of course.' One more hug and she was gone.

Dana headed back to the lounge and dropped onto the recently vacated spot, sighing deeply.

'Everything all right, babe?'

'Oh, Logan, shit went down today. Jackie didn't want to see me, not really, she wanted to spew secrets, lies, whatever, at Mum. It was awful.'

'Want to talk about it?'

'I'm not sure. I mean, yeah, I do. I think I need to.'

'Well, now you have to spill,' he said, smiling, but when he saw the look on her face, he stopped. 'What happened?' he asked quietly.

'Kelsey, love, why don't you go into your room and play with your dolls? I'll be in there in a few minutes to play tea party with you.' Kelsey smiled and ran to her room. 'I thought she wanted to see me,' Dana said, tearing up. 'I thought she cared about me and my life, but really she wanted to have a go at me and Mum. She told me my father committed suicide because of me. Because she told him she was pregnant. My mum told Jackie today that my father Danny had asked her to marry him and she'd said yes. My mum was cheating on my dad.'

Logan looked away then blew out a breath. 'Wow, that's some heavy shit. Why did she call you there in the first place? I thought she wanted to meet you, get to know you before she passed away.'

'Nope, looks like she just wanted to hurt us both. It worked.' Dana drew in a shallow breath.

Logan put his arm around her. 'I'm so sorry that happened to you. That wasn't fair, especially on top of everything else.' Dana could tell that he had more to say but was holding back so he didn't make it worse and she loved him even more for it.

'I really thought that she loved me, regretted giving me up, that maybe she wanted me in her life.'

Dana couldn't put it out of her mind for the rest of the night. As she made dinner, as she bathed and helped dress Kelsey in her pyjamas even though she was a *big girl* now, she thought about her family. When she tucked in her daughter and kissed her goodnight, she whispered, 'You are the best thing in my life. I hope you know I love you so much.'

Belatedly, Dana realised that Jackie hadn't mentioned her rounded stomach or the fact that she would be a grandmother soon. But it had become clear almost immediately that Jackie didn't care about that, or her, at all. She had called Mischa after all these years, out of the blue telling her that she was dying, yet all she'd really wanted to do was unload and play the blame game with Dana's mum after decades. Dana felt as if she had been cast aside for a second time by her real mother. She felt the sadness well up inside her again. She would never do that to her daughter, deliberately hurt her, make her feel as if she wasn't wanted, nor would she do it to the baby growing in her womb. She put her hand on top of her stomach just as Logan was walking up to her.

'You OK?'

Dana wrapped her arms around him and rested her head on his shoulder.

'No, not really. I just can't believe how today went down. I just... Logan, I don't want to turn out like her. She's my mother – what if I end up hurting those closest to me?'

'Dana, you're a wonderful person. You would never hurt those you love. You have a good heart.'

'Thanks. I needed that. Uh, while we were out, Mum asked us

to come over on the weekend for a BBQ. She wants to get the family back on track and she wants me to talk to Alesha, try to find some common ground or something like that.'

'So James will be there?'

Dana laughed. 'Yes, my love, your drinking buddy will be there too.' She cupped his cheek and planted a small kiss on his lips.

8

Days blurred into each other. The world was perpetually dark, Dana's pain drowning out everything and everyone around her. The world had been leached of colour and happiness, her very existence hanging in the balance. Kelsey had been gone for two weeks now. Her funeral was finally happening today after the coroner's findings had been handed to the police. Dana and Logan had been informed that Dana would not be charged for the death of their daughter. Logan had broken down. He'd been so stressed that he would lose all of his family and that Dana would go to jail. Dana, on the other hand, showed no emotion whatsoever when told the decision. All her pain in that moment was internalised.

Logan was helping her as much as he could, but he simply couldn't understand her guilt at her role in Kelsey's death. Maybe she was projecting her anger at the world onto Logan and her family, but they had to hate her as much as she hated herself, surely.

The grief-stricken mother was supposed to be getting dressed for the funeral. Her own mother was there to help her and was now waiting in the lounge. She had laid out a dress for Dana to wear. A bright pink maxi dress that would be more comfortable than any of her other clothes as she was now thirty-four weeks pregnant, not far from having her baby. It was Kelsey's favourite colour. The service was to be attended by family only as Logan thought it best to keep it small and private. He drove them to the service, but when they arrived Dana couldn't get out of the car. Logan eased her out before holding her up under one arm while her father took the other side, supporting her. Together the three of them made their way slowly inside. Dana sat in the front row of the small chapel, Logan on one side, her mother on the other.

Pippa appeared in front of her, leaned forward and gave her a gentle hug. 'I'm so sorry, Dana.' She was fighting off tears but lost the battle. 'So damn sorry. She was the most wonderful human being I've ever known.' Pippa dabbed at her eyes with a tissue then bent down and hugged Logan, whispering not so quietly in his ear, 'How's she really doing?' Dana pretended not to hear her or see when Logan shook his head. How could they not see that she deserved to be in perpetual pain? Her mother grabbed her hand as the minister stood in front of the lectern, holding some cards in front of him. He looked appropriately sombre, perfect for the occasion. Dana wondered how many speeches he gave a week about people he didn't know. None of her family had decided to speak, choosing to write down anecdotes and their thoughts on Kelsey's short life instead.

The man cleared his throat, the sound grating across Dana's already shot nerves. She saw Alesha and James quietly take their place next to her father. Alesha tried to catch her eye, but Dana looked straight ahead, ignoring her, ignoring everyone. She was numb right now; she hadn't properly processed what had happened to Kelsey and who had played what role in the tragedy. All she knew was she was dying inside and wished more than anything else that Kelsey were alive and home with them, giving her a kiss, rubbing her baby bump, eating Dana's home-made pancakes and not mentioning the lumps in them.

'...Tea parties with her mother, her favourite doll, Emma, and her best friend, a bear named Boo Boo.' She had drifted away, not even noticing that the service had begun.

Boo Boo. Kelsey's most treasured possession, her constant companion, the reason why she had been standing behind the car in the first place. Dana could only speculate that Kelsey had come out to drive home with her to find the bear. The real question, though, was who had let the little girl out of their sight? They had all been there and Alesha had offered to watch her, and Dana had told Logan to keep an eye on her, so why then had Kelsey ended up out at the front? Dana had to take the time to process this. If she was right, then she wasn't alone in bearing the guilt of her daughter's death. Thinking clearly finally, she wondered if any of her family had come to the same conclusion and if they realised the role they had all played in Kelsey's death, especially Alesha.

She wanted to jump up then and there and demand answers from each and every one of them. Five adults and not one of them had seen her slip away? Who had been watching her? Dana's body was filling with rage and it was all she could do to keep from screaming. She refocused her attention on the minister, staring at his face so intently that she forgot to blink. Logan took her hand, squeezing it firmly, looking over at her. He'd been drunk that day, drinking with James from the moment he had arrived. Dana couldn't even say how many beers he'd consumed.

And Alesha – they hadn't even fixed their relationship, coming off the back of the adoption argument. Where had she been when her niece had snuck away? Dana hadn't expected anything from James, also very drunk and talking loudly with

Logan when she had left. Her father had been grilling lunch, the scent of cooking meat drifting on the breeze, but he'd also known she was leaving and her mother should have been the one holding everything together. Where had she been during all of that?

Breaking her thought pattern, her mother grabbed Dana's other hand, rubbing it in small circles, as if that would make her feel better. There was a large printed poster of Kelsey leaning on an easel beside the minister. She was dressed in a pink frilly dress that her nan had given her along with her fairy wings. Dana had taken the photo and it was how Dana chose to remember her. Kelsey's smile was like sunshine; she really did look like a fairy princess. Dana hadn't chosen the photos for the montage that played across the television screen, so she figured her mother had taken care of that since she was incapable of doing anything. Since the accident, she dressed in whatever was laid out for her, she sometimes ate whatever was put in front of her because she had to keep eating for the baby. She hated being pregnant now. The kicking was a constant reminder that she would soon become a mother to someone else when she was still mourning the death of her first child. What if she hurt this one too? She never raised any of her fears with her family, choosing to barely speak at all.

Mercifully, the service ended, and Dana was helped to her feet by Logan and her mum. Dana walked down the aisle, completely numb, mournful piano music playing from the corner of the room. Why hadn't they chosen one of Kelsey's favourite songs? Just one more thing to hold on to, to obsess over, to prove that she was a terrible mother. The summer sun shone down on Dana's face, making her sweat lightly under her bright pink flowing dress. Logan opened the car door for her and gently helped her into the front seat where there was more room for her and her large bump. He slid into the driver's seat, her parents buckling themselves into the back. She didn't know where the others were and she didn't care.

The cemetery wasn't far away. It felt as if she had barely clicked in her seat belt when Logan slowed the car, then parked on the large dirt parking lot where there were a few other cars parked. He helped her back out of the car and draped his arm around her shoulder to steady her as she walked over the uneven grass, headed towards the freshly dug grave, the coffin already poised, ready to be lowered into the ground. She stifled a sob. How could she leave her baby here, in the dark, unforgiving ground? She wanted nothing more than to throw herself into the grave and be with Kelsey always, but she had her other child to think of. She pushed the thought away; she just couldn't think about the baby right now.

Her mum and Pippa must have decorated the coffin. Pink balloons blew in the breeze as if waving goodbye to their favourite little princess. There were pink and white streamers adorning the side of the coffin and when Dana went and stood in front of it, she placed her hand on the top, noticing the remnants of pink glitter, mostly blown away by the breeze. Using her finger, she drew a love heart in the remaining glitter. The minister gave one final speech about delivering an angel to heaven as the coffin was lowered into the ground, taking her baby with it.

Someone pressed a pink carnation into her hand. She looked down at it, having no idea what she was supposed to do with it. Then she saw her mum walk forward, lean over and throw the carnation onto the disappearing coffin. She turned, tears sliding down her face as she pulled Dana into a desperate hug, then moving to hug Logan.

'So sorry for your loss,' she whispered. It sounded like an

inadequate thing to say, given what they had lost, what Kelsey had meant to them all.

Dana could see other people in the cemetery, mourning their losses as she was. One couple bent over a headstone, a bunch of fresh flowers lying on the grave. They stood up, hands clasped, and looked her way. They were too far away to see their faces but she could imagine they wore identical looks of grief to hers. She felt wrong staring at them, but she couldn't help it. Dana stopped intruding on their moment and watched as Pippa, her dad, James and finally Alesha threw their flowers in one by one. Alesha sobbed, and as she turned she caught Dana's vacant stare. She didn't try and hug her, but hugged Logan instead, perhaps instinctively knowing that Dana would have recoiled from her touch.

Finally they had all thrown in their flowers except for her. She just couldn't seem to make her feet move towards the grave. Eventually Logan whispered into her ear, 'Dana, love, you have to throw your flower in and say goodbye now.' He grasped her elbow and gently propelled her forward. As it loomed closer with every step, she resisted. That couldn't possibly be the last memory of her daughter today. Just as she was about to take the final step, Dana spun around, breaking Logan's hold on her, and hurried as fast as she dared back to the car, the pink carnation clutched tightly in her hand, the stem bending with the force of her grip. She threw herself into the car, slammed the door closed and screamed as loud as she could.

* * *

They argued about Logan going back to work, Dana holding a grudge against him for going back the day after Kelsey died. It had been four weeks since Kelsey passed away and Dana still hadn't got over him returning to work so soon. Logan had said that he couldn't be in the house surrounded by Kelsey.

'I know this is hard to accept, but I needed to go back, for myself. Besides, we need the money. We have a child coming.'

'What, so we can just replace one dead child with a living one?'

'You know that's not what I'm saying at all,' Logan said in a calm and controlled voice that only angered her more to the point of screaming at him. He laid it out for her, told her she needed to get on board, then rolled over in bed, turning out the lamp. Dana fumed, cried and cursed him for hours.

He was being patient with her, but she could tell he wanted her to start moving into the next phase of grieving, as he had. The pink carnation still rested in a small rosebud glass vase in her bedroom, slowly withering, a constant reminder of the day she'd said goodbye to her daughter. She felt that she needed to punish herself by looking at it every day. Maybe when it was no longer there she could start to heal.

The second day after Kelsey had passed away, she'd expected Logan to change his mind about going to work, but he'd dressed and left the house after a quick kiss on her turned cheek. Pippa had appeared, ready to take care of Dana for the next four weeks. She unlocked the front door with the key Logan had had cut for her.

Pippa had told her that Logan was worried about her and wanted the best for her and the baby, but Dana hadn't wanted to hear about all the things Logan wanted for her. What she wanted from him, was... actually, she wasn't quite sure what she wanted. Dana needed to remember that he had lost his daughter too and he probably felt as if he was losing his wife piece by piece as she retreated into herself, no matter how he acted.

Dana was depressed, she knew that. She didn't need to go to a doctor to diagnose her. Her hair was falling out in chunks and her mind felt as if it were fractured in a million different directions. She couldn't focus and she had considered suicide, even going so far as to devise a plan down to the last detail. Nothing could shock her any more. She felt as if depression was a dark, endless pit full of misery, guilt and self-loathing and she belonged there. Each day, a little more of her crumbled, threatening to plunge her into the darkness forever. She couldn't tell anyone about this – they'd put her away *for her own safety*. So she suffered alone, trying to work out a way to live in a world without Kelsey, because this wasn't living.

After Pippa had arrived that second morning, the days had begun to bleed into each other. Pippa would arrive as Logan left for work. They quite often crossed paths at the front door, where Dana heard them whispering, presumably about her. Eventually Pippa was over for her last day before she had to return to work.

'I can arrange to have some more time off if you need me,' Pippa said yet again, her guilt at not being there for Dana obvious. When she had told her that she wouldn't be coming around during the day any more, Dana's breath had caught in her throat. How was she going to be able to cope? But she deserved to be alone. She had killed her daughter.

Pippa must have noticed the colour draining from her face as she quickly said, 'How about I call your mum to come round again tomorrow? I'm sure she'd love to see you, spend the day with you.'

Except for the day Logan had gone back to work, Dana hadn't heard much from her mother. It was Dana's fault. She wouldn't pick up when either of her parents called and she had refused to answer the door the few times when her mother had popped round. Her mum respected her privacy and didn't use her key to get in. It hadn't taken Dana long to figure out why she was behaving like this, shutting her mother out: she had lost Kelsey at her mother's home and she now associated her with loss, grief and anger. It wasn't fair, but it was how she felt.

All she could see was that she was alone again. Abandoned. She would get through it eventually, but for now, she was wrapping herself in a cloak of guilt that no one could penetrate. Soon she would be responsible for another person and the very thought terrified her. She was thirty-six weeks pregnant and every second that she was awake was uncomfortable both emotionally and physically. She was tired all the time, and numb. Dana felt as if she was sleepwalking through life and she supposed she was.

When Logan came home from work, he had his usual whispered chat with Pippa about her, but they'd started having that outside on the front veranda now where they were out of earshot. It was just as well – she didn't want to hear Pippa's report or hear the disappointment in her husband's voice when he heard she was the same. He saw it, he lived it every day, but they were experiencing different things; they were in different stages in their grief. Dana was still firmly stuck in the past, whereas Logan was moving on with his life, whizzing through his grief and even talking about the baby with joy and anticipation, something she wasn't capable of doing yet.

* * *

Pippa started coming over in the evenings and having tea with them, usually bringing food with her. She talked and laughed with Logan, touching him on the arm as she walked by, trying to entice Dana into the conversation. Dana sat there, her eyes sliding from Logan to Pippa, wondering how they were able to smile, to laugh, to feel. She couldn't help but compare herself to

Pippa these days. Pip was young, beautiful and slim, as Dana had always been. Dana, on the other hand, was to the point of being emaciated despite her baby bump, her skin a grey colour and smudges of darkness under her eyes.

Pippa brushed Dana's hair, using dry shampoo because she wouldn't wash her own hair. Logan sometimes laid out clothes for her in the morning, but usually found her in her pyjamas when he came home because everything he picked out reminded her of a snapshot in time with Kelsey. If she was ever going to wear clothes again then she needed to go shopping, but she wouldn't leave the house, because she couldn't. She was *that mother*. A tragic figure, a cautionary tale.

Dana pushed her chair back from the table, her dinner uneaten yet again. She caught the look of exasperation on Logan's face, but she couldn't help it. This was the way she was now. A shadow of her former self. The house was devoid of laughter, except Pippa's and Logan's, which seemed out of place and downright insensitive. Dana walked from the kitchen and into the lounge, where she sat heavily on the couch. She heard Pippa's gentle laughter, which was cut off by the house phone ringing. The house was hushed in between rings as if holding its breath until Pippa picked the phone up.

'Hello?' There was a pause. 'Hi, Mischa, how are you?' she asked, keeping her voice low. A pause. 'She's not doing too well, I'm afraid. Logan and I are trying to keep her afloat, get her spirits up, but... I just pray when the baby comes it gives her something to do. Someone to love.'

Dana did love someone: her daughter, Kelsey. Why couldn't they all see that she wasn't ready to move on? To say goodbye? Dana knew that her emotions were driving Logan away slowly. They still shared the same bed and he still did things for her, but she feared he did them out of duty now, the memory of love, not actual love.

'What kind?' asked Pippa, Dana honing back in on the quiet, one-sided conversation. 'OK, I'll talk to her about it. See you later.' Pippa put the phone down and came into the lounge. 'That was your mum,' she said unnecessarily. 'Just ringing to say hi, but she didn't want to interrupt your tea,' Pippa said, aware that Dana hadn't touched a bite.

Dana nodded. She had nothing to say about her mother calling. She didn't want to hear from her just yet, let alone speak to her. That first day with her mum had been hard enough, she wasn't ready to repeat it any time soon.

'Dana, Mischa suggested something that I think is a good idea. Hear me out.' Both Dana and Logan looked at her and for a moment Pippa seemed to squirm under their gazes. 'There's a group, in town... a special group where people who have lost someone can go. Well – it's a grief counselling group, a support group,' she said in a rush. 'You meet people who are in a similar situation to you, having lost someone that they love,' she finished quietly. 'I think it's a good idea to go, Dana. You need to talk and share with people and if that can't be us then that's fine, but you need to talk to someone. The meeting is tomorrow at six in the evening. I can take you.'

Pippa looked over at Logan, who nodded. 'I think it's a great idea too,' he said, injecting enthusiasm into his voice. 'Dana, what do you think? Will you go? If not for you, then for me?'

Dana felt pressured. They were both staring at her, waiting for her positive response. Surely they knew that talking to a group of strangers about Kelsey's death wouldn't help her? But they wore identical looks of hope, and she didn't have the energy to argue with them. Logan nodded at her when her gaze fell upon him.

'Please, love, you need some help, more than I can give you.'
He smiled tentatively at her.

She didn't return the smile, but she did whisper, 'OK.' If it
would get them off her back, it was worth trying.

'What did you say?' asked Pippa.

'I said yes.' Dana's voice was flat, drawing out each word as if it
were being pulled from the depths of her soul. This would make
them happy and someone should be happy. She put her hands on
her knees, pushing herself up, and walked from the room. She
could hear Logan and Pippa start to talk in low voices as soon as
she headed down the hallway. Dana turned back and looked at
the doorway to the kitchen. It would be so much easier if she
could walk back in there and tell them how deep down she was,
how the blackness, the darkness, was taking her over piece by
piece and she wasn't sure that she'd ever make it back. She
pushed the impulse from her mind, walking to her bedroom and
lying on the bed. She was already in her pyjamas, so no need to
get changed. She hadn't even bothered getting dressed that day.

Later on, she heard the front door open. She could hear
Logan and Pippa head out onto the veranda of the small house
and Logan gently closing the door so as not to disturb her. They
were out there for ages, probably talking about how they clearly
thought that this group would restore her to the *normal* Dana, but
that was the thing: this *was* the new normal. There *was* no going
back.

Dana fell asleep without hearing Logan come back inside but
she woke when his weight moved the mattress. He must have
heard the change in her breathing. He lay behind her and sighed.
She could smell toothpaste on his breath, a light waft of beer.
'This support group is a good thing. I think it'll really help you.'
He slid his hand onto her back then over her side to reach her
belly, where he rubbed the baby. 'Not long now. We'd better start

thinking about long term. For the baby, I mean. We'll be fine for the first few months to make feeding easier for you, but then... we'll need another room for the baby.'

She stilled, unable to even breathe. He wouldn't...? Angrily, she snapped on the bedside lamp and rolled over, sitting up with difficulty. 'And where do you propose we put the baby, Logan?' she demanded, her eyes boring into his.

He sat up too, the sheet falling from his bare torso. 'Dana, you know where I mean,' he said in a tone meant to soothe her, but she would not be soothed.

'So, what? You just want to erase any trace that Kelsey ever existed? Throw out her things and move our new child in there? Is that it?' she yelled, untangling herself from the sheet.

'You're taking this the wrong way. I've spoken to your parents and Pippa about this. We all agree it's the right thing to do, to help you move on.'

'Oh, well, if you all agree about *my* life, then who am I to complain?'

'You're not moving on,' he said, his voice rising. 'You're not even beginning to let go. You're either angry or distant all the time. I can't reach you and when we do talk, we end up in an argument like this one. It's got to stop, or something has to change. We won't throw anything out, we'll just box most of it up and store it at your parents' place. Your mum said it was fine.'

'You discussed this with them but not me? I need that room. I need it to stay exactly how it is so don't you dare touch it. You hear me?' she screamed.

'Yeah, I hear you,' Logan said firmly, grabbing his pillow and walking out of the door.

Dana was horrified her family had dared to put a time frame on grieving. They had allocated her a certain amount of time and it appeared that time was now up. She was to move on, but how could she when she lived with the guilt each day, each minute? She rolled over, putting her hand across her mouth while she cried. This grief group, they'd understand. They'd be people like her, not wanting to let go, holding onto those they loved tightly. Their memories the only thing sustaining them. Maybe it was a good idea for her to go. Besides, she'd already said yes, there was no going back now. Dana thought about the pink carnation that had finally withered and died. She had cried as she had thrown it in the bin.

9

Pippa offered to drive her to the meeting, which started half an hour after she finished work. It ran for an hour and Pippa was going to wait in the car for her. Dana knew that Logan and Pippa were worried that she would change her mind when it came down to it, but she'd said she'd go and she would. She couldn't guarantee that she'd talk, but she'd listen to the sad stories of other people who'd lost loved ones – at least, that was what she assumed happened in these meetings. You shared your grief, but did they actually tell you how to deal with that grief? The guilt? Was there a formula for her to follow to move on?

Dana opened the door but was hesitant to step out of the car. 'You'll be OK, honey. I promise. They're just people, like you, trying to deal with something bigger than themselves. This will be good for you and the baby,' Pippa said, smiling at her. 'I'll be right here, waiting. Good luck.' Dana closed the door and saw Pippa pull out her phone. Texting Logan to let him know that Dana was going inside or something else?

The baby. Most days Dana didn't even think about the baby, so consumed was she by thoughts of Kelsey. It was due soon, so she'd better start getting used to the idea of being a mother again. It was hard. Part of her wanted to be present and live again for this new child, but part of her couldn't even handle the thought of living without Kelsey. Her mind and heart were at war with each other.

Dana walked through the doors of the building where the group was being held, not knowing what to expect. There were twelve chairs in a semicircle with a lone chair at the other end. She guessed this was where the counsellor sat. She wondered if you went around the room and introduced yourself then told your story. She began to panic at the thought of telling people what she'd done. She turned to run away – she would tell Pippa that it just wasn't for her – but as she turned she bumped into a woman. She was a bit shorter than Dana was, blonde with a dazzling smile, which she turned on Dana.

'Sorry,' Dana mumbled and went to walk around her, awkwardly moving her bulk to the left of the woman.

'Hey, you're new, right?' she said as she smiled at Dana.

'Um, yeah, but I'm not actually staying. I was just leaving.' She looked guilty as she said it.

'Oh. Well, I'm Melanie Cullen. I've been coming here for a while now. It really does help, you know. You should stay, at least for a few minutes. I'm here because I lost my daughter, Mindy.' She said it so matter-of-factly and without prompting that Dana was a little shocked at her candour and she wondered if she would ever speak like that about Kelsey's death. 'She was the love of my life,' Melanie said as she guided Dana towards the white fold-out table and set about making a cup of tea in a plastic cup, dunking her teabag in and out of the hot water, barely flavouring the water.

'What's your name?' Melanie asked cheerfully.

'My name?' Dana asked. Melanie's head bobbed up and

down. It was as if she had forgotten how to talk to people. 'Dana O'Connor.' She reached out her hand to grasp Melanie's small one.

'Nice to meet you, Dana. Who did you lose?' Melanie took a sip of the tea, staring at her intently.

Dana's face fell and her eyes immediately filled with tears.

'Oh, shit. I'm so sorry. I'm always putting my foot in it, being so blunt with people. I forget that not everyone is like me.' She seemed apologetic but still smiled. 'I'm sorry, Dana. What a beautiful name. Are you married?' she asked.

'Yes, I am. His name is Logan,' she said, feeling as if she had to expand upon her answer.

'I was too, but when my Mindy passed away, my husband couldn't handle it and he left me, the bastard.' Her sunny features clouded over and Dana realised that she wasn't the only one with problems. 'I was all alone, trying to cope by myself before I received a flyer in the letterbox advertising this group. It's helped so much that, a little while ago, I helped with another letterbox drop that covered the whole town. There are so many people in need, I want to help them all.' Melanie grabbed her hands. 'Dana, please stay. It'll help more than you think. How far along are you?'

'Thirty-six weeks.'

'Such a wonderful miracle.' She seemed sincere and nice, if a little forward and blunt, but Dana found it kind of refreshing.

'OK, maybe I'll stay for a few minutes,' she agreed.

'That's great!' said Melanie in an upbeat voice. Dana was dragged along behind her as she led her to a grey plastic chair, gently pushing her down into it but keeping hold of her hand, as if to give her comfort. Surprisingly, it *was* comforting.

People started sitting down and Dana looked at the clock. It was almost time. She had no idea what to expect and it made her nervous. She just wanted to fade into the background, listen but not say anything. There were fewer than ten people there. A woman sat down in the chair at the head of the semicircle. She caught Dana's eye and smiled at her reassuringly.

'Evening, all. For those of you who are new, I'm Janet Michaels and I'm the counsellor running this support group. I'm glad to see you all here today. Does anyone want to say a few words to get the meeting started?'

Beside her, Melanie immediately threw her hand up. Dana looked at Melanie then at Janet. Melanie seemed eager to talk. Dana wondered where she got the guts to speak about her loss so easily.

'Yes, Melanie,' said Janet.

'Well, I'd like to introduce our newest member, Dana O'Connor.' Dana flushed with embarrassment when everyone started clapping politely. She smiled briefly, nodded, then waited it out.

'Dana, welcome.' Janet smiled at her. 'Did you want to share something today or not yet?'

'I... um... I...'

'It's OK, you don't have to speak today, no one will force you.'

Dana stayed silent for the rest of the hour-long meeting. She listened to heart breaking tales of love and loss. Some had lost husbands and wives, some children, like her, but to illness. It was gut-wrenching listening to these people tell their stories, crying over their collective losses. It hurt her heart just to be there and she decided not to come back next week. It was too difficult. She felt her hand being squeezed and looked down to see Melanie gripping her hand in hers.

Melanie leaned over. 'You're so brave. I can tell we're going to be the very best of friends.'

Surprisingly, Dana realised she liked the cheerful woman with her loose blonde curls and winning smile. Soon after, the meeting ended and Janet made a point of coming over to her. 'Melanie,' she said, glancing at her briefly.

Melanie smiled.

Janet turned to Dana, smiling gently at her, her voice soft and modulated. 'Thank you for joining us today, Dana. The first step is always the hardest to take. Will we see you again next week?' Again she smiled, head cocked slightly to the side, her silver hair falling over her eye as she waited for Dana to speak.

'I... um... I'm not sure. I found today—'

'Difficult?' finished Janet.

'Yeah. I found it hard to hear other people's stories. It's heart breaking. With where my head is at, I'm not sure that I can do it.'

Janet touched her left shoulder, patting her twice. 'Coming here will help. Talking will help. Being around people who don't know you but do know what you're going through will help.'

'Right,' chimed in Melanie. 'And you've already made a friend in me,' she said.

Janet glanced at Melanie. 'Yes, you'll make friends here because we've been, or are, where you are now.'

Dana found Janet's reassuring way of speaking comforting. Maybe she would come back.

'I'll think about it,' Dana said, noncommittally. She swung her bag over her shoulder and headed towards the exit. Melanie fell into step beside her.

'Can we exchange numbers? You can call or text any time. I'll always answer, I promise.' She smiled again, lighting up the room. Dana found herself giving her a hesitant smile back. Smiling felt almost unnatural now, as if her face were made of stone, stuck in a mask of grief, one little happy movement and she might crack, falling to the floor, shattering. The women exchanged numbers.

Melanie walked her outside. Dana could see Pippa in the car

waiting, looking in her direction. Pippa waved. 'Who's that?' Melanie asked, smiling.

'My best friend, Pippa. She drove me here. She's been... concerned. Logan too.'

Melanie didn't say anything for a moment. 'Want me to come and pick you up for next week's meeting? I would imagine that driving is difficult,' she said, placing her hand on Dana's swollen stomach. She touched it so quickly that Dana wasn't even sure it had happened. Dana went to leave but Melanie grabbed her and hugged her. 'I'll text you,' she said before walking towards Pippa's car. Dana wondered what she was doing. Melanie opened the passenger side door to Pippa's surprise.

'Hey, I'm Melanie, Dana's newest friend, how are you?' she asked in her bubbly voice.

Pippa looked a little taken aback before smiling in return. 'Nice to meet you, Melanie.'

They stared at each other for a beat longer before Melanie stood up, gave Dana one last hug and headed off towards her own car. Dana slid into Pippa's car, slamming the door.

'Who was that?' asked Pippa as soon as she dropped into the passenger seat.

'My new friend apparently. She lost her daughter too. Mindy. She's a little forward but it's kind of nice. She took me under her wing today. She offered to pick me up next week.'

'So, there will be a next week?' Pippa asked, smiling.

'Possibly. Hearing their stories was... confronting,' Dana said, struggling to find a word that accurately conveyed the sadness and despair that filled the room. She still didn't know if this was for her, but she'd give it another go. She owed it to Logan at least to try.

Pippa drove her home in silence, pulling up into the driveway, turning off the ignition. 'You coming in?' asked Dana, surprised.

'Yeah, just to say hi to Logan and make sure you're OK. I know today was hard but I'm so proud of you for going.'

Dana unlocked the front door to find Logan walking down the hallway. 'Hey, how was it?' he asked, giving her a hug.

Dana gave him a wan smile. 'Exhausting.' She pushed past him in the narrow hallway and went to change. She felt as if she needed to remove the sadness from her body.

Logan didn't follow her, so once she was dressed she poked her head out of the bedroom and saw Logan and Pippa talking in the hallway. She couldn't hear what they were saying, so she walked back into the bathroom to scrub her face. It had felt strange to have been out of the house when she'd been inside for such a long time. She knew Logan would tell her that he was proud of her, but she wasn't sure if he should be proud. One meeting didn't cure her of her grief, make her the woman that she used to be. She'd never be that woman again. The baby kicked, and her hand unconsciously cradled her stomach.

She heard the front door close. Pippa hadn't even said goodbye to her. She heard Logan coming down the hallway. He stood in the bathroom doorway and watched as she dried her face.

'I'm really proud of you, honey, I know that must have been very hard on you.' He walked into the small bathroom and took her in his arms, planting a chaste kiss on her forehead. They hadn't made love since the accident. Before, they had done it a few times a week. Now, nothing. Logan never brought it up, but she wondered how he felt about it. She had caught him masturbating to porn a few nights ago. He'd had a guilty look on his face, but she'd closed the door and they'd never spoken about it. It had made her feel like shit, as if she was letting him down, but she felt the same way – he was letting her down. Their daughter had died; didn't he care? She knew it was wrong of her to think that way, she knew he grieved Kelsey too, but she just couldn't help it.

Logan had a few beers with dinner and some more while lounging in front of the TV. She had counted them: six. A lot even for him. He came home with a carton of beer every few days now, where one used to last him two weeks or so. It was his way of coping and who was she to try and tell him what to do, even if that was what they were doing to her?

Her phone pinged in the kitchen, where it was charging on the counter. She picked it up, looking at the name. Melanie. She looked at the time; it was past nine.

Hey, just checking in to see how you're feeling after the meeting. You doing OK?

Dana didn't know what to say. She started her reply several times, erasing each one before she could send it before finally settling on:

It was rough, thanks for checking in.

Melanie wrote back immediately.

No problems.

Dana thought about Melanie's daughter, Mindy, and how she had said that her husband had left her soon after her death. Maybe she just needed a friend. Maybe she had no one else. Dana knew how isolating grief could be.

I have to go to bed.

Dana had no idea how to make a friend any more. She felt embarrassed, unsure of herself.

OK, talk tomorrow. Sleep well, no nightmares x

Dana took the phone to her room and turned it on silent before putting it face down on the bedside table. She crawled under the covers and within half an hour Logan came into the room, quietly sliding in beside her.

'Do you want to talk about it?' he asked.

'No.' She rolled over, pulling the blanket with her. Suddenly the cover was ripped from her hands. She sat up and turned towards Logan.

'What the hell?'

'No more!' he yelled at her. 'I am so sick of you being this way.' He glared at her, daring her to argue with him.

'Like what?' she spat.

'Your attitude, Dana. I can't stand it. It's time for you to start at least trying to move on.'

'I went to that fucking meeting you wanted me to go to! I'm about to become a mother again and I'm still grieving. What the hell do you want from me?' she screamed, hand swiping at the angry tears that ran down her face.

Logan looked taken aback at her outburst, whether it was her yelling or her words, she didn't know, and she didn't much care.

'It's just, you're not moving on. Pippa agrees with me,' he said, as if that mattered, his eyes sliding from hers.

'Oh, well, if Pippa agrees, then I must be in the wrong,' she said sarcastically.

'Don't be a bitch, Dana. She's your best friend and she's worried about you, as am I. Can't you see where we're coming from? The baby is coming soon and you won't even let me pack up her room.'

'You can't even say her name, can you? When was the last time you said Kelsey? It's like I'm the only one who remembers her, like she was a dream for the rest of you, and, yeah, I'm still mourning, so what? I lost my daughter. What's your excuse?' She felt as if she was repeating herself and justifying her emotions. She couldn't deal with this, so she did what she always seemed to do lately. She stood awkwardly and picked up her pillow, ready to run away.

'Don't bother,' Logan said coldly. 'I'll take the couch.' He grabbed his pillow and bunched it under his arm as he left the bedroom.

Dana didn't feel much after her argument with Logan. Logan didn't, and couldn't, understand how she was feeling. Him yelling at her was out of character, but, lately, who was to say what was and wasn't in character? After Logan left, she simply pulled up the covers, rolled over and tried to sleep.

She must have fallen asleep at some stage because in her dream she was stuck in a loop of hitting Kelsey then waking up on the ground, going over to the car and seeing her lifeless body jammed under the wheel. She screamed every time, longer and louder, until finally her screams transcended her dreams and became reality. She woke herself up with her panicked screaming. Through her confusion, she heard footsteps running down the hallway and then Logan was behind her, cradling her, whispering, 'You're OK, it's gonna be OK,' but how was anything supposed to be OK ever again?

'Get off me!' she yelled, pushing herself away from him, her belly hindering her escape from his arms.

'What? What is it now?' Logan demanded.

'I don't *need* you to comfort me. I don't *need* you at all,' she yelled, knowing that she was being deliberately cruel but not being able to stop.

'Fine. I'll leave you alone, then,' he said, defeat in his voice. She watched as he swung his legs over the bed then walked back down to the lounge. She sighed, her breathing ragged, her nightmare still all too real. She rolled over and closed her eyes, praying that she didn't drop right back into the same nightmare.

* * *

The next morning when Dana stumbled out of bed, Logan had already left for work. The house was quiet. So quiet that she almost welcomed the noise when the home phone rang. Only one person called her on her home phone: her mother.

'Hi, Mum,' she answered quietly. She had been avoiding her calls, but it was time to talk to her. To take one tiny step forward.

'Hi, darling. I'm not going to ask you the question, I just wanted to make sure that you're OK after last night.'

'What?' she said, breath stuck in her throat. How did she know about the fight?

'Logan called, said you had a fight and that I should check up on you this morning.'

'Oh, he did, did he? I'm fine, Mum, it was just a fight.' She sighed wearily.

'But you should be there for each other, not at each other's throats. He said it wasn't the first time that you'd fought or had nightmares.'

'He told you about those too?' She felt betrayed.

'Yes, darling, he's worried about you. That you're not coping, that you can't move on. Alesha and I are going to come visit you today. Just us girls. I'll bring the morning tea, since I know you haven't been out shopping.'

She didn't want to see Alesha and she said so. In fact, her sister was the very last person she wanted to see.

'Don't be silly, Dana, she's your sister. It'll be good for you.'

Dana didn't have the energy to fight her mother, so she stayed silent.

'Great, we'll be there at eleven. See you then, love.' Her mother hung up and Dana took a deep steadying breath. It would be the first time that she'd seen Alesha since the funeral. The days had blurred together, rolling into one long nightmare. She could barely keep track of time.

Dana looked around her. Dishes piled high in the sink. Dirty clothes hung over the couch, work gear for Logan, some clean clothes in the basket, ready to be folded but now full of wrinkles. She opened the fridge. Condiments and beer. Two cans left out of the carton he'd bought only two days ago. How much was he really drinking a day? She knew she should care, but she just... couldn't.

There was a knock at the front door and Dana pulled her phone from her pocket. Eleven. She had been wandering from room to room looking at her failings for nearly two hours.

'Dana?' There was more knocking at the door. Had they forgotten that she was heavily pregnant and couldn't move that fast? She made it to the door just as another barrage of knocking rattled the old door.

'I'm coming!' she yelled, yanking the door open. 'I was at the door,' she said snippily.

'Then why didn't you answer it?' Her mother waltzed past her, followed by her sister, who met her eyes briefly then looked away.

Her mother held a white box in her hands. Dana recognised the label; she'd gone to her favourite bakery for sweet treats.

'Mum, you know... I'm really not in the mood for guests. Could we do this another day?'

'We're not guests, darling, we're family and family stick together, see each other through thick and thin. And this is your time of need and, yes, I know you haven't been picking up the phone, but I thought it was time that we rectified a few things. I love you, *we* love you. Me, your father, Alesha, we all agree that it's time to get some things taken care of.'

Dana ran her hand through her unwashed hair. She studied Alesha, who was looking at the sink. Was she judging her on her housekeeping skills or just avoiding her gaze? Dana hadn't known how she was going to react to seeing her sister, but she did now. She felt rage. How dare she show her face here, as if they were still sisters, still anything to each other. Her mum didn't seem to sense the tension in the room even though the air crackled with it, or perhaps she was just ignoring it.

'For one, you could start to pack up Kelsey's room. You really do have to make room for the new baby, you know,' Dana's mum prattled on, unaware of the look of murderous rage on Dana's face. Alesha had her head hung low, only looking up occasionally.

'Mum, I don't want to pack up Kelsey's room and I have no intention of doing so,' she snapped, hands on her hips, her mouth downturned.

'Well,' she said, turning to face her daughter, 'you're going to have to when you move, so might as well get a jump start on it. I brought some boxes over. They're in the car.'

'Move? I'm not moving. What gave you that idea?'

Her mother looked at her.

'Oh, God, it was Logan, this whole thing was his idea, wasn't it? He thought I'd be more likely to pack up her room if you forced it upon me. Well, I won't do it!' she yelled, slapping her hand down on the kitchen table. It cracked loudly in the otherwise quiet room. She saw Alesha flinch, but her mother stood strong enough to weather Dana's emotional storm.

'And you,' Dana said, finally rounding on her sister. 'How dare you set foot in my house? Did Logan or Mum tell you it was a good idea for you to come here?'

Alesha opened her mouth to speak.

'You know what? It doesn't even matter, you're not welcome here. You killed my daughter.' There, she'd said what had been on her mind since the funeral. Once she was past the initial shock, Dana had gone through everyone that had been at the BBQ, and while all of them were culpable in one way or another, including herself, Alesha was the only one who had volunteered to take care of Kelsey.

'Dana! You mustn't blame your sister. She didn't do anything wrong.' Her mum defended her, enraging Dana even more.

'Didn't do anything wrong? Didn't do anything wrong?' Dana screeched, her voice getting higher with each word. 'She offered to watch my child, but she didn't. My child died because of *you*, you fucking bitch!' she said, glaring at her sister.

Alesha snapped her head to the side to look at their mother, her eyes wide with fear. 'I—' she said, still looking at her mum for help.

'Don't look at her, goddammit. What was so important that you couldn't keep an eye on my daughter for half a fucking hour?'

'I...' Alesha started to cry.

'Don't you dare fucking cry! Don't you *fucking* dare! You have no right! Why? Why weren't you watching her?' Dana cried angrily.

'I got a text,' Alesha admitted quietly, not meeting her sister's eyes.

'A text?' Dana was beyond furious, she had moved past full-blown rage now, unable to see anything other than her daughter's face. 'Get out!' she screamed, pointing towards the front door.

'Darling, there's no need—'

'You too. How could you come here expecting me to forgive her? I will never forgive. I lost my child. I'm a mother without a child, because of you all, especially *her*. Leave, now, before I do something I won't regret.'

For a long moment, Dana thought her mum wasn't going to leave, but then finally she moved, picking up her bag and sighing deeply. 'I expected forgiveness from you.'

'And I expected better from you,' Dana said coldly. 'Now get the hell out of my house.'

Her mum and sister both walked quickly down the hallway in single file. When just outside the door, her mother said her name but she never got a chance to finish her sentence because Dana slammed the door in her face. She felt better, as if she'd purged herself of something toxic.

Dana walked back down the hallway. Her mobile rang on the kitchen bench. Dana thought it might be her mother – she was tempted to not even look at it, but it kept ringing, so she went back into the kitchen. It was Melanie. She picked it up. In her upbeat and cheerful voice, Melanie said, 'Hello, love, how are you?'

How was she indeed? That was the million-dollar question, wasn't it?

Actually, she felt like crying but she held it together – she had only just met this woman after all. 'Yeah, fine, just tired, I guess. How are you?' With Melanie, it seemed easy. She knew what she was going through and didn't make demands of her.

'I was ringing to see if you wanted to catch up today, have a chat and a cup of tea? We can go wherever you want or stay in at your place.'

Dana thought about it for a moment. She could do with some cheering up. 'You can come here for a little bit if you want.'

'Sure!' Melanie said excitedly. 'What's your address?'

Dana gave it to her and she said, 'I'll see you soon.' She hung up and Dana cradled the phone to her chest.

In no time at all, for the second time that day, there was a knock at the door. Dana opened it to see Melanie standing there, holding a gift basket. 'Hey, beautiful,' she said, smiling.

Dana stood back and let her in. Her new friend walked straight past her, down the hallway and found the kitchen. 'This is nice,' she said, taking it all in. 'Nice and cosy. My house is too big for me, I rattle around in it with no husband or daughter.' She put on a brave smile, but Dana recognised the pain behind that smile. It was what she saw in the mirror every day.

'Coffee or tea?' asked Dana, finally remembering her manners.

'Coffee, please. This is for you.' She pushed the gift basket at Dana, who reached for it. It was large and heavy and Dana immediately put it on the bench, looking at it.

'I made it myself.' Melanie beamed proudly. It was full of body products, stuff to pamper herself with.

'You didn't have to do that,' Dana said. It was such a generous gift. This stranger was showing her more kindness and compassion than her family was.

'Sure, I did. We're friends now and, besides, I'm teaching myself a new skill. Did I do a good job?'

Dana looked at the basket. It looked like one of those professionally designed gift baskets that you got from the florist. She told Melanie so.

'Oh, you're so sweet!' She beamed, leaning forward to hug.

'How did you know your husband was pulling away from

you?' Dana blurted out. It was blunt, yes, but she was curious – did he start out doing what Logan was doing?

Melanie looked at her, the expression on her face turning sour. 'He was distant. Cold. Made me pack up Mindy's room too soon, within weeks of losing her. It was just crazy, the things he did to me under the guise of love. Sorry, what's your husband's name again?'

'Logan.'

'Right, does Logan say things like that to you yet?' Melanie asked, narrowing her eyes as if it was a given that he would eventually.

Dana swallowed down the lump of pain in her throat. 'Yeah, actually. He's mentioned a few times about wanting to pack up Kelsey's room, but I won't let him, then I find out this morning that he has spoken to my mother about us moving house. Can you believe that?'

'What? That's terrible. This is where all your memories of Kelsey are. You can't let him do that to you. Promise me you'll stand strong, tell him he can move out, but you're not going anywhere. Take a breath, it's all going to be OK. I'll help you through this. I will be like your sponsor – you call me if anyone needs an arse kicking.'

'Thanks. But I don't want him to move out. Besides, I'm about to have another baby soon and I'll need help. I don't want to rely on my mother for anything right now.' There was bitterness in her voice, but Melanie didn't say anything or ask any questions, and for that Dana was grateful.

Melanie reached out and laid her hand on Dana's stomach. 'No matter what, this baby will be loved. You love it, right?' she asked, eyebrows drawing together.

'Yes... and no.'

'What do you mean?'

'I mean, I want to do right by this baby and it was, is, so wanted, but it's not going to be Kelsey, you know?' Dana was close to tears. How was she telling a virtual stranger these things when she couldn't verbalise them properly to her own family?

Dana discreetly wiped at her eyes, wondering where this woman had come from and how she got her so quickly. Melanie stayed for the next hour and they talked about lots of different things, not just their shared grief. Melanie even managed to make Dana laugh at one point.

'I can't stay any longer today, but I'd like to see you again if that's OK with you.'

'You make it sound like the end of a first date.' Dana smiled slightly.

'Well, isn't it? We just met, I come over, we talk, I bring you a gift... sounds like a first date to me. The only thing that's missing is the awkward kiss at the front door.' Melanie had a fit of uncontrollable giggles at her joke. 'Call me or I'll call you.' She stood, grabbed her handbag and headed to the front door. Dana followed her. 'Thanks again, Dana, for the invite, and remember, any time you need me, I'm there.' She leaned forward and put a kiss on Dana's cheek. 'Bye!' she said loudly as she opened the door.

Dana closed it behind Melanie, feeling... lonely.

Just as she was walking back down the hallway, another knock on her door. Dana hesitated.

'I know you're in there. Where else would you go? Let me in, Dana, or I'll just use my key,' a voice called out. Dana opened the door.

'Pippa, hi.'

'Don't hi me – why didn't you answer my text this morning? I wanted to make sure you were doing OK, you know, checking in just like a good best friend should.' Pippa flipped back her hair, giving her a tight smile.

'Logan told you about the fight, didn't he? You're here to make sure I'm all right. Don't feel special. He told my mum too, who also agrees with him that it's time to pack up Kelsey's room, that we should move away from the memories, but he doesn't realise that those memories are all I have left.' She said it all in a rush, feeling the need to explain herself yet again, hoping Pippa would get it this time.

Pippa looked at her, sadness in her eyes. 'Babe, we are all grieving for her and for you, but you need to realise that we all grieve in different ways, and Logan, well, Logan's way is to pack up all the memories, good and bad, and put them away in a box inside his heart.'

'How do you know this?' Dana asked.

'We're just close, that's all, always have been.'

'No, you haven't always been, Pippa. I've seen you whispering with him. Don't lie to me. I can't handle another person I love talking about me behind my back.'

'Yes, we talk about you, but we don't want you to hear, so we whisper. There's nothing going on and the fact that you could even think either one of us would do anything to hurt you shows that you're not in your right mind. Are you going to your support meeting next week? Want me to drive you?'

'No,' Dana said curtly, 'I have another friend picking me up.'

'Oh. Who? That chick?'

'Her name is Melanie. Actually, she came round this morning to check on me after Mum and Alesha came around, badgering me to pack up Kelsey's room. I just can't handle it any more. No more telling me what to do.' Dana threw her hands up in the air in frustration.

'It's best for you, love, you know it deep down.'

'No, I bloody well don't, and stop pushing me!' Dana yelled, fed up with all of them on her back about Kelsey's room. 'I think you should leave.'

'Dana, don't do this.'

'Do what? Protect myself? I have to, no one else will. Pippa, I need you to go. Now.'

Pippa gave Dana a look that conveyed sadness with a hint of frustration. 'I'll call you tomorrow.'

'Don't bother. Not if you're going to side with Logan on everything.'

Pippa didn't say anything, just left the house, closing the door behind her quietly. Now Dana was truly alone and unhappy. She rarely fought with Pippa and had the urge to run after her, but then she remembered her and Logan whispering, bodies close together, and she decided not to. In her grief, she saw betrayal everywhere. Overcome with a wave of exhaustion, Dana decided to lie down for a short nap. She headed towards Kelsey's room, needing to feel close to her daughter after her rough day.

Dana fell asleep in Kelsey's room, surrounded by her toys. It gave her comfort, making her feel as if she were close to her girl again. She was facing the window and was woken hours later by... something. Intuition maybe, but she felt that someone was in the room, staring at her. She could feel the hairs on the back of her neck stand up.

'Logan? Is that you?' Dana thought she could hear breathing behind her but was too scared to turn around. What if it wasn't Logan? She didn't dare look. She stayed frozen in fear for what felt like minutes. Then she swore she heard the back door click closed. She stayed on the bed for a long beat before rolling over slowly, expecting to see some remainder of the intruder behind her. She forced herself to get up, quietly walking towards the door.

Suddenly someone appeared in the doorway in the half-gloom and she screamed in terror, her voice tearing from her throat in fear.

'It's me! It's Logan,' her husband said, grabbing her wrists and holding them tight.

'Were you just in here?' Dana asked, frantically looking around.

'What? No, I just got home.' His beer breath washed over her.

'Logan, there was someone in the house.'

'When?' he asked, slurring his words a little. He'd had more than a few beers with the boys then.

'Just now. Before you came home. I was asleep and I woke up and I could feel someone behind me, then I swear I heard the back door close. I'm scared.'

'All the more reason to move house,' he said straight away, insensitive to her feelings.

'Is that what your reaction to an intruder in our house is? To pack up our lives into boxes and leave? This is where Kelsey was born and grew up. I'm not leaving.'

'Then maybe I'll leave!' Logan exploded.

'Fine! You do that!' she yelled back. The baby moved within her, kicking out painfully, and she moved her hand to settle the baby down, a look of pain on her face.

'Is the baby coming?' Logan asked nervously.

'No, the baby isn't fucking coming. It's upset we're fighting and, frankly, so am I. Why can't we make this work?' she asked gently, tucking a piece of hair behind her ear, her hair wild and unbrushed.

'Because you won't move forward and I want to. Something tragic happened to us, yes, but we need to live again, love again. Please. For me.'

Dana stared at him for so long he started to look uncomfortable. 'I just... need more time. Can you go and check the house, please?' she begged, wanting more than anything to be out of this conversation.

'What? Looking for imaginary intruders?' He laughed at her, mocking her.

She knew she was being sensitive and he was being insensitive because he was drunk, but she couldn't help but feel that she wasn't being heard.

'Come out, come out, wherever you are!' Logan said in a joking voice. He checked the whole house, moving through each room, looking in wardrobes, under the beds and even in the back yard. Then he came back inside where Dana was anxiously waiting in the lounge.

'Dana, there's no one here, although you need to remember to lock the back door, OK? It's not safe.'

Dana had locked the back door, she was positive. She was a pregnant woman alone all day who slept a lot, so she always locked her doors.

Her encounter scared her. For the rest of the night she thought about the intruder. She made her way down to the bedroom. Her phone lay on the bedside table – she could have sworn that she'd left it in the kitchen. It had been there when she was with Melanie. Had she moved it without remembering or had someone else? She was beginning to not feel safe in her own home. Dana threw back the blanket and lay down on her side, the only comfortable position at this point. Logan had brushed his teeth but the beer stench still clung to his body, leaching out of his pores. It made her wrinkle her nose in disgust. It hadn't bothered her before when he'd had one or two but now he was drinking the better part of a carton every few days it bothered her.

He slipped under the sheets behind her. She lay on her side, thinking about why someone was in her house, if not to scare her. But how did they get in? And why were they moving things around in the house? Logan snuggled up behind her and she felt his hard cock rub up against her. For the second time that night, she froze in fear. It had been so long since they'd had anything resembling a sex life. It had been the furthest thing from her mind and still was.

She moved away from Logan, but he reached out, grabbed her and pulled her back against him, then began kissing her neck. He trailed his kisses down her skin, gently massaging one of her breasts. She moaned just a little bit and he saw that as an invitation.

'I want you so bad it's killing me.'

Suddenly the imagine of Kelsey stuck under the wheel of the car flashed into her mind and she could hear her screams echoing. She choked out a strangled sob, which he interpreted as one of pleasure.

'Yeah, that's it,' he whispered, pulling on her nipple.

She pulled away and slid from the bed and flicked the lamp on, struggling to her feet. He sat up, sheet falling from his body so she saw everything. The sheen of sweat covering his body, his cock hard and ready to go. But she wasn't ready and doubted she ever would be.

'That's not fair, Dana. Stop being a cock tease and come back to bed.'

'I can't,' she whispered. 'I really wish I could, but I'm—'

'Not ready,' he finished. 'Yeah, I get that a lot.' He flopped onto his back.

Dana left the bedroom closing the door behind her as she walked into the hallway, unsettled by everything that had happened today. Dana was still freaked out by the intruder in her house. Why would someone want to scare a grieving mother?

Turning on the lounge lamp, she made her way into Kelsey's room. As she tried to get comfortable in the bed, she kept hearing noises coming from within the house. Was someone inside right now, sneaking around her house trying to scare her? Dana's nerves were frayed as it was, she couldn't handle going to check the house out.

She eventually fell asleep, curled up in Kelsey's bed, clutching Emma to her chest, Boo Boo stuck under her back. Her sleep was broken, dreaming of Kelsey, smiling, laughing, doing cartwheels on the grass in their small back yard. Then, as usual, her dreams turned to nightmares as she relived the day of Kelsey's death. She was back on the ground, waking up, struggling to free herself from unconsciousness. She managed to get to her feet somehow and run towards the car, remembering that she had hit something. That something had turned out to be her precious four-year-old daughter. She threw herself on the ground, looking under the car. She saw her arm and reached out to hold her hand, checking her wrist for a pulse, but she was gone. She screamed.

Her scream echoed around the room and must have carried down the hallway as, the next moment, Logan was snapping on the light, striding across the room to pull her into his arms.

'Dana! Calm down, sweetheart,' he said as she thrashed in his arms. 'You're safe now. Stop,' he said, grabbing at the fists that tried to strike him. Finally she slowed down, her anger dissolving into tears instead.

'I was dreaming the nicest things, but then it turned into a nightmare.' She gulped.

'The same nightmare?'

'Yes, the same one. I can't break out of it. I just keep seeing her broken body, Logan. Don't you? Don't you dream about her?'

'No, I don't. I think about her sometimes, but I don't dream about her. I think it's my mind's way of protecting me from the pain.'

'That or you're too drunk to remember,' she commented bitterly.

'Nice, Dana, real nice.' Logan let go of her and stepped back, rubbing a hand over his stubbled face. He smelt bad, his body odour taking over the room. He looked at her then said coldly, 'Goodnight, Dana.' She heard the bedroom door shut with a ringing finality.

10

Dana was about three weeks away from the due date of their second child and she still wasn't ready emotionally. She had some of the stuff that she needed, like the cot and pram, which was Kelsey's old one, but now she was rethinking that decision. The cot was already set up in her bedroom, but she had no nappies, bottles, steriliser, or any of the things that should have been arranged already. Maybe she would have to ask her mother for help, which was the last thing that she wanted to do right now.

She didn't shower, she didn't brush her hair, she just tied it up in a messy bun and left it at that. She brushed her teeth, but she didn't even bother to look at herself in the mirror any more. She knew she looked like shit, but she didn't want to see the haunted look in her eyes.

Melanie was coming to pick her up at later for the support group meeting. In a strange way, she was looking forward to it. She wanted to hear that people had it bad too, unlike the first week when she could hardly deal with all the sadness that filled the room. She needed to know that she wasn't alone.

Melanie arrived an hour early at five o'clock, to take her out for a quick cup of tea before the meeting.

When the hot liquid hit the back of her throat, Dana sighed.

'You OK over there?' Melanie asked with a smile.

'Yeah, just thinking.'

'You gonna talk at the meeting? Share your story?' Melanie seemed eager for her to talk, to get her grief off her chest.

'I don't think so, not yet. I think I just need to watch and listen for a little while longer. Hopefully I will be able to soon though.'

When they got to the meeting, the chairs scraped along the wooden floor as people sat down and Janet began her spiel. 'Hi, everyone, welcome to the group. I'm Janet and I'm the counsellor for this meeting. I see we have no new members tonight, so would anyone like to share something?' She looked around the room, not actually staring at individuals, just kind of skimming faces waiting for someone to put up their hand. Someone did. A young woman, maybe twenty or so.

'Hi, I'm Emma.' Emma, the same name as Kelsey's favourite doll. Dana was immediately drawn to her. 'I lost my mother about a month ago. She had stage four breast cancer. I was so close to her.' Emma began to cry softly and Dana's heart went out to her. 'My father... he kind of lost it after she died. He went away. I don't mean he died too or left or anything, but his mind just seemed to slip away. He's in a nursing home now. I go to visit him every day. He always asks me where Mum is and it breaks my heart. I don't tell him any more. They say he has dementia. I think he does too.'

Dana wanted to hold Emma's hand and made a move to reach out to her, but Melanie grabbed her hand and pulled it back.

'Emma doesn't like to be touched, bit of a germophobe, you know?' she whispered with a wink. The wink felt out of place in such a distressing setting. Dana had just wanted to do what Melanie had done for her, but she let it be.

The meeting ended with other people speaking but not Dana or Melanie, though Dana assumed that Melanie must have shared her story a lot in the beginning. Melanie dropped her home and Dana waved as Melanie tooted her horn as she drove off.

The phone was ringing when she got into the house. Dana made sure that the door was locked this time, not wanting her night-time visitor to be able to get into the house again. Pippa was waiting for her in the lounge, sitting on the couch. She stood as soon as she saw Dana, who squeaked in fright before realising who it was.

'Pippa! What the hell are you doing here?' The phone stopped its incessant ringing. There was total silence in the house. 'Pippa, what's wrong? Why are you here?' Dana watched as Pippa swallowed, as if trying to get the words out was physically impossible.

Dana shrugged. 'What is it?' She couldn't take any more bad news.

'Your mum called me just before to tell me something and I rushed right over to you to give you my support, but you weren't here.' Pippa's tone was almost accusatory.

'I went to my meeting,' Dana said, confused. 'Why, what's going on?'

'Honey, I don't know how to tell you this—'

'Start at the beginning, then.'

'All right, your mum told me about the brunch that you all had here last week.'

'You mean the ambush. Yeah? So?'

'She said it got heated and you ended up telling Alesha that she's the reason that Kelsey is dead.' Pippa looked down at her hands, clasped in her lap.

'I did and I stand by that. If Alesha had been watching Kelsey like she said she would, like she asked to, then Kelsey wouldn't have been out the front now would she?' Dana was starting to get worked up. Who was Pippa to come in here and act all high and mighty with her? She hadn't even been there that day, or seen Kelsey's broken little body. Dana stifled a sob, remembering.

'Dana... she tried to hang herself last night.'

'What did you just say?'

'I said your sister tried to kill herself. Your mum found her, only because she called her and she didn't sound right. She could have died. She *wanted* to die for what she'd taken from you. Like you said, she feels it was her fault and she couldn't live with the guilt any more. She left a suicide note.'

'I didn't mean for her to hurt herself,' said Dana, tears gathering in the corners of her eyes then freely running down her face. 'Is she OK?' she asked, tears running down to touch her top lip. She wiped at the mess, rubbing her hand on her trousers.

'Yes, she will be, eventually, but she's suffering, Dana. You need to go and see her, forgive her.'

Dana was crying heavily now, her breath coming out in hitches. 'I can't.' She gulped, hand to her heart. 'It's too hard. I just can't.'

'Then your sister is going to go on blaming herself forever for the mistake she made. Forgiving her will at least release the burden of guilt that she feels. Think about it.'

Pippa left Dana alone with her thoughts. Her jumbled and traitorous thoughts. She didn't know what to think so she did the only thing that came to mind.

'Hello? I need you.' She hung up.

Before she knew it, Dana was opening the door and immediately starting to cry as she fell into caring arms.

'What's wrong?' asked Melanie. 'What happened?' she asked.

'My sister, Alesha. She... she tried to kill herself last night.'

'Oh, I'm so sorry, Dana. How awful.'

'It's my fault.'

'How could it possibly be your fault?' Melanie asked, concern written all over her face, her eyes narrowed.

'I blame her for Kelsey's death. I told her that I blame her.'

Melanie directed Dana to a chair in the lounge. 'Why don't you tell me why you blame her?' She sat on the couch, opposite Dana, and crossed her legs, waiting for the story to begin.

Dana wasn't sure that she could tell her story, but she found that once she started, she couldn't stop. 'We were at my parents' place. Logan forgot Kelsey's bear. He was drunk so I said I'd go back home and grab it. Alesha, my younger sister, offered to watch Kelsey. She didn't and Kelsey slipped out the side gate. I was reversing—'

'Oh my God,' breathed Melanie. 'You hit her?' There was only sympathy in her voice. 'You poor thing.' She stood, moving towards Dana as she continued talking, her words interspersed with sobs.

'I backed over her. I didn't even realise what I'd done at first. I thought I'd hit Dad's dog. It wasn't until I got out of the car to look for it that I saw her. I started screaming and I couldn't stop. Eventually I passed out. They must have carried me so I couldn't see her, but I ran, I looked at her. Bloodied and broken. I did that. I ran over my baby girl, but Alesha promised me that she'd watch her. Now you see why I blame her?' Dana was sobbing again, words muffled by her tears.

'Yes, of course,' answered Melanie. 'I can't believe what you're going through. So much tragedy for one person to handle. Obviously your sister felt extreme guilt to try and commit suicide though. Are you going to go see her?'

Dana looked up, wiping her tear-stained face with the sleeve of her top. 'I don't know. Pippa says I should, that I should forgive her, stop blaming her for what was an accident, but I'm not sure that I can.'

Melanie looked at the ground then back up at Dana, who was waiting for her opinion. 'I don't think you should. You should hang onto your anger, let it out at the people who deserve it the most. Your sister played a part in the death of Kelsey, so why shouldn't she suffer too?'

'You really think that?' asked Dana, wondering why her and Pippa's views differed so widely. They both wanted what was best for her. Pippa knew her and her family the best, but Melanie had lived through this herself. 'Are *you* still angry?' she asked.

'You're damn right I am,' Melanie said. She had yet to share what had happened to her daughter, just that she'd passed away. 'I wouldn't forgive her in your position, but it's up to you, of course. Maybe if you went to see her, you'd know for sure if you wanted to or not.'

'I think I'll do what you said, go with what I'm feeling when I see her. Forgive or hold onto my anger – they seem to be the only two options that I have.'

Dana heard the key turn in the front door and stood up. 'Looks like you're about to meet Logan after all.' She waited for his heavy footsteps to fill the silence, but instead they were light ones.

'Oh. It's you. What are you doing back here?' Dana asked Pippa.

Pippa looked confused and stared at Melanie. 'I'm sorry, Dana, I didn't realise you had company. Nice to see you again, Melanie,' she said, raising a hand in greeting. Melanie nodded her head rather than saying hello.

Pippa cleared her throat and stood there awkwardly for a beat before she said, 'I didn't like the way we left things earlier and I wanted to come by and make sure you were OK.'

'She's fine,' Melanie butted in.

'Excuse me? I was actually asking Dana.' Pippa frowned at the newcomer, who glared back at her. Dana didn't know what to say, but she knew she had to intervene.

'Melanie, thank you so much for coming around and for your advice. I'll see you later, shall I?'

Melanie got up. 'Sure, I'll call you.' Dana walked her to the door.

As Dana came into the kitchen she saw Pippa rustling round for teabags. Pippa turned, tucking her hair behind her ears, and said, 'Well, she's a bit full on, don't you think?'

'She just cares. She seems to be very protective of me.'

'Not sure if that's a good or bad thing, seems a bit much a bit quickly. How many times have you called or texted since you last saw her?'

'I don't know, Pippa, a lot. Why the third degree?' Dana demanded.

'No reason, just want to make sure that you make good choices, beginning with going to see your sister. Logan agrees it's a good idea and might be cathartic for you if you forgive Alesha.'

'You spoke to Logan about this?'

'Yes I have. He called me.'

'He hasn't even bothered to call me yet. Why does he need to go through you before he speaks to me?'

'I think it's more a case of he doesn't know what to say, so he gets advice from me who knows you best. He'll talk to you when he comes home, I'm sure, and drive you to the hospital.'

'If I go there, everyone will think that it's OK, that I forgive her, release her of her burden, but what about the stone around my neck? In my heart? What *I've* lost?'

Pippa sighed deeply, putting her arms around Dana. 'Please, Dana, just go. Forgive her.'

Dana felt as if she was disappointing Pippa, as she was disappointing Logan, her mother, Alesha, everyone.

'Fine, I'll go,' she said eventually. It was the easiest way to get Logan and Pippa off her back. Just do what they wanted her to do.

'That's the right choice to make, honey.' Pippa almost sounded condescending, which confused Dana. Pippa gave her a kiss on the cheek. 'I'll call you tomorrow.'

Dana nodded, then went into the lounge, collapsed on the couch and thought about tomorrow. Did she really forgive Alesha? She had no fucking clue.

* * *

Logan came home late that night. He waltzed into the kitchen where Dana was making a cup of tea. He went straight to the fridge and cracked open a can, taking a long pull from it.

'I guess it's too much to ask that you're cooking tonight?' he asked, pissed off at her already.

Dana turned to face him as he burped loudly. When had things become so bad between them?

'No, I'm not making dinner, Logan.' She could still barely stomach food and although her mum dropped around dinners, she didn't eat much of them. Logan was living on microwaved meals from her mum and clearly he was sick of it.

'Pippa says she convinced you to go see Alesha.'

'Oh, did she now?' Dana said sarcastically.

'What the hell does that mean?'

'Means you shouldn't have called Pippa before calling me. I should have been your first call. It should have been you trying to convince me to forgive her, not Pippa.'

'Honestly? I thought she had a better chance because, in case you haven't noticed, we're not exactly in sync these days.'

He took another gulp of beer and left the room. She followed him.

'And whose fault is that?' she demanded, pushing him into fighting with her.

'I'm not doing this with you, Dana.'

'It's your fault! You push me to do things that I don't want to do. You push me to move on, you push me for sex, you push me into packing up Kelsey's room. Push, push, push! That's all you ever do!' she screamed at him.

'I may push you, but at least I don't tell you the truth.'

'And what is the truth? Go on, say it. Say it! Say it, you fucking coward!'

His face was bright red as he tried and failed to hold the words in. 'You killed Kelsey!' he yelled right back at her, throwing his beer at the wall where the can exploded in a smash of foam and liquid. She flinched. 'You wanna know the truth? *You* killed our baby, *you* ran her over, she's dead because of *you*. That what you want to hear? That make me into the monster you so desperately need me to be? Well, fine. You killed her,' he said, raising his hands in the air.

Dana began to cry, holding onto the back of the chair for support, her other hand curved around the baby, leaning away from him as if preparing to be struck. Could the baby hear the hurtful, hateful but devastatingly true words its father had just hurled at her like knives finding their mark? Could it feel her tension? Her tears? Thing was, he was right about her killing Kelsey. She was the one driving, after all.

Logan stood there breathing hard and ran his hands through his hair, pulling tightly. 'Jesus fucking Christ, Dana.' He looked up at her, crying, something he hadn't done properly since the funeral. 'I'm so sorry, I didn't mean what I said.'

'Yeah, you did. The truth comes out when we're angry. You

meant every word and I agree, I killed her and I have to live with it, but you all played your part too. If you hadn't been drunk that day, you would have kept an eye on her and seen that she left. If Alesha had done what she said she'd do, Kelsey would be safe in her bed right now.'

'You can't go blaming yourself or others.'

'Why? You just did.'

'I said I was sorry,' he sulked.

'It doesn't matter,' Dana said, walking off to the bedroom to have a shower. She felt strangely lighter, as if their fight had taken some of the weight from her shoulders. It didn't even touch the sadness and guilt in her heart, but she felt a little less fragile now. She hopped into bed and pulled the covers up. Too hot, she pushed them down and pulled up the sheet instead. She was fast asleep, almost unconscious as soon as her eyes closed. She didn't hear Logan come to bed that night and when she eventually woke the next morning at about five, she was surprised he'd come to share the bed after their terrible fight. She would have stayed on the couch.

'You awake?' he asked sleepily.

'Yeah.'

'I'm sorry about what I said.'

'You were just saying how you felt. Can't stop you.'

'It's not how I feel. I just said it in a split second of anger.'

'Doesn't matter,' she said, ending the conversation.

He sighed and rolled out of bed. 'I don't know how much longer I can take this.'

'You want to abandon your pregnant wife? Go ahead. No one will think that's cowardly at all.'

'You're putting me in an impossible position, Dana. Stay or go, I can't win.'

'Make a fucking choice, goddammit, and stick to it!'

He grabbed his clothes and went into the bathroom. She fell asleep again and woke when the front door closed. Staring at the ceiling, she ran through what had happened both yesterday and already this morning. Something really had to change. She loved Logan; she didn't want to lose him. He'd been in her life for over a decade but, although she loved him dearly, she just didn't really like him that much right now.

* * *

It took Dana a week to go and see Alesha. She couldn't put it off any longer. She couldn't drive so she waited until a decent hour and messaged Melanie.

Morning. How are you? Just wondering if you might be able to take me to the hospital this morning. I need to see Alesha.

As usual the response was almost immediate.

Of course. What time do you want me to pick you up? Maybe we can stop for a tea somewhere.

Dana found herself wondering if Melanie had other friends. It didn't matter either way to her, but Melanie seemed always available. Right now, it was helpful. Dana's mum had offered to come and pick her up, but Dana didn't want to drive to the hospital with her mum. She would either lecture her or give her the silent treatment, which was worse, or even go as far as to defend Alesha. Just because Alesha had tried to hurt herself didn't mean that what she did was erased. Dana planned to tell her sister that when she had recovered. She had to own her part in this tragedy.

Dana dressed in a mismatching top and skirt. It was going to be hot today, so she wore a long floaty skirt covered in blue and white swirls. It had been a favourite when she was pregnant with Kelsey. She had kept all of her maternity clothes, knowing she would fall pregnant again. She changed over her bag to a bigger one, a tote, and filled it with snacks for the road. She actually felt like eating today, or, rather, the baby did. She began daydreaming about how life would look shortly. She and Logan would get back on track, be on the same page, be happy with their new baby but never forget their other daughter.

The knock brought her out of her musings and she let Melanie in the door. Melanie gave her a gentle hug, mindful of the baby belly, then kissed her on her cheek. Dana was getting used to Melanie's enthusiastic greetings and farewells, which actually made her feel special. Maybe that was the point.

'Ready?' asked Melanie.

'Yeah. Let's go. The sooner I get this done, the better I'll feel.'

Once they were on their way Melanie asked the question. 'Do you know what you're going to say to her?'

'Like you said, I'll know in the moment, but I do need to say a few things first. I'm sorry that she did what she did, but it was her choice. Not mine.'

Melanie nodded. 'That's right. She has to take personal responsibility for her actions, before and after.'

Melanie was such a good listener, giving sound advice that made sense to Dana. She thought, as she'd done many times before, that Melanie was the only one to *get* her right now. She loved Pippa, but she could feel her slipping away and she didn't know how to stop it. They just didn't understand. Pippa. Her family. The people who were supposed to know her best.

'Dana? We're here,' Melanie said as she pulled onto the service road to the car park. Dana felt her stomach drop, her insides tighten with stress, a headache developing behind her eyes already and she hadn't even got inside yet. She swallowed loudly.

'You OK? I can turn the car around and take you home.'

'No. I have to see her. Besides, my mother messaged me this morning and I told her I was coming.'

'All right. I'll come up with you.'

'You're such a good friend, Melanie. Thanks for driving me here and giving me the push I needed.'

Melanie smiled. 'I just want to help you, that's all.'

They made their way to Alesha's room.

'I'll go get a coffee then wait outside the room.'

Dana nodded, her mouth dry. She knocked then pushed open the door. Immediately her eyes were drawn to the pale figure lying on the bed.

Alesha.

Her mother, who had turned at the sound of her knock, jumped up and came over to hug her. 'You came,' she said, tears in her eyes. 'I didn't think you would, but then Logan called—'

'I didn't come here to talk about Logan, Mum.'

Her mother seemed taken aback with her tone and, perhaps anticipating trouble, she said, 'Your sister is feeling much better. She hasn't been sleeping much but they gave her something a while ago, a pill of some sort. She's been inconsolable. Please tell me you're here to forgive her, Dana.' She smiled hesitantly, her voice wavering.

'Honestly, Mum, I don't know.'

'Dana?' Her sister woke, her voice croaky and sounding a little slurry.

'Hi, Alesha.'

Alesha looked at her, her eyes slightly unfocused. She sat up and had a sip of the water her mother offered her, then she looked up at Dana. 'Hey, Dana.' She blinked a few times, as if trying to clear away the medication fog. She seemed more alert now though, enough to hear what Dana had to say to her.

She didn't want to do the whole pretend pleasantry thing, instead wanting to say what she had to say then leave. Dana knew what her mum wanted her to do, to give absolution, but there were some things that had to be said first. It had all started when Alesha had told her that she didn't belong and had ended in her trying to hang herself. It was a circle of life: Dana's birth, Kelsey's death, Alesha's attempted suicide and the baby about to be born. Dana felt her heart beat faster as they stared at each other in uncomfortable silence.

'I'm sorry, Dana,' Alesha said in a soft voice, breaking the loaded tension that filled the small room.

'For what?' Dana asked, wanting to make her say it. She wouldn't be giving her a free pass today.

'You know,' Alesha said, glancing at her mum, who stood back watching her daughters talk it out.

'You don't get to say that to me, Alesha. Tell the truth. I want to hear you say the words,' Dana demanded, not wanting to hear vague apologies.

'I'm sorry for not watching Kelsey. I'm sorry for the part that I played in all of this.'

'All of this? You mean her death? The part you played in her death?'

'Dana,' warned her mother.

'It's OK, Mum, this has been coming for a while now and I need to say it. Yes, I'm sorry that I was part of the reason that she's dead. I didn't mean it. She slipped away when I was on my phone, I didn't notice and I'm so sorry. I should have kept a better eye on her. I'm so sorry,' Alesha repeated.

'And that makes it OK? I lost my daughter because you were

playing on your phone. What the hell was so important that you couldn't ignore it for half an hour?'

'It was... another man, someone I'd been seeing for the past few months. He sent me a text message.'

Dana was shocked. 'You're cheating on James? Who are you?' Alesha had the decency to look down at her hands, ashamed.

'Please don't tell James. He'd leave me,' she begged quietly.

'Are you fucking kidding me? You want a favour from me? No bloody way. I'm not helping you at all. Ever.'

Alesha looked crestfallen but Dana didn't give a shit. 'You are a disgusting, selfish woman who disrespects everyone and everything. I don't know how you can look at yourself in the mirror. If it wasn't for you, Kelsey would still be alive. You robbed me of birthdays, graduation, marriage, grandchildren, everything! Do you understand what you stole from me?' Dana was getting worked up now and she could feel her blood pressure rising, the heat travelling through her body to colour her face. The baby kicked her in the kidney and she inhaled sharply.

'Are you all right?' Alesha asked, concerned.

'Don't you worry yourself about me and mine, not ever again, because you won't be seeing us, ever again. *This* baby won't know you. I won't let you harm it like you harmed Kelsey and tried to harm yourself. I know you're suffering for what you did, but you can't even begin to imagine what I'm going through. If you did, you'd understand why I will never forgive you.'

'Dana—'

'Don't even say it, Alesha, I'm warning you. As you so eloquently put it, I don't belong to you, to any of you.' She looked at her mother. 'I'm just the mistake you adopted.' Dana turned and strode out of the door, closing it and her heart firmly on her family.

Melanie was waiting across the hall, leaning casually against the wall. 'Well, that was intense. I could hear you from out here. I am so impressed by you right now. You really gave it to her. Let's get you and baby home and comfortable.'

'I need to lie in bed for a while and process what the hell I just did. My mum's going to be so pissed at me.'

Melanie reached over and grabbed her hand. 'You have me now. I'll be your family.' She smiled at Dana, who was grateful for her support. 'I'm so lucky to have found a friend like you.'

Just as they turned to leave Dana's mum came out of Alesha's room. 'Dana, wait. I have something to tell you.'

'Mum, I'm not in the mood for a lecture. Please, just leave it be. It's done now.' She sighed.

'I just wanted to tell you that Jackie passed away this morning. She asked me to inform you when she went.' Her mum turned and went back into Alesha's room, closing the door behind her.

Melanie looked at her. 'Who's Jackie?' she asked.

'No one who matters.'

They drove home largely in silence as Dana ran through what had happened. Logan was going to be furious with what she'd said and done and no doubt her mother had called both him and Pippa, filling them in on what had happened already.

Melanie dropped Dana off with the promise of picking her up for the support meeting later that day.

11

Logan called her just before Melanie was due to pick her up. He was angry, she could tell from the way he barked her name.

'What's wrong now, Logan?' she asked wearily, not sure she could take any more drama today.

'Your mum called. Alesha is distraught and your mum thinks she's going to try and kill herself again. She's beside herself with worry. Why the hell did you say those things to her, Dana? You could have just forgiven her and been done with it. Instead, you're dragging it on.'

'Why? Because I didn't want to forgive her, that's why. You all don't get it and I'm sick of repeating myself—' The knock at the door ended her rant. 'I have to go. Melanie's here to pick me up for the meeting.'

'Fine. Tell them what you did tonight, see what they think.' He hung up on her.

'Fucker,' she whispered to the empty silence on the other end.

'Hey,' Melanie said when she opened the door. Her smile was infectious and Dana found herself smiling back despite the stressful day.

'Hi. I'm ready to go,' Dana said, bag in the crook of her elbow. Suddenly she gasped.

'Dana! Are you all right? Is it the baby?'

'I don't know, I just had a stabbing pain. I think I'm all right,' she said, breathing through the sharp pain. 'Don't worry, I'm not going into labour or anything. Let's go,' she said, ignoring the lingering burn. She would not be having this baby today. She wasn't anywhere near ready yet but she couldn't deny that it was coming and fast. She had a constant back ache, couldn't sleep, and the baby had dropped down low, making everything she did uncomfortable.

'Dana? Are you sure you want to go tonight? We could blow it off and go somewhere else.'

'No, it's fine, I actually want to go.'

'Are you ready to talk?'

'No, I don't think so, but I'm ready to listen.' And she was. She needed to know how to handle this new baby situation. Maybe she'd ask Janet after the meeting – surely she would have heard just about everything, being a counsellor. She made up her mind to pull Janet aside at the end of the meeting.

But the meeting didn't quite turn out the way she thought it would. The group sat down in their little semicircle and waited for the meeting to begin. Janet began with her usual introduction but tonight, there was a new member to their support group. His name was Matt, and he spoke with candour.

'Hi, I'm Matt Wallis and I'm here because I recently lost my son. My wife died so it's just been the two of us since then. I'm here because I need to talk to people who understand, to hear their stories. My friends try, but they don't realise that all I want to do is be with my boy. I'm not suicidal, I just want him back.' His gaze landed on Dana and she smiled tentatively at him. He smiled back, his handsome face transforming. He had salt and pepper hair, he was tall and very good-looking. He was wearing a T-shirt that showed off a nice body. Dana froze – what the fuck was she thinking? She looked over at Melanie, who was staring at her intently.

'What's wrong?' Dana asked at the slight frown on her friend's face.

'Nothing. Why?'

'I don't know, you just look... worried.'

'I'm fine,' Melanie said quietly, but she looked anything but fine; she looked pissed off.

At the end of the meeting, Dana walked over to Matt to introduce herself, her intended conversation with Janet forgotten.

He was pouring himself a cup of coffee. 'I wouldn't drink that if I were you,' she said, a small smile on her face.

'That bad, huh?'

'Yeah. Hey, I just wanted to welcome you to the group. My name's Dana.'

'Hey, Dana,' he said easily, 'I'm Matt. How far along are you?' he asked and for a moment she had no idea what he was talking about.

Then she realised. She felt as if she had been pregnant for a lifetime. 'Oh, um, actually I'm due in a couple of weeks.' She gave a little smile.

He smiled again. 'That's great news. There's nothing like a new baby.' *To replace the old one?* She pushed the thought from her mind. Now was not the time.

Her smiled slipped a little at the thought but then Matt said, 'So what do you normally do when you're not pregnant?'

'Um... I've been a stay-at-home mum for over four years, and before that, I worked at a supermarket, but it's been a while. You?'

She caught sight of Melanie in her peripheral vision. She didn't look happy. Matt started talking. 'I'm in sales. I don't like it, but I just wanted a job that I could numb the pain with. I travel around the country so I'm not around my house all the time. I go away about once a month or so. Do you like to travel, Dana?'

'I haven't been anywhere really.' And it had never bothered her until that instant. Why had she and Logan never gone anywhere?

'That's a shame, this country is a beautiful place. You should see it some time.'

Suddenly Melanie was at her side, pulling on her arm. 'We have to go, Dana, I have something else to do tonight.'

A look passed over Matt's face as he glanced down at Melanie's hand wrapped tightly around Dana's arm. 'How about I drive Dana home since you have somewhere else to be? We haven't been properly introduced. I'm Matt.' He put out his hand to shake Melanie's. She looked at him with a blank expression before grasping his hand, pumping it up and down twice. Perfunctory. It was obvious that she'd taken an instant dislike to him, but Dana couldn't work out why.

'Nice to meet you.' She smiled a bit, but to Dana it looked off. 'No, it's OK, I'll reschedule. It's not important,' Melanie said.

'Well, now that you don't have anywhere to be, do you want to go for some real coffee, or tea for you? Or do you have to be home soon?' asked Matt. His smile was infectious.

Dana thought about Logan. Did she have to go home? 'No, I could go for a cup of tea.' She was decisive. Logan could wait. Their arguments could wait.

'Let's go, then. Melanie, would you like to come too?' he asked, as if she wasn't already invited.

Melanie frowned at him, looked at Dana, gauging her reaction, then said, 'Sure, let's go.'

Dana went over to Janet and thanked her, her earlier questions forgotten. She looked back at Melanie, standing next to

Matt, not speaking, and decided to rescue Matt. She wondered why Melanie, normally talkative and lively, was wound tighter than a drum tonight. She looked as if she were about to burst as both she and Matt waited for Dana to say goodbye.

They enjoyed their drinks, talking about stuff that was inconsequential, nothing serious or life-changing, which was a relief to Dana. She had spent so many weeks talking about her loss and grief or ignoring her loss and grief. Matt was a lovely man. Funny, intelligent and full of fun stories from his travels. He didn't speak about his son, she didn't even know his name, but after half an hour of talking, she felt as if they were firm friends. The only one who didn't seem to be having much fun was Melanie.

A little later, she looked at her phone. It was after nine in the evening – the time with Matt had flown past. She was surprised to realise that she actually felt comfortable with him.

Once they had paid the bill, Matt asked for her phone number. 'I don't have many friends. I kind of lost a lot when my wife passed and the ones that stuck around didn't know what to say when I lost my son, so...'

'Of course,' Dana sympathised. She rattled off her number, then took his.

'Do you want my number too, Melanie? I think it would be nice if we all caught up again.' Melanie nodded her head politely and put his details into her phone.

'See you next week, ladies,' Matt said as he walked off to find his car.

The drive home was very sombre, Melanie sullen and quiet, angry almost, whereas Dana felt great. She had met another person that she clicked with, who seemed to understand her. You could never have too many of those, right? She looked over at Melanie's profile as she drove. Her jaw was clenched, knuckles white on the steering wheel.

'Are you OK?' she finally asked her.

'Yes. Well, no. Don't you think he, Matt, was just a little too flirty with a pregnant married woman?'

'What are you talking about? He's lonely and was just being friendly. I like him,' she said quietly, 'and I don't have many friends.'

'You have me,' Melanie said, as if that were all she needed.

Melanie pulled up to the kerb in front of Dana's house. Logan's car was in the driveway, and the front light had been left on for her. It was a nice gesture on his part, given everything that had happened over the past few days, but he hadn't called to see how she was doing or when she was coming home. She would have answered, no matter how upset or angry she was. She never wanted to worry him on top of everything else that was going on. Obviously he wasn't that worried.

'Night, Melanie.'

'Night, Dana,' Melanie mumbled.

In the glow of the streetlight, as Dana was walking past the letter-box, she saw something sticking out of it. She grabbed the mail and pulled. It stayed stuck in the letterbox and she grunted as she tried to pull it out again. The postman must have doubled over the newspaper. With a bit of wiggling and a few swear words, she managed to pull the paper free. There was a newspaper in there and, on top, a folded piece of paper, now ripped at the edges. Angling it towards the streetlight so she could read it, Dana opened up the paper, assuming it was junk mail ready to be recycled. She'd put it in the bin while she was out here.

It was a printed copy of Kelsey's death notice page from the local paper. Dana felt as if she had been hit in the stomach with a bat, the air whooshing from her lungs. The small notice was circled aggressively in red pen, ripping through the white paper. A word was scrawled across the page.

Murderer.

Someone had written the ugly word on the top of the page. Dana didn't know what to do. She stared at the paper for a long time before finally tearing her eyes away from the word and noticing a small blob of ink at the top of the page in the left-hand corner. She couldn't stop staring at it. It might not have been a huge deal, except *her* printer left the exact same shape ink blob in the same spot at the top of her printed pages. What they hell? Had this come from inside her house? Had someone broken into her house and used her printer?

Scrunching the paper, Dana looked around her fearfully. Was someone watching her right now? Happy to see her so scared? She stuffed the paper into her bag, not wanting Logan to see it. He already thought that she was nuts thinking that there was an intruder in the house. Didn't this prove her theory though? Someone was harassing her, had it in for her. But when would they have been able to print a document from inside her house? Dana hurried to the front door, still looking behind her. What if the culprit was closer to home?

The front light might have been on, but the hallway light was off, and Dana stumbled down, dragging her hand along the wall. The bedroom light was off as well, as was the lounge light. Dana headed for the only light on in the house, the kitchen. Logan was sitting at the table. She didn't feel like getting into it with him, not after what had just happened. Her heart was still beating so hard, thumping in her chest as if she'd just run a race. Fear. It was fear. She was scared and didn't know who to talk to about it.

'I was worried,' he stated as soon as he saw her.

'You didn't call,' she countered, placing her bag on the kitchen bench. She needed to throw away that piece of paper as soon as possible. It was all she could think about.

'I didn't want to bother you.'

'Then you couldn't have been too worried.'

'I need Melanie's number.'

'Why?' she asked, surprised. He didn't even know her.

'In case I can't get hold of you, I can at least call her to make sure you're all right. Please, Dana.'

'Fine.' She pulled out her phone and recited the number. Matt didn't come up in the conversation, not because there was something to hide, she simply didn't feel it was any of Logan's business. Some things she just wanted to keep for herself.

'I saw Pippa today,' he commented.

'Oh, yes?' she said, watching his face carefully.

'She's worried about you, about your friendship with each other.'

'Why?'

'She feels you're slipping away from her and she misses you. You should give her a call tomorrow.'

'You notice how you're always telling me to call people? You pretend it's a suggestion, but I feel like I can't say no.' Dana stared at her husband, wondering what was going on inside his head. 'Why is Pippa bothering you with this kind of shit anyway?'

'Dana, I'm trying to help you. The wider your circle, the more people who care about you, the more people you can rely on.'

'Thank you for your concern, Logan, but I've made two friends from the group now.'

'Two? I thought you only knew Melanie.'

'And Matt, I met him tonight. He lost his son.' She didn't know why she blurted this out after she'd decided not to tell him, but now he knew.

'Who's Matt?'

'I just told you, Logan, he's new to the group and needed some friends so we took him for coffee.'

'Ahh, I see,' he said, his fingers under his chin. He did this when he was thinking really hard about something important. 'Should I be worried?' he asked.

Dana stared at him in disbelief. 'Are you fucking kidding me? That's where your mind goes? I just met him tonight and he's a friend, a support person like you just suggested I find, and there is not and never will be anything going on. I can't even think about shit like that – you of all people should know that.' She was angry, furious now. Her eyes were narrowed, her face pinched with hurt.

'I don't want to fight with you. I really don't. Just go to bed,' she told him. He stared at her, the sharpness of her voice making him sigh with resignation.

'Fine,' he said, turning his back on her and striding down the hallway.

12

Dana's mother called. She had known it was coming eventually and it came quicker than expected. Her mother would have rationalised that Dana needed a day to cool off before she contacted her and on any other topic or situation she was probably right. Dana was a people-pleaser, someone who went out of her way to keep people happy, and some used that against her. But Dana felt very strongly about Alesha and forgiveness; she was not going to be a people-pleaser this time.

'Mum,' she said without greeting her, hostility in her voice. 'What do you want?'

She heard the intake of breath as her mum steeled herself to speak to her eldest daughter. 'Well, I was just calling to see how you were after that regrettable catch-up yesterday.'

'Regrettable catch-up? It wasn't a catch-up, it was a set-up. I regret nothing about it, Mum. Alesha's suicide attempt didn't change my feelings, nor did they bring Kelsey back. I'm not going to apologise, not now, not ever.' Dana hung up the phone, stabbing at the button angrily.

Her phone rang a second time. It was her mum again. 'What is it now?' Dana asked.

'I'm sorry, I really am, I shouldn't have pushed, I just want you girls to be OK with each other. I'll stop now until you're ready. I'll stop pushing, all right?'

Dana smiled in relief, nodding. 'Thank you, Mum. I appreciate you apologising and not getting in the middle of this. I'll talk to you later.' She hung up the phone, this time in relief.

Dana heard the soft ping of a text message come through on her mobile. She checked and found it was from Melanie, reiterating her feelings.

Morning, how weird was that Matt guy last night? He was a bit too friendly, didn't you think?

Dana read the message twice.
Sigh.

I liked him actually. I told you that.

She wasn't into playing games right now. She really liked Melanie, but there was enough of her to go around. She didn't have to restrict herself to one friend in the group – as Logan had said, the more support, the better.

Melanie quickly backtracked.

Oh. Well, I guess he was all right.

The phone pinged again but this time it was Matt. She was popular this morning.

Morning. I hope this isn't too forward, but I was wondering if I could buy you a cup of tea today? I had fun last night, as weird as that sounds, and, as I mentioned, I don't have a lot of friends, well, any if I'm being honest. What I'm trying to say, very ineloquently, is that I want to be your friend. But as I'm typing this I realise how lame that sounds.

Dana could imagine the sheepish look on his face. She laughed, the noise startling her and she immediately stopped. Quickly, without thinking, she wrote back.

Sure, we can be friends. Tea would be great. I don't drive, bump and all, so could you please pick me up?

Dana sent Matt her address.

Changing her clothes and dressing in a black maxi dress and her favourite sandals, she grabbed her bag and waited. Matt messaged her to say he'd arrived.

Standing beside his car, watching her walking towards him, he broke out into a grin and opened the door for her.

'Hey, Matt, how are you?' She dumped her somewhat heavy bag in the car.

'Good. You look lovely, Dana.' He turned away and she knew that he probably felt guilty for saying it. As if he was betraying his wife's memory by complimenting another woman. She understood.

'Thanks.'

He pulled away from the kerb smoothly, starting up the conversation.

'So, should we go back to the café near the community centre or try somewhere else?'

She looked at him and his eyes glanced sideways at her while he drove.

'The same place sounds good. Thanks again for coming to pick me up. I just can't drive any more.' She pointed to her stomach. It was a good enough excuse, and it was true anyway.

'I'm so happy for you, Dana. To have a child is the most precious thing in the world.'

She nodded, momentarily unable to speak, thinking of Kelsey, but she knew that Matt would have his son in his thoughts as well. She hadn't asked his son's name at the meeting, or how he'd passed. It wasn't her business. Maybe today they would share their stories or maybe they'd pretend they were normal people untouched by tragedy.

'I miss him,' he said, out of the blue. Dana turned to look at him as he swiped at his eyes.

'I understand.'

'It's my fault.' Then he shut down and stopped talking. Dana wondered what he meant. Was he actually responsible, like her, or did he just blame himself? She was sure he would tell her when he was ready.

Matt pulled into the car park and as she opened her door he ran around to the passenger side and offered her his arm, his earlier emotional outburst forgotten.

'Gotta take care of you, in your condition,' he said, smiling.

Once they were seated, Matt said, 'So, Dana, tell me about yourself.'

It was a loaded question and she wasn't sure if he wanted to hear about Kelsey, or something else. She decided to go with the easiest topics. 'Well, I'm married, over ten years now; my husband's name is Logan and we've known each other forever.' Dana meant to stop talking there but the words rushed out of her. 'Oh, and I recently found out that I was adopted – my parents kept it from me my whole life, so that threw me for a loop. Then my biological mum died of cancer and I'm about to become a mum for the second time, but I'm not quite sure how I feel about it as my daughter died not that long ago.' She hadn't meant to say that last part but her brain seemingly wasn't connected to her mouth. The tears burned behind her eyes and threatened to spill over.

'I'm sorry,' she blurted out, embarrassed.

Matt saw her face fall and reached across the table to lightly touch her hand. 'Do you feel any better?' he asked with concern. 'Sometimes talking to a stranger is the best thing for you. That's why I joined the support group, to find the understanding I needed and to talk about how I feel. Clearly you needed to do the same. It doesn't need to be a big deal, Dana. Please don't get upset.'

'Yes, actually I do feel better. You're a good listener.'

The conversation flowed with Matt. He made an effort to be attentive and tell her anecdotes that made her smile, even laugh a little.

'Hi, guys, what a coincidence running into you two here,' a voice interrupted them.

Dana looked up to see Melanie standing in front of their table. Melanie glanced over at Matt, and Dana saw a quick shadow pass over her face. For his part, Matt didn't seem very happy that Melanie had crashed their time together either. Dana couldn't help wondering if it was a coincidence that Melanie had showed up, but then she rationalised that Melanie would have had no idea that they would be here at this time.

'Would you like to join us, Melanie?' Matt asked.

'Well, if you don't mind,' Melanie said, already pulling up a chair.

'Of course not, do sit down,' Matt said, moving a bit to make room for her. He waved over the waitress and ordered another coffee. 'Ladies? My treat.'

Melanie ordered a latte but Dana stuck to tea. She was thinking about her conversation with Matt – was she ready to become a mother again? A question that had tied her up in endless knots ever since Kelsey's death.

'Dana?'

She looked up and realised that both Matt and Melanie were staring at her.

'Sorry, off with the fairies. What did I miss?'

They both had a chuckle at her expense and Dana smiled, defusing the situation.

'Actually,' Matt said, 'it was the waitress, who was asking you if you wanted anything else, but you were elsewhere.' He smiled and crossed his legs, his foot touching her calf. A small jolt of electricity ran through her, then she shut it down. Had it been on purpose? Dana diverted her attention away from Matt and looked up at Melanie.

'What are you doing over this way, Melanie?' she asked.

'I was doing some shopping and suddenly was craving a latte. You know this place makes the best latte.'

'Have to agree with you,' Matt said, raising his mug. 'What's on for today, Melanie?' he asked politely.

'Errands then back home to do housework, but these days the housework doesn't take long since there's only me.' It almost sounded like a challenge.

'That's me later,' Dana said. 'I have to tidy up before Logan gets home.' Not really, she had no intention of cleaning the house, but she wanted to make Melanie's answer seem less out of place, and it didn't hurt to mention her husband again.

Once the drinks were finished, the bill paid, Matt stood up and said, 'Come on, Dana, I'll drop you back home.'

'I guess I'd better get going too,' Melanie said, pushing her chair back and standing.

When they walked towards the car, Dana was surprised to find that Melanie had parked right next to Matt. *How bizarre.*

'Was it just me, or was that a little odd?' Matt finally asked as they drove home.

'I was thinking the same thing, but I'm trying to keep in mind that Melanie has lost everything and she's lonely, in need of friends.'

'Do you know her well?'

'Not that well. I met her when I first started going to the support group, as you know. There's not a whole lot that Melanie has chosen to share with me yet, but she's been very supportive of me.' Realising that she didn't know much about Melanie, like where she lived, or what she did for a living, Dana wondered if Melanie was keeping her at arm's length or just didn't like to talk about herself.

'I'm sorry, I have to ask – do you get a weird vibe from her?'

'I think she's just intense and a little protective of me. But she is lovely,' Dana quickly added, giving her new friend the benefit of the doubt. Within the space of a few weeks, she'd made two new friends but seemed to be losing her oldest friend. Dana would have to call Pippa soon to talk. Dana couldn't imagine life without Pippa or Logan in it, but it kind of seemed as if they were forming a bond separate from her. Did she actually believe that or was she just imagining something that wasn't even there?

Matt pulled up outside the house. Logan's car was in the driveway. He was home early, and she wondered why. Then she saw Pippa's car parked up the road from their house. Pippa must have come round to visit but found Dana wasn't there. So why was Pippa still there, then?

'Hubby home? Guess you won't get to clean before he gets back after all.' Matt smiled. 'I had a good time. Thanks for coming out with me today.'

'I really enjoyed myself too. Thanks for the invite and the lift.'

'Can we do it again some time?' he asked shyly, and she thought about his foot touching her, how it had made her feel.

'Sure,' she said, feeling anything but sure.

Dana unlocked the front door and, with keys in her hand, walked down to the lounge, hoping to apologise to Logan and Pippa and try to regain some of their closeness, but they weren't there. Dana looked in the kitchen but they were nowhere to be seen. With a horrible sinking sensation, she walked quietly back down the hallway and pushed open the closed door to the bedroom. She knew what she expected to see; her husband and her best friend entwined on their bed, but neither one of them would do that to her surely, especially not now.

The room was empty. She sighed in relief, let out a shaky breath, embarrassed for doubting them, and went looking for them outside. There was a small table and chairs under the back veranda, so Dana figured they must be out there. Looking through the laundry window, she saw them sitting outside, chairs pulled close together. Then, to her horror, Dana realised they were holding hands. She wanted to run out there screaming, demanding to know what was going on, but, instead, opened the door, plastered on a smile and faked it.

The two of them pulled apart as soon as Dana stepped out onto the veranda, although neither looked guilty, Dana noticed bitterly. Wondering how long this had been going on for and if it had moved past hand-holding, she longed to ask. Logan and Pippa were so comfortable with each other, and she had had suspicions about them, of course, but had put it down to paranoia and hormones. But now it seemed as if her instincts might have been correct all along. Logan was having an affair, if not a physical one, then an emotional one at least. She guessed she could understand Logan looking for an out, but with Pippa? What was Pippa's excuse for betrayal?

Coming out of the back door, greeting Pippa calmly, as if she hadn't seen them touching each other, was difficult. Dana touched her stomach as she moaned lightly, a gesture not lost on Pippa, whose eyes slid away from Dana's, not full of guilt, but something else. Jealousy perhaps? Envy? Pippa had expressed a desire to have kids numerous times but had never found the right guy to settle down with. Had that changed?

'Hey, Dana,' Pippa said, returning her stare. Now Logan was the one looking away. 'Where have you been? I came over to see you.' *Yeah, right,* Dana thought.

'I've been out to tea with Melanie.' Not sure why she omitted Matt's presence. 'We have got pretty close.' She didn't want to add that she was growing closer to Melanie while growing more distant from Pippa, but the implication was there.

'You're home early, love,' Dana said, finally addressing Logan. He looked up, shading his eyes against the late afternoon sun.

'Yeah, the boys and I knocked off early.'

'No pub today?'

'Nah, came straight home.'

To meet Pippa. In their house under the guise of checking up on Dana.

'That's good, an early mark is probably just what you need. Want a drink, Pippa?' she asked, wanting nothing more than for her to just fucking leave. Dana wouldn't confront Logan, not yet – more evidence was needed than just holding hands. Though even this small betrayal hurt her deeply. Two people who claimed to love her were going behind her back. How long had they had feelings for each other? She wished she knew.

'No, I'd better get going. Thanks though.' Pippa gave Logan a look that Dana couldn't decipher.

'See you, Pip,' he said casually, looking out over their small back yard.

Dana walked Pippa through the house and to the front door. 'Sorry I couldn't stay longer, I have some things to do.' Pippa leaned forward and gave Dana a brief one-armed hug around her huge belly. 'See you later.'

Dana closed the front door, heading into the bedroom. She lay down on the bed, rubbing the pain from her stomach. Logan came into the room and sat on the side of the bed. He stared at her rubbing her belly.

'Everything OK?' he asked, forehead creasing with concern.

'I don't know, is it?' Dana countered, a small frown on her face.

'Sure, I'm fine, we're fine.' Logan couldn't look at her as he said it and Dana knew. He was definitely feeling guilty about something; whether it had to do with Pippa or not, she didn't know. He left and she watched him go with mixed feelings. Yes, the love was still there but could she hold onto him? Her thoughts moved to Matt, and Melanie. Two new and two very different friends. They both had their own stories; Matt had confided in her, Melanie was yet to open up about Mindy, but they were both of great support to Dana.

* * *

At the next meeting, Dana still didn't share her story. Instead, she sat in between Matt and Melanie, her mind elsewhere. She was thinking about Logan and Pippa holding hands and what it meant.

Dana had been obsessing about it ever since, wondering if anything more was going on. Things at home had deteriorated with Logan; they were barely communicating at all. He'd taken on some extra overtime and was spending the week working a couple of hours away from town. Trying not to let her imagination run away with her, Dana wanted to believe that Logan and Pippa touching was a one-time thing. Logan seeking comfort in a good friend. Nothing more than that.

Her stomach pains were getting steadily worse, moving into her lower back. Inching closer to giving birth to her second child, Dana was still unsure how she felt about being a mother again. Not that she had a choice – the baby was coming whether she was ready or not. But what if she couldn't love it?

Dana was pleased when Matt called her the next day, just to say hi and check in on her. 'I just had a feeling that there was something going on with you. That perhaps you needed something. Everything all right?'

'No, I don't think so. I think I've begun labour – actually, I think I've been in labour since late last night.'

'What? Is your husband there with you?' Matt sounded a little frantic.

'No, he's at work, he's working away on a job site. I didn't want to bother him until I was sure.'

'I'm coming over to check on you, right now.' Matt hung up the phone abruptly. It was funny how quickly Matt had integrated himself into her life. She was rocked by another wave of pain, bending forward and grabbing onto the kitchen table for support.

The next thing she knew, Matt was banging on the door, yelling to her to let him in. 'Dana!' he yelled, thumping on the front door again. She hobbled to the door, holding her back, her stomach hanging low, uncomfortable and full. The baby was ready to come soon, she could feel it. Opening the door, he barged in. 'Is it time?' he said, taking in her pale sweaty complexion and eyes narrowed in pain. She nodded. 'Where's your bag?'

'What?'

'Your overnight bag, Dana. Where is it?'

'I never packed one, I... was busy.' Matt tried the first door to the left and strode into her bedroom. 'Sit,' he commanded. He randomly pulled open drawers, dragging out a small pile of clothes. 'Your husband can grab the rest later. Let's go.' He gently pulled Dana to her feet and wrapped his arm around her middle, walking her to the car.

He just about broke the sound barrier getting her to the hospital in record time. He ran ahead and she heard him call for a wheelchair, yelling that she was in labour. He behaved as if he were the father-to-be and she found it amusing. Then she was hit with a wave of pain, nausea grabbing at her at the same time. She breathed shallowly, the stabbing pain coursing through her entire body.

Matt came running out with a nurse, who helped her into the wheelchair and rolled it up to the birthing suite. Dana gripped the arms, trying not to cry out in pain and failing.

'Dana!' Matt was holding onto her hand; she curled her fingers around his and squeezed tightly, afraid.

'My husband,' she gasped, 'can you call him? He... he needs to be here. I need him.'

Matt rummaged around in the bag and pulled out the phone.

'Code?' he asked, quickly entering in the numbers. 'Logan? It's Matt, a friend of your wife's. She's in labour and is asking for you. She's been in labour since last night. You need to get to the hospital now.' Matt hung up the phone, put it back into the bag and said, 'I'll see you when you're holding your new baby.' He smiled reassuringly. 'You got this.' Grimacing in pain, the door swung closed slowly. She didn't want to be alone and prayed that Logan arrived soon.

A nurse helped Dana get dressed into a gown ready for the delivery. Dana moaned in pain, then screamed. She didn't know how long it took but eventually a doctor bustled into the room and took a look under the gown they had put her in.

'Almost there, my dear,' he said, looking at his watch.

Feeling a wave of pain pulling in all directions, she grunted loudly as it rolled over her, threatening to drown her. Once it had passed, she lay back on the bed, panting. Her eyes rolled towards the clock. Matt had rung Logan, but it could take him an hour or more to get to the hospital. She had heard that sometimes the second baby came on quickly and she hoped with all her heart that Logan would be here to see his child born. It would mean the world to him. Dana felt the familiar pain building up again and grabbed at the sweaty sheets underneath her body. A nurse wiped her brow with a cool washer, which distracted her for all of a second before she was screaming in agony again. The contractions started to speed up, beginning to crash into each other with frightening speed. It wouldn't be long now.

Suddenly the door was thrown open and Logan stood there, panting almost as much as she was.

'Did I make it?' he puffed, eyes wide.

'Well, you're about to become a dad, so hurry up and get in here,' said the doctor, throwing him a quick smile.

Logan hurried over to her, kissed her sweaty brow and held her hand while the next lot of contractions slammed into her.

'One more push, Dana, and you'll meet your baby,' the doctor instructed.

Gathering up all the strength she had left and with one final push, she felt the baby slide from her body. Over her laboured breathing, she heard the baby cry and began to sob with joy. With that one cry, Dana felt hopeful. She felt a connection and knew without a doubt that this baby would be loved with every part of her heart. She was ready to be a mother again.

'It's a girl,' the doctor said. He handed the baby to a nurse, who passed Dana her daughter. Opening up her gown, she placed the baby girl on her breast where, after a little time, she began to feed.

Dana looked down at her beautiful new daughter and whispered, 'Hi, Kelsey.'

* * *

Logan didn't shock easily, but when his wife whispered the name Kelsey, ice water coursed through his veins. He stared at his wife dumbfounded. Was she confused from the stress of the labour and thought she had given birth to Kelsey? Was she stuck in the past?

Logan couldn't bring himself to look at the baby and had to be prompted by the doctor to go to his wife. 'It's OK now, Dad, go be with your family.'

Logan walked the three steps in a daze, not knowing what the fuck to say. His wife looked up at him, tears in her eyes. 'Isn't she beautiful?' she exclaimed, already in love. She looked at him expectantly.

This was what he had wanted to happen, that she fell in love immediately with their new child, but not like this. 'Yeah, she is, but you know this isn't Kelsey, right? This is our second daughter; we haven't named her yet.'

'Her name is Kelsey,' Dana repeated, the name stabbing him in the heart, piercing the fragile shell he had built around his grief.

'No, Dana, it's not,' he said forcefully.

'Maybe now's not the best time to be having this conversation,' the doctor said, looking rather embarrassed. Logan knew he was right; his baby girl had just been born and it was a bittersweet moment to see Dana nursing her, the baby nestled in her arms, held tenderly. He longed to hold her, to smell her sweet smell, to hold her slight weight in his arms. His mind flicked back to when Kelsey was born and how different it had been. He'd been there every step of the way; they'd been so in love back then, their future so hopeful. Now, they were barely speaking, almost strangers existing in the same house.

He reached out and touched his daughter's tiny hand. She was so soft, her mouth popping off Dana's breast as she let out a cry. 'Would you like to hold her?' his wife asked quietly.

He nodded and leaned in to take the baby, instinctively rocking her back and forth. He stared at her intently. He couldn't believe she was finally here. He had loved her since they had found out they were having another baby, but it was surreal to finally be holding her. He looked down at his exhausted wife.

'How did you get here, Dana? Why didn't you call me yourself?'

'I didn't want to bother you until I was close.'

'Dana, I just made the birth of my child by minutes. What if I'd missed it? I'd never have forgiven you.' Logan felt his blood pressure rising with his anger. 'And what the fuck is Matt doing here?' Logan asked loudly, the nurses glancing over at him. One of them frowned, but he didn't care. He needed answers.

'I asked him to come over and drive me to the hospital since you were out of town.'

'So, you've been seeing him, then?'

'No, not in the way you think, Logan. He's a good friend. Just like Pippa is a good friend to you.'

Logan swallowed. He couldn't say anything now; he knew what he was doing was wrong.

'All right, Daddy, time to get Mum and baby down to the ward and a little more comfortable,' said an older nurse, carefully taking hold of the baby while Dana settled into the wheelchair. 'Not far now, I promise, then you three can have some bonding time,' she said cheerfully, obviously feeling the tension in the room.

Dana had just got settled in the bed in the private room, the baby placed in her waiting arms, when there was a soft knock at the door.

'Dana?' A short, petite woman pushed open the door. 'Oh my God, are you all right? Matt called, he was worried about you, wanted me to come and say hi to you and the baby. Oh, she's so beautiful, Dana. What's her name?' The woman spoke quickly, ignoring Logan completely. It was as if he were invisible.

'Kelsey.'

'Gorgeous.'

'Who are you?' Logan asked, confused. Had he not been paying enough attention to Dana and what was going on in her life? Who was this woman?

'I'm Melanie,' the visitor said, as if that explained it all. 'Matt went home but he said to say he'd call later.'

'Remember, Logan, Melanie is a friend from the support group. I met her the first week I went. She kind of took me under her wing.'

'Well, aren't you just making new friends left and right?' Logan said, more sarcastically than he intended to. He was aware of the tension in the room and, on some level, he knew that he was creating it, but he couldn't seem to stop himself.

'What's that supposed to mean?' snapped Melanie. 'Is Dana not allowed to have friends?'

He was taken aback by the question. 'Yes, of course, I just meant... I don't know what I meant,' he said, rubbing a hand over his tired face. He felt old, as if he couldn't keep up. How was he supposed to raise a baby when he felt like this? He thought about Pippa and he wished she were here. He should call her; she'd want to know that Dana had had the baby. They were still friends, no matter how strained their relationship was right now.

'I'd like to have some time with my wife and daughter, if you don't mind,' he said pointedly to Melanie.

'Fine, but I'll be back tomorrow, OK, Dana?' Melanie leaned in and gave her a kiss on the cheek. Dana said a tired goodbye. 'Congratulations again, Dana,' she said, still ignoring him.

'I'm going to call Pippa and tell her that you've had the baby.' Logan walked from the room without waiting for a reply. He was bone weary and imagined that Dana was exhausted too. Pippa's phone rang and rang before she finally picked up.

'Hey, Logan, how's it going?' she asked cheerfully, so at odds with his wife's demeanour since the accident. It was a balm for his drained soul.

'Dana had the baby. I'm at the hospital now.'

There was silence on the other end and he pulled the phone away from his ear, wondering if they'd been disconnected. 'Pippa?' he said. 'You still there?'

'Yeah, I'm here. How is she?'

'She's... not well. Exhausted.' He needed to tell her, to unburden himself. 'Pip, she's called the baby Kelsey.' It hurt his heart to even say her name out loud.

'What?' she replied, shocked.

'She called our daughter Kelsey. What the hell do I do now?' More silence. 'Can you come to the hospital, please? She could do with a friend who really knows her.'

He could hear the hesitation in her voice before she replied, 'Yes.'

Logan didn't want to go back inside the room until Pippa arrived, but he had to; he needed to support his wife and newborn baby. 'Dana?' She opened her eyes slowly.

'Yeah?' she asked, reaching out her hand for him to hold. He grasped it gently, patting her with his other hand. He still loved her. No matter what, he loved her. 'What about Grace?'

'Grace? Who's Grace?'

'Our daughter, Dana. Why don't we call her Grace?' He waited for her to explode. She was so unpredictable these days.

'No, Logan, her name is Kelsey.' She stared him down and he eventually looked away. If anyone could talk her round, it was Pippa, in fact he was pinning his hopes on it.

Pippa appeared in the doorway about half an hour later, striding into the room. She touched his shoulder then gave him a warm hug. Smiling at him, she said, 'Congratulations, Dad.' Then she turned her attention to Dana.

'Dana, congratulations, honey, I'm so proud of you.' Pippa put her hand on Dana's cheek lovingly, then finally looked over at the baby girl who was making tiny noises in her sleep. 'She has your nose, Dana,' she whispered so as not to wake the baby. 'Absolutely beautiful. What's her name?' she asked expectantly.

'Grace,' Logan answered quickly.

'Actually,' Dana said tiredly, 'it's Kelsey.'

Even though he had told Pippa what Dana had called the baby, Pippa still looked shocked at hearing her say it out loud. 'Dana, sweetheart, you can't call her Kelsey.'

'Why not?'

'You do realise that this baby isn't the little girl that you lost, don't you?'

'Of course I know that!' Dana snapped. 'But I can at least get back some of what I lost, a piece of Kelsey.'

'I won't let you name our new-born after the daughter we lost. It's crazy talk. She's gone and nothing you do will bring her back. It's not fair to treat this baby like a replacement. I won't let you do it.'

Dana hung her head. 'I don't want to fight you both. For once, let me just have something I want.' She looked so small, so forlorn; her black hair hung sweaty in her face. 'Please.'

Logan looked at her, fighting the wave of sadness he felt for his wife, and said sternly, 'Her name is Grace and that's the end of it.'

'Well, you don't get to decide everything, Logan,' Dana snapped. 'She's my daughter. I carried her and I gave birth to her, I'll name her what I please and her name is Kelsey.' Dana's head rolled limply to the side on the pillow as if all the fight had been taken out of her with those few words.

'Well, whatever her name is,' Pippa said, trying to defuse the situation, 'she's a gorgeous little girl.' Pippa beamed at Logan and this time he felt a surge of happiness. Dana must have looked up and seen it on both of their faces, because she cleared her throat and said, 'I'd like to be alone with my daughter now.'

He understood. She wanted time to bond with the baby. That was a good sign.

'OK, we'll leave you to be with Grace, but I'll be back tomorrow after work to see you both.'

'You're not taking tomorrow off?' Dana asked incredulously, ignoring the name he called the baby... for now.

He looked at her in bewilderment. 'No, why would I?'

Dana and Pippa both stared at him. 'Maybe you could work a half-day then come up and see your girls,' suggested Pippa, and he realised the error he had made. Now Dana would think that he didn't care about either one of them, which wasn't true.

'Of course. I'll try and take the day off. I'll call you and let you know.' Logan walked over to the side of the bed and gave Dana a kiss on the cheek, before gently planting a tiny kiss on his daughter's cheek, whispering, 'I love you, Grace.' And he really did. When he stood, he didn't miss the look of annoyance on his wife's face.

'It's Kelsey,' she whispered furiously.

'No, Dana, it isn't.' But he wasn't willing to fight any more today. He'd had enough.

Next it was Pippa's turn to say goodbye and he could see her hesitate for a second before kissing Dana on the cheek too. 'Rest now, you've done a wonderful job. Night, beautiful girl,' she said as she touched the baby's cheek with her fingertip. They left the room together.

Once in the hallway and out of earshot, Logan said, 'Thanks so much for coming over. I doubt I would have had the courage to say what I did without you there, supporting me.'

'It's OK, I don't mind. I love Dana, she's my best friend, and I love Grace.' Pippa hesitated and he thought she was going to say that she loved him too, but she didn't.

'Have you met this Melanie?' he asked.

'Yeah, I have. She seems very interested in Dana.'

'That's what I thought. She bit my head off when she thought I was saying Dana couldn't have friends. That's not what I said at all.'

'I'd keep an eye on that friendship if I were you.'

'What about Matt? He brought Dana into the hospital, although I'm not even sure why they were together. They seem very close.'

'We're very close,' Pippa murmured.

'True.' Logan looked at her with longing, but she turned her gaze away, her eyes sliding away from his. She pulled at a loose thread on her top, much more interested in that than talking to him.

'Pippa,' he began.

'Don't. Now is not the time. Your wife just gave birth. Grace is your main priority now. We'll talk another time when everything has settled down. There's no hurry.'

He stayed silent for a moment. 'I'll walk you to your car, just hang on. I have to make a quick call.' He pulled out his phone and dialled his mother-in-law to tell her the good news. Mischa must have had a gut feeling because as soon as she answered the phone she said, 'She's had the baby, hasn't she? A boy or girl?' she asked excitedly.

'We had another little girl.'

Mischa squealed with glee and he couldn't help but smile. She'd been looking forward to this baby almost as much as he had. Kelsey's death had left a hole in all of their hearts and this baby would help, not replace, never replace, but be loved and cherished in her own right, helping heal some of the festering wounds. Eventually scar tissue would grow over those wounds and he would be able to think of Kelsey without feeling as if his still beating heart had been forcibly removed from his chest.

Mischa's voice brought him back. 'Is Dana up to visitors just yet?'

'I'd wait until tomorrow. She basically kicked Pippa and me out to bond with the baby. I don't mean to be rude, but do you think she'll see you? You guys have been strained lately.'

Mischa sighed and paused. 'I have to try, Logan, she's my daughter, and my granddaughter. Goodness me, what's the child's name? I forgot to ask.'

He paused, wondering how much to tell her.

'I actually named her – it's Grace.'

'Why did you name her? Shouldn't that have been a joint decision?'

'Not when you hear the name Dana had picked out for her. She wants to call her Kelsey. She's still fighting me on it.'

'Why on earth would she want to do that? That's a terrible idea. This child needs her own identity.'

'I wholeheartedly agree. She's her own person and such a burden shouldn't be put on tiny shoulders. Always being compared to a sister that she'd never live up to would be devastating for a child. I won't have that for my daughter.'

'How long will they be staying in the hospital?'

'I think the doctor said two days providing everything goes according to plan and I don't see why it wouldn't.' Logan realised he had said Kelsey's name more in the past half an hour than he had since she died. He said goodbye and went back to Pippa, who was waiting for him.

He walked her to her car, resisting the urge to take her hand in his. Pippa had made it clear that things would be staying just as they were for now. Dana having the baby had obviously made her take stock of her feelings for him.

'Pippa—'

'Not now, Logan... just... not now. We can't be having this conversation. I don't want to, it's not right. That's your wife and new baby up there – you need to focus on them.' Pippa crossed her arms, perhaps so he couldn't touch her hand, yet she gave him a lingering look, at odds with her body language. She slipped behind the steering wheel. 'Be with them. We'll talk some time soon.'

Dammit. He *liked* her. More than liked her. And he knew that she liked him too.

13

Logan didn't take the next day off, nor the day after that. When he finally turned up at the hospital to bring Dana and Grace home Grace was three days old. He had brought Pippa with him for support for both Dana and him, although it had been a bit of a battle to get Pippa to come.

'What the hell do you want me there for?'

'I need you there. Besides, you're still her best friend and she's going to need someone since she's not really talking to her mum. You're kinda all she has besides this Melanie and Matt, and I'm not sure either relationship is healthy. Please, Pip.' He looked at her imploringly and she gave in as he knew she would. He was terrified that there would be a silent, awkward ride home, the divide between him and his wife too great to bridge without help.

With the baby firmly strapped in, and Dana sitting in the back seat with her, Pippa in the front, they began the drive home.

'How are you feeling about coming home, Dana? I bet you can't wait to have the baby all to yourself,' Pippa said with cheer that sounded false even to his ears. All three of them were putting on a front, and they all knew it, but couldn't help but be cast in the roles they were playing.

'Happy. Kelsey and I need to settle in.'

Logan gritted his teeth before saying, 'Her name is Grace. Do you understand me, Dana? Her name is Grace, not Kelsey. Grace.' Pippa laid a fleeting hand on his arm and he knew it was a warning to leave Dana be for now. She'd come round in her own time – at least that was what Pippa thought. But Logan wanted to smash something, to punch a wall so hard he drew blood. If he couldn't ease the ache in his heart, then he wanted to hurt something.

When they arrived at the cottage, Logan took the car seat and gently put it down in the lounge, staring down at the sleeping face of his daughter. No matter how he felt about her mother, he would do anything for Grace. Losing Kelsey had been traumatic, but he decided that he really did want to be a dad again as Dana had clearly decided now that she really wanted to be a mum again. This would be good for them both, even though he had his reservations that it would bring them back together as a couple. He sighed as he remembered a simpler time when they had loved each other so deeply, but now he had feelings for another woman. It made him feel like shit. Grace's arrival meant he couldn't be with Pippa just yet, but he had a feeling that it wouldn't be long. He could hold out until then, until Dana had worked everything out within herself and Pippa agreed to give their relationship a go. He felt like a traitor thinking of Pippa in this way, but it was beyond his control. He had fallen for her, but he still loved his wife too.

Pippa made them all a cup of tea while Dana settled Grace in the cot in their bedroom. He'd have to approach Dana again about packing up Kelsey's room to make way for Grace. Dana was adamant that they not move house and just as adamant that

Kelsey's room be left exactly as it was. He disagreed but didn't want the argument – this was her first day home after all.

'Dana? I've made tea and I brought some cupcakes too. Want one?' Pippa said. There was no answer from Dana.

'I'll go get her,' he said, pushing himself up from the table with a groan.

'You OK?' Pippa asked, a concerned look on her face as she touched his arm.

'Yeah, just feeling old today, I guess.'

'Logan, this is a wonderful day. Your Grace is home, finally here. Enjoy it, no matter what else comes with it.'

She was right, of course. He walked down the hallway and as he got closer to their bedroom, he heard Dana talking to their daughter.

'I'll do better this time, Kelsey. I won't let anything happen to you like the other Kelsey. I'll tell you stories about her so you'll know her. Dad and I will always be here for you. We'll be a family again soon, I promise you.'

He threw open the door. 'Enough!' he roared, startling both Dana and Grace, who immediately began to wail in that high, hiccuppy voice that new-borns had. He was startled by his own outburst but pressed on. He walked over to his wife, took the screaming baby from her and said coldly, 'Her name is Grace, godammit, Dana. Do you understand me? Her name is Grace and if you call her Kelsey one more time, I'll take her from you.' He was breathing hard. 'You understand?' He was looming over her and he realised that he might be scaring her but he didn't care. Enough was enough.

'OK,' she whispered, clearly frightened.

'Say it.'

'Her name is Grace,' she said. He handed Grace back to her and walked out of the room, stunned that he had just done that.

He backed away from the doorway and went back into the kitchen, his face pale. Pippa looked up at him. 'Everything all right? I thought I heard yelling.'

'She's in there calling her Kelsey, talking to her about how we'll be one happy little family. I had it out with her. I'm just not sure how much longer I'll be able to keep this up. I love my daughter and I still love Dana, but...' He couldn't even finish his sentence. Pippa came over to him, leaning her forehead against his briefly, but the contact was enough to make him feel comforted.

They pulled apart reluctantly and Dana came back into the room, Grace held firmly in her arms.

'I thought the little one was asleep?' said Pippa with a smile. 'She must be exhausted, and you must be too. Do you want a sleep, Dana?'

'Don't talk to me like I'm a child,' Dana replied woodenly.

'Dana,' Logan warned, 'Pippa is just trying to help. Maybe you should go lie down – you look pale.'

'Cheer up, you just had a baby. You should be happy,' said Pippa. Dana stared at her as if she were wondering how insensitive Pippa could be. He knew Pippa was trying to make light of the situation, something that was lost on Dana at this time.

Dana frowned, clearly feeling ganged up on, even though he was just trying to look out for her, and the baby. She couldn't mother Grace properly if she was exhausted and he couldn't take any time off work. Dana would have to learn how to cope on her own during the day.

'Fine.' His wife took Grace back to the bedroom and he looked at Pippa.

'I know she's just given birth, but... I'm not even sure that I want to be here. You know?'

Pippa smiled sadly at him. 'I understand. You think you're

ready to move on but you're afraid of what that will do to Dana. I get it.'

'Do you really?'

'Yes. Really I do.'

'I love you.' There, he had said it. He held his breath, waiting.

Pippa looked shocked and just stared at him. 'You love me?' she asked with surprise in her voice.

'You find that hard to believe? Pip, I've been falling for you for a while now, I just didn't realise it. Do you feel the same way?' He waited, unsure of where her loyalties would take her. Would she give in? Love him back? Or would her loyalty to Dana outweigh her feelings for him?

'I – I don't want to betray my best friend. And I wouldn't hurt her if I could help it at all, but I can't.'

'What are you saying?'

'That I love you too.' Pippa was sobbing softly. 'I feel so guilty, being so happy with you when she's lost a daughter, but we have something special, we really do. I've known you for so long and if someone had told me a few months ago that I would fall in love with you I would have laughed. But here we are.'

She looked at him and sighed. He knew exactly what she was feeling. The realisation that they loved each other but couldn't be together was sobering them up quickly.

'I'd better go. Say bye to Dana for me.' Pippa looked as if she was going to say something more but instead she left.

Dana must have heard the door close and came out into the kitchen. 'Has she gone?'

'Yeah, she has,' he said wearily, not wanting to fight with her again on her first night home.

* * *

Later that evening, Logan fell asleep to the soft sucking sounds of Grace in her cot at the end of the bed. He dreamed of Pippa, her creamy skin, her figure that made him weak, her throaty voice. When next he woke, the room was silent, unnaturally so. Dana was asleep soundly beside him, her long black hair covering half her face. He wasn't sure what had woken him, but now that he was awake, he knew something was wrong. He untangled himself from the sheet, pushing it back, pulling it off Dana, who mumbled softly. He felt anxious as he hurried over to the cot, terrified that he would find Grace cold and blue.

She wasn't there.

His heartbeat sped up, thumping painfully in his chest, his blood boiled underneath his skin and his hands shook with shock. Where the fuck was she? He tore out of the room, neglecting to wake Dana, he was that terrified. He snapped on lights as he ran into each room, checking everywhere for his daughter. He stopped in front of Kelsey's room. The door was closed.

She wouldn't.

He pushed open the door and flipped on the light. Lying on Kelsey's bed, surrounded by pillows, was Grace, asleep.

'Shit,' he said quietly. With shaking hands, he picked up his daughter, cradling her tiny body to his chest. She was warm and snuggled into him. He carried her back to their room and put her back into her cot, tucking her in carefully.

A few hours later he sat at the kitchen table waiting for his toast to pop. He hadn't slept after putting Grace back where she belonged. He had made himself a coffee and nursed it in front of him, hands wrapped around the cup, almost too hot for him to touch. His toast flipped out of the toaster and landed on the bench. He buttered it then went back to the table where he continued to brood.

Last night had scared him badly. He'd decided in the early hours of the morning to call Dana's mum to ask her to reach out to her struggling daughter again. Dana appeared in the kitchen, and she frowned when she saw him sitting there.

'Why are you home? Don't you have to go to work today?' she asked, yawning.

'Dana, it's Saturday. I don't work on the weekend, you know that.'

She looked away, then nodded. 'I remember now.'

He watched her as she poured herself a glass of milk in a small plastic cup. She must have been able to feel his stare because she turned to face him. 'What?'

He blew out a frustrated breath. 'I know you love Grace, I know you do, and I know you care about her well-being and safety.'

She gave him a glare that normally would have silenced him, but he couldn't keep quiet about this.

'I woke up to find Grace missing from her cot and when I found her, she was in Kelsey's room, in Kelsey's bed. Can you explain that?'

'I should hope that's where you found her since that's where I put her last night.'

'Why?' Dana didn't seem the least bit fazed by what she had done.

'You wanted her in Kelsey's room, so what's the problem? I did what you asked.'

'I wanted to clean out the room, make it Grace's, not stuff her in amongst Kelsey's doll collection. She'll be staying in our room until we clean out and pack up Kelsey's room.'

'Well, she'll be in there with us forever, then.'

Every suggestion he made regarding anything was met with anger or silence. He was exasperated and just wanted a break from her, anything to get away from those vacant, dead eyes that he feared so much. 'What is wrong with you?'

'Me? You're the one trying to swoop in here like you're my saviour when, really, I don't need saving.' There was silence while he processed her comments. 'What are you thinking?' Dana asked. She hadn't cared enough to ask him what he'd been thinking for the longest time.

'I guess I'm wondering why you're doing all of this.'

'All of what?' she asked, draining Kelsey's small plastic cup.

'Resisting change, not even considering any of the suggestions that I make. It's as if, overnight, my opinions about Kelsey and Grace don't matter.'

'Because they're shit!' she screamed, hurling the cup past his head and into the sink, narrowly missing him. He wasn't sure if she'd meant to hit him with it or not. 'You push and you push with your constant nagging, never giving me a moment's peace to just be a mum to my baby. I'm so sick of it!'

He took a step towards her and she took one back. 'So this is how it is going to be from now on? Anything I say is just shit and that's that?'

'What the hell do you want from me, Logan?' his wife yelled.

'Right now? Absolutely nothing.'

14

Logan kept pushing her to pack up Kelsey's room. The sooner, the better, he'd said, but she was resisting. It was all too much to deal with right now, she'd told him that, but he just wouldn't listen. He might have won the fight on the baby's name, much to her sadness, but he would not push her around about this. She was *not* packing up Kelsey's things, that was just going too far.

'But we don't need to just yet. Grace won't need a room of her own for months.' It still felt wrong to call her Grace, but Dana knew she wasn't going to win the name war with Logan. He'd made that very clear. So had everyone else. So Grace it was.

'I'm not waiting months for you to do it. I'll do it if you can't.'

'Why are you so keen to have her things gone?' Dana asked, genuinely confused. This time her voice wasn't coloured with anger. She was curious.

'Why? Because it hurts, Dana. Every day that they're in there, it hurts. It's like we're waiting for Kelsey to come home and that's never going to happen.'

This was the most he'd ever said on the subject and it got her thinking. 'What if I compromised?'

'I'm listening.'

'Leave it a few months and by the time... Grace is ready for her own room, I'll be ready. Then we can pack up Kelsey's things, together.'

He shook his head no. 'That's not going to work, Dana. I just told you how much it hurts me to have her things in the house.'

'And I've told you how much it would kill me to have her things in boxes. I need her room to stay just as it is. Please, Logan.'

He turned away from her and strode from the room, no resolution reached. Would they ever be able to agree on anything again?

* * *

Grace was a demanding baby in some ways, but nothing Dana couldn't handle. She remembered Kelsey being more easy-going than this. Logan was at work during the day and didn't help all that much overnight. He loved Grace though – while he was home, before bed, he spent time with her, reading to her and hugging her to him gently. It was sweet and made Dana smile. It seemed as though things might be starting to get a tiny bit better between them. Yes, it was early days, but they had to work things out, didn't they? After all, they had a daughter together.

She thought about the first night they'd come home when she'd put Grace into Kelsey's bed. He couldn't understand why she'd do such a thing and was furious with her, but she didn't understand why he was reacting the way he did. He had wanted it so she couldn't understand why he was so angry at her. She had fucked up again and couldn't win.

Pushing the uncomfortable memory from her mind, Dana focused on the present, feeding her daughter. As she fed Grace while sitting on the couch, Dana thought about Matt, something she had done a bit of in the hospital. She had sent photos of Grace to both Matt and Melanie, and they had each said how cute she was and how much like her she looked.

As if he knew Dana was thinking about him, Matt messaged her.

What's up? How you feeling? You doing OK?

Was she OK? Logan and she were still fighting. Maybe this *was* settling in though.

Getting there. Logan's acting a bit weird.

What's there to be weird about? His wife and baby daughter just came home. I'd be so damn happy.

His words made her feel both good and bad.

What are you doing right now?

Right now? Feeding Grace. She's just about ready for a nap, falling asleep as I type.

How 'bout I come over and keep you company for a bit?

She thought about his question for at least a good minute. She liked Matt and it would be good for her to have some company; he was a good friend and made her smile. She could do with a friend right about now.

Sure, come on over.

On my way.

Dana put Grace in her cot and then went into the bathroom, running a comb through her hair so it hung untangled down her back. Then she changed out of the clothes that had dried spit on the top.

Dana was still playing with her hair when Matt knocked on the door. Quickly pulling it over one shoulder, she opened the door. He was dressed casually, but his hair was carefully done too.

'Hey, Matt, come in.' She stood back, and because of the narrow hallway, he had to squeeze past her. Halfway past her, he stopped and put his arms around her, giving her a quick kiss.

'Hey, yourself,' Matt said, his breath tickling her. He smelt like some woodsy aftershave. He headed into the lounge and sat down, crossing his legs and making himself at home. He patted the space beside him. She was about to speak when the wail of the baby cut through the silence.

'Ah, seems like little miss is awake. Can I have a hold? It's... been a while.'

Nodding, she went to get Grace. When she came back into the lounge, Matt was standing, waiting. Dana put the baby into his outstretched arms and he folded her very carefully into his chest. Her cries tapered off. He looked down at her, looking into her eyes, then he bent down close to her and breathed in her baby scent before kissing her on her nose. When he looked up, tears were streaming down his face. Dana's heart went out to him. Sometimes she forgot that they had met via their shared grief. That he had lost a child too. He handed Grace back to her, unable to hold her any more.

'I have to go. I'm sorry. I thought I could do this, but I can't.'

'Stay, Matt. I want you to stay.'

'It's too hard. Grace... you. I want a family again so badly, and here is a ready-made one, people that I care about and I can't have them. It's just painful is what it is. I just need time.'

Time. Wasn't that what she'd been asking Logan for? Time was the enemy of everything.

He left her alone holding the baby she now understood he so coveted. He had made his feelings pretty clear. He wanted to be in her life in more ways than just friendship.

Immediately she felt lonely again. Putting Grace back into her cot, she pulled out her phone. Her finger hovered over Matt's name but she hesitated. He needed time and space to deal with his emotions, a break from her, so instead, she pressed Melanie's name.

'Hey, Dana! I haven't heard from you in days. I've missed you. You know I can't go more than a few days without you!'

It was nice to hear Melanie's cheerful voice. A friend was a friend and she was in short supply of those these days, what with Pippa becoming more distant and Matt fleeing from her.

'It's nice to talk to you too. It has been a while.'

'Do you want to catch up?' Melanie asked, pausing for Dana to respond.

'Yeah, that would be nice.'

'We have a meeting on tonight, first one since you've had Grace. Want to go together? I'll come pick you up and we'll have a tea and latte across the street again.'

'Sounds good. I just have to wait for Logan to get home to watch Grace.'

'OK, text me when he's home and I'll come grab you. I'm so excited to see you and my baby girl!' Melanie squealed.

Dana hung up the phone with a smile. Her new friend was proving very entertaining, keeping her mind off things. While she'd been talking to Melanie, she'd missed a call from her mum. She was about to call her back when she felt a breeze lifting up tendrils of her hair. Curious, Dana went into the kitchen, heading for the back door. It was wide open. She stared at it, confused. She had definitely closed the door. She was sure she had. Dana grabbed the handle, closed and locked the door, jiggling the handle for good measure. How long was the door open for? Was she alone in the house? Dana started to feel jumpy, the noises of the old home settling sounding sinister to her. She worried how she was supposed to protect Grace if someone was able to get into her house whenever they wanted. She heard Grace fussing in the bedroom. She obviously wasn't going to settle any time soon so Dana headed down the hallway to give her a cuddle.

As she rocked Grace, Dana thought about the scrunched-up paper in the bottom of her bag. She still hadn't thrown out the death notice with the horrible word scribbled across it. She couldn't imagine anyone she knew doing something so disgusting to her, a grieving mum. The fact that it had come from her printer worried her no end, yet she made the decision not to tell anyone about it. Who would believe such a story? How could she prove who was messing with her? More importantly, *why* were they messing with her? It was something that had been weighing on her mind, but she wasn't ready to share just yet. Not after Logan had made fun of her the last time she knew someone had been in her house. The thing was, she was right: someone *was* harassing her and they obviously blamed her for Kelsey's death. Dana had no idea what to do. Grace began to wail, her cries piercing through Dana's fear.

Logan came home three hours later to a crying baby that still wouldn't settle. 'What's going on here? I can hear Grace crying from the street,' he said, taking her from Dana's arms. He cradled Grace and began to rock back and forth, shushing her.

'I've got my meeting tonight so you'll have to watch Grace.'

Dana had meant to ask him nicely, but she was afraid that he'd say no so she just told him instead.

'Sure.' She needn't have bothered about him being angry or annoyed. She was pleased with his attitude, saw it as a positive sign, maybe a thawing towards her?

She quickly texted Melanie, who sent a winky face then a heart emoji. She was there in under ten minutes.

'Hi, Melanie,' Logan said softly when she walked into the lounge.

Melanie didn't even acknowledge him. 'I missed you,' she said to Dana. 'OK, show me my baby girl,' she said before realising that Grace was in Logan's arms. Melanie walked over to him and smiled with a strained smile. 'May I hold the baby?'

Logan looked over her head at Dana and she nodded, so he gently handed Grace to her. She snuggled Grace against her chest and looked down at her with wonder. 'She's just so lovely, aren't you, my beautiful girl? Congratulations again, Dana.'

'Thanks, Melanie,' Dana said. Melanie gave Grace one last look before handing her back to Dana, who then passed her back to Logan.

'We have to get going. I'll be back in a couple of hours – we're going for coffee afterwards. There's bottles of milk made up in the fridge and she'll want to go down about fifteen minutes after her feed.'

'OK, see you in a couple of hours,' Dana threw over her shoulder as she pushed Melanie towards the front door.

Once they were in the car Melanie spoke. 'That guy.'

'He's not that bad,' Dana said. 'He really isn't.'

'He's pushing you to do things before you're ready. That's emotional abuse. That's not healthy, Dana, you know that, right?'

She did know that, she felt it, but she also knew that Logan was trying to do what he thought was best, as was she. They just didn't see eye to eye or have the same approach to life; not right now anyway.

'And what about Matt?' Melanie asked suddenly, breaking into Dana's thoughts.

Dana immediately went on the defensive. 'What about him?'

'Well, I get the feeling he really likes you. Am I right?'

Jesus, she was like a bloodhound or something, always sniffing out the dead bodies.

'Of course not. Matt and I are friends, good friends, but just friends. As you said, I'm a married woman.' Dana hoped her lie was convincing. She knew that Matt wanted more – he not only wanted more with her, but he wanted Grace in his life as well.

As they drove to the meeting, Dana wondered if she should confide in Melanie about the intruder. It was adding a whole lot of stress to her already stressful life, but she had no idea how to begin and was still trying to find the words when they arrived at the meeting.

She couldn't tell Matt; he was taking a break from her. She opened the door to the meeting room and saw a familiar sight. Matt, sitting in his normal seat, his large frame dwarfing the chair, long legs stretched out in front of him. He stood when they walked over. He looked in her direction when he said hi, holding her gaze for a second before he greeted Melanie.

'Dana, Melanie, how are you both?' he asked, coolly, as if a couple of hours ago he hadn't declared that he wanted to be with her. Melanie gave him a nod but ignored him after that. His eyes flicked Dana's way but she immediately looked away. He had already lost so much, a wife, then a child. He had so much sadness, he deserved better than a life alone, but she couldn't give him what he desired. She was committed to making things work with Logan.

When the meeting wrapped up, Melanie picked up her bag and said to Matt, 'Well, we'd better get going, things to do.'

He looked forlorn as Dana said goodbye but she knew that she needed to give him his space; he had to work things out within himself and how to deal with his friendship with her moving forward.

She pushed Matt from her mind as she shared a cup of tea with Melanie. Luckily her friend did not bring up either of the men in her life for a change. Afterwards, Melanie drove her back home and said, 'I'll call you,' as she drove off with a wave.

Grace was crying when she walked in the door and Logan pounced on her. 'You've been gone for three hours, Dana.'

Sighing, she put her bag on the kitchen table and walked to the sink to grab a glass of water. Logan followed her, the squalling baby held in his arms.

'I know. I told you, meeting, then the café. Besides, I'm home now,' she said, reaching out her hands and taking Grace from him. 'Did you not know how to settle her?' There was no judgment, but he took it as such and attacked her.

'She wanted her mummy,' he spat, making her feel like shit.

'You know, I was taking a few hours out of my life to catch up with a friend and discuss the meeting that we'd just attended for people who have lost those they love, so excuse me if I don't hurry away from someone who tries to understand me, to you, who *won't* understand me.' She hadn't meant to say those things but he was pissing her off. How could he not be happy that she'd made friends, that she was going to the group he wanted her to go to?

'Look, I'm sorry, it's just, she's a lot to handle after working all day. You get to stay at home, you don't really work, you know.'

Dana stood there fuming. So they were back here again? 'Who do you think takes care of Grace all day and all night? You did this with Kelsey too. You don't value my contributions as a mother and it pisses me right off.'

Logan stared at her as if contemplating her angry words. 'You're right.'

Dana was taken aback. 'About what?' she asked warily, still seething at his comments.

He took a deep steadying breath. 'I shouldn't have said those things to you and I'm sorry. I'll see if I can take a few days off next week to help you with Grace.'

'You are?' To say she was surprised was an understatement, he'd never acted like this before, offering to help by taking time off work, but she wasn't going to say no.

'OK, I'd like that. Thank you,' Dana said as Logan walked over to her and pulled her gently into his arms. It felt nice, it felt... familiar.

* * *

Alesha lay on the double bed in her old bedroom, her fingers tracing patterns on the bed cover. She stared at the ceiling. There were little glow-in-the-dark stars stuck above her head; they'd been there for years, slowly discolouring, their glow dimmed. This used to be her room up until she'd moved out of home. She'd lived in the bungalow at the back of her parent's place and by a twist of fate, she was back here again, lying under those same stars. Her life had imploded with one text. She should have been watching Kelsey as she had offered to do; it had been the perfect chance to mend things with her sister. She should have ignored the bloody ping of her phone and waited but she had been so happy that the man she was seeing had messaged her that she had checked it. James had ignored her the whole car ride over, making no effort to engage her in any conversation whatsoever.

Around other people, he came across as attentive and loving, but when they were alone, it was a different story. He had obviously fallen out of love with her a long time ago but was too much of a coward to pull the pin on their relationship. Then Kelsey had died and she'd fallen apart at the seams.

Instead of supporting his wife when she needed him most, instead of standing by her side, he was highly embarrassed by her suicide attempt. It was all over town what she'd done, their friends knew, their work colleagues knew, and his way of coping with that was to ask her to move out of their house. It had been humiliating and hurtful. He hadn't even come to visit her in the hospital, but once she arrived back home, via taxi, when all she'd wanted was to curl up in her bed and forget that the world existed for a while, she had opened the front door and found three suit-cases packed and waiting. He hadn't even let her through the door.

'James? What's this?' she'd croaked, her voice damaged by her... incident.

He stayed stone still, looked at her, taking in her dishevelled appearance and the mark around her neck. A mask came over his face. She knew it well: it meant that he was about to be a total prick. 'I'll get right to it. I want you gone.'

'What? Gone where?' she asked softly, confused.

'Out of my house and out of my life. You're an embarrassment and a liability to me and my career. How could you do something so reckless? Did you even think about me?' His voice was cold and his words calculated. 'I'll put your suitcases in your car for you, then you need to leave.'

'Just like that? You're throwing me out of my own home?'

'Yes. You can slink back to your parents' house and hide out there. No one will even miss you.'

Refusing to allow him to see her cry, or how much his words

had hurt her, Alesha bent down and grabbed hold of the smallest suitcase, wheeling it towards the garage and put it in her car. There was no point arguing with him. The next time they saw each other maybe he'd be more reasonable, but she wouldn't hold her breath.

Once the car was packed with her meagre belongings, she turned to say something to him, but he closed the door in her face. She heard the lock engage and knew that their marriage was over. This was how she found herself back in her childhood home, recuperating, trying to get her head straight, but it was hard, living with the guilt that she felt every day. Things were going downhill for her quickly. Yes, her life had imploded, and she blamed one person. Her sister.

15

Instead of waiting to be asked, Logan offered to stay at home with Grace while she went to her meeting the next week. He had become much closer to Grace ever since they'd had the talk about her contributions as a stay at home mother and he was even taking some time off to help out. He bathed Grace, fed her and hugged her more often and he was more kind to Dana. It made her think that they had a shot, that maybe they could make this work. Dana felt less angry and was beginning to see light at the end of the tunnel. Finally.

Logan had taken her and Grace for a drive to the paint store and they had picked out a colour to paint Grace's room. It had been a bittersweet moment for Dana to see Logan trying so hard while they talked about repainting Kelsey's room. In the end he had left the choice up to her and after swallowing the lump in her throat, she'd chosen a beautiful lilac.

Dana woke up the morning of the meeting to a message from Matt.

Just checking in. Need a lift tonight? Coffee and tea afterwards?

She knew that it must have been hard for him to reach out to her after the way they'd left it last week, but he had done it anyway. She really wanted to see him. Matt had said that he wanted to see her alone afterwards so she hoped Melanie didn't ask to come out after the meeting for a coffee.

That evening, Matt messaged her to let her know that he was outside.

Dana checked her phone. 'I'd better get going. Will you be right with Grace?' she asked.

'Yeah, we'll be fine, won't we, Grace?'

Dana dropped a kiss on her daughter's cheek and left.

'Hey, Matt, how are you?' she asked tentatively as she hopped into the car and clicked her seatbelt into place.

'I need to apologise,' he said quickly, as if needing to get it off his chest and out of his mind. He pulled away from the kerb. 'I'm so sorry, Dana.'

'For what?'

'Well, not being ready, I guess, most of all. You need something from me that I felt I couldn't give.'

'And what do I need?' she asked, wondering that same question herself.

'Friendship,' he said haltingly, as if scared she was going to stop him at any second.

'I understand why you were scared. You've loved and lost a partner – I can't understand how that feels – and then to lose your son, it's no wonder you want to be a part of something special again. Life is fragile and fleeting, Matt; we do the best we can do.'

He glanced over at her. 'Yeah, life is fleeting, so we need to make the most of it,' he reiterated.

'Matt, I like you. If I'm honest, if I wasn't married, this story might have a different ending.'

He looked crestfallen. 'So, the only way I get to be in your life is as a friend?'

'Yes. Matt, I'm married and I want to see if I can make it work with Logan. I'd be lying if I said I didn't have feelings for you, because I do – you're important to me.' Matt pulled up in the car park and they both saw Melanie waiting on the stairs.

'*Shit,*' she said under her breath.

'What if we didn't go in?' Matt asked, turning to face her.

'What?'

'What if I just drive out of here? We could go somewhere else, for coffee, skip listening to the depressing stories. We have enough of our own, don't you think?'

She laughed. 'I agree with you that they are depressing. They'll notice if we're not there, especially Melanie – she can actually see us right now.'

Without another word, he reversed out of the car park and Dana felt naughty, as if she'd cut class or something. He took her to a different café, one across town. Her phone vibrated in her pocket as they waited for their drinks. She quickly turned her phone over, hoping Grace was all right, but it wasn't Logan, it was Melanie.

'Everything OK?' Matt asked, seeing the frown on her face.

'Yeah, Melanie is calling. I'll call back when I get home.' Dana let it go to voicemail and turned her phone face down again, focusing her attention on Matt.

'So why are we skipping the meeting today?' she asked, one hand folded under her chin, smiling.

'Today is my son's one-year anniversary.'

The smile instantly fell from her face, her hand reaching to grasp his automatically. 'Oh, God, Matt, I'm so sorry. I didn't know.'

'How could you?' he asked, pulling back his hand and raking

it through his hair. 'I never told you when it was. I haven't even been able to tell you his name.'

'You didn't think that today of all days it would have been good to attend a meeting?' she asked quietly, looking into his eyes.

'No, I didn't want to share my grief with anyone... except you.' He exhaled a breath. 'I know that's probably inappropriate but—'

'No. It's not. You spend this time with whoever you damn well want. I can't imagine what you're feeling, although I'll be there eventually.'

Their food arrived, along with his coffee and her tea. She raised her cup. 'To your beautiful boy.'

He gently clinked her cup with his and said, 'Jeremy.'

'Jeremy,' she whispered. 'To Jeremy.' He smiled sadly at her.

'I'm glad my wife, Anne, isn't here. She wouldn't have survived a blow like losing her child.' It was the most he'd ever opened up to her and the most emotional she'd seen him. He was finally trusting her with his story.

'I'm sorry. To lose a spouse and a child...' She couldn't even finish the sentence; it tore at her heart.

'Yeah.' It seemed as if he was done sharing and that was OK. She was about to start talking about something else when her phone vibrated again. She turned it over. Melanie. She sighed. 'Go away,' she muttered under her breath.

'Do you just want to answer? Might be easier.'

'No. She'll want to know why I didn't come to the meeting and where I am. I don't want to play with her right now.'

That got a small smile out of him.

'I will listen to her message though, just to make sure that everything's all right.' She pressed the button to access her voice-mails and listened to Melanie's.

'Dana!' She sounded worried. 'Where are you? I saw you and

Matt leave and you're not at home.' *How the hell did she know that?* 'Call me back.'

'What did she say?'

'She's saying pretty much what I said she would, but I think she went to my house. Now I have to explain to Logan why I skipped out on the meeting.'

'And why you did it with me.'

'That part doesn't worry me, but he expects me to go to these meetings to get over Kelsey.'

'And *are* you over her?'

'Not even close. She will always be my baby. You just don't get over losing a child. I don't have to tell you that and I shouldn't have to tell him that either. He lost the same child, but we're in such different places with our grief.'

'Everyone grieves differently, Dana.'

'True, I guess. Is there a right and a wrong way?' she asked.

'Depends on the person you ask. I have no wife to compare my grief to, but I don't think she would ever have got over Jeremy's death either. She'd probably never forgive me and hate me forever.'

Dana looked up at him, her expression one of surprise. 'Why on earth would you say that?'

He looked at her, his mouth opening and closing, as if he were physically choking on the words trying to push past his lips. 'I killed him. It's my fault.'

He began to cry quietly; she reached over the table to touch his hand. 'Do you want to talk about it?' she asked gently while stroking his hand for courage.

'I really do.' She stayed silent, waiting for him to be ready to tell her his story. 'Ever since Anne passed away, I had trouble adjusting to being alone, to being a single dad. It was a steep learning curve taking care of Jeremy and I was grieving our loss. I hired a nanny so I could go back to work. I didn't want to, but I had to bring in money.' She nodded with understanding.

'I was doing OK. It had been four months and I was beginning to finally cope. I no longer cried myself to sleep, didn't break down at work. I was just Jeremy's dad from then on. I tried not to think about Anne but she was everywhere, so we moved. One day, the day Jeremy died, the nanny couldn't come in – she was sick with a fever and didn't want to pass whatever she had on to Jeremy. We had a day care near my work that I had sometimes used on a casual basis. I was supposed to drop him off, but I was running late trying to get everything done in time. Jeremy was having a bad morning and was screaming. I tried everything but he settled down as soon as I got him strapped in the car. He started sucking on his thumb and went to sleep. The car always did that to him and I was relieved. I had a presentation that morning and I was already stressed.' He stopped talking, then he ran both hands over his face.

'I was on a work call, some emergency with the client, I don't even know what it was, but it was important at the time. So important that I forgot to turn off at the street to the day care. I drove straight to work.'

She could see where this was headed but didn't say anything. He needed to get his story off his chest. 'I parked and went into work. It was just another day, a normal day. I forgot Jeremy was in the car and I went in to work.' He began to cry again. 'How could I do that to my son? I killed him, Dana,' he said, looking up at her. 'I killed him. Do you have any idea what that does to a person?'

She wanted to tell him, yes, she did, but now wasn't the time for her story. She stood up, walked around to him, and grasped his shoulders, pulling him to her, rubbing his back. He stood up and returned her hug.

'You didn't kill him, it was an accident, something that happened to you both. You loved him.'

He pulled back. 'That's not what Anne's family said. They told anyone who'd listen that I wanted no responsibilities since she died. That I deliberately left my son in a hot car to suffocate to death.'

His body heaved in her arms. She kept holding onto him, trying to take away some of the pain when he bent his head and pressed his lips to hers gently. She pulled away. 'Oh, Matt, I'm—'

'Sorry. I know. You're married and you feel sorry for me.'

'Yes, I feel for you, but that's not why... You're a good guy and what you just told me doesn't change anything. I don't look at you and see you as a bad person. It was a moment in time, an accident, one that will last forever for you but an accident still.'

'How can you not judge me?' he asked as she sat back down.

'Because I know what it's like to be the one responsible for your child's death.' Her voice wavered, her eyes filling with tears.

'Before you say anything, let's get out of here. People are staring at us.' Matt managed a half-smile. He paid and they sat in the car, silent until she spoke.

'My daughter, Kelsey, died in a car accident.' Matt was quiet, letting her talk this time. 'The car was being driven by me, but she wasn't in it at the time.' She couldn't believe that she was ready to share the most painful aspect of her life with him.

'What do you mean?' She looked away and he said, 'You can tell me, Dana. I won't judge, just like you didn't judge me.'

'My sister was supposed to be watching Kelsey, but she got a text message from a man she'd been seeing and took her eyes off her. I didn't realise that Kelsey was behind the car and I reversed over her. I killed her.' Dana burst into noisy tears.

'Let it out, sweetheart,' he said, rubbing her back. She did, she cried for a good few minutes before her tears started to taper off, turning into soft sobs. He pulled a tissue from his pocket and dabbed the tears from her cheeks.

'Sorry,' she mumbled.

'I think we both needed this. To come clean, to talk about what we've lost, especially today. It was ruled an accident for me and I'm guessing for you too?'

'Yes. It was an accident. I didn't see her, but I never checked my mirrors. I might have been able to save her life.' She hiccupped, tears in the corners of her eyes waiting to spring forth again. She held them at bay by biting on the inside of her cheek.

'So Logan expects you to get over Kelsey's death when you were the one driving?'

She nodded.

'No one should expect that. It's not fair. You have the added guilt of being the driver – he should know that you blame yourself. How could you not?'

Matt got it. Maybe because he was going through something similar.

'I wish you could have met him,' Matt said.

'Me too.'

'Dana, I... I just...'

'Matt—'

'I know, I know. I feel... deeply for you, Dana, and I don't want anyone else. Just you. I know you have Logan and Grace, but... I'm hopeful.' He smiled at her. 'Anyway, let me get you home before you get into trouble again.'

'Well, I haven't received any frantic calls from Logan, so all must be well at home.' Matt opened the car door for her and she hopped in.

'Thanks for tonight,' he said as they pulled up in front of her house.

'I think we both needed tonight, so thank you too.'

Dana headed inside.

'Hi, I'm home. Logan?' she called. She went into their room, expecting to see Grace asleep in the cot. She wasn't there, neither was Logan. Dana went down the hallway and found them asleep on the floor in the lounge, Grace on a blanket with cushions on either side of her. Logan had a cushion under his head and was out like a light. She smiled at the sight of them both. It was adorable so she pulled her phone out of her pocket and snapped off a shot. They must have been tired to not even make it to bed. She wondered what they had done that had been so exhausting.

After the emotional night she had had, both listening to Matt's heart breaking story and confiding in him about hers, she felt drained, so she put the kettle on and made herself a cup of calming chamomile tea, her favourite. She sat at the table, blowing off the steam, thinking about Matt and his declaration of affections. She had feelings for him, as a friend, possibly something more, but she wasn't willing to let them get in the way of her marriage. She and Matt were just friends.

Eventually, Dana stood up. After her emotional talk with Matt, Dana felt like she needed to be closer to Kelsey so she walked into her room, but when she flipped the light in Kelsey's room, all she could do was stare.

16

Logan had been waiting for Dana to leave for her meeting. As soon as she left, he put Grace in her cot and grabbed the boxes that he'd hidden in the shed behind the old fridge. He brought them inside and began packing quickly. He figured he had at least two solid hours before she arrived home, plenty of time to pack up Kelsey's room. Everything went into the boxes; there were no exceptions. While he was working, he cried a little, seeing all of her things as they went into the boxes. Dana wouldn't understand that this was hurting him too. She would only see her own pain. Boo Boo went in as well, the stuffed bear that had started it all. If not for this damn thing Kelsey would be alive.

When he taped up the last box, Logan looked around at the bare room. There was nothing left to suggest that a little girl had lived here except for one pale pink wall. He carried the boxes out into the trailer that he'd parked around the corner of their street. He'd thought of everything. He'd previously told Dana that when the room was packed up, all of Kelsey's stuff would go to her parents' place, but he decided against that, as she would just pack it up and bring it back home. Instead, he took Grace and drove to the storage facility in the industrial estate and unloaded all the boxes, snapping the padlock on the storage shed as he left. He was bone tired by the time he got back home, and Grace was asleep. He lay down on the floor with his daughter and before he fell asleep, he contemplated what he'd done and just how bad the fallout would be.

As expected, Dana flipped out when she returned and saw what he'd done, screaming at him to bring back Kelsey's things, but he wasn't going to do that; he knew what was best for her. He'd been with her long enough to know that this was the right course of action. He didn't tell her where Kelsey's things were, instead he calmly told her why he'd done what he'd done, picked up his bags, took his daughter and left. Dana was so angry she didn't even come after him. She wasn't thinking of Grace, she was firmly stuck in the past, a place she'd been in for months. It was time for her to be shocked out of it.

He could have gone to a motel and stayed the night there, but he knew where he wanted to go, somewhere where he and Grace would be appreciated, with someone who would welcome them with open arms.

He knocked on Pippa's door, bags slung over his shoulder, baby wrapped in his arms. She opened the door, dressed in jeans and a low cut white top. 'Logan! What are you doing here? And look who's with you! Hi, Grace, hello, darling.' Pippa held out her arms for a cuddle of the sleepy baby and Logan immediately handed his daughter over to her as he hefted the bags on his shoulder.

Pippa took them both into the cosy lounge. 'Not that I mind, but what are you two doing here?'

'We had to leave home for a bit. I packed up Kelsey's room while Dana was at her meeting.'

Pippa looked shocked. 'Well, that might push her over the

edge. Then again, maybe it's time she stepped up, finally moved on.'

'Exactly what I've been thinking,' he said, glad Pippa agreed with him. 'Dana will never move on with all that stuff in there, like a shrine.'

'So I take it you two want to stay here the night, then?' she asked, kissing a sleepy Grace on her cheek.

'If that's OK,' Logan said, wondering if he'd made a mistake coming here. Would spending the night be putting himself in a dangerous position? Probably, but he couldn't seem to make himself leave.

'Of course it is. Now, where are we going to put Grace to sleep?'

'Her bassinet is already in the car. I packed it earlier. I'll go grab it.' As Logan walked out to the car he thought about how different the two women in his life were. He could see how Dana had been trying ever since Grace was born and he had almost thought that they could get back to being a family, but tonight had shown him that she wasn't willing to move forward yet. She loved Grace deeply, he knew this, but she just couldn't let go of Kelsey. She had forced his hand.

As he walked back inside, his phone rang. It was Dana. He ignored the call then she called back straight away and left a message. He didn't bother checking it. He heard Pippa talking to someone and at first he thought it was Grace. He heard a door close; Pippa must have gone into her bedroom. He could hear her voice pitched low, and when she came out there was a look of guilt on her face.

'You all right?' He took Grace from her arms and placed her gently into the bassinet, tucking her in.

'It's a low day when a woman has to lie to her best friend about her husband's whereabouts.' She had tears in her eyes.

Logan's phone rang again, and this time Mischa's name flashed across the screen. He felt that he couldn't ignore her call, so he answered it. She was calling on behalf of Dana who she said was at their house looking for Kelsey's things. He told her that he hadn't thrown anything away and that they were safe. After a pause, he informed her that he wouldn't be home that night. He knew that would hurt Dana but a part of him didn't care.

He went to Pippa, hand on her arm. 'Thank you for covering for me. I just need some distance and if she knew I was here, she'd be over here like a shot causing a scene. I'm done with the drama, at least for one night. I was just trying to help.' He could say that as much as he wanted, but a small part of him wanted to hurt Dana too, to punish her for how miserable he'd been since Kelsey died. They could have shared their grief; instead she had mourned deeply and alone, accusing him of not caring, which cut him to the bone.

'Do you want something to eat?' Pippa asked quietly, breaking into his thoughts.

'I'd rather have a hug.' Pippa took a step towards him and he folded her into his arms. She tilted her face upwards and he kissed her gently on the lips.

'We shouldn't be doing this, Logan,' Pippa whispered in between kisses.

'Why not? I love you and I know you love me. It feels right, Pip. Don't over-think it.'

'Yes, I love you, it's just—'

'No, no more, Pippa.' He led her by the hand down the hallway to her bedroom.

Logan turned on the lamp beside the bed. He wanted to see her the first time he made love to her. She was beautiful. He watched her get undressed slowly, revealing each part of her creamy skin. First she took off her jeans, dropping them to the floor, next came her top, and underneath was a crop top, covering most of her breasts. She was moving ever so slowly, making him wait for it. He was hard and when she took off her crop top, exposing her breasts with her perfect pink nipples, he could see she was just as turned on as he was. Then she took off her underwear and stood naked in front of him. His eyes roamed her body before lingering on her face.

Pippa lay on the bed and waited for him. He didn't bother with a striptease, he just wanted her. He didn't want to over-analyse his decisions. He'd waited so long for the chance to make love to her. He hurriedly pulled off his jeans, no underwear for him, then his shirt joined the pile of clothes on the floor. She stared at him, his cock hard, desire written across his face.

He kissed her deeply; she nibbled on his bottom lip, driving him crazy.

'Logan,' she whispered, her breath tickling his ear.

He wanted to take his time, but she had other ideas. 'Are you sure, Pippa? No going back,' he said, praying that she wouldn't change her mind.

'No going back.' She smiled at him slowly, eyes half closed with passion. He slid inside her, burying his cock in all the way. She gasped and for a second he thought he'd hurt her, but then she dug her nails into his back; he felt as if it were on fire, but in a good way.

'Jesus, Pippa,' he whispered, his face inches above hers. 'I love you.'

She clenched around his cock and, as he moaned, said, 'I love you too.'

He began to thrust harder and faster, much to her pleasure. He felt his orgasm building, his balls tightened and he came inside her. Before he'd even stopped pulsing, he reached his hand down between them and began to play with her clit until she too came with a small gasp.

He rolled off her and she snuggled up in the crook of his arm. She spoke about their future. Of how she wanted to be married within the year and have babies. Lots of babies. He listened to her, a contented smile on his face.

'I've always wanted kids but I wasn't sure that I would make a good mother,' Pippa confessed.

'Don't be silly. You're great with Grace and she's not even yours and you were always so close to Kelsey.' Saying her name hurt so he pushed her aside.

'That's the thing – I'd like to be a part of your and Grace's life on a more permanent basis.'

'What are you saying, or asking, Pippa?'

She laughed. 'OK, you found me out. I want you to leave Dana. I love her but I love you more; you and Grace. I need you.'

He didn't know what to say to that. It was a lot to throw at him just after he'd cheated on his wife. Now Pippa was asking him to leave Dana when she was at her most vulnerable?

'Pippa, don't you think that's a bit quick?'

'You love me, yes?'

'Yes, but I'm not sure that I can leave Dana and Grace.'

'No, you misunderstand. I want you to bring Grace with you. I want to be her mum.'

Logan looked at her in surprise. This was Dana's best friend – how long had she been thinking about this for?

'What you're asking me to do is not something that I take lightly, you know? I still love Dana, and Grace is her baby, not yours.'

'Logan—'

'Pippa.' He exhaled loudly. 'I need to think. Maybe we should just go to sleep. So can we just drop it, please?'

Pippa stared at him, anger colouring her face. 'I thought you wanted this – wanted me – but if I'm just a piece on the side then you can fuck right off.' She stalked naked from the room, leaving Logan wondering what the hell was wrong with the women in his life.

17

The room was bare. All of Kelsey's things were gone. Her bed, her clothes, her toys, Boo Boo, the lot. Dana dashed back into the lounge, screaming, 'What did you do?'

Logan's eyes popped open just as Grace started to cry, her tiny eyes screwed up, very unhappy about the noise. 'Would you please calm yourself? You're scaring our daughter,' he said in a soft but patronising voice.

'Please tell me you didn't throw away her things?'

'It was time, Dana. It was for your own good.'

'That wasn't your decision to make!' she screamed. 'How could you do this to me?'

'Not *to* you, *for* you. There's a huge difference,' Logan said, picking up the baby and rocking her in his arms.

'Put it all back, right now,' she demanded.

'I can't do that. It was anchoring you to the past, making you blind to your present. This baby, our baby. Grace. She needs you now, not Kelsey.'

His words broke her heart. How could he do this to her? She wasn't ready yet, she'd told him that she wasn't ready yet; he went and did it anyway. She looked around the lounge, her breath stilling in her throat. 'You took down her photos too?' she whispered. 'It's like she was never here. What's wrong with you?'

Logan picked up an overnight bag and the nappy bag that was beside the couch, something she hadn't noticed before when she'd come in. He swung them over his shoulder. 'I'm leaving until you get a hold of yourself and I'm taking Grace with me. We'll have this conversation when you're ready to listen to reason.' Delivered in a monotone voice, it was like a slap in the face how quickly he could replace Kelsey and move on. She began to cry, great heaving sobs. She dropped to her knees, arms hugging herself, unable to even move, let alone fight to keep her daughter. She heard the front door close with finality. They were gone.

After curling up in a ball and sobbing on the lounge floor for she didn't know how long, Dana finally pulled herself together. She was frantic with worry. He hadn't said where he was going and he'd taken her daughter with him. She called his mobile a few times but it just kept going to voicemail. She left only one message: 'Bring my fucking daughter back!'

Then, on a hunch, she called Pippa. She said she hadn't seen them, but Dana didn't believe her. She thought they were probably having a laugh at her expense – the stupid, unsuspecting wife – but she knew what was going on. She considered driving round there and confronting them both, but she was just too angry; she'd only make it worse. The only option for her now was to go out to her parents' place and get Kelsey's things back. If he could strip the room when she wasn't there, she could fill it back up when *he* wasn't there.

Dana slammed the door closed on her way out and headed to her car. Her dad had shown up one day with a second-hand hatchback for her to use. At first she didn't think she could drive it but here she was, about to drive the damn thing out of necessity. As she threw herself into the driver's seat, she looked over at the passenger seat, ready to throw her bag onto it when suddenly she stopped. There, in the glow of the interior light, was a small box, wrapped in pink wrapping paper with a pink bow. Dana just stared at it uncomprehendingly until the light slowly dimmed to nothing. Her heart started hammering and she realised that she didn't want to sit in the dark with that thing. She fumbled for her phone, turning the light on and shining it on the present.

'What the fuck?' she breathed. Placing the phone on the seat, she picked up the box with shaking fingers. She pulled on the end of the pink satin ribbon until it fell from the box. With care, she slowly unwrapped the present, the paper sliding off the seat and onto the floor. She was left holding a cardboard box. It seemed harmless enough but Dana was terrified. She pulled the lid up and looked inside. It was a small pink baby's rattle. It looked almost identical to the one she had found when she had been helping her mum clean out their shed. She picked it up between two fingers and as she did, a piece of paper fell onto the seat. It was small, just a tiny rectangle with even tinier writing on it. Dana put the rattle back in the box and used her phone to shine the light on the piece of paper.

Grace.

What the hell? Someone had broken into her car to leave a gift for her daughter? Dana whipped her body around and slammed down the lock on the driver's side, locking the car. She peered out into the darkness, trying to see if anyone was out there, watching her. She wished with all her heart that she weren't alone. She threw the piece of paper into the box, which she then threw into the back seat, and sped off towards her parents' house.

Most of the lights in the house were out when she arrived but she thought she saw the lounge light on. The bungalow behind the house was dark too, where Alesha was staying. Surely her parents wouldn't be in bed at nine o'clock in the evening? She banged on the door, waking up their old dog, Max. She must have banged loudly as he was hard of hearing now.

The front veranda blinked to life and her mother peered out of the screen door, checking who was there. 'Dana? What are you doing here at this time of night? Where's Logan? Where's the baby? Has something happened?' she asked, opening the door for her, a worried look on her lined face.

'Where is it?' Dana demanded.

'Where's what?' her mother asked, confused, ushering Dana into the house.

'Mum, I know that her stuff is here.' Dana barged through the lounge door as her father came out to see what was happening.

'Dana. What's going on?' he asked, taking in her wide eyes and dishevelled hair.

She was still freaked out about the present, but she didn't say anything about it – where would she even begin? Things kept happening to her. She was being punished and it frightened her.

She focused on what she had come out here to do. 'Dad, where is it?' Dana asked tearfully, grabbing at his arm, fingernails digging into his skin.

'Slow down, love. What are you looking for?' he asked.

'He brought it out here, I know he did. So, where is it?'

'Calm down, start from the beginning,' her dad said.

'Logan... he packed up Kelsey's room while I was out. Where are all her things?' she begged, tears flowing down her face. She really wasn't in the right frame of mind to be dealing with this, yet here she was.

'Darling,' her mother said, 'we don't know anything about this. We haven't heard from Logan in days. He hasn't been out here, we promise.'

'No, that's not right. He moved it somewhere and he said before he'd bring it out here to the shed, that you said it was OK. Please, Mum, where is Boo Boo?'

'Come sit down, we'll figure this out. We'll call Logan and see where he put Kelsey's things. I'm sure this is just a big misunderstanding,' her father said, clasping his hand around her wrist. 'Come inside, love, while your mum calls Logan.'

'No, I have to find it and if it's not here... Unless you're lying to me... for my own good,' she said. 'Just like Logan did.'

'I can't even imagine what you're going through, love. Just stay here and I'll ring Logan,' her mother said, heading deeper into the house. Dana could hear the low murmur of her voice, pausing for him to answer, then silence.

'Well?' Dana asked as her mum came back into the room.

'I got a hold of him, and I asked him where all the things are. He said that they're somewhere safe and that he hasn't thrown any of it out. He's not coming home tonight though. I'm so sorry, Dana.' Her mother looked at her with pity.

Dana was bawling, tears streaming down her face. She couldn't seem to stop crying. Everything just kept piling up on top of her. She watched her parents exchange worried looks.

'I'm not crazy. I just want her stuff back. I need it. How could he do this to me?' she sobbed.

'I think you should stay here with us for the night. You're in no condition to be driving home,' her mum said, laying a comforting hand on her shoulder then pulling her into a hug.

'I want to go home,' Dana sobbed. 'I want Kelsey's stuff back.'

Her parents eventually managed to convince her to stay for a cup of tea and while she drank it in silence, Dana stopped crying, wiping her eyes with the tissues her mum handed her.

Dana heard a noise outside. She wondered if the person, the intruder, had followed her out to the property. She felt the hairs on the back of her neck rise. She wanted to confess what was happening to her, to hear her mum's comforting words, to have her dad offer to keep her safe. Instead she said, 'I'd better go now. Thanks, Mum, Dad.' She gave her parents a tearful hug goodbye, terrified that someone was waiting in the dark for her. She watched the road behind her in her mirrors the whole way home, and when she arrived, she quickly ran from the car to the house, locking the front door after her.

Being in this house caused her so much pain; there were too many memories that she just couldn't let go of. Logan had not only left her, but he had taken her baby with him. Now this... present. What did it mean? Who was messing with her? And why?

Dana had been so distraught about Kelsey's things being packed up that she hadn't even fought for Grace to stay. She knew where they were, well, she suspected anyway, and she couldn't handle it, knowing that another woman was playing happy families with *her* family and probably doing a better job of it. Sobbing, she walked into the empty room, empty save one lonely pink wall. *What the fuck was she supposed to do now?* She lay down on the carpet and cried herself to sleep.

* * *

Dana woke up to a creaky neck and a sore back. Disoriented, she wondered why she was on the floor. She looked around and realised that she was in Kelsey's bare room. She wanted to cry but she was so exhausted she didn't have any more tears to shed. Groaning, she stood up, rolling her neck from side to side, trying to work the kinks out. Looking down, she saw something on the floor underneath the window that hadn't been there last night. It was a scrap of paper and when she got closer and picked it up, she saw it had words on it. Angry, black scrawled words written into the paper so hard that it was torn in places and almost unreadable.

You killed her.

Dana stared at it so long the words blurred. What did this mean? That someone had been in her house last night while she'd been passed out on the floor? Did they leave her this to mess with her? With a shaking hand, she carried the piece of paper into the kitchen and threw it on the bench, no longer wanting to touch the poisonous words. Was it because they were true? She left the room but kept coming back, standing in the doorway staring at the paper. How was the intruder getting into her house? And why were they doing this to her? She was suffering enough, blamed herself for what she'd done, she didn't need these constant reminders. She remembered that the death notice with the word *murderer* was still crumpled up at the bottom of her bag. Suddenly needing to rid herself of the truth, she grabbed her bag, finding the ball of paper at the bottom. She grabbed the latest message and threw both threats into the sink, using the gas lighter to set them on fire, as if their words could be erased that easily. As if her guilt could be cleansed by fire.

She walked down the hallway to the bedroom, tears in her eyes, thinking about the angry words. Had Logan left it for her to find? No, he had already had his say, surely he wouldn't do something so cruel to her. Yes, he'd packed up Kelsey's room last night, something that had devastated her, but he would never do *that* to her. Never deliberately torture her.

'Logan? You in here?' She pushed open the door and peered in. The bed was made but there was no sign of Logan or Grace. She slowly closed the door with a sigh. She felt empty inside. It felt as if both her girls were lost to her. One she had killed, one she had driven away.

Dana sat at the kitchen table for what felt like hours. Finally, her phone beeped, startling her so she slopped her now cold tea over the table. Absently, she wiped her sleeve over the mess, cleaning it up. She quickly checked the phone, hoping that it was Logan, but instead she saw Melanie's name.

I haven't heard from you in days, can we catch up?

She read the message again. Melanie had been acting odd lately, being rude to Matt, trying to convince her that she could do better than Logan. But Dana didn't want to do better than Logan. She loved him, him and Grace. She needed them both back home again.

Her phone beeped a second time.

Dana?

Sighing, she picked it up and tapped out a message.

Sorry, been busy.

She didn't want to tell her what had happened last night. Melanie would just use it as another reason to dump on Logan. Then again, she could do with the distraction.

I wouldn't mind getting out of the house.

You got it, I'll come and pick you up. Be there in ten.

True to her word, Melanie was there in ten minutes, which had left Dana just enough time to get dressed, brush her teeth and pull herself together. She didn't want to think about the words any more; they weren't true. They couldn't be. But in the back of her mind, she knew this person, this intruder, was just saying what she already thought about herself: *murderer, you killed her.* It was just so menacing coming from someone else, found in her home and car, her personal spaces. It shocked and scared her. If she wasn't safe at home, then where was she safe?

Melanie knocked on the door. 'Dana! You in there?'

'Hey, Melanie,' Dana said as she opened the door. 'How are you?'

'Great. Where's my baby girl? I need a cuddle.'

Dana panicked. 'Uh... she's not here.'

'Oh, that's a shame. Where is she?'

'She's actually out with Logan, having father-daughter time.' She hoped she sounded less panicked than she felt on the inside.

'Everything all right, Dana? You seem a bit jumpy.'

'I'm fine. Let's get out of here.' It would have been the perfect time to tell Melanie what had been going on, but she found she couldn't find the words, so she left it alone.

Melanie drove, heading out of town. 'Where are we going?' Dana eventually asked.

'Well, I was going to take you out for a coffee but since you don't have to hurry home to be with Grace, how about a spa day? I feel we've kinda lost touch. I'm not saying it's your fault,' she paused, 'it just is what it is. I don't want there to be weirdness and hurt feelings, no matter who might try and come between us.'

Dana knew that she was referring to Matt. 'I don't either. Let's go then, we could both do with a relaxing massage.'

'Do you think that Logan and Grace will be home when we get back?'

Dana felt like saying that she didn't know if Logan was ever coming back. She had no clue what was going on in his head. 'Maybe we should go to your house one of these days. I'd like to see where you live. We never go to your place for a catch-up. Is that where you hide all of your dead bodies?' She smiled, trying to take the focus off her, Grace and Logan.

A shadow passed over Melanie's face and Dana wondered what she'd said that was so bad. 'Oh, my house isn't interesting,' Melanie said in a voice that discouraged further questions, 'just the place where I used to live with my family. It hasn't been the same since Michelle died.'

'You mean Mindy?'

'Did I say Michelle? She answered to both, first or middle name.' Melanie laughed, a tense sound, and Dana felt bad for bringing it up at all.

'You know, I'm so sorry for your loss, Melanie.'

'I know you are. That's why you're such a good friend.' She reached out and grabbed Dana's hand, squeezing it for a second before letting it go.

'My husband was a piece of work, just like yours. When we lost Mindy, I didn't cope very well.' It was the first time that she was opening up to her and Dana let her speak. 'We had been having problems already, so her death just made everything that much harder. I was walled off from him, but I still loved him. He chose to bury himself in someone else's pussy.' Her voice was bitter and still so full of hate. Dana reached over, touching her hand, letting her know that she was there for her. 'Not even six weeks. He didn't even stay for six weeks. The sooner you realise that all men are lying dogs only out for themselves, the better off you'll be, Dana. I promise you.'

This was some heavy stuff, Dana thought. 'I'm so sorry you went through that on top of everything else...' she started, then she realised that this could be her situation. She knew that Logan and Pippa had feelings for each other. They were probably together right now but she knew that Logan would never leave her. He loved her. Her and Grace. This whole line of thought was making her feel ill.

Then her phone beeped and she tore into her handbag looking for it.

'Is that Logan?' Melanie asked shortly.

'No, it's Matt.'

'What's he want? Tell him you're busy,' Melanie said.

She replied by text.

Hey, Matt, how are you?

Can't stop thinking about you.

She smiled.

I'm in the car with Melanie, spa day. Talk later?

Yeah. Say hi for me.

'Matt says hi,' she said, not turning her head, but she didn't miss the look of contempt on Melanie's face out of the corner of her eye.

'Hmm,' Melanie responded. She didn't seem impressed with him interrupting their day. 'Why don't you just turn off your phone and be done with it?'

She didn't want to turn her phone off. She wanted to hear from Logan; she wanted to know when he was home.

Four hours later they were on their way back to town, refreshed, pampered, and relaxed after having a full body massage and a facial. Dana was surprised to realise she felt as if she could handle things a bit better now.

When Melanie pulled up at the front of her house, Logan's car still wasn't there. Was he ever coming back?

After heading inside, Dana made a snap decision: she decided to drive past Pippa's house to see if Logan's car really was there. She knew that she shouldn't torture herself like that, but she had to know they were safe, and, like it or not, Pippa's house was the most likely safe place for Logan.

Dana drove slowly to Pippa's house, afraid of what she'd see there. But she was right, of course: there was Logan's car parked right outside Pippa's house. That meant that Logan had been there all night and all day and they'd been playing happy families with *her* daughter. She could just imagine Pippa cuddling Grace close, inhaling the sweet baby scent, maybe even singing her to sleep last night. She drove around the corner trying to decide if she should confront them both. She realised that it was exactly what Logan thought she would do, and if she did he would be calm, as would Pippa, and he'd win again. They'd make her out to be the crazy one, adding to the list of her bad behaviours that he could use against her later. She decided then to be the bigger person and drive home. He had to come back eventually and this way he'd see that she had grown.

She was still pissed about Kelsey's room and how he'd packed it up behind her back, but she tried to look at the big picture. Every time she went off at him, it just pushed him further away and she didn't want that. She didn't want to drive him into Pippa's arms; she couldn't imagine another woman's hands on her husband. So she went home and pulled on a pair of jeans and a flowing white top that Logan loved. She went barefoot and decided to do something to show him and herself how much she wanted this to work. There was paint in the shed, ready to paint Kelsey's... Grace's room, the beautiful lilac that they had brought together. Tying back her hair, she put the roller into the tray of paint and rolled it across the edge of the pink wall. It was like covering up Kelsey, layer by layer, and she cried as she did it, but it had to be done. She'd barely finished when she heard the key in the door. She stayed in the room, finishing off the skirting boards with the small paintbrush.

She was still on the floor a few minutes later when Logan found her, Grace in his arms. She turned to see him staring at the wall then at her. He smiled at her and held out Grace for her to hold. Dana smiled back at him, standing, tears in her eyes as she took hold of her daughter, automatically rocking her, feeling the flutter of her heart. She was home.

Logan looked at the wall for a long time. It was a symbol of hope for them all, something to signify that she was ready to let the room go, not Kelsey, but the room. It was something. A big step forward. Logan came to her, leaned his forehead against hers and whispered, 'Thank you.'

18

Logan had woken that morning, tangled up in Pippa's long limbs. He freed himself and went to check on his daughter, who was just beginning to stir in her bassinet. She had had a great sleep last night; he'd only needed to get up twice during the night for her. He looked down at her. She looked so much like Dana: she had a little bit of dark hair now and a cute button nose. He couldn't see much of himself in her yet; she was a Dana mini-me.

Thinking of his wife made him feel guilty and he wondered if he should just leave Pippa's house and go home. He was having second thoughts; almost regretting having made love to Pippa last night. This was moving way too fast for him. Did he really think that he could jump from his wife to a girlfriend straight away? How would he explain that to people? To her parents? Dana would always have his daughter so he would always be linked to her. Was it easier to stay with Dana? Was it going to be too hard to be with Pippa? He realised that he was going back and forth between the two, weighing up the pros and the cons of both women, but he kept coming back to the mother of his child versus his happiness with Pippa. If he could recapture what he had with Dana, would that be enough? He needed to think so. He was pretty sure that she knew where he'd been last night – spending the night with Pippa. Her imagination would run away with her, but in this case, she'd be right.

'Morning, baby,' whispered Pippa behind him so as not to disturb Grace, but she was waking up anyway. He looked at his phone; it was early in the morning and he was trying to figure out a way to tell Pippa that he should go home.

'Hey,' he said, picking up the stretching Grace. He turned, facing her, the woman he'd had sex with. He avoided her eyes.

'You OK, Logan?' Pippa asked, trying to meet his eyes.

'Yeah, just tired, I guess. I should think about taking Grace home soon. She needs a feed and a nappy change.'

'Oh, I thought you might stay the day so we could hang out, maybe talk about last night and what happens next.' He knew what she wanted from him, but he just didn't have the energy.

'I'll change Grace,' Pippa said, sliding from under the sheets, then taking Grace from his arms, grabbing a nappy and heading to the kitchen to organise a bottle for her.

He followed her into the kitchen.

Pippa insisted that he stay with her for most of the day. She wanted to talk about what had happened between them last night and their future. Logan was still trying to process what he'd done but he let her talk. She seemed to take control of the conversation and he let her. He held Grace in his arms, rocking her back and forth to settle her down after she'd had another nap and a feed. She'd been good most of the day but it was beginning to get late and she was getting fussy now, probably missing her mum. He decided that it was time to go home. 'I'd better get home soon. Dana will be worried,' he said.

The word *home* wasn't lost on her, neither was Dana's name. She stared at him for a beat then said, 'Sure, I guess I'll just catch up with you another time. Will you call me?' She sounded a little desperate. That wasn't what he needed right now.

'Yeah, I'll call. Just let me get settled back in and work out what's what.' He knew it was a lame brush-off. Dana hadn't come over as he'd expected her to. She had left an angry message last night, but he hadn't heard from her since and he was beginning to worry about her. What if she'd done something silly because of what he'd done to her? He felt bad about leaving Pippa after what they'd done, but inside he was getting more and more worked up. He loaded the bassinet into the car, then their bags, then put Grace into the car seat ready to drive home.

'Can I do anything for you?' Pippa asked.

'No, thanks. I'll call you,' he said through the open window of the car.

She gave him a strained smile and waved them off. He looked in his rear-view mirror and saw her standing out on the road, watching him until he turned the corner. It wasn't long before he pulled into the driveway, grabbing his stuff and his precious daughter. He unlocked the door and peered in the bedroom, expecting to see Dana lying down in defeat. She wasn't there.

He heard a noise and walked down the hallway, Grace gnawing on his shoulder. The noise was coming from Kelsey's room. He stopped just outside the doorway as his wife turned to face him. She had painted over the pink wall with lilac, the colour they had chosen for Grace. She stood, staring at him. He walked forward and gently leaned his forehead against hers. She had finally put Kelsey to rest. He smiled and she returned his smile lovingly. He had his wife back.

* * *

Dana was in the middle of feeding Grace several days later when her phone beeped. It was Melanie.

I had fun at the spa the other day. Want to catch up today?

While she liked Melanie a lot, she was beginning to feel a little bit crowded by her. She needed to put at a bit of distance between them. Dana wanted to make things work with Logan desperately and felt like they were moving in the right direction so Melanie's tirade against men the other day was off-putting. Dana had been a little taken aback by her outright hostility. Not just towards her own husband, which she could certainly understand, but against all men, so it seemed.

I can't today, it's a Grace kinda day.

She hoped that she hadn't offended Melanie.

How is my baby girl?

She's great, just feeding now. Will call you tomorrow.

Melanie didn't write back so Dana was sure that she had offended her. She sighed. Dana didn't have time for hurt feelings unless they were her own. Her thoughts turned to Matt.

It had been five days since Dana and Matt had caught up for coffee. In that time, Dana had decided she would not be going to the meetings any more. They weren't helping her. She still hadn't spoken about her loss there and the more time that went on, the less she wanted to. She would still catch up for coffee with Melanie and Matt though, she'd become close to them both.

'Come, little one, how about we go see your new room?' Grace drooled and Dana took that to mean yes. While it was only a few steps from the lounge, those steps felt as if she were walking a million miles to a destination she wasn't sure she wanted to arrive at. But arrive she did. Standing in the doorway of the bedroom holding her baby, she looked at the lilac wall and thought about her other baby. Was she wiping her memory just to please Logan or was she truly ready to begin moving on? She wasn't exactly sure just yet, but she'd figure it out.

'This is your room now, Grace. It used to belong to your older sister, Kelsey. She would have made the best big sister ever. She was so excited to meet you but she... she passed away.' Dana's cheeks were wet, her tears falling noiselessly.

You killed her.

Dana let out a sob and, realising that she couldn't be alone, picked up the phone. 'Hey, it's me, can you come over? I need to talk.' Her voice was thick with emotion.

* * *

Dana put the baby into Matt's arms and he immediately began bouncing her gently, just like a pro. Time had not dulled his instincts as a father. Dana scraped her chair out as she sat down. Kelsey's chair. She still sat on it, feeling close to her daughter.

'Do I love Kelsey any less because I let go of a big piece of her? I know it was just a coat of paint, but at the same time it wasn't just paint. Does that make sense?'

'Perfect sense. You're worried that by putting her stuff into storage, by painting the room, by having Grace move in, you're somehow forgetting about Kelsey, you're saying goodbye forever. Are you ready to say goodbye, Dana?' he asked as Grace grabbed his finger and hung on tightly to it.

'That's the thing. I just don't know. Part of me wants to hold onto her forever, to keep her as mine, but the other part wants to be a good mother to Grace, to be a good wife to Logan.'

'And you don't think you can be those things if you're holding onto Kelsey?' He winced a little at the mention of Logan's name but she ignored it. He wanted to be there for her, talking about Logan was part of that deal.

'I don't think Logan thinks I can.' Dana gave a brittle laugh, smoothing back her long hair.

Matt glanced at her before commenting. 'I think you're a wonderful mum and I know you're a great wife. If you weren't already married, I'd marry you in a heartbeat.' He laughed but she knew that behind the laughter was truth and longing.

'So, what do I do?' she asked Matt, Grace now asleep in his strong arms.

'I can't answer that. I mean, I can, but I can't really be objective.'

Dana was in deep thought. She was staring at a pile of Grace's clothes balanced precariously on the arm of the couch. She was sure that she had put those away this morning. Yet there they were again. Was it possible she had just thought she'd put them away? This seemed to be happening to her a lot. Dana thought of the notes. Could they be connected?

'Dana? Dana, you all right?'

Matt was standing beside her, Grace facing her in his hands.

'What?'

'You're crying. You OK?'

'Yes, I'm OK. I just...' She thought about the notes, the present, the clothes. How much more of this stress could she handle? 'Actually, I'm not feeling that well. Would you mind if we caught up another day? Please?'

He put a hand against her cheek. 'You are a bit warm.' He

handed Grace to her mum and gave them both a kiss goodbye. 'I'll catch up with you later.'

Matt saw himself out and closed the door behind him.

Dana stared at Grace, who then burped, spitting up on Dana's top. It made her laugh. 'Such a lady,' she whispered. 'Let's go put you in the cot while Mummy changes out of this dirty top, OK?' She walked into the bedroom, careful not to bounce the baby before putting her gently into the cot in the corner of the room.

Dana then walked into the small bathroom and noticed two things. One, the bathroom was hot, two, the hot-water tap was gushing, steam billowing out of the spout, fogging up the small mirror. 'What the hell?' Dana mumbled. Who had turned on the tap? She leaned forward to turn it off and happened to look in the mirror above the basin. There, in the steam, was an outline of a love heart. Dana's heart began to race. She looked closer; it must have been done recently but who could have done it? Matt was gone; besides, he hadn't gone into her bedroom. Dana looked over her shoulder. Was it the same intruder from before? The one who she had sensed in Kelsey's room? The one who had left the notes with the messages scrawled across them? She felt as if she couldn't talk to anyone about what was happening to her. It was making her paranoid, feeling as if she was going crazy, beginning to not trust anyone because anyone could be doing this to her.

Dana hurried back into the bedroom, her change of clothes forgotten, and picked up Grace. She then went around to all the doors and windows in the house and made sure that they were locked up tight. They were. So how was the intruder getting in? She held Grace closer to her; her daughter reached up and tangled her fist in Dana's long hair, pulling on it.

'Ow,' she said, distracted for now, but she was going to get to the bottom of this. She refused to be scared in her own home.

19

Logan was busy connecting pipes in the bathroom in the new house they had been working on for months. It was a beautiful place, large and airy, and he couldn't help but compare it to his own house. He wanted to move to a bigger place, maybe buy something, but Dana was steadfast in her refusal to leave the home where Kelsey had lived. Personally, he thought it would do her the world of good. Dana had come so far and a simple thing like painting a wall signified so much more to him than to her. It was a turning point, and he interpreted it as a sign that she was ready to start scaling down her grief, moving on. She didn't talk about Kelsey as much. It wouldn't be long until Grace would fill the empty room with her things and, finally, her cot with her in it. He smiled at the thought of his precious daughter. She was the one constant bright spot in his life, but thinking of her invariably made him think of Dana and their relationship and how fractured it was and how he'd made it so much worse by sleeping with Pippa.

His phone rang and he stood up, his back creaking. He looked at his phone and saw it was Pippa calling him.

'Hey, Pippa, how are you?'

'Great. How are you?' She was always so cheerful.

'Good, just at work. What's up?'

'I was wondering if you wanted to come round for dinner tonight? I think we need to talk.'

His mind flashed back to him gently sliding his cock all the way inside her.

'Sure, I'll tell Dana I'm going to the pub, but I can't stay for long.' He felt guilty even saying it, but Pippa had asked, and he loved Pippa. He loved Dana too. He was so confused and he knew that eventually he would have to make a decision, but not today.

'I'll see you later, then.'

Logan knew she wanted to talk to him about what had happened between them and he wasn't sure how he felt about it. He had actively avoided thinking about Pippa for days now and she had been giving him space. He sent Dana a quick message.

Won't be home til late tonight, going to the pub with the boys.

He felt bad lying to her. He didn't know if she suspected that he'd slept with her best friend. He hoped not. She was in a world of her own and had been for a long time now. He didn't want to hurt her any more than she was already hurting.

That evening he drove down Pippa's street, still unsure and kind of wishing he *were* going to the pub with the boys.

'Hey, Logan, come in,' she said when she opened the door, but before he even had a chance to come inside she wrapped herself around him, squeezing him tightly. He felt the air rush out of his lungs. 'I've missed you.'

'Why are you so happy?' He asked.

'Come inside and I'll tell you.' He followed her into the lounge where she had laid out a juicy steak with beer battered fries plus a beer, condensation running down the sides. She pointed to the spread. 'Eat, drink.'

He sat down feeling as if something was going on here, but he had no clue as to what it was.

'What is it, Pippa?'

She looked fit to burst. 'Well, I was asleep last night then something woke me up so I lay there for an hour or so thinking about you and me, then I came up with a solution to our problem.'

'We have a problem?' he asked warily.

'Yeah. We do, and her name is Dana. I've thought about it and I've decided. You have to break up with her but do it in such a way that she thinks it's her decision. That way you can walk away looking like the injured party, with your head held high, not the other way around. You just need Mischa's help. You need to convince her that Dana would be better without you, alone, starting again. Without Grace either.' She smiled as if that were a normal thing to say. 'Dana isn't fit to be a mum anyway. Mischa will be able to convince her to give Grace to you – she doesn't really want her anyway. It'll just take a few well-placed comments to her parents and everything will work out just as it should. How great is that? You can both move straight in here. I'll set up a nursery – I have the spare room. You just need to have a heart-to-heart with Mischa about how you're no good for Dana any more, too many memories or such, and that you'll take Grace off her hands. You can come up with whatever words you want. Then, down the track, you can get a divorce from her and marry me. So, what do you think?' She sat there, staring at him expectantly, smiling. 'Logan? What do you think? It's a good idea, isn't it?'

She seemed to need his approval but he was unable to organise his thoughts, so he reached forward and grabbed the beer, taking a long swig of it, buying himself some time.

'So, you want me to divorce the mother of my children and steal her baby?' Logan asked slowly, still not sure he'd understood that garbled and crazy plan. 'Not only that, but you want me to make it out like it's *her* idea?' He must have been looking at her strangely because her smile faltered.

'You can't steal something that doesn't belong to her in the first place. Don't you want to be with me?' she asked.

'Pippa. Are you listening to yourself? You're not making any sense.'

'Well, then, we'll take Grace and move across the other side of the country. You can ask for a divorce then. Simple.'

He couldn't believe what he was hearing. 'What about Dana? I can't do that to her.'

'Oh, who the fuck cares?' Pippa said, her voice raised. She stood, running her hands through her hair. 'You'll always be able to find a way to justify staying with her forever: she's fragile, she has your daughter, she's the mother of your daughter who died. You know you could take Grace at any time. Dana's not exactly a fit mother. No court would deny you full custody. You love me and I love you, so why shouldn't we be happy, together? I'm sick of hiding how I feel about you, sneaking around behind Dana's back. Besides, she has to know about us, so what's the big deal in taking the next logical step?'

Logan sat back in the couch, mulling over what Pippa had said.

'It all comes down to whether you want to spend the rest of your life with me,' she said, demanding, pacing the room, staring at him intently. 'Well? Do you?'

'I do, yes.'

'More than her?'

'It's not that simple. I love you both.'

'That's not what I asked, Logan. Will you leave Dana and

choose me?' Pippa waited. She was expecting him to make a decision about the rest of his life right now. Logan knew he loved her and he couldn't face losing her. Pippa had her hands on her hips, a frown on her beautiful face. He just wanted to make her happy.

'I choose you,' he said quietly, wondering what this would do to Dana. How it would rip their little family apart just as the fractures were starting to heal. 'I'll talk to her.' He was such a coward.

'When?' Pippa pushed.

'In the next few days, I promise.'

She seemed satisfied with his answer. While he watched, she took off her clothes, walked over to him, rested one leg on his knee and started to touch herself between her legs. He stared, mesmerised by her. He unbuckled his jeans, pulled his cock out of his pants and began to stroke himself, his hand moving up and down while she rubbed her clit, pushing her fingers inside herself. It didn't take long; he felt the orgasm building up. She pushed her fingers in deeper, then just before he came, she straddled him, sliding down on his cock, riding him until he came inside her. She continued to ride him, while he played with her clit until it was her turn to come. She gave a small yell then sighed deeply. 'God, I love you,' she whispered, leaning down to kiss the side of his neck.

'I love you too,' he said, but he wondered if he had just made a fatal mistake.

Logan went home half an hour later. As soon as he walked through the door, he went and had a shower, washing Pippa from his body. He knew what he had to do and he wasn't looking forward to it.

20

Dana was holding Grace in her arms when Logan arrived home and walked into the kitchen. 'Oh, hey,' she said distractedly. 'I thought you'd be later. You hungry?' she asked.

'Um, I need to talk to you about something.' He looked at his wife, who waited expectantly. 'Can you put Grace down, please? I need to talk to you.'

'Why do you need me to put Grace down to talk? Is everything all right?' A look of worry crossed her face.

'Come sit down with me,' he said, taking her shoulder and guiding her towards the couch. He took Grace from her arms and placed her on the play mat.

'Dana, I want to talk to you about something important.'

'What is it?' Dana asked with concern edging her voice.

I don't know where to start. Look, Dana,' he started, pausing mid-sentence, 'you know we've had our issues since Kelsey passed away.'

Saying nothing, she just stared at him, biting on her bottom lip.

'We haven't been the same since Kelsey died. I thought you'd get better, that we'd get through this together, but we haven't. I can't keep going on like this.'

A change came over his wife's face. She glared at him, brow furrowed, eyes narrowed. 'Of course I haven't moved through this. She's my daughter and I can't just forget her as easily as you seem to be able to do. It's like you don't care that she's dead.' He saw her eyes glinting with unshed tears.

'That's not what I'm saying at all. Christ.' He rubbed his hand over his tired face. 'What I'm trying to say is that you should have moved on by now. You have Grace to love. Hanging onto the past is no good for you, for either one of us, and it's frustrating me,' he said with more anger than he'd intended. He knew he was hurting her, he could see it reflected in her expression. He didn't want to be so cruel to her, but he couldn't seem to stop himself once he started.

Dana sat on the couch staring at him, her hands clasped so tightly he could see her nails digging into her flesh.

'I know that I have Grace, Logan, but it's not as easy as replacing one daughter with another. Kelsey is our daughter too, you can't just erase her from your life, from your memory. You've already packed up her room and removed all of her photos – what more do you want? I love Grace but she's not Kelsey and she never will be.'

'Just get over it!' he screamed at her. Logan felt like a total arsehole when she suddenly burst into tears.

'Why are you doing this to me?' she asked. 'Why now?'

He stood up, looming over her, and she shrank back as if he was going to physically hurt her.

'I would never hurt you,' he said, angry at himself as much as he was with her.

'But you are!'

He couldn't bring himself to apologise to her; this was not

the way he wanted this conversation to go and he needed to just say it. 'I'm leaving you,' he blurted out, dropping back onto the couch, shoulders slumped. This was not how he'd planned it.

'What?' Dana said, her eyes wide with shock. He saw her look over at Grace, as if the baby could understand why her family was being ripped apart. 'Why? Why would you do this to me, to us? Why now?' she sobbed, her hands covering her face, trying vainly to stop her tears.

He felt like a shit-head, watching the great heaving sobs that shook her thin body.

'Because I love someone else.'

'Who is she?' Her voice was suddenly devoid of emotion.

'You know who. Pippa,' he said. 'I love Pippa.'

Her breath came out in ragged gasps. She stood up slowly. 'Please don't, Logan. Please don't leave us.'

'Don't you get it? I'm leaving *you* and I'm taking Grace with me.'

'What? You can't do that! I won't let you.'

'I'll take you to court. The way you've been behaving, no judge would let you be a mother to anyone.' Pippa's voice was echoing in his mind.

'Please, don't take my daughter,' Dana begged, grabbing his hands.

He stood, pulling them from her grasp. 'I'll be back for her. This is best for all of us, especially Grace.'

He went to their bedroom to pack, throwing things into a duffel bag, almost in tears himself. He hadn't known he was capable of such cruelty to someone that he loved. And he did love her, he just loved Pippa too and he couldn't help but think she was the easier solution. He could hear Dana crying in the other room and when he walked back into the hallway, heading for the front door, he turned back and looked at her, their eyes meeting. She was on the floor holding Grace in her arms.

'I'm sorry,' he said.

'No, you're not, but you will be.'

He wondered if he'd just made the biggest mistake of his life.

* * *

Dana stood and dropped onto the couch, holding Grace to her chest. Tears ran down her cheeks. She didn't bother wiping them away. What was the point? She was devastated, broken. How could Logan say those things to her? How could he be so cruel as to threaten to take away the only good thing she had left in her life? She was too ashamed to call her mum – what would she even tell her? So she called the only other person who would understand her loss.

'Hey, Dana.'

As soon as she heard his calm voice, she burst into more noisy tears.

'God, Dana, what is it? Is it Grace?'

'He left,' she managed to choke out. 'He left me, for her. Pippa.'

'Logan left you? I'm coming over right now.' Matt hung up the phone and was banging on her door soon after. She opened it and fell into his arms.

'Shh, sweetheart, it's gonna be fine.' He backed her inside the house, still holding onto her, kicking the door closed. He stroked her hair gently, her tears soaking through his shirt.

'How is it going to be fine?' she said, backing away from him, her eyes signalling her defeat. 'He threatened to take Grace away. Matt, I can't lose another child, I just can't. I'll die.'

'Let's go sit down,' he suggested, leading her to the couch. She looked down at her beautiful daughter and wondered if Logan would make good on his threat.

'What happened exactly?'

Dana took a deep breath. 'He came home from the pub, he'd been out with the boys, and he told me it was over, just like that. He was leaving me because he is in love with Pippa. I think he... I think he wants her to be Grace's mother. He said he'd take her, that I'm not a fit mother.'

Dana's breath hitched and her eyes filled with tears again. She couldn't stop crying. He grabbed her hand, grasping it tightly. 'I'm staying here tonight. You shouldn't be alone right now.'

'Thank you,' she whispered, resting her head on his shoulder. What the hell was she to do now?

* * *

Logan drove to Pippa's house, speeding the whole way, driving recklessly, almost hoping he would crash. Tears slid down his cheeks, obscuring his vision. He pulled over to the side of the road and put his hands up to his face. How could he have just done that to Dana? How could he have said those horrible things to his wife, who he still loved? She was devastated. He'd done that to her. He was ashamed of his behaviour, for threatening to take her daughter away. What a fuck up! He wanted to go back home and tell her that he didn't mean any of it. *Home.* It was never going to be his home again; he'd seen to that.

He wiped his eyes and pulled back onto the road, heading for Pippa's house even as he wanted to turn around and go back to Dana.

When he got there, he turned off the engine and stepped out of the car. He pulled back his shoulders and knocked three times.

She opened the door immediately. Clearly she had been waiting for him.

'Oh, Logan, you've been crying! You told her. How did she take it? Did she try to convince you to stay? Where is Grace?' she asked, firing the questions at him. He just wanted to turn around and leave. Be by himself, not play twenty questions with Pippa. 'Logan?' she prompted.

'Yeah,' he said in a monotone voice.

'Are you OK? How's Dana?' Pippa asked, her forehead creasing with concern.

'Like you care. How could you make me do that?' he demanded. 'I broke her. She's devastated.'

'You chose me, Logan, that was your choice. Don't blame me.'

Logan began to cry, so she hugged him tight. 'We're in this together, sweetheart. Let it all out.' Pippa held him as he cried.

He buried his head on her chest while she held him. 'It will be all right, love, we'll get through this. I love you,' she said, kissing the top of his head. Eventually he pulled away from her and wiped his eyes. 'It'll be all right,' she repeated. 'We'll get Grace back.'

'I can't do that to Dana. I just can't. I won't. Grace is all she has left.'

'But what about what you said to me? That I'd make a good mum? You said I was a natural with Grace. Logan, I want kids. Grace or a baby with you.'

He didn't think he could take Grace but maybe, just maybe, he could start again with Pippa. He thought about the look on Dana's face when he told her he was taking Grace. She had been shattered and totally blindsided. He had half a mind to go over there to make sure she was coping. Instead, he said, 'I'm going to call her.'

'Why?' asked Pippa sharply. 'You'll just confuse her, give her mixed signals.'

'I'm calling her.' Logan pulled out his phone and tapped Dana's name. The phone rang and rang in his ear. 'She's not answering. Maybe I should go back and check she hasn't done anything stupid.'

'Logan. You're done with her now. Just leave it.' Pippa pushed him back on the couch and lay beside him. 'It'll be all right. We'll work it out. Just relax.'

Pippa spent the next hour or so outlining their new lives as she cooked dinner for them. He ate, chewing each mouthful in silence while she kept up a steady stream of conversation that exhausted him after his emotional outburst. She didn't seem to need him to contribute to the conversation, so he stayed quiet, thinking about what he'd done. Eventually they went to bed. Finally, Pippa fell asleep, a gentle smile on her lips. Her body felt different from Dana's. It felt wrong somehow. When the darkness of the sky started to recede, giving way to the light tendrils of dawn, he drifted off to sleep, only to be woken what felt like minutes later. Eyes still closed, he felt his cock being sucked, a tongue flicking over the tip.

'Dana,' he moaned, reaching out to push his fingers into her hair.

'What the fuck? It's Pippa, not Dana!'

He sat up quickly. 'Shit, I'm sorry, I guess... I guess it's just habit...' He couldn't even finish his sentence in the face of her anger. Instead, he got up and went into the shower, still hard. He was screwing up in every aspect of his life. After last night, he didn't even know what he was doing any more or why.

'I've got to leave for work early today,' he said as he was walking out of the door.

'Fine.' Pippa was pissed at him.

What a great way to start a new relationship.

On the way to work, he decided to go and check on Dana and Grace. Dana probably hadn't slept all night. He knew her – she'd be a wreck and it was his responsibility to make sure she was coping.

Logan slid his key into the front door just after seven o'clock. He couldn't hear any noises, so clearly Grace hadn't woken yet. Dana was probably sitting in the kitchen nursing a cup of tea just waiting on him to come back home to her, ready to beg him to reconsider. She would be hoping he hadn't meant what he said, that this was just a temper tantrum, and maybe it was. Maybe he could apologise and take it all back.

He walked into the lounge and stopped suddenly. Dana was stretched out asleep on the couch, hand draped over the edge, dangling down towards the man sleeping on the floor.

'What the fuck is going on here?' Logan demanded, waking up Dana and the man. Dana sat up in a hurry, while the unwelcome visitor yawned and looked at Logan as if he belonged there in the house and not Logan.

Dana got off the couch and stalked over to him. 'What are you doing here?' she demanded coldly. 'You don't live here any more, a fact you made very clear last night.'

'So what? You just replace me with another man?'

'Matt, could you please go and check on Grace for me? Please,' she said when he didn't move.

'What's he doing here?' Logan demanded, confused.

'I called him last night after you left. I was a mess and I needed someone. He was there for me, we stayed up late talking and he didn't want me and Grace to be on our own so he stayed. Not that I have to explain any of this to you. You don't belong here Logan, so what are you doing in my house?' She ran her hand down her hair and pulled it over her shoulder. A move that he knew well. She was furious. She had every right to be.

'I was just coming to see that you're all right.'

'Oh, how sweet.' Sarcasm filled the room. 'Pippa know that you're here?' she asked, one hand on her hip, her stare drilling into his.

This was a whole new Dana, not like the inconsolable woman from last night. This Dana had a spine made of steel. 'No. I told her I was going into work early. She wouldn't understand.'

'Great way to start a new relationship off, by lying. Seems to be what you do best.'

Matt came into the room holding Grace. He stood beside Dana.

'She was awake. You OK here?' They looked like the family now, with Logan the outsider.

'She's fine, man. Why don't you give me my daughter?'

Matt looked at Dana for approval and when she nodded, handed the baby over to him. Logan kissed Grace on the forehead and told her he loved her, then passed her to Dana. 'Well, looks like you're coping just fine without me here so I'm going to go, but I'll be back to see Grace.'

'Logan?' He turned and waited. 'Knock first? This is my home. In fact, why don't I just take your key right now?' She said it with such contempt, a tone he'd never heard from her before.

She was right though: this wasn't his home any more. He realised he'd made a huge mistake. No matter what had passed between them, or maybe because of it, Dana was the woman for him, he'd just allowed himself to be swept away by his lust for Pippa. What a fool he'd been. He clenched his teeth as he slowly removed his house key from the ring and put it in her outstretched hand.

* * *

'Well, that was an interesting way to start the morning,' Matt said as he watched Dana cuddling the baby. 'Are you all right?'

'Better than I thought I'd be after the first time I saw him. Maybe it was easier because I didn't have time to stress about it. I'm just glad you were here. I might not have been able to say those things if I'd been alone. He's the father of my children – you don't stop loving someone just because they no longer love you.'

'That's true. I know it's not exactly the same, but I didn't stop loving my wife just because she was no longer here. Same with my son. Same with Kelsey, I know.'

'You're right, but it's worse, they're gone forever and you'll never have the chance to say your goodbyes to them. I'm sure when he calms down, Logan will share custody of Grace with me – if Pippa doesn't make him go for sole custody. I know I wasn't exactly perfect when I was pregnant with Grace. I was wrapped up in my grief, not letting anyone in, until I started going to the meetings. Then I met you. You helped me come out of my shell a bit more, made me interact with the world. Thank you, Matt.' She leaned over the baby and kissed his cheek.

'Dana, you know I want more, but Logan only left last night. You need time to deal with your feelings about him before I officially ask you out on a date. So I'm going to go home now, and leave you and the little one alone.' He hugged them both goodbye and left.

Immediately the emptiness crowded her in. No Logan, no Matt. She was alone.

Or so she had thought. Until Logan started calling. He called three times that day, and each time she picked up then hung up on him, just so he'd know that she was deliberately ignoring him. She wondered if he was calling to set up a time to see Grace, but she reasoned he would have left a message if that was all he wanted.

Later that day, Dana decided to do the thing she had been dreading for weeks. She was going to build the proper cot and put it in Grace's room, Kelsey's *old* room. After a kiss on her cheek, Dana placed Grace gently into the cot in her bedroom so she would be safe while Dana built her new, permanent cot. She went out to the laundry where they had been storing the flat-packed cot. She dragged the box into Grace's new room and began unpacking the pieces. After half an hour, Dana took a break to grab a drink and to go and check on a very happy Grace.

Dana stretched out the kinks in her back and went back into the bedroom to finish the job. Soon after, she stood proudly in front of the now assembled glossy white cot, admiring her handiwork. Who said she needed a man? The faces of the two men in her life flashed before her eyes. Dana then started to cry. Seeing the new cot in the room was overwhelming and more emotional for her than she had thought it would be. It was as if she couldn't control her feelings any longer. She needed to sit and focus on something else.

21

A week went by, with Logan calling each day. Dana didn't want to speak to him and was making him wait until she was ready to deal with his issues without wanting to scream. And she wasn't there just yet.

Dana hadn't heard from her mum for a while; she knew she was giving her space but she missed her. She still hadn't told her about Logan leaving, preferring not to bother her with her problems all the time, especially since she knew, now that her sister was at home, she'd be demanding all of her mum's time. But as Dana finished up washing the dishes, her phone pinged and she pulled it out of her pocket. It was a message from her mum.

Hi love, what are you up to?

Funny story

Dana was about to launch into what Logan had done but she paused, fingers hovering over the keypad. She deleted the message and called her mum instead.

'Hey, Mum,' she said wearily.

'What's wrong? I can tell by your voice that something is wrong. Is Grace all right? Are you OK?' her mum asked quickly.

'I guess, if you call being threatened with legal action and being dumped all in one night OK, then I'm fine.'

'What? I don't understand.' Her mum sounded confused. It had been confusing for her too, but Dana could see everything perfectly clearly now.

'Well, Logan left me for Pippa a week ago, said he wants to take Grace away from me.'

'Oh, God, Dana. I'm coming over.'

'No, Mum, it's actually OK. I finally get it. We're broken, he broke us, but now I'm free. I can do what I want.'

'But Pippa? How could he do that? How could *she* do that? After all you've endured these past few months since Kelsey passed away. I can't believe this. I... we... have seriously misjudged Logan. If he takes you to court for custody Dad and I will help out with the costs, I promise.'

'Thanks, Mum, I appreciate it, but I honestly don't think it'll come to that. He's just angry, with me, with the world. He's a very unhappy man right now. I can see that he's using Pippa to make himself feel better. It's sad really. Anyway, please don't worry about me, you have enough to worry about,' she said, alluding to her sister. She knew what a handful Alesha could be, especially when she was needy. 'I'm actually all right. I thought, well, I guess I was devastated, but he's done me a favour. I can move on now. Put some of the past behind me.'

'Oh, darling, I'm so proud of you. You've always been the strong one. I'll call you later today.' They said their goodbyes and Dana hung up. Already she was feeling more positive, now she was over the initial shock of what Logan had said to her when he left her.

Logan now only represented a lost time in her past; Matt, she hoped, was the man who represented a possible future.

Her phone rang as she was walking back into the bedroom to get Grace, who she could hear had woken up from her afternoon nap. Dana wanted to show her the cot and introduce her to her new room. She was finally ready to do it. It was Logan *again*. She picked up but this time didn't hang up on him.

'Why do you keep calling me? There's nothing left between us now,' Dana said, frustrated with his inability to take a hint. She blew out a breath that moved a chunk of hair that had escaped from her messy bun.

'Don't hang up, Dana,' Logan said quickly.

'Why not? I have nothing else to say to you.' Which, of course, wasn't strictly true. She wanted to say, *Why wasn't I enough for you?* but she wouldn't give him the satisfaction.

He sighed, the sound ripping from his chest. She tried not to care. 'I just wanted to see if you were really all right,' he said quietly.

'You mean after you left me, broke my heart and threatened to take my daughter from me? I'm great, wonderful. I don't even miss you so you can stop calling to check on me now. You have no obligations towards me whatsoever. I'll be seeing you in court.'

He ignored her last comment. 'Matt helping you out, is he?' Logan asked bitterly.

Dana was almost amused by his jealousy. 'Are you serious? You don't get to ask me that,' Dana replied heatedly, even though she *had* been leaning on Matt a bit. 'How's Pippa?' she countered after a long pause.

This time, he was the one who paused. 'That's one of the things I wanted to talk to you about, but you keep dodging my calls.'

'What now, Logan?' Dana sighed. She was done with all the

bullshit. He couldn't drag her down any more than he already had.

'Can I come over tonight after work? I'd like to see Grace.'

She hung up without responding. She picked her little girl up, taking her to her new room to show her her new cot.

Taking a deep breath, she stood for a moment in front of the door she didn't remember closing. Dana began to sob as she couldn't help but remember her other little girl. Pale skin, dark hair, light smattering of freckles and big eyes that were always full of questions, her cheeky smile and her sweet laugh that had always captivated everyone. Dana held Grace, thanking God that she had her to comfort her. She knew that Grace wasn't a replacement for Kelsey – she never had been – she was a wonderful gift to her and Logan.

Dana turned the knob and pushed open the bedroom door wide. She stood there, stunned, unable to tear her eyes away. The cot, pristine white, was just where she had left it, in the middle of the empty room, but now there was one huge difference. The carpet was now streaked with fresh lilac paint. It was everywhere.

'What the hell?' Dana whispered, unable to comprehend what she was looking at. She had only been gone from Grace's new room not even twenty minutes before when she'd put a pile of new stuffed toys in the corner of the room, but, in that time, the intruder had broken into her home yet again and destroyed Grace's floor.

What the hell was going on? Why was someone hell-bent on making her life an absolute misery? What was she supposed to do? Who was she supposed to turn to now?

Logan. She wondered what he wanted but reasoned he couldn't possibly be the one hurting her – he wasn't that cruel, despite his actions over the past week to the contrary.

Dana couldn't face cleaning up the floor, she'd do it later, so she closed the door on the room that was meant to be a fresh start for her. She refused to cry even though she was terrified. Someone had been in her home again. How the fuck were they getting in? Holding Grace to her, she stifled her tears of fear, not knowing what the hell to do next.

Dana sat down on the couch, in shock. She put Grace on the play mat on the floor. She had no idea how long she'd been sitting there, staring into nothing, but when there was a knock at the door she jumped. She went down the hallway and cautiously asked who it was.

'It's me.' Logan was standing outside in his work gear, obviously having come around straight after work. It was just past six o'clock. No pub for him – she couldn't smell beer on him at all when she let him in and she was glad for him, for all of them. She turned, hiding her tears, and walked down the hallway and into the kitchen, where she put the kettle on out of habit. He followed her and sat down at the table. Briefly, she thought about showing him Grace's room and what the intruder had done. Surely he'd believe her now? What if Grace had been in there? Just the thought made her breath catch in her throat. She swallowed hard and moved around the kitchen, fixing herself a cup of tea, not asking him if he'd like a drink. She knew she was prolonging the inevitable, avoiding having to actually talk to him. She was only just keeping her shit together. Dana wanted to run away, hide under the covers with Grace and cry.

'Dana? Please sit down. I have things I need to say.'

'I thought you'd already said everything you wanted to say to me. What more could there possibly be?' Dana sat down on the edge of her seat with her tea cupped between her hands. She felt scared and nervous; she sensed something was off with him. After so many years of marriage, she had learned to read Logan well. 'What is it now?' she asked, striving to keep her voice neutral. 'Is this a talk about custody? Because if it is, you should know—'

'No, it's not. I was a prick when I said that to you. It was unforgivable. I won't fight you on custody, I just want to see her as much as I can. We'll do what's best for Grace.'

'That sounds reasonable. Is that all?' she asked. 'Because I have things I need...'

He sighed, stood, raked his hands through his hair then sat back in the chair heavily. He looked as if he had something heavy weighing on his mind. 'Pippa's pregnant,' he blurted out.

The air felt like it had been sucked out of the room. Dana sat there staring at him uncomprehendingly. 'Excuse me, what?'

'She's pregnant. Pippa's pregnant.'

'But... how is that possible? You only just left me like a week ago.' Then it dawned on her. 'Oh, I'm such an idiot,' she said, putting a hand to her forehead. 'You slept with her before that, didn't you?' She raised her head and looked at him, eyes blazing, drilling into his.

'Dana—'

'When?' she demanded. 'When the fuck did you sleep with my best friend?' She needed the answer, needed her suspicions to be confirmed.

'The night I packed up Kelsey's room and took Grace to Pippa's place. I didn't mean for it to happen and she's only just taken a pregnancy test, but I thought I owed it to you to tell you first.'

'*That's* what you think you owe me? Fucking hell, Logan. As if things weren't bad enough already, you go and knock up your mistress! What is happening to you?' She couldn't believe this. She had thought she had been imagining things, blown things way out of proportion in her mind, yet here he was, confirming her worst fears about him. It wasn't just hand-holding or an emotional affair, they had slept together. It was a proper affair, with her best friend. And on the very night Kelsey had been ripped away from her for a second time. Dana couldn't believe it. And now, here he was announcing to her that Pippa was pregnant.

'Actually...'

Dana didn't even get a word in before Logan spoke again.

'Pippa wants to be married before the baby arrives, so I will need a divorce.' He looked at her, the embarrassment and shame written all over him. She thought she was done being hurt by this man. She was wrong. He wasn't the man she had married and borne children to. This man before her, sitting at the table they once shared meals at, was a complete stranger to her.

It only took her a moment to sever her relationship with him. Dana knew there was no point drawing out the pain. 'Sure, have your lawyer draw up the paperwork and I'll sign it.'

He looked surprised.

'What? Were you hoping for a fight for your affections? No way. I finally get it, Logan. You have made me see you for what you really are. Now get the fuck out of my house,' she said calmly, her tone at odds with her cutting words. He sat there for a moment as if unable to move a muscle. 'Logan, I swear to God, get out. Now.' This time he stood up, looking down at her.

'I really didn't mean for this to happen, Dana, and I'm sorry things turned out like this.'

She said nothing, just stared at her tea, swirling the nearly full cup in between her hands. He left, closing the front door behind him. He hadn't even asked to see his daughter. After a long while she went to lock the door, locking out the world. She just wanted to hibernate with Grace, but someone had other ideas. Her home phone rang.

'Mum?' she said, picking up the phone, the anger coursing through her now dissipated into weariness.

'Hi, love, how are you and Grace doing now? I've been worried.'

'Mum?' Dana interrupted. 'Pippa is pregnant with Logan's baby. He asked me for a divorce.'

Dana said it in a rush and her mother was silent for a beat before she said, 'Well, that was quick.' Dana didn't know whether to laugh or cry.

'Apparently they slept together the night Logan packed up Kelsey's room, the night that I came to your place looking for her stuff. He didn't even wait until we were separated. I don't know why I'm even surprised by anything this man does any more. It's like he's a stranger to me.' She felt the tears burning behind her eyes but she refused to let them fall. He would not make her cry ever again.

'Want me to come round? Let me keep you company.'

'Nah, it's OK, Mum, I just wanted you to know what was going on in my fucked-up world.'

'I'm so proud of you, honey, the way you are handling yourself when things just keep getting thrown at you. Maybe one night, Dad and I could take Grace for you overnight so you can have a decent break. I doubt that you'll be giving Grace to Logan any time soon so you might want some time to yourself, you know, to process things. I just can't believe he's doing this. How badly we misjudged him.' She sighed, repeating her earlier sentiment from last time they spoke.

'Thanks, Mum, that might actually be a good thing. She's such a contented girl. She'll behave for you. But a night to myself does sound nice. I'll let you know. Gotta go. Love to you and Dad.'

* * *

Living back at home was hard on Alesha. One minute she had been part of a successful power couple with the best of everything and the next she was back living with her parents. As if that wasn't hard enough, she had so much going on that she hadn't yet dealt with. Kelsey. Her niece's death had weighed so heavily on her that she'd tried to take her own life. And despite her mum pushing her to speak to a professional, she had yet to do so. In fact, she had no intention of talking about it to anyone, preferring to feel the weight of her guilt.

Alesha didn't even remember the night she had tried to kill herself. That day, she had been thinking about Kelsey and her sister, how broken Dana was, how Alesha was just as broken, but no one saw that, did they? Not her husband and certainly not her parents, who were all about Dana. Dana this and Dana that. Well, Alesha had suffered a loss as well. James blamed her. She didn't have to guess, he'd told her outright.

The last meal they'd had together, she had ordered in, and he'd ignored her except to make a deliberate dig at her ordering in rather than cooking.

'I see you're letting everything go these days,' he had commented, drilling her with the stare he reserved for court. Alesha had nearly crumbled but had managed to hide her tears. She knew he saw them as a sign of weakness and would have thought even less of her. Although he'd been at the BBQ as well, he took no responsibility for not watching his niece. Kids weren't his job. He didn't even like them and was very vocal about not wanting any, ever, even though she did.

Alesha had been pushing her meat around her plate when he'd spoken. 'Do you feel bad?' he'd asked her. She had frozen. He hadn't brought up the accident since they had attended the funeral, where he had pretended to care about her, holding her as she'd cried, but when they had got home it had been another story. He hadn't been able to get away from her fast enough.

'You know I do,' she'd replied, taken aback by his question. 'If I could change things, I would.'

'You are responsible though. You see that, right?'

His words had hurt her even though she knew that her sister felt the same way. It *was* her fault, hers and everyone else's at that BBQ, including her sister's.

Alesha tried not to go into the main house during the day, choosing to stay alone in the bungalow. She only went in if she thought the coast was clear. She'd already had enough awkward run-ins with her father to last a lifetime. He blamed her too. She could tell. The way he looked at her, with such disappointment in his eyes, the coldness of his voice when he was forced to speak to her. Her mother tried to make it better between them but had earned herself harsh words from her husband, which had sent Alesha hurrying back to her bungalow. Her mum was the only one on her side, knowing it was an accident. A horrible accident.

Alesha could feel herself slipping away piece by piece. Her life was ruined. She couldn't show her face anywhere, and one morning divorce papers were delivered to the house. James was making good on his promise. She was spiralling out of control, lying on the bed, holding the papers to her chest, sobbing. If she could make things right again, she would.

* * *

As the days passed, Dana started thinking about Melanie. She seemed to have taken a step back at last. Dana had had a few texts asking her to coffee, but Dana always made up some excuse not to go. She no longer went to the support meetings, feeling she didn't need them any more. The only helpful thing to come out of them was her friendship with Melanie and Matt. He had been giving her space too, checking in via text every couple of days. He knew that she needed to process all of the information that had been dumped on her recently. She knew she really should call Matt, see how he was.

One evening, the TV droning on in the background while she folded laundry and tidied up the house, it was time to put Grace down to bed. Tonight was going to be the first night that Grace was going to sleep in her new bedroom. This was a trial run for both Dana and Grace, to see if they both could handle it. She was nervous but it was another huge step forward in life. Dana changed Grace into her sleepsuit and took her into her new bedroom. She opened the door. Dana looked at the paint stains on the floor, she'd tried to clean it up herself but hadn't had any luck so she'd ordered the new carpet but it would take a few days to arrive. Just the thought of someone being in this room had her tied in knots. She didn't know what to do or who to trust any more. She was terrified of being alone at home, and in the darkest part of the night she wished for Logan to be beside her. She was barely sleeping, between Grace's schedule and the fear of the intruder breaking into her house and leaving threatening messages for her to find. Dana felt as if she was beginning to unravel at the seams.

Cradling Grace in her arms, Dana whispered, 'Time for sleep, beautiful,' nuzzling her neck gently, kissing her sweet-smelling skin.

Once Dana had put Grace down into the cot and watched her sleepy eyes close gently, she turned off the light and left the door wide open. She headed to her bedroom to get changed, turning on the lamp in the lounge and the main light off on her way through. She planned to watch a movie once she had changed and brushed her teeth. It had been a while since she had truly laughed so Dana thought she'd treat herself to a comedy. Dana washed and moisturised her face, brushed her teeth and changed into a pair of comfortable tracksuit bottoms and a loose jumper. Not long after, she walked down the hallway and into the lounge. The lamp was off and the main light was blazing away overhead, taking all the shadows from the room. The TV was on but the sound was turned off.

'What the hell?' she mumbled in the silent room. 'I know I turned the light off. And I sure as hell didn't turn the TV on.' Feeling a small chill creep up on her, she left the lounge light on and went into the kitchen. She couldn't put her finger on what was different, but she knew something was out of place. She felt it. It was then that she noticed that Kelsey's chair was missing. It hadn't just been moved, it was gone altogether. Dana turned in a circle, staring at each corner of the kitchen trying to find the chair. *What the hell was going on?* Dana went into the lounge and checked the room, already knowing that she wouldn't find it. Who the hell would steal a chair from her kitchen? Was it because it was Kelsey's chair? Dana could feel tears of loss welling in her eyes. Another connection to Kelsey gone. She was sure that the chair had been there before she had made tea, but she had eaten in the lounge tonight. Struggling to remember the last time she'd seen it, Dana began to fear that the intruder was back again.

Why did these things keep happening to her? Needing to calm her nerves, Dana went to the sink and grabbed a glass from the drying rack. She filled it up and took a big sip, draining half the glass in one go. She looked at herself in the darkened window above the sink. Her reflection stared back at her. A pale, smudged woman with dark, hollowed-out eyes. She put down the glass and said, 'Am I going crazy?' Her voice was loud in the quiet house, scaring her even more. She felt chills race across her arms, goose bumps rising to cover her skin. She spun around expecting to see someone behind her but there was no one there.

Dana knew that she had been under extreme stress and suffering from crushing grief for a long time now and she couldn't help but wonder if it was all finally catching up to her. She thought about what she'd been through in the house, the notes, the threats, the accusations, the things that she hadn't told anyone about, and began to wonder if there was an intruder at all. She closed her eyes, hand resting on the back of a chair for support. Dana had to face the very real possibility that she might have been doing this to herself the whole time. That maybe there *was* no intruder, just Dana and her inability to move on from her part in Kelsey's death. It started with Kelsey, and Dana was terrified that if she was threatening herself, then where was her limit? Could she really be behind all of these threats? Just the thought that she might be doing this and not realising it was causing her such fear. She was already scared all the time, worried about what she'd find once she left a room. How could she prove if it was her or an intruder?

Starting to panic now, she went to check on her daughter. Dana flipped the light on and let out a stuttering breath. Grace was wearing a different sleepsuit from the one Dana had dressed her in at bedtime.

Dana felt her vision swim fleetingly as she looked down at Grace. 'Oh, God!' she said loudly, quickly leaning into the cot to lift Grace out. The baby sighed lightly in her sleep as Dana grabbed her nappy bag with one hand, then ran from the room, and threw her phone into her handbag then slung it over her shoulder, picking up the car keys as she hurried down the darkened hallway. She had to get out of here; someone was obviously in the house with them. Who knew what they would do next? Ever since Logan had left the house, she had been living in fear for hers and Grace's safety. This just proved that her fear was justified.

She strapped Grace into her car seat as fast as she could, constantly looking back at the house, expecting to see someone sneaking up on her. Once inside the car, she locked them in and everyone else out. On autopilot, she drove to the one place she knew they'd be safe.

'Mum!' Dana yelled as she banged on the screen door. The veranda light burned bright above her, then her mother appeared at the door. She opened it slowly and was shocked when Dana grabbed the door, pushing it open quickly, trying to get inside. 'Let me in!'

'Dana... what's—?'

'Inside,' Dana gasped, pushing her mother backwards into the house. Dana was crying. She couldn't stop the tears that flowed down her face, dripping off her chin, some landing onto her daughter.

'Dad!' she yelled urgently. Her father appeared, responding to her desperate call.

'Dana, what are you doing here? What's wrong?' he asked, catching sight of her tear-streaked face.

She passed Grace to her mother and pulled back the curtain, looking out of the window into the inky night.

'What's wrong?' asked her mother, fear beginning to creep into her voice.

'We might have been followed. I'm not sure. We have to be careful,' she said, talking very fast, still peering out of the window.

'Careful of what? You're not making any sense. Tell us what's going on,' her father demanded.

'Are we safe here?' she questioned. Her parents exchanged confused glances with each other.

'Safe? Of course we're safe here,' her mum replied, looking down at Grace's sleeping face. 'What on earth is going on, Dana?'

'Someone was in my house. Someone touched my daughter! She could have been hurt!' Dana began to sob uncontrollably, collapsing on the couch, burying herself in her dad's strong arms as he sat beside her.

'What do you mean someone was in your house? I think I'm going to call Logan,' said her mother, taking Grace into the kitchen with her.

Dana didn't even acknowledge her mum's comment, she was just grateful that she and Grace had made it here safely and that someone else was going to take over for now. She felt as if she were losing her mind.

22

Logan's phone rang and when he saw his mother-in-law's name flash up he quickly answered despite the late hour. 'Mischa? What's wrong?' asked Logan, instantly on high alert. After everything that had happened, Mischa wouldn't call him if it wasn't an emergency.

'Oh, thank God you picked up, Logan! You need to get over here to our place, now. Something has happened,' she said, sounding a little breathless and very worried.

'Is Dana OK? What about Grace? What's happened?' He was aware of Pippa watching him closely as he moved away from her.

'I can't explain it because Dana isn't making any sense. She's absolutely distraught. Can you come, please? She needs you.' Dana's mother hung up and Logan turned to face Pippa, who was standing right behind him, her face looking annoyed at the intrusion.

'I have to go out to Robert and Mischa's place.'

'What? Now? It's late.'

'Something's happened with Dana. I don't know what, but

she's upset, and Mischa said Dana needs me, which means Grace needs me.'

'Logan, you're seriously going to leave now? We're in the middle of an important conversation,' Pippa said, putting both hands on her stomach, making her point very clear.

'I have to go. We'll talk about this later, all right?' He grabbed his car keys and wallet, kissed her forehead and headed for the front door.

'Seriously, Logan?' Pippa yelled after him. 'Dana snaps her fingers and you go running?'

'I am not doing this with you now, Pippa.'

Logan left, revving the car as he backed out of the driveway. He saw her come outside, crossing her arms over her chest in anger as she watched him drive away. He knew he'd pay for this later, but Mischa had sounded... scared. Soon he was turning onto the driveway to the property where his wife and child were. He pulled up right in front of one of Robert's boulders and it flicked through his mind that he hadn't been to the house since Kelsey had died. Pushing the sobering thought aside, he got out of the car.

Dana threw open the door and launched herself into his arms, crying hysterically.

He pushed her back inside the house, hugging her tightly in his arms. Logan looked over her shoulder at Dana's parents. 'What the hell is going on?' he said over Dana's cries. It was as if she had fallen to pieces.

'We don't know exactly what has happened. Dana just arrived on our doorstep with Grace, bawling uncontrollably. Saying she thought that she might have been followed. She's acting kind of paranoid,' Mischa said, obviously worried about her daughter's state of mind. Logan stepped out of Dana's arms, wiping the tears from her face. Her tearful eyes connected with his. She ran her hand through her hair, struggling not to cry again.

'Dana, sweetheart, what happened? Is it Grace?' he asked, looking over at his daughter resting in her nan's arms, asleep, despite the commotion around her.

'I... uh... Grace is fine. *For now.*' She sniffed back her tears and Logan knew she was close to completely losing it again. He hadn't seen her like this since they'd lost Kelsey.

'Explain it to me – what's got you so scared?'

Dana looked up at him with terrified eyes. 'Someone was in our house,' she whispered.

The words chilled him. 'Someone was in the house? How do you know? Tell me.'

She pulled away from him and began to pace the lounge, her parents standing off to the side, watching as Dana tried to tell Logan what had happened.

'Well, I was getting ready for bed. I wasn't gone for long. Grace was asleep in her new room.'

Logan didn't know that Grace had moved into Kelsey's old room; he knew how hard that must have been for Dana to say those words. He was so proud of her. Then he realised that he had no idea what had been happening with his own family. The past two weeks had flown by and he'd barely seen Grace. Shame burned through him. He should have been there to support Dana and Grace when they needed him most. Instead he'd spent the last two weeks playing house with Pippa, too ashamed to speak to Dana for fear that she'd tell him the truth about what he'd done to their family.

'When I came out, the lounge light was on, but I'd definitely turned it off and had the lamp on instead. The TV was on too. Maybe I could have forgotten that I did that, but when I went into the kitchen, something... something didn't feel right.

Kelsey's chair was gone. I went looking for it – it's not misplaced, just gone.' Dana seemed to choke on Kelsey's name. She wiped her eyes and started again. 'I just knew that there was something else, I just knew it, so I ran into Grace's room to check on her. I put Grace to sleep in a sleepsuit that had balloons on it.' They all looked at Grace, who was now wearing a sleepsuit with cherries on it. There were confused glances all round.

'Are you saying that someone was in our house and changed our daughter's outfit?' Logan asked, his face expressing disbelief.

'Yes! That's exactly what I'm trying to tell you. Someone was in the house! They could have hurt Grace. I grabbed her and drove straight here. Who would do this to us? Why would they break into our house and do that? Just to scare me? Well, I'm scared all right.' She was babbling now, and he had no idea what to make of any of this. She threw herself into his arms again and he automatically hugged her to him. He looked over her shoulder at Robert and Mischa and raised his eyebrows. Had someone really been in their house? If so, who?

'Dana, I need to talk to Robert and Mischa for a little bit. Would you hold Grace, please?' Looking after their daughter would give her something to focus on instead of her fear while he talked to her parents. She nodded and took the baby from her mum.

The three of them walked into the kitchen and Logan began whispering. 'Look, Dana has been under incredible stress these past few months – Kelsey, Grace, me. It's taken a toll on her. Is it more likely that someone broke into the house and changed our daughter's outfit, or that she is confused as to what she dressed Grace in tonight? She could easily have mixed up Grace's outfit – balloons and cherries are similar, especially in the lamplight.'

'Are you saying you don't believe her?' asked Mischa. 'She

seems adamant and her fear wasn't faked. She came here, terrified.'

'I don't doubt that she was scared. If it's not her and someone did break into the house, then I'm as concerned as she is. But as I said, great stress, everything with Kelsey, plus add a new-born to the mix, she's probably not sleeping either, I just don't know. But either way, we all need to be there to support her. Having said that...'

Robert nodded and Mischa touched his hand.

'Thanks for coming out. She really needs you tonight.'

They all headed back into the lounge where Dana sat, holding Grace, her cries finally stopped.

Logan touched Dana on the shoulder, squeezing her gently. 'You're all right now, Dana, you and Grace. You'll stay here tonight and I'll work out what to do, OK? I've just got to ring... Pippa, let her know that I'm staying the night, here, with you two.'

He took out his mobile and went into the kitchen for some privacy, tapping Pippa's name on his phone. It rang once before she picked it up.

'Logan, are you all right? What's going on?' She sounded frantic.

'Yeah, I'm all right. It's Dana, she's really upset. She thinks someone broke into the house tonight. She's at her parents' place now but she's really shaken up, so I'm going to stay here with them tonight.'

There was a long pause on the other end of the phone. 'What?' she said, her voice low.

'Pip, please don't be angry, they need me. I have to take care of them.' He felt as though he shouldn't have to explain himself to her, yet here he was doing just that.

'I need you,' she snapped. 'I'm having your child too, you know.'

'Trust me, I know,' he said, trying, and failing, to keep his voice even. Why was she doing this now? Couldn't she see that they needed him? Where had it all gone so wrong with her?

'Logan? Logan?' He came back to the present. Pippa was talking to him, well, at him really.

'What?' he said, more sharply than he had intended.

'You need to come home.'

'I don't know where home is any more,' he said before hanging up. 'Jesus,' he whispered to himself. His wife was a mess and his girlfriend was demanding he come home to her, acting all territorial, but Dana was distraught, he couldn't just leave her. He had a duty to both Dana and Grace to make sure they were safe.

He walked out of the kitchen and back into the lounge. Everyone was quiet and he knew without a doubt that they had heard his side of the conversation with Pippa. It was very awkward. Robert busied himself with touching Grace's hair, Dana was staring down at their daughter, only Mischa acknowledged the call.

'Everything OK?' asked Mischa softly. He knew that Dana's parents must despise him for what he'd done to their daughter, yet she was treating him kindly when he didn't deserve it.

'Yeah, just... stuff at... home,' he finished weakly, only realising what he was saying halfway through saying it. These people had been his family. They were important to him and he had thrown that all away. He loved Pippa, but he missed Dana, the way she used to be, the way she had been coming back to these past few weeks. He was still in love with his wife. He looked out of the dining room window; the bungalow was dark. That could be a potential problem, he thought. What if they ran into Alesha while they were here? He didn't see her car but figured it was parked around the back.

'I'm staying here with you. We'll go back home tomorrow and I'll check all the locks.'

'Should we call the police?' Mischa asked.

'And tell them what? That your granddaughter's clothes were changed by someone who might have broken into the house? Do you know how crazy that sounds?' He didn't intend for it to come out harshly, so he softened his voice and tried again. 'I'll check the house, make sure it's safe. But for now, we stay here. I won't have Dana upset.'

Robert and Mischa just stared at him. 'Any more than I've already upset her,' he added. What else could he say? He had hurt Dana terribly and he would give the world to take it back, but he couldn't. He was with Pippa now; she was having his baby and he couldn't very well leave her and go back to Dana. Besides, Dana wouldn't take him back – just as Pippa had predicted, she had changed, grown more independent, someone he didn't quite recognise. He knew tonight wasn't who she was any more. She was scared and afraid for her daughter. Logan knew she would do anything for Grace.

'I'll sleep on the couch, Dana and Grace can have the spare room and I'll take them home in the morning.'

Dana kissed her parents goodnight as they went to their room. Logan stood in the lounge with Dana and Grace. 'Thank you for believing me,' Dana whispered. 'I know it sounds made up, but I'm not imagining it. Someone was in our house.'

He grasped her hand. 'I promise we'll sort this out. Now, why don't you and Grace go to bed?' She moved backwards, pulling her hand from his. He tried not to take it personally. After all, Mischa had called him, not Dana. She did not forgive and she did not forget.

'Yeah, all right. I'll see you in the morning.'

He leaned forward and out of habit went to kiss her goodnight.

'Logan, don't,' she whispered. She wrenched herself backwards and covered her mouth with her hand. 'This isn't why we called you. I'm not going to do this with you. You made your choice. I'm going to bed.' She turned and walked away, Grace clutched to her chest.

'*Fuck!*' he whispered in the quiet house. Eventually he unfolded the blanket Mischa had left out for him and lay down on the uncomfortable couch.

Dana didn't sleep much that night, waking at every little noise in the usually comforting old house. But tonight, every creak and groan just put her on edge and so by the time the sun came up, she was a wreck. Logan pretty much pounced on her when she came out of the room with Grace. He was obviously on high alert too. Her parents were still in bed, their door closed.

'Morning,' she said, handing a sleepy Grace over to Logan to cuddle.

He looked concerned. 'Did you sleep at all?'

'Not really, you?'

'No, too worried about you and Grace. I'm going to the hardware store this morning and installing a deadbolt on the front and back doors. It's such an old house, everything is breaking down in there and I can't have you living in fear. I wish you'd just pack up and move to another place.'

'We've been through this; I'm not leaving the house that Kelsey grew up in. I just can't, won't. I've moved Grace into her own room, and that was a hard enough step for me.'

'Are you still going to your support meetings?' he asked.

'I don't need them any more,' she said wearily.

Logan didn't push and for that she was grateful. Besides, it was no longer his business.

'Want to follow me home... back to your place? I'll take a look around then go to the hardware store.'

'I'd appreciate that, Logan. I have to call Matt too. He's going to be so worried. He messaged me last night, but I was too upset to message back.' She saw the frown on Logan's face but he held his tongue. 'And Melanie, she's left me a dozen messages over the past couple of days. I need to finally catch up with her – besides, she'll be desperate for a Grace cuddle.'

'You don't worry about her? I mean, she is ever so slightly crazy.'

'At this point, I only have two friends.'

'Isn't Matt your boyfriend?' he said with more than a hint of jealousy.

'Not that it's any of your business, but no. I'm not ready for a relationship. My husband did a real number on me, you know? Made it hard for me to trust again.'

Logan had the decency to look ashamed. 'Look, why don't you go get your things and follow me back to the house? We'll leave a note for your parents and you can call them later.'

Dana nodded, grabbed the nappy bag, putting all of Grace's stuff into it, while Logan wrote her parents a note, leaving it on the kitchen table.

Dana didn't want to go home; she was frightened. She remembered back to the afternoon she'd been in Kelsey's bed, weeks ago, and had felt a presence in the room. Had someone really been in the house, or had her imagination got the better of her? The back door had been unlocked and she'd been positive she'd locked it.

She followed Logan home and pulled into the driveway while

he stayed on the street. A car drove off as she was taking Grace out of the car seat. She looked up and could have sworn it looked like Melanie's. She dismissed it immediately. Melanie would have come barrelling up the path had she seen her coming home, a million questions on her lips about where she'd been, her hands stretched out for a cuddle with Grace.

It was a little after nine in the morning. Logan used her key to unlock the door, helping her inside. It looked like her house, everything in its place, but it still didn't feel right. She wondered if it would feel like home ever again. Logan went round and checked each window, making sure that they were locked, then looked at the front and back doors.

'I think a deadbolt on each of these doors is the way to go. Do you mind if I leave you to go and get them? It'll take me about half an hour, maybe forty minutes at the most.'

'OK,' she said, twisting a piece of hair around her finger. She was nervous and it showed.

'Dana?'

'Yeah?'

'Has this been happening to you a lot?' Logan asked, his forehead creased with worry.

'Has what?'

'You know, like last night? Have things been happening to you in the house?'

She didn't really know where he was going with this but decided to be honest. 'Yes, it has. Logan, someone has been harassing me and breaking into my home. It's been getting worse. I've just been trying to deal with it on my own.' She shrank back under his intense stare.

'What kind of things?'

'Some of it is harmless, clothes and bottles moving around, things like that, then the morning after you cleaned out Kelsey's room, I found a scrap of paper with something horrible written on it, then out of the letterbox, on a piece of paper, someone called me a murderer,' she said, her voice drifting off into silence. 'There was also a present left in my locked car – it looked like a rattle that I had as a child, wrapped up in pink paper. How would they know that?' She was aware of how crazy she sounded; as she said it out loud she realised that *she* thought she was crazy too. Why would anyone play games with her like this? What was there to gain? *You killed her, murderer.*

'Why didn't you tell me about this?'

'Well, Logan, in case you haven't noticed, we're not exactly close any more, and we haven't been in a long time.'

He frowned. 'That ends now. From now on, you tell me everything. No matter how small.'

'Do you believe me?' she asked, holding her breath.

He stilled and she waited. Did he believe her? She knew it sounded far-fetched and she began to feel those feelings of doubt creep back in. Was she responsible for everything that was happening to her? Was she doing this to herself or was there truly an intruder?

'I believe you, but I also know that you are under such stress with everything that's been happening to you these past few months. Losing Kelsey, giving birth to Grace. Me leaving. It has to be taking a toll on you. I worry about you, Dana.'

Dana was about to question him further when the moment was broken by her phone vibrating in her pocket. She pulled it out, checking who it was, expecting it to be her mother, checking in.

'Why's *he* messaging you so early?' Logan asked, jealousy colouring his voice.

'*He* is a friend and, not that it's any of your business, but he wants to come over to see Grace and me.' Dana was annoyed with

Logan's possessiveness; she wasn't his any more. He'd seen to that. And just when they'd started to get along.

Logan frowned again, pissed off. 'I'd better go get those dead-bolts. Tell your boyfriend he can come over.' He stormed off angrily.

'He's not my...' but Logan had gone. Dana messaged Matt back and said to give her half an hour or so. She wanted to change out of the clothes that she had slept in and brush her teeth and hair. She fed Grace then took her to her bedroom with her so she could keep an eye on her. She would be sleeping in the same room as Grace for a while, that was for sure. Just the thought of a stranger's hands on her daughter caused fear to settle in her heart.

Once Dana had changed, she took Grace into the lounge, where she put her on the play mat. Exhausted, Dana lay on the couch and closed her eyes while she waited for Matt to come over.

She must have dozed off because next thing she knew, she was woken up by knocking on the door. Frantically, she looked down at the floor, and, finding Grace where she'd put her, she breathed a sigh of relief. Dana hadn't meant to fall asleep but the last twenty-four hours had taken their toll on her, physically and emotionally. She was exhausted. There was another knock and Dana went and opened the door.

Matt stepped into the house, bent down and gave her a gentle kiss on the cheek. Logan was waiting by his car, locks in his hand. This was very awkward.

'Hey,' she said to Matt.

He filled the small space with his large frame. 'Hey, yourself,' he said, closing the door on prying eyes. He obviously hadn't seen Logan waiting out at the front. She'd deal with that in a minute.

'Where's the little one?' he asked.

'She's in the lounge on the play mat, enjoying some tummy time.' Matt walked into the lounge and picked Grace up carefully and held her in his arms. She looked so tiny, so defenceless, but Dana knew that Matt would protect her no matter what. Grace looked up at him, gurgled, then smacked him on the cheek with a tiny hand.

'I think that means that she likes you,' Dana said, laughing for the first time since yesterday. It felt good. He smiled at Grace then at Dana.

'How are you? You look tired.'

'You never tell a woman that she doesn't look her best,' she teased.

'Sorry. You look beautiful.'

'Better. Actually,' she said, her voice turning serious as she took Grace from his arms to cuddle her, 'we had some... drama here last night.'

'Drama? Why, what happened?'

She told him about what had happened the night before.

He put one hand on her shoulder, carefully, as Dana held Grace in the other arm, pulling her in for a gentle hug, making sure he didn't squash the baby. 'Why didn't you call me? I would have come straight over,' he said, and she was touched that he cared.

'I couldn't even breathe, let alone think clearly. I just knew that I had to get out of here, get Grace somewhere safe. I wasn't sure if anyone was still in the house, so I grabbed the bags and just ran. I drove straight to Mum and Dad's place, checking the mirrors the whole time, terrified that I was being followed. Mum called Logan to come over to their house.' Matt looked crestfallen at her revelation that her estranged husband had come to the rescue. 'He followed me back home this morning and checked the locks, but it's an old house – if someone wants to get in, they'll

get in. He's going to put a deadbolt on the front and back door.'
She sighed. 'I think it will make him feel better. He's actually
outside with the deadbolts now. I'd better let him in so he can
install them.'

Dana let a surly Logan back into the house, where he
installed the locks silently, glaring at Matt every time he saw him
holding his daughter. Finally he was done. He dropped the new
keys on the table and left without saying another word.

'You know, I could sleep here for a few days until you feel safe
again if you want,' Matt offered.

She was touched that he'd do that to make her and Grace feel
safe. 'That's really sweet, Matt, and, as much as I want to be self-
sufficient and only rely on myself, I think I could use the back-up
this time.'

'Dana, this wasn't some little thing. And you're not being weak
asking for help, if that's what you're worried about.'

Her phone vibrated in her pocket. It was Logan.

We still need to talk about things. I'll call you later on.

She sighed. She was not really looking forward to talking to
him about anything.

'You OK?' Matt asked, concerned.

'Yeah, I will be. I have to go down to the supermarket for some
things. Would you mind coming with me?

'So much for being independent.'

'Yup, sure will. I'll drive.'

Matt strapped Grace in and gave her a sweet kiss on the forehead, then he drove them to the supermarket, constantly
checking the mirror.

They went shopping, Dana holding Grace in her arms,
unwilling to let her go, Matt pushing the trolley. She was just

thinking how nice it was to be with him, doing something as normal as grocery shopping, when someone called her name.

'Dana!'

She turned, and Melanie was standing behind her, smile on her face.

'Oh, hi, Melanie.' Dana felt a little uneasy around her with Matt there, although she knew that was ridiculous.

'Melanie,' Matt said evenly.

'Hey, guys,' Melanie said cheerfully, like the Melanie she'd first met. 'Funny running into you two here. Sorry, you three. How's my baby girl?' she said to Grace, taking her from Dana's arms without asking.

'How have you been, Dana? I haven't heard from you in a while, and here you are, with the charming Matt.' Was there sarcasm in her voice? She was still smiling what looked like a genuine smile. Dana couldn't tell.

'We've been OK,' Dana said, not wanting to go into the details of stuff with Logan or the hassles she'd had last night and this morning, and she especially didn't want to talk about why Matt was chaperoning them. 'Just the usual, looking after the little one,' Dana said, reaching out for her baby. She didn't think Melanie was going to hand Grace over, but then Melanie smiled and gave Grace back to her. 'Speaking of which, we've got to finish the shopping so I can take Grace home for a nap. She'll start getting grumpy soon.' Dana smiled as she told the lie.

'Oh, sure. Maybe we can catch up some time this week?' Melanie asked.

'Yeah, maybe, I'll call you later on, all right?' Dana just wanted the moment to be over.

'Nice to see you again, Melanie,' Matt said politely.

'Hmm,' she responded. 'See you, Dana. Bye, my baby girl,' Melanie said, wiggling her fingers at the happy little baby. She turned and walked off in the opposite direction, heading for the exit. Dana noticed that she didn't have any groceries with her.

'That was weird,' Matt finally said on the way back to Dana's place.

'Yeah, it has been a bit off with her lately. Even over the phone, it's like there's this distance between us, but I'm not sure what went wrong, to be honest. She just started in on Logan and you and hasn't really let it go since. I've got to the point where I've ignored a few of her calls and texts because I don't want to deal with the drama. Had enough of that to last me a lifetime.' She smiled at Matt when he looked over at her.

Ten minutes later, they were sitting in the lounge, Dana on the couch and Matt sitting next to her on the floor, playing with Grace while they ate their lunch.

'She really is such a sweet baby. Gorgeous, actually. Just like her mum.' He turned his head towards her as he said it and she felt her stomach do a slow roll when he smiled lazily at her.

'Thanks,' she whispered, ducking her head in embarrassment. She knew that every compliment he gave her was done through the lens of love, but she wasn't ready for any of that yet.

23

Logan was in a foul mood by the time he arrived at work.

'Hey, boss, someone's here to see you,' his number two, Petey, said to him. Logan didn't have time to deal with any shit today. He'd seen his wife with another man, albeit it looked like they were just friends, but he was still pissed. He knew it wasn't his right to be angry any more, but he was.

'Who is it? The owner again?' He didn't have time to deal with this; he was already hours later than he'd expected.

'Nah, not the owner, some chick.'

As he turned, his heart dropped. Pippa was standing there, watching him.

Logan walked over to her, hands in his pockets. 'What are you doing here, Pip?' he asked, aware that the eyes of his men were on him. They didn't know that he had split from Dana and was now with Pippa, so this could start rumours.

'Don't Pip me. Why haven't you been answering my calls? I've been trying you all morning.' She was angry. He'd have to work hard to talk himself out of this one.

'I'm sorry, Pippa, I had to install deadbolts at Dana's house this morning.'

'Deadbolts at Dana's house? That's what we're going with?' she asked sarcastically, hands on her hips. He looked sideways at his guys, who were all staring, not even pretending to work. This was clearly much more entertaining.

'It's the truth. Look, can we do this somewhere else?'

'Why? Are you embarrassed by me? Ashamed of me?' Pippa was working herself up now and he knew it wouldn't be pretty.

'No, of course not, but you knew where I was.'

'Exactly! You were with *her*,' she said, her jealousy obvious.

Logan sighed, gripped her by the elbow and walked her behind a stack of pallets. 'Dana and Grace were in trouble. I told you that. They needed me and I had to go. Someone was in their house last night.'

Pippa couldn't see past her emotions when it came to Dana any more. She had no love for her former best friend; it had evaporated each time he talked to his estranged wife, or went running to her rescue like last night. Pippa wanted Grace in her life, but Logan was only allowed to spend time with his daughter at Dana's house and he hadn't even done that yet. He had agreed to Dana's demand because he understood that was the way it had to be, for now. Pippa had changed from fun-loving to jealous of everyone and everything; he couldn't help but wonder if he'd done this to her. She was a different person before she got together with him, but he knew how she became when in a relationship – Dana had told him. She went in too deep, too fast, scared men off. Was this what was happening here? Dana was different too. Now she had someone else. He'd done all this to her, to them, to himself. He was making Pippa suffer and had driven his wife into the arms of another man.

'Are you even listening to me, Logan?' Pippa had her hands on her hips, glaring at him.

He touched her hand, then grasped it tenderly. 'I'm listening to you, Pippa.' He tried to put her mind at ease. 'But last night someone broke into their house and could have hurt Grace. I had no choice but to go, and I'd do it again. Do you understand? You and the baby are important to me, but so are Dana and Grace.'

Pippa swallowed and it looked as if she was going to say the right words, but instead she said, 'You're never going to love me the way you love her, are you?' Before he had a chance to reply, she pulled her hand from his and walked back to her car. She got in and locked the door and when he knocked on the window she ignored him. She reversed out, tyres spinning on the dirt. He looked at the fleeing car, worried about her state of mind. She was so pissed at him. He turned to find his men staring at him.

'Get back to work, guys,' he yelled, pissed off at them for listening in. It was a while before he realised he was angry because what Pippa had said was the truth.

* * *

'Are you sure you don't want to come with me?' Matt asked as he took Grace from Dana's arms, kissing the baby goodbye before putting her onto the play mat.

He gave Dana a hug goodbye as she said, 'No, you're only going to get some clothes and you won't be long, right?'

'No, I won't be long, but I'd feel better if you came with me.'

'We'll be fine for half an hour, I promise. The sooner you go, the sooner you get back.' She shooed him with her hand and he headed for the door. Not even a minute after he left, she heard a knock at the door. 'Miss me already?' she yelled before opening it. 'Oh, it's you.'

'Yeah, it's me.'

Dana was confused. 'What are you doing here? I'm a bit busy now, Melanie.'

'I just saw Matt was here, you can't be that busy,' Melanie said as she pushed past Dana, storming into her house.

'Melanie! You can't just come in here like this!' Dana yelled as she followed her, leaving the door wide open. 'What the hell do you think you're doing?' Dana demanded as she strode into the lounge. Melanie had hold of Grace. Dana put both hands out. 'Melanie, I need you to give Grace to me. Right now.'

But instead Melanie wrapped her arms tighter around the little girl, who began to cry. 'Melanie, she needs her mum, please give her to me.'

'She doesn't need *you*. She needs someone who'll love her properly, not see her as a replacement for another child.'

'Is that what you think? Melanie, I love Grace, I have since the first second I laid eyes on her.'

'You hated her! You told me you weren't even sure if you wanted to be a mum again. Grace deserves better than you. I'm taking her with me. And you can't stop me.'

'Melanie! Stop! You're scaring me!' Dana shouted.

But Melanie shoved past her, Grace wailing in her arms. Melanie turned, walking backwards towards the front door so she could keep an eye on Dana. 'I can do for her what you can't. I can love her for herself.'

'You're fucking insane! Give me back my baby!' Now Dana's cries were so loud they hurt her own ears. Grace was red in the face as she screamed her lungs out too. Just as Melanie reached the doorway, backing out of it, someone grabbed her from behind, pinning her arms to her chest, and Grace to her body.

'Get the baby!' Matt yelled and Dana launched herself forward and wrenched Grace from Melanie's arms.

Dana hugged Grace closely, rocking her back and forth. 'Shh, Grace, it's OK now, honey. Mummy's here.' Grace continued to scream, her voice seemingly filling the entire small house.

Melanie, still encircled by muscled arms, threw her head backwards and connected with Matt's nose, with a sickening crunch. Matt yelled, letting go of her, and she whirled, running past him and to her car, where she hurled herself in and sped off.

'Thank you, oh, God, Matt, thank you!' Dana threw herself into Matt's arms, crushing Grace, who began to scream again.

'The baby, Dana,' he said, one arm loosely wrapped around her, one hand cupping his bleeding nose. Dana backed away, crying, her cheeks stained with tears.

'What the hell happened?' he asked when she let go of him to comfort Grace. 'What was she doing?'

Dana was in shock. 'I don't know... she... she said something about me not loving Grace and saying that she could give her what I couldn't, be a better mum, I guess. She was trying to kidnap her, Matt. Oh, God, if you hadn't been here—'

'But I was.'

'You... what are you doing back?' she stammered, rocking Grace, who had finally begun to settle down.

'I left my phone on the kitchen bench. I heard you screaming. I saw Melanie... I just reacted. Dana, we need to call the police, right now. Melanie's fucking nuts. She's obviously the one who's been harassing you. We need to call them now.'

Dana, still crying, nodded. 'Make the call,' she said, wiping her eyes.

24

Two hours later, Matt opened Dana's front door and ushered them through the doorway. Dana felt drained emotionally and could barely function, she was so tired. During her questioning by the police, she'd realised that she had let a woman she knew nothing about into her home and, worse, into her and her daughter's lives. How could she have been so stupid? She'd known Melanie had a thing about Grace, that she had since Dana had first gone to the grief support meeting before Grace had even been born, and it had only intensified over time.

She didn't even remember Melanie's last name, even though she knew she had told her. Cullkin? Collins? The police had checked with the support group register, but Melanie must have given a false name because she wasn't listed on the police database or on the driving licence database. By the end of the interview, Dana couldn't·even be sure if her first name was actually Melanie. She had lied about everything; Dana knew nothing about this woman. Matt knew even less; his interview was quite short. His nose was swollen, his eyes the slightest bit black underneath. Melanie, or whatever her name was, had done a good job.

Matt ushered Dana into the lounge, where she clutched her daughter to her, not sure if she was ever going to be able to let her go again.

Matt dropped a kiss on Dana's head. 'I'll make you a cup of tea, although you look like you could do with a shot of bourbon instead.' He smiled but she was too distressed to even play along.

'I opened the door,' she said woodenly. 'I opened the door, Matt. She almost took Grace because of me. I did this.'

He squatted in front of her, one hand on her knee, the other holding Grace's hand. 'You are not responsible, Dana. Do you hear me? This is all on Melanie. The police will find her and arrest her.'

'How?' she cried tearfully. 'We don't even know her name. I don't even have a photo of her. How are they going to find her?'

Matt seemed to have no answer to that. He simply gave her a comforting hug. 'It's not your fault,' he repeated.

When a knock sounded at the door, she let out a startled scream and jerked her body, upsetting Grace, who began crying again, picking up on her mum's tension. 'Who's that?' Dana cried, looking at Matt.

'I'll go check.' Matt walked up the hallway, Dana standing at the end, watching him, tears streaming down her face, a screaming Grace held in her arms. She was terrified it was Melanie back to take Grace away from her, for good this time. Whoever it was knocked again.

'Dana? You in there?'

She let out a cry of relief. 'Logan?'

Matt opened the door to Dana's husband, who walked down the hallway. Logan took one look at Dana's face.

'What's wrong?' he immediately asked, fear burning in his eyes.

Dana began to cry harder and walked into his arms, laying her head on his shoulder, Grace between them. 'What the hell is going on?' Logan demanded, looking at Matt for answers, his arms snaking around Dana's body.

'Dana, talk to me,' he said. 'What's wrong? What's happened?'

She wanted to tell him, but she just couldn't find the words; she was completely spent and collapsed on the couch. Matt took Grace from her arms and passed her to Logan, then he sat down next to her and hugged the distressed woman.

'Will someone please tell me what's going on here?'

'Sit down, Logan,' said Matt. Dana could tell that Logan wanted to say something to him about being ordered to sit in his own home by a complete stranger. Still, he sat, staring at his baby girl in his arms, soothing her.

'Melanie tried to kidnap Grace this afternoon.'

'Your friend Melanie?' he asked Dana. She nodded.

'I thought it was Matt at the door. I opened it. Logan, I opened it and we nearly lost our daughter. Our daughter!' Dana started to sob again. Matt filled Logan in on what had happened and the police interviews. 'They're looking for her. They'll find her, I'm sure of it.'

'Fucking hell.' Logan rocked Grace and after a few minutes her tears turned to muffled sobs; he put Grace down on the play mat and sat on the other side of Dana, hugging her to him. She remained stiff in his arms. She didn't want to be comforted now that the shock was wearing off. She'd done this. She'd let Melanie in. No, she deserved anger, not empathy.

She pushed Logan away. 'Get off me,' she said, standing up. Both Logan and Matt looked at her.

'What?' Dana said. 'We're not safe. None of us are safe. Melanie's a maniac, insane, and she wants my baby. Logan, you have to do something. Now. We can't stay here and we can't stay at Mum and Dad's. I won't put them in danger too.'

'You could stay at my place,' Matt interrupted. 'Melanie doesn't know where I live, not even you know. I can protect you there.'

'Don't I get a say in this?' Logan asked.

'No, Logan. We're going with Matt to his place. It's a good idea. She won't find us there. Watch Grace. Don't let her out of your sight, either one of you. I'll pack us both a bag.'

She left them sitting in uncomfortable silence in the lounge while she went into Grace's room and quickly packed her a bag. She looked at the lilac wall, then let her gaze wander to the skirting board on the right-hand side. There was a tiny patch of pink paint there that she deliberately hadn't painted over, a small reminder of a girl who'd left a huge hole in their hearts. Wiping tears for Kelsey from her face, she promised her that she'd never let anything happen to her baby sister again.

Dana dumped the nappy bag and overnight bag just inside the lounge then went to her bedroom to pack herself a bag. She threw open the wardrobe, pulling out clothes, not even really aware of what she was packing. She grabbed a couple of pairs of underwear from the top drawer, then hurried into the bathroom to grab some toiletries. Once she was finished, she looked around at the room that she had no intention of ever sleeping in again. Logan was going to get his wish; she would be moving to another house just as soon as she could. One where Melanie couldn't find them.

'I'm ready,' she announced. 'Let's go. Now, please.' She looked at her husband. 'Logan, I'll call you when I'm at Matt's house.'

'And where is that?' he asked Matt, but Dana answered for him.

'We're not going to tell you just yet. We'll be back soon, maybe a couple of days, then we'll discuss looking for a new place to live. But for now, I don't want anyone knowing where I'm going.'

'Are you sure?'

'I'm too scared, Logan, don't you see? She could follow you. Then it would all be for nothing. Grace has to stay safe. Please understand. I'll call you, I promise.'

Logan looked angry and she didn't blame him, but this was what she needed right now and, when it came to Grace, she was the one making the decisions, not him.

Matt picked up her and Grace's bags and said, 'I'll go wait in the car. I still have a car seat in the back from... from when...' He couldn't bring himself to say it so Dana simply nodded and he left gratefully.

'Dana, this is insane. You're going to hide out with our daughter and not even tell me where you're going?'

'I'll come home when I think it's safe. Could you call my mum? I just can't tell the story again right now.'

'Yeah, sure, I'll call her shortly.'

'I have to go. Give your daughter a kiss goodbye.' Logan kissed Grace three times, and Dana knew he was wondering if he'd ever see her again. 'We'll be back in a few days or so, OK? Just hold out until then, but you'll see her, I promise. I won't deny you contact, I promise,' she repeated.

Dana knew she was babbling and Logan must have heard her panic levels rising because he said, 'I love you, Dana. I still love you. You and Grace, we're a family, nothing will ever change that. I'll be there when you need me. Just don't wait too long to call.' He smiled at her and she gave him a small smile back through her tears. He walked them out of the door, pulling it closed behind him.

Dana turned to look at him one last time and could see that he was fighting back tears of his own.

'Bye,' she mouthed as she strapped Grace into the car seat. Logan lifted a hand as they drove off, but Dana didn't look back.

* * *

Logan was in shock. He wondered if he'd just said goodbye to his family for the last time. What was stopping Dana from just leaving with Grace and not coming back if she was scared enough? He had to hold onto the thought that she would never do that to him. Never. She just wasn't like that. She always did the right thing, unlike him, and a part of him couldn't help but wonder if this was karma for what he'd done to her.

Logan looked at the little house where he'd lived with Dana and Kelsey, then Dana and Grace. *Kelsey.* He pulled away from the kerb and tried not to think about Kelsey. It hurt too much. He had to focus on Grace and on his and Pippa's little one. It was still early, but he loved him or her already. He might not be that sure about Pippa any more, but he loved that child and would make it work somehow. He wasn't about to make any huge life-changing decisions on top of the day he had had.

He walked in the front door of his new house, calling to Pippa.

'Pippa? I need to talk to you. It's important. Actually, I need more than that. I guess I need a hug and a beer, not necessarily in that order.'

But Pippa wasn't in the lounge or the kitchen, so he headed to the bedroom. She was sitting on the bed, facing the window, her back to him. He sat on the other side of the bed, then swung his legs up, hands behind his head.

'What a fucked-up day. I don't even know where to start. Jesus. I just... Grace... was almost, God, I can't even say it – she was almost kidnapped from my house today. That crazy friend of

Dana's, Melanie, she tried to take her, kidnap her. The police are looking for her. I can't believe how close we came to losing my baby today. I can't even think about what would have happened if Matt hadn't been there. I may not like the guy much but, right now, I'd buy him a round of drinks. Dana's gone. She's gone to Matt's house, taken Grace with her and she won't tell me where he lives. I don't even know the guy but Dana seems to trust him, so I guess I have to too. Don't have much choice really.'

Logan realised that he'd been speaking for a while and he was telling her something shocking and upsetting, yet she hadn't turned around or spoken once, not even to ask how he was coping. 'Pippa? Are you all right?' He reached out and touched her lower back.

She turned slowly. He couldn't quite put his finger on the expression on her face at first, then he recognised it. Shock. Pippa looked just like Dana had looked when he'd last seen her.

'Yeah, I knew you'd be shocked too. It's terrifying. I just don't know how to process this. Losing Kelsey, we're still trying to work through our grief and we almost lost our Grace.' Still Pippa said nothing, staring at him with a wooden expression on her face.

'What's wrong?' he finally asked, pausing for a breath. She was beginning to worry him with her silence. It wasn't like Pippa to be silent.

She opened her mouth to speak but no words came out. 'Pip?' He rolled off the bed and walked round to her side; he called her name again and she turned to face him. 'What's wrong with you?'

'The baby,' she whispered.

'It's OK, Grace is fine. She's safe now. I told you, Dana has taken her to Matt's house. She'll be safe for a few days while we work out what we're going to do.'

Tears gathered in the corners of her eyes before rolling down her face. She didn't wipe them so he did, tenderly touching her face with his fingertips. She leaned into his hand and he rubbed his thumb over her cheekbones.

She sighed. 'Not Grace,' she said, finally meeting his eyes.

'What's that?'

'Not Grace. *Our* baby.'

He felt the colour drain from his face; his heart started to beat faster and faster. He knew what she was going to say. He had to stall her; he couldn't hear the words, not today, not after what had just happened. His mind was fuzzy, the thoughts not connecting to the words fast enough.

'Logan. Our baby,' Pippa repeated.

'You lost it?' he whispered, hating the way it sounded. As if she'd lost her keys or some stupid fucking shit like that, not their baby. He sounded accusatory, as if it were her fault somehow when of course he knew it wasn't. These things just happened sometimes. He tried to process what was going on, but it had been such a terrible day, so much had already happened. And now this. He couldn't believe that this was happening to them, to Pippa. Poor Pippa, she had wanted this baby so badly. He put his fingers under her chin, lifting her face up towards his. 'I'm so sorry, Pip,' he whispered, feeling as if he was going to lose it at any moment. Sorry was such an inadequate word.

'I never had it.' Her expression was carved in stone and she was now stony-eyed.

'What? I don't understand.' What did she mean she never had it? The baby?

'I went to the doctor to confirm the pregnancy. He told me I wasn't pregnant.'

'Not any more?' he asked, still feeling the emotion well up inside him.

She swallowed. 'Not at all. I wanted a baby so badly that my body was mimicking the signs of pregnancy. Logan, I was never pregnant with your child. I couldn't even get that right.' She turned away from him, unable to look him in the eyes.

He was quiet while he tried to process this new and devastating information.

'You hate me now, don't you? I basically tricked you into leaving your wife and demanding a divorce, all because I thought I was pregnant with your child. Well, now you're free to go home,' Pippa said bitterly.

Logan's head was swimming with information. Pippa had never been pregnant. He'd asked for a divorce from Dana because Pippa wanted to be married before the baby came. She had wanted to be a mother so bad that her body tricked her into thinking she was. He couldn't even comprehend what Pippa must be going through. He slid his arms over her shoulders and rubbed her back.

'I'm so sorry, Pip. I didn't even know that was a thing. I knew how much you wanted a baby. I just thought you were lucky to get pregnant the first time we slept together.'

'Don't you mean *we* were lucky?'

'Yes, of course. *We* were lucky. What can I do to help?' He looked into her eyes, which changed from vacant to burning brightly.

'Fuck me.'

'What?' He thought he'd misheard her.

'Fuck me. Get me pregnant for real this time.' She stared at him, pleading. 'Please, Logan. I need this.'

He backed away from her, bumping into the wall. He turned and headed for the door. 'Now is not the time, Pippa. Did you not hear anything that I said? About how Grace was almost kidnapped today? Dana had to make a statement to the police and everything. I have no idea where my daughter is right now... and Dana—'

'I don't give a fuck about Dana!' Pippa screamed. 'I am so sick of hearing her name. Dana won't let you see Grace unless you go over there, Dana won't let me near your daughter, Dana wants this and Dana wants that and now Dana is gone and you're *still* talking about her. What the actual fuck, Logan? Are you still in love with her?' She glared at him. 'Tell me the truth, you owe me that at least. Do you still love her?'

Now was his chance, his chance to release them both, set them free, to tell the truth that he'd wanted to deny, but he just couldn't any more.

'Are you in love with her? Answer me!' Pippa demanded when he didn't reply quickly enough.

So it had come down to this. It was now time to tell the truth. 'Yes. I still love her. I am in love with her. I'll go,' he said as he began to pull his clothes from the wardrobe, dumping them into his bag.

'Don't go,' she whispered. 'You can give me what I need. Please stay with me.'

'That's not a good enough reason to be together, Pippa. I'm sorry but I'm going home. This isn't going to work, I realise that now. Not when I still love my wife. It's not fair on you or me.'

'She won't take you back, you know,' she said furiously. 'You forget, I know her just as well as you do, maybe even better. You broke her trust and her heart; she won't forgive you. Ever.'

'I have to try,' Logan said simply. He slung his bag over his shoulder. 'I really do care for you, Pippa. I hope you find someone who deserves you, not someone who's damaged like me.' He wanted true happiness for her, not the half-arsed *love* he'd given her. She deserved better than him.

What a fucking day. One family, he'd almost lost it all, and the other? Well, he'd never had it to begin with.

Dana. What would she make of all of this? Was Pippa right?

Would Dana never forgive him for what he'd put her through? *She shouldn't,* the voice within him said. He didn't deserve a second chance, but he hoped with all his heart that she would give him one anyway. Considering where she was right now, he might have already missed his shot. He'd been so selfish. He was ashamed of himself and everything he'd done to her. Maybe Dana shouldn't forgive him. He deserved to be miserable, alone.

Logan drove around for a while because he had no idea where to go. Then it dawned on him: go back to the one place you were truly happy. A place that just happened to be empty. He'd work things out with Dana when she came back home. By then, he would have sorted out in his head everything that he wanted to say to her. She might even forgive him once she saw how sorry he was and just how much he loved her and Grace. That he was ready to do whatever it took to make it right, to be a family again.

Dana had taken his key away when he'd left for good and he'd hated the humiliation of having to knock on his own front door to get in. He used the new spare key, kept inside a hanging pot plant out the front, and unlocked the front door. It felt so familiar. He was home.

He dropped his bag onto the hallway floor and walked into the bedroom he had shared with his wife in another life. He just wanted to crawl under the covers that smelled like her, but he'd promised to call her mum, tell her what had happened. As was to be expected, she freaked out.

'What the hell happened?' she yelled down the phone. He felt for her. It seemed as if every time she picked up the phone these days it was more bad news.

'Her friend Melanie? I don't understand. What does she want with Grace?' Mischa was having a hard time understanding the sequence of events.

'I don't know, except what Dana told me. She said Melanie

told her she'd make a better mum to Grace and that Dana had never loved or wanted Grace, or some such shit. I don't know the full story – she was understandably upset. So Dana and Grace are going to spend a couple of nights with her friend Matt so Melanie can't find them. She just wants to feel safe.'

'And you can't keep her safe, can you?' Mischa asked. There was a hint of anger in her voice as if she blamed him for what had happened.

'I guess not. Anyway, she wanted me to let you know. She was so scared when she left. Mischa, I'm worried about her. She's been through so much these past few months, especially since Grace was born. She's come so far and I don't want this Melanie thing to set her back.'

There was a long pause, and he knew what Mischa was thinking; she didn't have to say anything. He knew how much he had contributed to the hard time Dana was going through. In fact, it was *all* his fault, he could finally accept that. He heard the back door at Mischa's house slam and heard her murmur something to Alesha, who answered back.

'Mischa, I'd better get going, let you get back to... things. I can't even think straight not with my family gone, but I'll have Dana call you in the next few days, when things settle down, all right?'

'OK, Logan. When you hear from Dana, let her know that we love her, her and Grace. I... I just can't believe this.' They said their goodbyes and she hung up on him. Now he was finally able to crawl into Dana's bed, where he fell asleep inhaling her perfume, content for now.

* * *

Mischa hung up the phone, but still clutched it in her hand tightly.

'Mum?' Alesha came to stand beside her in the kitchen. 'What was that about?'

'I... I don't even know where to begin love. Your sister...'

Alesha stared at her mum and Mischa slammed the phone down onto the bench, hard enough to crack the corner of her case. Alesha jumped.

'I swear to God she just can't catch a break. When will life become normal for her again?'

'Back up, Mum, I have no idea what's going on right now.'

Mischa turned to face her youngest daughter. 'I don't even know what to think. Dana is gone, with Grace. She's left home for a few days.'

Alesha watched as her mum struggled to speak. 'Where has she gone?' Alesha asked.

'To Matt's house. That friend, well, I guess she's not a friend after all, that Melanie, she tried to kidnap Grace today.' Mischa's hand went to her heart and she stumbled. Alesha quickly pushed her onto a stool, grabbing her a glass of water, which shook in her hand as she raised it to her mouth.

'Someone tried to kidnap Grace? Why?' Alesha's eyes were wide, the light brown irises catching the sun streaming through the window, and Mischa looked, really looked at her.

She was thin, so thin, pale with dark smudges under her eyes. She looked... she looked like Dana. Her daughters had more in common than they thought but she would never get them to meet, let alone see eye to eye. They were both struggling so much in life, weighed down by guilt and regrets.

'I have no idea when I'll hear from her. She's already having a hard enough time. She came out here last night. I didn't tell you but someone was in her house, an intruder who touched Grace.

She was so scared and now this. Alesha, could you please find your father? He needs to know what's going on.' She saw the look pass over her face. 'Please, for me?'

Alesha nodded and slammed the back door behind her, heading off to look for her father.

25

Matt drove up a short driveway and, looking at the gorgeous house before her, Dana realised that Matt was well off. His house sprawled across a large area of land, and lush green lawns, clipped neatly, surrounded the house. He took Grace from the car seat and handed her to Dana, while he grabbed their bags. 'Whatever you've forgotten, I'll buy for you, so don't worry.'

Dana was silent. She thought about Matt lounging on the threadbare carpet of her tiny home and she felt the heat of embarrassment rise up her neck.

'What's wrong?' he asked, looking back at her when he saw she hadn't moved.

'I just, I didn't know your house looked like this. It's huge. Don't you get lonely?'

'Well, not any more. I have you and Grace now.'

It was kind of an odd thing to say but she put it down to a poorly timed quip. 'We won't be here for long though. Grace needs stability and familiar surroundings, and she needs to see her dad too. But I really want to thank you for asking us to come and stay when we needed a friend the most.' She meant it. She did appreciate the fact that he was offering them his house to lie low in for a couple of days.

He smiled at her. 'It's no trouble. It'll be nice to have company, no matter how short the stay.' He smiled again and Dana felt safe for the first time in a long time. 'It is a big house for just one person,' he said, unlocking the front door.

Dana nodded in agreement as she wandered into the lounge, then the kitchen, with Grace. It was beautiful, spacious and probably decorated by Matt's wife. Matt cleared his throat.

'Let me show you to the guest room.' The guest room turned out to be a huge room with an en suite. He moved Grace's bassinet in and set it up for her. The back wall of the room featured double glass doors that led out onto a brick-paved area with a small table and two deck chairs.

'Matt, it's beautiful. I can't thank you enough.'

'Relax, Dana, you're safe here. No one knows where you are.' He was right, not a single soul knew where she and Grace were. Dana's breath stilled in her throat. Melanie would have no idea where to find them; she couldn't take Grace if she didn't know where they were. Then again, *no one* knew where they were.

That evening, after she and Grace had taken a well-needed afternoon nap, Dana got up and roamed around the house, looking for Matt. Eventually she found him in the kitchen, the aromas enticing her into the room. 'You cook too?' she asked, surprised. 'You rescue women and children, provide safety in a gorgeous home and you cook? I'm impressed, Matt, impressed, and thankful.'

'Dana, you don't have to keep thanking me – you know how I feel about you and Grace. I'd do anything for you both. I... I miss having a family.' He didn't elaborate but she knew what he meant.

She missed Kelsey and Logan as well. Just then she heard Grace cry from the other end of the house.

'Matt?'

'Mmm?'

'Can I bring the bassinet into the lounge, please? I'd feel safer if Grace was where I could see her.'

'Of course. I'm sorry I didn't think of that. Let's go get her.' She followed him towards her crying baby, picked her up while Matt picked up the bassinet and carried it into the very spacious lounge. Dana rocked Grace in her arms as Matt went back to cooking.

'I didn't know what you liked, and it occurred to me that we've only ever had coffee or tea together, never a proper meal, so we could consider this our first date. I made honeyed chicken with rice and I have a cheesecake in the freezer for dessert.'

Dana couldn't remember the last time someone had cooked for her. Logan was never big on things like that.

Logan. He must be so worried about her and Grace. Not knowing where they were or if they were even safe must be killing him. Dana knew he wasn't happy; she could see that even though he tried to hide it. And while it made her sad, it wasn't her problem. Not any more.

'You OK?' Matt asked her.

'Yeah, just thinking about Logan,' she said without thinking.

Matt frowned, his forehead creasing, his eyes darkening so briefly, Dana wondered if it even happened at all. 'He's happy you're safe. Maybe you could give him a call tomorrow and let him know you're all right, but for tonight, let's just enjoy ourselves. I'll serve dinner now. How about I put Grace back in the bassinet?' He took Grace from Dana, kissing one cheek, then the other. 'It's like I have a family again,' he whispered to Grace. He was such a sweet man and she was so happy that she had found him. His friendship was very important to her and he'd helped her through a lot since she'd known him.

Dana sat down at the dinner table while Matt served up a plate of chicken and rice for her, then he handed her a glass of white wine. He held up his glass, sitting opposite her. 'To babies.'

Dana thought it was an odd choice of toast given the circumstances, yet she raised her glass then clinked it against his before taking a small sip. She didn't want to get drunk, there was too much at stake, but Matt obviously didn't have any such worries. He drained his glass within a minute or so and refilled it from the bottle that he'd put in the middle of the table then drained it again, refilling it for a third time. She had never seen him drink anything but coffee. He must have seen the surprise on her face when he poured another drink again so quickly. 'Oh, yeah, I'm a big drinker. I've always been a big drinker, never get drunk though,' he said, smiling reassuringly at her.

Dana, uncomfortable with this line of conversation, commented on a framed photo of a woman, presumably his wife. 'Anne was beautiful, Matt. You must have been very happy together.'

'She didn't really get me,' he said, slurring ever so slightly after three glasses of wine in quick succession. 'Not like you. You get me.' He smiled at her and she smiled back cautiously. 'She died in a car accident.'

'Oh, I'm sorry, Matt. That's so tragic.'

'Tragic is the fact that I was driving.' This time Dana really didn't know what to say. It hit too close to home for her.

'We were coming back from dinner, fighting as usual, about my drinking and driving. She never let up on me. It was raining that night.' He seemed lost in his memories so she let him speak. 'We spun out and we hit a tree, but, honestly, I can't remember much of the accident. I can't remember if I killed her deliberately or not.'

Dana tried to cover the look of horror on her face at what he'd just said. Surely that was a slip of the tongue? He couldn't actually be suggesting that he'd deliberately crashed his car, could he? He kept talking.

'Her family seemed to think so. Had it not been for Jeremy, they would have taken me to the cleaners. Then I lost him too. They never forgave me. I never forgave myself. You know?'

She nodded, having absolutely no idea what to say. Had Matt just confessed to maybe killing his wife? She raised her fork to her mouth slowly, chewing the now tasteless chicken.

'Is it all right?' he asked. She had no idea what he was talking about.

'Pardon?'

'The food?'

'It's lovely, thanks, Matt.' Even though the chicken felt like paste in her mouth and she could barely swallow it. Dana was very uncomfortable now. He watched her as he ate. He'd certainly made his feelings clear and he'd been patient up to now. She might never be ready to move forward with him. And now she had even more reservations. Dana couldn't think of a worse time to start up any kind of relationship than right now. Surely he had to know that and wouldn't even try.

Once they had finished the meal, Matt cleared the table. 'I'll help you do the dishes,' she offered.

'Don't be silly, I'll do them tomorrow.'

'Well,' she said, stifling a pretend yawn, 'Grace and I should be going to bed.' But before she could lift the bassinet, Matt's hand on her arm stopped her.

'I thought we could spend some time together, you know, just talk or something.' He paused.

'Matt, I know what you want, and, as much as I appreciate the desire, I'm just not ready. I'm on tenterhooks with what happened to Grace and it's the last thing on my mind. And I should really tell Logan where we are. You understand, don't you?' She was worried that she'd offended him or hurt him, which was something she didn't want to do. But after his musings about his wife's death, there was absolutely no desire there at all. He had let his guard down. Had she caught a glimpse of the real Matt or just a man who was hurting? She didn't know any more.

'You're right, I'm sorry, I didn't mean to make you feel pressured to do anything you don't want to,' Matt said, sadness in his eyes. 'I'll walk you down to the bedroom,' he said, ever the gentleman.

'Matt,' Dana said, once he had put the bassinet down in the room, 'I am sorry. I don't want to hurt you, I really don't.'

'It's fine,' he said, but she knew he was upset. He left the room without touching her and she knew she had offended him. She had made some serious mistakes along the way. Her life had started to unravel the moment her car had struck and killed her beloved daughter and had carried on unravelling ever since. She thought maybe it might be a good idea to go back to the support group, but what if Melanie was staking out the place, just waiting to follow her back to wherever she was hiding? No, she couldn't take the risk. Melanie wanted her baby and she had proven herself willing to do anything to take Grace from her.

* * *

The next morning, Matt was gone when she woke up. She looked everywhere for him, calling his name but getting no response. Eventually she found the note resting on the table.

Be back soon, help yourself to breakfast x

She thought, while he was out and Grace was still asleep, she'd take the opportunity to call Logan, give him her undivided attention. But first, a cup of tea. As she waited for the kettle to boil, Dana make a slow loop of the lounge looking at the knick-knacks on the small end tables. There was a bookshelf that ran along one wall and as she ran her fingers along the spines, she suddenly stopped in her tracks. Her heart stilled and she found it hard to draw breath. She walked to the last shelf at the end of the bookcase and stared at the object. It was out of place, that much was obvious. It belonged here about as much as she did. Reaching out a shaking hand, she put her hand around the rattle that had been left wrapped on the front seat of her car. The rattle that she threw into the back seat. How did it get here?

'What the hell?' Dana turned the rattle over in her hand. It was definitely the same one. Old, hand-painted, but *how* did it get here? In a rush, Dana realised that the intruder had followed them; they knew where she and Grace were. They weren't any safer here than they were at home. How could she have been so stupid? This was never going to end.

She hurried back to the kitchen, where she'd left her phone. Logan answered straight away. 'Dana?' His voice was filled with fear. 'How are you and Grace?'

'Yeah, we're all right. We're out of town, but I'm still worried. Logan, something has happened. I don't know how but the intruder who's been breaking into the house found me here last night. They left me something for me to find.' Her voice was high and reedy with fear and all she wanted to do was go home.

'What? How is that even possible? Did they follow you? Listen, Dana, I've been up all night – I think you should come home and this just tells me it's the right choice to make. We barely know this Matt guy and you're out there staying with him, alone, and I don't even know where and now you're saying that someone found you anyway? You have to come home. Please.'

Dana could hear how worried he was and she completely understood where he was coming from. This was his daughter too. This place wasn't the safe haven she'd thought it to be.

'I can keep you safe at our house. Your house. I'll take some holiday and be there for you and Grace. I've fixed the locks so no one will be getting in. Just tell Matt that I want you home. It's not like he's going to say no – he can't keep you there. Dana, please.'

'But he's been so lovely and he really cares about Grace and me.'

'Do you trust him, Dana?'

She paused as she considered the question. Thinking about what he'd told her last night after several glasses of wine. *Did* she trust him? Did he kill his wife during an alcohol-induced episode? Suddenly she had misgivings about the man who'd been so caring towards her.

'It's a yes-or-no question, Dana. Don't over-think it, just go with your gut.'

'I don't know,' she whispered. 'I trust you because you know me the best, you always have, and you love your daughter more than anything. What about Pippa though? She's not just going to let you come back home and stay with us.'

'Uh,' he said.

'What's wrong?'

'Well, I was going to tell you this when everything had settled down, but I guess now might as well do. She's... she's not pregnant.'

'Oh, Logan, I'm so sorry. To lose a child before you've even had a chance to hold them must be a special kind of hell.' No matter what had happened between them, her first instinct was to comfort her soon-to-be ex-husband.

'There was no baby. I caused you all this pain for nothing.' He sounded sorry; his voice pitched low. 'I can never make it up to you, but I'll spend the rest of my life trying. I love you, Dana, I never stopped loving you.'

She didn't know how to respond so instead she said, 'I'll call you when I'm home.' Dana knew she was going to head home that morning; she and Grace might as well be there. Now she just had to tell Matt.

'I understand. I'll wait as long as it takes.' She hung up the phone.

'Who was that?'

She let out a little yelp of fear as she turned to see Matt standing close behind her. She laughed nervously under his intense gaze. 'How long have you been standing there?' she asked, her smile slipping a little.

'Long enough. Are you leaving me, Dana? After everything I've done for you and Grace? Despite the way we feel about each other? You're going to choose him over starting a life with me?' He was intense, coiled tight; she could feel the anger coming from him.

'It's not like that. I will be eternally grateful for what you've done to help Grace and me, but I think it's best I head home. I can't stay hiding here forever, and Logan wants to see his daughter. He's worried about us and he is her dad. I was so scared that I didn't think about the fact that I was running away with his child. I hope you understand, Matt.' She chose not to tell him about the rattle; she wasn't sure why, only that she wanted to go home immediately.

For a moment, she thought he was going to refuse to take them home. His face darkened, his eyes narrowed, and he was tense, but then he smiled and she thought she must have imagined what she'd seen. 'All right, then, let's get you packed and home. It was nice while it lasted.'

He stared at a photo of his wife. 'Anne would have been happy that I found you. Making a new family for myself, not being alone and closed off like I have been for a long time. You know?'

'I know all about being alone, but I can never truly understand losing a spouse, not forever anyway.'

'Things will calm down soon enough.' Matt went round the lounge collecting Grace's things, putting them in her nappy and overnight bags, then took the bags out to the car. However, once they were in the car, his mood seemed to deteriorate with each passing minute. Dana didn't dare ask what was wrong and suddenly her mind flicked to an image of him and his wife arguing, a horrible accident... but was it? He'd even questioned it himself. Dana kept looking in the back seat, checking on her precious daughter, the only person that truly mattered to her.

When they arrived home, Dana breathed a sigh of relief. She knew that overnight wasn't a long time to be gone, but it had felt like an eternity since her life had been normal and it was comforting to be around the familiar. So much had happened in the past few days, weeks, ever since she had lost Kelsey – it had been never-ending.

As Matt went out to the car to bring in their things, Logan appeared from the kitchen. Dana was surprised and even a little scared, until she realised it was him.

'What are you doing here?' she asked.

'I came back yesterday. I needed... I needed to be here, to be in your and Grace's home.' He was about to say more when Matt walked in, arms loaded with the bags and bassinet.

'Logan,' he said flatly, eyes dull and unwelcoming.

'Hey, man. Thanks again for what you did for the girls – we really appreciate it.'

Dana felt uncomfortable. She hadn't realised that Logan was here, in her house. Now it looked as if she had come home to be with Logan, which wasn't the case.

She had to break the tension. 'Matt, thanks again for the help last night. Letting us stay with you was so lovely. I'll give you a call, OK?'

He nodded. 'Of course. You take all the time you need.' Matt smiled tightly at her, then kissed her on the cheek.

'Bye, Matt,' she said as he walked out of the door.

'Bye, Dana.' And then he was gone. The breeze whipped around the corner of the eaves, making a moaning and grinding sound as the trees brushed up against the house.

'So what are you really doing here?' she asked Logan, passing him Grace for a cuddle. 'She kick you out?'

He had the decency to look away. 'No, I left her. It wasn't working out.'

'Can't say I'm surprised, Logan.' She felt the familiar anger welling up within her but decided to let it go, for now. She would be the bigger person here. 'What are your plans, then?'

He readjusted Grace in his arms. 'Well, about that. Given what's been going on here, all the stress and drama you've been having, I'd like to come back home. Not to be with you or anything like that – I know what I did there.' She nodded so he continued, 'But sleep on the couch for a while until things settle down a bit. Maybe we can even have a proper, civil conversation about the future. I still love you, Dana. You and Grace.'

'Don't,' she warned, and he backed off, waiting.

She stood in her kitchen, eyes glued to the ground while she thought about things. He'd hurt her so badly and she'd never really got to say her piece properly. There were still so many unresolved issues that, yes, did need resolving, and him being under her roof would make it easier. For now anyway.

'You can stay for a little while, until I say otherwise. We'll talk when I'm ready and you're not to push anything. All right?' Her voice was stern; this was her heart she was protecting. No leaving it open for him to stomp all over again.

He smiled at the baby as he murmured his thanks.

26

Later that night, they sat at the table eating; neither of them mentioned Kelsey's chair being missing although he knew it had to hurt Dana. He didn't want to break the mood, but he wanted to do something nice for her – she deserved it.

'I have something for you,' he said, getting up from the table and heading into the lounge where he had left his bag. He unzipped it, then went back into the kitchen, holding something behind his back. She looked up, expectantly.

'What do you have behind your back?' Dana asked.

Logan thought about changing his mind for a split second, then he handed it to her.

Her sharp intake of breath and the colour leeching from her face made him think that he had made the wrong choice.

'It's Boo Boo,' she said softly, running her fingers over the bear's worn face. 'Where did you get this?'

'I stored all of Kelsey's stuff. I would never get rid of it, Dana. I just wanted to help you move on, and you have. We will always love Kelsey. She will always be in our hearts, but we had to move on, for our sakes and Grace's.' For the second time that day, he waited for the anger to come.

Dana looked at her hands, folded around the bear. She was quiet and he could see she was fighting back tears. 'For a long time, I hated you. For the way you seemed to move through your grief with such ease, for trying to make me move on when I wasn't ready and for packing up her room when I told you not to. But even as I say it now, it makes me more sad than angry. I can see now that it was coming from a place of love. It took me quite some time to get over what you did, and I'm still not sure that I forgive you for packing up Kelsey's room.'

He nodded. 'I just thought you should... you know... have Boo Boo. It meant so much to Kelsey and I shouldn't have taken everything away from you.' He was relieved that she had taken the bear; it was a step in the right direction.

Logan looked around at the homey kitchen where they'd shared so many meals, the lounge, carefully filled with their photos, knick-knacks and memories. He had returned some of the photos of Kelsey, but she hadn't noticed yet. He hoped to create many more memories here with his family.

'Dana—' he began, not sure of the reception he'd receive. 'I – I told you that I want to come home. But for good, not temporarily. I miss you. I love you.' He decided that honesty would work best.

She held Boo Boo up to her face and inhaled. 'I know she's gone, but I swear I can still smell her.' Dana looked up at him, the freckles across her nose standing out starkly against her pale face. She inhaled deeply again and his heart seemed to seize in his chest. She was going to tell him no, he could feel it, and he wouldn't blame her.

'I've thought about this day, Logan. I've thought about you coming back into my life and how I would handle it. What I would say. You hurt me, I mean really hurt me. You left our daughter as well and I'm not sure that pain can ever be fixed.'

Logan stared at her, his eyes pleading her not to say the words. 'Dana—'

'Let me finish, I need to talk.' He stayed silent, hands clenched, resting on top of the kitchen table.

'You ran away with my best friend, you cheated on me, you made me feel like I was doing the wrong thing, being a bad wife and a bad mother. You did that to me, Logan. What's to say that you won't leave me again for someone else? I don't think I can ever fully trust you,' she said bitterly. 'I need time.'

She stood up, pushing her chair back, and went down to the bedroom, taking Grace with her. That was all he could hope for for now. He couldn't deny any of what she'd said because it was all true. Every last, hurtful word. He'd done this to her and he too had to live with it.

* * *

Dana's phone rang on the bedside table; it was her mum. 'Hey, Mum? Everything OK?'

'I should be asking you that after everything that's happened. I was worried.'

'Sorry, Mum, I should have called you, but I just couldn't. Grace and I are back home now. Logan is here too.'

'Does that mean he's back?' her mother asked cautiously.

'In the sense that he's staying here for the near future, but that's all.'

'Why did you come back after only one night? Did Logan want you home?'

Dana said yes, because it was easier than telling her about the rattle she had found. She still didn't know how it had got there.

Had they been followed from her house to Matt's and if so, by who? Or, as she was beginning to fear, had she put it there herself? Last seen, it had been in the back seat of her locked car. Dana ran a hand over her face, the exhaustion beginning to get the better of her. She felt as if she was losing it. Too many coincidences in her life, easily explained away if she was threatening herself and wasn't aware of it.

'Are you getting back together?' her mum asked quietly.

'No, we're never getting back together, but we need to work some things out in terms of custody and the house, just haven't found the right time to talk about it.'

'Have the police caught that woman yet?' her mum asked, her voice dropping to a whisper as if talking about Melanie would somehow conjure her up.

'No, not yet, so I assume she's probably left town, what with the police looking for her and everything, but we're still on high alert around here,' Dana said. 'How's Dad?' she asked, worried that this new stress might bring on another stroke.

'He's all right, love, just so worried about you and Grace, the three of us are,' she said, including Alesha, but Dana ignored her. 'I was ringing to check on you, but also to see if we could have Grace come stay for the night. Sounds like you and Logan have some stuff to work out. We could have Grace, make it easier on you to have some uninterrupted time to talk.'

'Mum, I'd like that. I'll message you tomorrow and we'll work out a day.'

'All right. Talk tomorrow, love.' Dana knew that there was much more to be discussed with Logan. She hadn't even scratched the surface yet, so her mum's suggestion was a good one.

Dana slid the phone into her pocket, checked on Grace and walked down to the lounge where Logan was playing with his phone. *Texting Pippa?* she wondered. No, that was none of her business any more; besides, he said it was over. Dana felt a pang of loneliness. Pippa had been her best friend and she missed the closeness they once shared. She quickly shut her feelings down.

'Mum wanted to know if she could have Grace one night so we could have some time to talk about things, work out a plan. I said I'd call her tomorrow.'

'Why don't you ask her to have Grace tomorrow night? I know you still have things to say, things that I need to hear...'

He was right, he needed to hear what she had been going through. It was funny how quickly things could change. Last night she had been with Matt while he was trying to convince her that being a family with him was the best move she could make. And today she was back in her own home thinking about all the things she wanted to say to Logan, the other man in her life. Would she end up breaking both their hearts?

27

Dana woke up the next day, a headache at the base of her skull. She had cried herself to sleep after she'd set Logan up on the couch last night. He had looked a little forlorn when she had walked down the hallway, but she was not letting him back into her life that easily. He hadn't earned that right. It was hard, having him under her roof; she had just been getting used to being alone, her and Grace.

Dana's thoughts drifted to Matt. She knew she'd hurt him by leaving him, a fact made clear since he hadn't responded yet to the message she'd sent him last night. She didn't want to lose his friendship, she cared a great deal for him, but she had to do what she thought was best for her and Grace; she'd told him that.

Sighing, she pushed the covers off her. Grace was still sleeping but Logan was not; she could hear noises coming from the other end of the house. She found him in the kitchen making breakfast.

'Morning, how'd you sleep?' he asked as he slammed a cupboard door closed.

'Yeah, good, thanks,' she said politely.

They were dancing around each other but that was to be expected. It was a bit awkward with him living in the same house when they weren't together any more. She didn't quite know how to act with her soon-to-be ex-husband.

'Don't forget to call your mum about tonight,' he said.

'Tonight?'

'Yeah, babysitting Grace, remember?'

'I forgot. Sure, I'll call her and we'll go out to eat and have a discussion, I guess. I'm less likely to yell at you in a public place.' She meant it to be a joke, but she wasn't smiling; obviously there was truth to it. She looked at the time. 'I'll give Mum a quick call now, then have a shower and pack Grace's bag while I wait for the little miss to wake up.'

Dana padded back down the hallway thinking about how much her life had changed. After losing Kelsey she had felt sure no one would be able to pull her back into the land of the living. But once she'd had Grace, the little girl had turned out to be the only one that could begin Dana's journey towards healing. She still missed Kelsey every day, but it hurt a little less now. She could think of her without the soul-shattering pain that had previously accompanied her name or the memories. Dana looked into the cot at her sleeping beauty. She filled Dana's broken heart with love and hopefulness for the future, and Dana couldn't love her more if she tried. No one was going to take that from her.

Dana quickly had her shower, leaving the door cracked a little so she could hear Grace if she woke up, but she stayed sleeping. She was still sleeping when Dana had finished dressing, so she went and packed an overnight bag for Grace then went into the kitchen to make a cup of tea and call her mum.

'Hey, Mum, it's me.'

'Hi, love, are you calling to arrange us to watch Grace?'

'Yup, is tonight good for you and Dad?' she asked, turning on the kettle.

'Well, we might have to rearrange our busy schedules... Just kidding, we'd love to have her tonight.'

'I'll get Logan to drop her out later this afternoon. Will you be all right with her?'

'I have done this once or twice before,' Her mum joked.

'Right, Mum, Logan will see you later. I... uh...' Dana paused.

'Alesha won't come into the house. I'll ask her to stay in the bungalow until after Logan has picked up Grace tomorrow, OK?'

Dana could hear the pain in her voice as she spoke of barring her other daughter from the family home but that was Dana's only request, that Alesha not be allowed near her precious daughter.

'I'm not going to apologise for my feelings, Mum. I'm just not. If you want to see Grace, that's fine, and if it's too hard, then just say so, but that woman does *not* go near my child.'

'I understand. We'll see Logan later on.' Her mum hung up.

'Hey. Everything OK?' asked Logan.

'Yes. Mum is expecting you this afternoon, I thought you could go out after I've bathed Grace, save Mum from having to do it, but you'll have to drop her off, OK? I just...' She was aware that she was rambling and talking too fast, but she couldn't stop. Just the thought of the house made her think of Kelsey, of Alesha, of what she had lost.

She was close to tears and obviously Logan could see the pain on her face. 'It's fine. I'll take her out there. You don't have to come, all right? I know that house is hard for you to visit. Just stay here and relax. I won't be long anyway. This is a huge step for you, having Grace stay with your parents. And I'm proud of you.' He looked at her intently and she turned away, not wanting that level of intimacy from him.

She pulled out her phone and checked. Still no word from Matt. She heard Grace fussing down in the bedroom and hurried to pick her up and cuddle her. She squirmed in her arms. 'Sorry, sorry,' she mumbled, 'I just love you so much.'

While Dana spent the day feeding, playing with and bathing Grace, Logan stayed outside working on all of the odd jobs that he'd been meaning to do over the past few months, as if trying to cram everything into one day. She heard banging and the chainsaw ripping through the air and, looking out of the front window, she saw the branches that rubbed against the house were finally cut down, and now in a messy pile in the corner of the yard.

Once she had Grace bathed and ready to go, she kissed her little girl goodbye and fought back the swell of tears that came over her. This would be the first night that she would be spending away from Grace voluntarily and she was scared. Could she really let her out of her sight?

'Don't over-think it, she'll be fine.' Of course Logan knew what she was thinking; he'd always been good at reading her.

'Yeah, I know. Drive safely, please?'

'Will do,' Logan said as he clipped Grace into her car seat.

Waiting for Logan to come back was torturous, so she spent the time out on the back veranda. There were many toys of Kelsey's out there and she was sorting out what could be kept for Grace and what needed to be donated to charity. She heard her phone ring and dashed inside, thinking it might be Logan, that something was wrong. She pulled the back door closed behind her and picked up the phone. It was an unlisted number, but she answered it anyway.

'Hello?' she breathed into the phone.

'It's me.'

Dana paused.

'Pippa.' It had been a while since Dana had heard her voice, but before all this had happened, she'd heard it every day for years.

'Yeah, it's me.'

'What do you want?' Dana asked coldly.

'To talk.'

'I'm pretty sure we have absolutely nothing to talk about. The time for you to come and talk to me has been and gone. I have nothing to say to you now.' Dana was about to hang up on her when Pippa started to cry.

'I have nothing left,' she sobbed. 'You stole it all from me!'

'What? *I* stole it from *you*? Are you fucking kidding me?' Dana was furious now. 'You stole my husband, forced him to demand a divorce, you wanted to take my daughter from me, then you faked a pregnancy to keep Logan. What the fuck did I ever do to you, you crazy bitch?'

Dana hung up, absolutely livid. She was shaking, she was that angry. Clearly Pippa had taken Logan leaving her very badly. So badly that she had felt the need to call Dana and blame her for all the bad things that had happened to her in her life recently. It wasn't Dana's fault that Logan had left. Dana no longer had or wanted a say in Logan's life or what he did. He was a grown man who could make his own decisions.

Fuck Pippa! How dare she ring her and say those nasty things? Dana paced the house, trying to calm down, and when Logan walked back in the front door, her furious look must have been evident from the minute he saw her.

'What's wrong?' he immediately asked, looking at her thunderous face.

'Your girlfriend called,' she said, still in a rage.

'Pippa? What did she want?' He looked confused.

'She just wanted to tell me that I stole everything from her and that now she has nothing. I can't even speak about it, I'm so angry.' She continued to pace the lounge, wishing she could smash something, anything to get rid of her anger.

'Forget about Pippa, about Melanie and about... Matt. We have our own shit to sort out and we're going to start right now.'

She saw the flicker of anger in his eyes when he said Matt's name.

'So go get dressed. I'm getting you out of the house for a bit.' He smiled, trying to lighten the mood, but she just glared at him before stalking off to the bedroom.

Logan took her to the Italian place that they'd been to a few times before on date nights. Dana wondered if Logan remembered that or if it was just a coincidence. They ordered and sat through an uncomfortable period of silence where they waited for their drinks to arrive. Dana was just about to open her mouth when Logan started talking.

'Dana, I just want to say I know I—' He stopped talking abruptly and stared out of the window. 'Oh, no, you've gotta be kidding me,' he said shocked.

'What's wrong?' Dana asked, turning to see what he was looking at. Pippa stood outside the window, looking in at them from the footpath. 'Oh, God,' Dana said quietly. 'What is she doing here? How did she even know where we were?'

'She must have followed us from home. She's been watching us,' Logan said angrily.

'What the hell, Logan? This woman has it in for me. We should just leave. This is embarrassing. I want to go home. I should never have agreed to this anyway.'

She saw the look of frustration cross Logan's face. 'No. I'll go talk to her,' Logan said sternly, and Dana knew better than to try and talk him out of it.

She watched as he stalked towards the front door, Pippa nervously rocking from side to side. Dana, watching from inside, couldn't hear what they were saying but she could see enough to guess that Pippa was begging Logan to take her back, grabbing onto his arm, crying, trying to hug him. Logan was having none of it. He removed her hand, putting it firmly down to her side. When she tried to hug him again, he stepped back and held her at arm's length.

'Enough of this drama,' Dana said to herself. She settled the bill then walked out of the door and stood there awkwardly waiting. She had no idea what to do in this situation so she did nothing.

'We can still have a life together,' Pippa said. 'I forgive you for going back to her. I know it was only for Grace's sake, but we can take Grace. I can be her mum now. Dana's never been fit to be her mum, even you agreed.'

Logan looked over at Dana and she shook her head. She couldn't believe that he'd say that about her. And he wondered why she didn't want to take him back.

'Pippa, I'm sorry you're hurting, I'm sorry I hurt you, but we're not going to be together. You have to understand that.' Logan was firm but Dana could see that his words weren't getting through to her.

Pippa sobbed, tears running down her chin. 'You fucking bitch!' she yelled at Dana. 'You never made him happy. I did. You just sucked him back in using Grace. How could you do that to me?'

Dana didn't want to get into a slanging match with Pippa on the street, so she just turned and walked off, confident that Logan would follow her.

'You'll regret leaving me. You'll never be as happy with her as you could be with me,' Pippa screamed at Logan's retreating back.

They got into the car and Dana locked the doors. 'I can't believe that just happened. She followed us. I just... I'm shocked.'

They drove home in silence but when they went inside Logan said, 'I broke her heart, Dana. All I am is poison to those around me. No wonder you don't want me in your life.'

'I may not want you in mine, but I want you in Grace's.'

He smiled at the crumb she had thrown him. 'Tell me honestly, is there any way back from this? Can you ever forgive me?' He waited, holding his breath.

'No.' She didn't want to give him false hope. 'You said it yourself, you're poison.'

* * *

Dana exhaled her nervous pent-up breath then sat down on the lounge, Logan sitting next to her. 'Right,' she said once they were settled on the couch. 'Since we didn't get to do this before, we're going to do it now. I propose that you get your own place as soon as you can. You can't sleep on my couch forever – it's an uncomfortable reminder of my former life. We will share custody of Grace, with me being the primary parent. You can have her every second weekend and a portion of the holidays, but Pippa is to have no access to my daughter. Ever. Also, any future girlfriend isn't to meet my child unless I give my permission for her to do so. If you want to take me to court to fight it out, then fine, Mum and Dad will help me out, but I'm hoping that we can work it out between ourselves. And as for the divorce you wanted, you got it. How does that sound?' she said, hands folded in her lap.

'Clinical and like you've had a lot of time to think this over. Is this what you really want, Dana? To divide our family like this? Why can't we just be a family again?'

'Logan,' she said sternly. 'You broke this family apart, you utterly destroyed me and the only way I'm ever going to pick myself back up is for you not to be here, reminding me every day of what you did to Grace and me. Can't you understand that?'

'I guess. So you're saying there's no hope for us, ever?' He looked so sad and she felt sorry for him.

'You've already asked me that and I've already told you no. You're the father of my children and I love you for that, but that's all you're ever going to be to me. Grace's dad. I don't think you will ever comprehend what you've done to me. Losing Kelsey was the most devastating thing that ever happened to me and you couldn't or wouldn't see what I was going through. You couldn't even support me while I was grieving. It's like you and everyone else put a time limit on my grief and when I didn't meet it, you forced my hand. First with the meetings, then by packing up Kelsey's room. I can never forget the pain I felt when I walked into that bare room, every scrap of my daughter gone. You had no right, Logan. You *have* no right to tell me what to do any more. I'm moving on. Grace and I are moving on. You have no power to hurt me any more.'

Dana felt wrung out emotionally, every scrap of energy inside her expended. She just needed to finish this chapter of her life. To start fresh, a clean slate for her and Grace. *Murderer.* She also had to find a way to forgive herself for Kelsey's death.

'I'll start looking for a place tomorrow. Good chat,' he said as he stalked into the kitchen, slamming cupboard doors as he made coffee.

She felt like a heartless bitch, but this was about what *she* needed, not him. Dana unfolded herself from the couch and went down to the bedroom, closing the door gently behind her.

28

Mischa held the sleeping Grace in her arms. She stared down at her, marvelling at the child who had brought *her* eldest child back to life. She had watched in helplessness as Dana had spiralled out of control in her grief after the death of her daughter. She'd thought she had lost her for good. Losing Kelsey was the most harrowing and heart breaking thing that she could ever have imagined. She had tried to help Dana while she was working through her own grief.

It was hard on all of them – even her marriage to Robert had nearly broken down, although she had made sure no one had known that. When Dana had had the car accident and Kelsey had died, Robert had been torn apart by what had happened. Like Dana and Logan, Mischa and Robert had grieved in different ways, and he had found it hard to empathise when Alesha had gone off the rails; he didn't seem to want to know about it. In fact, he ignored her completely and had even tried to stop her from moving back home. Now when they saw each other, he was cold towards her. It broke Mischa's heart but she understood that she couldn't put everyone back together again. Hopefully Robert would forgive Alesha in time. She looked out of the back window; the bungalow was dark. Alesha must be having an early night.

As she thought of her youngest, memories from the day Alesha had tried to hurt herself came rushing back. Alesha had called her mum before she'd tried to hang herself.

'Mum? I'm so sorry.'

'Alesha, baby, I know you think you caused this, but you didn't. Kelsey was a little girl, she got away from us all. It was an accident. Neither one of you girls did this. You can't take it on, Alesha. Please.'

'I'm done, Mum,' she said in a clear voice, no tears now.

Mischa knew something had shifted within her youngest. Alesha hung up the phone after telling her mum that she loved her and then Mischa went into the lounge where her husband was sitting in his chair, reading the newspaper.

'Robert? Can you go over to Alesha's house?'

'Why?' he said, not even looking up.

'Because I think she's in trouble, real trouble.'

'She's fine, probably just being dramatic as usual. I'm not going over there. I'm in my pyjamas.'

Mischa was astounded and angered by her husband's lack of empathy. 'Well, I'm going over there. She just didn't sound right. Please, Robert,' she begged, 'come with me.'

He ignored her so she went on her own, grabbing her car keys and reversing out of the driveway, almost clipping one of his stupid rocks. Alesha lived on this side of town and Mischa drove above the speed limit the whole way, even running two red lights. Finally she pulled up at Alesha's place, just short of hitting the fence. She banged on the front door, then used her key to let herself into the house.

James was nowhere to be found. 'Alesha! Where are you?' There was no answer so Mischa went from room to room calling out her name, increasingly frantic. Eventually she found her. In the back yard. In the shed. She had a rope around her neck, and she was hanging from the wooden crossbeam.

'Alesha!' she screamed, grabbing at her kicking legs, trying to hoist her up onto her back. Alesha tried to kick her way free, but her mum held fast, grabbing at her bag with one hand to try and call for help. She managed to call emergency services then dropped the phone so she could grab Alesha with both hands. Mischa was panicking, not knowing what to do when she spied the small saw and the step ladder in the corner. Sliding out from under Alesha, she grabbed the ladder, forced it open and used the saw to cut through the rope.

How much more tragedy could their family take? Alesha had taken the time to write a note to her sister before going into the shed in the back yard, putting a rope around her neck, and kicking the stool out from underneath her. Mischa had read the note. It had consisted of five words.

I don't deserve to live.

Mischa had sat by her daughter's bedside for a week before Pippa had finally convinced Dana to come and visit. It hadn't ended well. But despite Dana not forgiving her, Mischa thought she could help heal Alesha. The night of Alesha's attempted suicide, James had been out with his mistress and didn't even bother to visit Alesha in the hospital, instead kicking her out of the house the moment she was released and returned home. It was natural that Alesha was acting secretive and detached from her family. She rarely came into the house, preferring to spend all of her time in the bungalow, alone. Mischa worried about her. Alesha went out even though she no longer had a job, quitting from her hospital bed. Her so-called friends had deserted her when James had. She was alone in the world except for her mother.

Mischa looked down at the baby who had started to heal one daughter, and contented herself that the other was recovering slowly too. Dana and Alesha, had they just talked, would have found out that they had a lot more in common than they thought, but Mischa no longer tried to coerce Dana into meeting her sister halfway. She knew that risked losing her again, and, by extension, losing Grace. This overnight stay was a huge leap forward in their relationship. She knew it, Robert knew it and Dana knew it.

Carefully Mischa put Grace into the bassinet, her back twinging as she stood up. She was not a young woman any more but she would do anything for this sweet little girl. She stared at her for so long that her husband came looking for her.

'She's such a gorgeous baby,' he said, 'so special. She brought our Dana back to us. I thought she was gone forever.' Mischa came around to stand in front of him, cuddling into his chest, feeling content when he wrapped his arms around her.

She wanted to ask him about his other daughter, Alesha, but managed to restrain herself. It wouldn't do to get into a yelling match this night. Mischa just wanted to stare at her granddaughter and remind herself that everything would be all right eventually, if they could just keep Grace safe. Robert hadn't had much to do with Alesha since she had moved home but, if she was honest, it had been like that since Kelsey had died. While they had never really delved into it, both she and Alesha knew that he blamed her. He rarely spoke directly to her and Mischa knew that it really hurt Alesha, as she and her dad had always been close before all this happened.

Robert and Mischa were woken soon after heading off to bed by the sound of screaming.

'What the hell?' she heard Robert say groggily, obviously not remembering that Grace had stayed over.

'It's Grace. I'll go get her. You go back to sleep.' Only it wasn't that easy. Despite being a mother of two and a grandmother, she could not settle Grace back down. The baby cried and screamed, her small face red and angry, tears sliding down to soak her sleep-suit. She didn't need burping; she wasn't hungry or needing a nappy change. Mischa was at a loss as to why she wouldn't stop crying. She walked up and down the lounge and kitchen rocking her until finally Robert came down and yelled over the baby.

'Call Dana, for God's sake. She's obviously wanting her mum.'

'I can't. She'll be asleep and this is the first break she's had since Grace was born.'

'Mish, she's getting more and more distressed. I'll go and call her now. She needs to go home.' Mischa felt like a failure; she should have been able to do this. With resignation in her voice, she agreed.

* * *

Dana was having the sleep of her life, deep and uninterrupted, luxuriating in the knowledge that she didn't have to keep an ear out for Grace, although she had put her mobile on the bedside table, just in case. She was dreaming of the tea parties that she used to have with Kelsey, squashing herself into the tiny chair and drinking imaginary tea, only there was one huge difference this time: an older Grace sat at the table with them.

'Do you want some tea?' Kelsey asked Grace, who nodded politely.

The big sister poured the tea, then passed a plate of imaginary biscuits to her young sister. 'Have a biscuit too,' she said sweetly.

'Thanks,' said Grace.

Dana sat there, beaming, watching the two loves of her life meet for the first time. It was a beautiful dream and when she heard the buzzing, she tried to ignore it. She didn't want to leave this dream, this special place, ever. Her Kelsey, alive, her two girls in one room together.

Dana felt the dream slipping away from her. 'Oh, hell!' she yelled before grabbing the phone, looking at the screen, instantly alert. 'Mum? Is everything OK?'

'It's Dad, darling.'

She could hear Grace screaming in the distance, and not her *pay me attention* scream; it was her *'I'm never gonna stop screaming'* scream. Dana sighed. 'I'll be there in twenty.'

She hung up and sighed again. Logan rolled over. 'That your mum?' he asked sleepily.

She wondered what the hell he was doing in the bed beside her, but she guessed that, while sleepy, he had probably come down to the bedroom on autopilot. She would talk to him about boundaries tomorrow. Now wasn't the time; she had to go and get Grace.

'Dad, actually, but I have to go and get Grace. She won't stop crying. It was great while it lasted.'

She dressed quickly and drove out to her parents' place. The closer she got to the property, the more anxious she became. She hated this place now but since Logan hadn't offered to go and get Grace, she had to. It felt as if it had only been yesterday since she had felt a thump and had got out of the car, leaning down to inspect the damage, only to find her baby wedged under the back tyre.

She shook her head. She couldn't think about Kelsey right now, not when Grace needed her. How things had changed. The driveway needed work, she thought as she bumped along the rutted dirt track. Dana pulled up at the front and opened the door, hurrying inside.

'Mum?' she called, following the screaming. Her parents were both in the kitchen. Her father looked up.

'Oh, thank God, Dana, you're here.' He hugged her to him and she wrapped her arms around him briefly.

'Give her to me Mum.' Her mum passed Grace to her and she began rocking her and talking to her in a soft and soothing voice. 'What's all this noise about, young lady?' Dana said in a sing-song voice. Grace stared up at her and slowly began to wind down, her cries eventually turning into hiccups before she drifted off to sleep in Dana's arms.

'Wow, Dana,' whispered her father, 'how did you do that? You're like the baby whisperer.'

'With *my* baby, sure.'

'I'm so sorry, darling, I thought we'd be able to handle anything, I guess we're out of practice with babies.'

'It's all right, things didn't quite turn out as planned anyway, so it's fine. I'll just take her home.'

Her father packed Grace's bag and carried it and the bassinet out to the car for her while she strapped Grace into the car seat. The baby barely even moved, she was so exhausted from all the crying.

'Thanks, guys, we'll try again another time, maybe just a day visit. She's obviously not ready for an overnighter just yet.'

'OK, honey. Love you.' Dana kissed her parents goodbye and reversed carefully, steadfastly refusing to think about... anything. The drive home seemed shorter than the one out to the property and she was pulling into her driveway in no time. She put Grace into the cot in her room; the baby snuggled down and let out a contented sigh. She smiled then touched her soft cheek lovingly. 'Love you, sweet girl,' she whispered.

Dana crawled back into bed, closing her eyes, hoping to salvage some more sleep before Grace woke up again. Logan mumbled in his sleep and Dana thought about waking him up to kick him out, then she decided not to – what was the worst that could happen?

29

The breeze swept through the old house, ruffling the curtains in the lounge as the back door was opened then closed. The house still smelt like toast, scenting the air delicately. The intruder cautiously walked into the kitchen and stared through the filtered streetlight at the table where the O'Connor family ate their meals. The hands of the clock above the kitchen sink glowed faintly green, ticking softly in the quiet house. It read just past one in the morning. Time was important.

The cottage was small, old, stuffy with no windows open, but this was the way it had to be. The stove, an ancient gas contraption, sat in the corner of the kitchen. The intruder stared at it for a moment before turning all of the dials to the on position. The distinctive smell of the gas began to quickly scent the air.

The intruder stood waiting as the gas filled the room and then inhaled deeply, the gas surging through lungs and tissue. Walking through into the lounge, the intruder used the light on the mobile phone to inspect the numerous photos that lined the bookshelves and were dotted around on the small nesting tables. Pictures of a little girl, with a huge smile, who looked just like her mum. There were family photos, Dad, Mum and the little girl. A nursery photo and a hand-painted plaster of Paris cat adorned the end of the lowest shelf. The intruder noticed that the photos that had been displayed then removed were now back again. The stained-glass window allowed no light into the room and the curtains were half drawn despite looking out onto an empty block. The intruder knew this, the intruder did their homework.

More photos, the young girl again, holding a bear, grinning into the camera. There was one photo of a baby. A different baby, eyes open, staring slightly to the left of the camera.

Kelsey and Grace.

The intruder knew this. How? The intruder knew the family. Knew that Dana would be home tonight and that Grace was gone. The intruder felt powerful knowing this intimate information about the family, almost as if they were a part of it... which was important somehow.

The gas was filling up the house now and the intruder was beginning to feel a little sleepy, a headache forming behind the eyes and the base of the skull. The intruder felt tired, as if they couldn't breathe properly; all the oxygen was being sucked from the room.

The couch looked inviting, but instead the intruder walked cautiously down the darkened hallway heading towards the front bedroom.

* * *

Matt paced the length of his house, mumbling to himself, formulating a plan about how to get Dana and Grace back. He wouldn't stop until they were his again. They were his family; they belonged to him now.

He drove to Dana's house and parked three doors down. The

lights were on, the two cars in the driveway until the pair of them came out and Logan's car reversed. Matt knew that his car didn't have a car seat in it, so obviously Grace wasn't inside. The house now sat wreathed in darkness, only the streetlight providing low light.

He saw a car pull out behind them, following closely, but he didn't take much notice of it. By the way Dana and Logan were dressed, he could tell they were going out. He felt the physical stab of pain inside his body, the betrayal that she would fall back in love with her husband so quickly. He felt used, abandoned. He had opened himself up to her. He had fallen in love with her. Life had been looking up, especially when she was in his house with her daughter – he could see a future together.

Then she went back to her husband, tearing his heart out. He should have known it wouldn't last. It never did. How could she do this to him? Should he follow them and watch through the window as they rededicated themselves to each other? While he had the urge to do it, he just didn't think he was strong enough to handle it emotionally. After all Logan had put Dana through. What was she thinking? He *had* to get them back. They belonged to him.

* * *

Pippa didn't even feel humiliated at how she behaved at the restaurant. She wanted Logan back at all costs and she wasn't above begging. She had been waiting outside, sitting in her car watching as Grace had been driven away and hadn't returned with Logan. She knew where he must have gone: the in-laws'. Mischa and Robert, people she used to be close to, back in another life. A life where she had a best friend, now a rival for Logan's love and attention. To see them sitting opposite each other had been more than she could handle. He'd never taken her out for dinner, so worried was he about other people's opinions of their relationship.

Logan had spotted her, of course, and she just knew that he'd apologise to her, take her in his arms and tell her everything was going to be OK. She chose to ignore the fact that Dana was there, staring at Pippa with sadness on her face. But instead of saying sorry, Logan was angry and she could see now how this might not have been the best time. She begged, she actually begged for him to come back to her. To try for another baby, to make Grace hers. She didn't care which, she just wanted him and a baby, a family. She grabbed him and he firmly removed her hand, she threw herself at him, hugging him as if she'd never let him go – if she had her way, she never would – but again, he removed her hands, stepping out of her desperate grasp. She cried, she knew she did, crying and begging, drawing the attention of the other diners who were looking out of the window at them.

Dana didn't gloat about winning, but she didn't have to. She was able to walk away, and Logan followed, leaving Pippa standing on the footpath, crying. She didn't follow them, there was no point; she knew where they were headed.

30

Staggering into the room, the intruder saw bodies outlined in the bed. Two bodies. Two people, not even aware that they were dying. It didn't matter. They would die together. The intruder bent down in front of Dana and whispered in a croaky voice, 'You don't deserve to live.'

There was something nagging in the back of the intruder's mind. Slowly scanning the room, the intruder saw the pale shine from the streetlight finally illuminating it. Realisation came slowly. It was a bag. A nappy bag.

Barely able to move, body hunched against an unseen force, the intruder walked on unsteady feet. The gas was filling the house quicker than anticipated; the intruder had to hurry. Hands gripping the edge of the cot, the intruder looked over the side.

There she was. *Grace*. What was she doing there? The intruder had watched her being driven away. Safe. Out of harm's way. The intruder let out a sob. With a trembling hand the intruder touched Grace's tiny chest. It wasn't moving. Grace was gone. The intruder had intended on her parents dying in their sleep, putting an end to all the suffering, all the hurt, all the pain, but not Grace. Grace wasn't supposed to be here. She was supposed to live. Why was she even here? What had gone wrong?

The intruder let out an anguished groan before slumping to the floor; the last thought before falling into unconsciousness was of Grace.

31

Melanie frequently sat outside Dana's house, across the road or up the street, watching her home every other day. It was a compulsion to be close to them both, especially Grace. It made her feel connected to the baby, who she loved with all of her heart. She had spied on Dana's house sometimes for hours on end, using her binoculars to get a better view. Tonight, she had been waiting outside for two hours. She knew that Logan was back in Dana's life. He'd reappeared after she had tried to take Grace. She had seen him at the house. Melanie wondered where Matt was in all of this; she hadn't seen him around lately. Tonight Melanie planned to rescue Grace and take her away and give her the life that she deserved. She would be a better mum that Dana ever could be. She loved Dana but Melanie felt she didn't deserve Grace. She killed Kelsey and Melanie wasn't about to let that happen to Grace.

Melanie would never be found by the police because she wasn't in the system. They could fingerprint the scene all they wanted to, but her name was fake and she had never told anyone where she lived, not even Dana. These days she didn't actually have a home. She lived in a motel; she paid cash for everything. Melanie had filled her room with baby things, just waiting for the right person to come along. Then she'd met the grieving mother-to-be at the support meeting that she frequented, one of many, talking about her dead daughter, Mindy, whom she sometimes forgot the name of and called Michelle by accident. Dana had pulled her up on it once, but she had explained it away easily and with a laugh.

The truth was, there *had* been a Mindy; she hadn't lied about that. Of course, her name wasn't Mindy. She wasn't felled by some kind of act of God either. Melanie had murdered her. Her husband had left her, that much was true, but their daughter was alive when he left. He had been having an affair and Melanie did hate him, but, at the same time, she loved him still. Melanie knew that she was fucked up; she'd accepted that a long time ago. She was crazy. She smiled. How many things did the word crazy excuse?

When her husband had left, she'd fallen into a deep depression. She'd spent a week or two in bed – she'd lost track of time – staring at the ceiling, wondering how on earth she was supposed to move on. He'd said he'd be back for his daughter but when he had come back, he'd found Melanie alive and his daughter lying dead in her cot. In her depressive state, Melanie hadn't bothered with her, leaving her in the cot until she'd stopped crying. She hadn't meant to kill her, it was just something that had happened. Melanie missed her every day. She owed her husband a child. That was what he'd said to her. A child to replace the one she'd murdered. So when Dana came to the meeting she was a grieving, vulnerable gift from God.

Melanie had watched the lights go out, plunging the house into darkness. That had been a few hours ago after she had arrived, parking a few cars away from the house, but still close enough to see what she thought was a figure dressed in dark clothing run from a car. The figure ran down the driveway and around to the back of the house. What the hell was going on? She decided to wait and see what would happen. Did she really see someone? And if so, who was it? What did they want? An hour later they still hadn't reappeared so Melanie did the only logical thing. She decided to go and see for herself. See if someone really was in there; besides, it was time to go and get her baby girl, finally.

She tried the back door. It pushed open easily, making minimal noise, but, to her, it sounded like a firecracker in the quiet house. She left it open for a quick getaway with Grace. The house was quiet, too quiet. There were no human noises, no snoring, no rustling of sheets as someone rolled over, stealing them from the other person. Melanie wondered how she'd react when she saw her beloved friend sleeping with the man who stole Dana from her. She crept through the darkened house, not game enough to use the light on her phone. As she reached the kitchen, she was hit with the smell of gas.

Oh, God! She hurried over to the stove and turned off the jets, wondering how long they'd been on. Her eyes watered and burned and she pulled her shirt up to cover her mouth, glad she'd left the back door open. It was a breezy night; it would clear out the gas quicker.

But why? To incapacitate them? Kill them? Melanie made her way to the bedroom and had just entered the room when she saw two lumps in the bed. There was just enough streetlight to see by. It was Dana and Logan. So she had taken him back after all. Silly girl, after all he'd done to her. She touched Dana's neck fearfully and she felt a slow and barely there pulse, but a pulse nonetheless. She didn't give a shit about Logan, but she grabbed Dana under the arms, pulling her from the bed, thumping her body on the ground before slowly dragging her through the house. When she got to the kitchen, she stopped to catch her breath before continuing. What if Logan lived? Dana would stay with him. But this way, when Dana woke up safe and sound, she'd know in her heart who had saved her.

Melanie dragged Dana out onto the grass, checking her breathing. She was alive and out of that house, that was a start. Melanie re-entered the house and went back down to the bedroom. She stared down at Logan in the half-light from the opposite side of the bed and whispered sarcastically, 'Couldn't have happened to a nicer guy.

It occurred to her that she still didn't know where the intruder was or who the hell it was. Melanie turned to walk around the other side of the bed to check if Logan was alive or dead when her foot connected with something solid. She bent down, hands outstretched. It was a body. She took out her phone and risked shining the light at the body. She gasped, the sound loud in the dying room.

She knew this woman – where did she know her from? Then it came to her. She was the person Melanie had seen sneaking into Dana's house on many occasions when Dana was home. The woman had a key. Who was she? And why did she break into Dana's house so often? What was she doing in there? Melanie had also seen her ducked down in a car watching the house, just as Melanie did. Why was *she* stalking her?

It was then that Melanie realised how she knew her: she had seen her photo on Dana's bookshelf. It was her sister, Alesha. She felt around for her pulse, which was thready but still there. So it wasn't only the men in Dana's life that were out to screw her over. The two men had fucked up *her* life, made Dana hate her, run from her, and now this woman was trying to finish what they'd started. No way. Melanie had no intention of saving *her* life. She saw a jumper lying on the ground, turned off her light and firmly pressed the jumper over Alesha's face. She didn't struggle. Her death didn't take long. Melanie checked for signs of life, but there were none. All she had left to do was take Grace and begin their new life together. She stepped over Alesha's dead body and leaned over the cot, waiting for the sweet sound of her breathing. But there was no sound and when Melanie bent down to touch Grace's neck, there was no pulse either.

Oh, God! Melanie panicked, leaning down to put her head to the baby's chest, but Grace was gone. Turned to stone by Dana's own sister.

Melanie reached down and lifted Grace up gently, cradling her in her arms, sobbing quietly. This house was a tomb. Grace didn't belong here. She picked her way back to the door, feeling light-headed, worried that she was going to pass out with her precious baby girl in her arms. She headed back through the open back door past Dana's body lying in the moonlight. She wanted to lean down and kiss her, to tell her how much it meant to her to have her baby, but she didn't have time, they needed to leave. Instead, she whispered, 'Thank you, Dana.' She began to feel better in the fresh night air, felt her head clear. She had to leave; she had things to do.

She took Grace down the driveway and over to her car. She had turned off the interior light earlier so no one would see her. She put Grace in the car seat that she had purchased for this exact reason and clicked the door closed.

She slid behind the wheel of the car, put her own seat belt on and pulled out onto the two-lane road. She still felt a little light-headed so she wound down the window all the way, letting in the coolish breeze to flush the toxin from her body.

She looked in the rear-view mirror at Grace. Silent, beautiful Grace. Now her Grace, finally. She stared at her cherubic little face, longing to get as far away from Dana as possible so she could never track her down, never find her and take Grace away from her ever again. Dana would wake up, knowing that her sister had tried to kill her. She would know in her heart that Melanie had taken Grace and know that she would be loved and cared for.

'Let's go, my baby girl.' Melanie smiled. She finally had her little girl. This was everything that she had desired for so long. She drove across the border and into the next town over, pulling up outside the pre-paid motel room. She'd paid for a week in advance. This was her final stop before she left the area altogether, starting her new life. She gently lifted the car seat from the back seat, careful not to jostle the baby. Unlocking the door, she set Grace down on the floor and sat on the bed. She quickly tapped out a text and waited.

It didn't take long for the quiet knock to rouse her from her thoughts. She had been thinking about Dana and how much she had genuinely loved her. They had started out so promising, but Melanie had been playing a part the whole time, someone Dana had liked, but sometimes that persona had slipped, her storylines getting tangled with real life. Nearly everything she had told Dana was a lie. The truth was stranger than any story Melanie could have made up.

Melanie opened the door. 'Took you long enough,' she said. 'Where have you been?' she asked, stepping back and opening the door wider.

'Don't start with me, Amanda. I'm not in the mood.'

Matt walked into the room, his large frame dwarfing her as he dropped a kiss on her head.

'I got her, Jude. I finally got her.'

He smiled, his white teeth showing through full lips. 'So you beat me, then? You were nowhere near close to getting Grace when I spoke to you the other day. I was so close too, after you tried to kidnap Grace. Told her I wanted to be a family, with her and Grace. She was at my rental house, falling for everything I was saying, then that fucker Logan convinced her to come home. I swear to God I could kill him.'

'He's not going to be a problem any more. Dana's sister saw to that.'

'What? Alesha? How did that happen?'

'No idea, but she's the one I've been seeing sneaking into Dana's house, so I'm guessing Alesha was the one messing with Dana the whole time. I knew I'd seen her somewhere – photos in Dana's house. You were so close to Dana, yet you still couldn't close the deal.'

She smiled cheekily as she teased him. Amanda and Jude, they had never been separated for long, always been drawn back into each other's webs. They still loved each other deeply despite their flawed marriage and wanted to be a family again. Grace was going to cement that family bond for good.

'So, let me look at my new daughter.' Jude was smiling. All Amanda had ever wanted to do was make her husband happy. When he'd left her, it wasn't because he didn't love her any more. He was a womaniser, he couldn't help himself, but he always came back to her. But that time had felt different for her – she couldn't handle it again and had become depressed. By the time he had returned to her, he had found their daughter still in her cot, dead.

Amanda waved in the direction of the car seat sitting on the floor near the bed. He walked over, then bent down ready to pick up his new baby daughter.

'What the fuck? Oh, God, what have you done, Amanda? She's dead!' he said, frantically feeling for a pulse in her tiny neck and finding none. 'You killed this one too?' he asked, incredulously. 'What's wrong with you?'

'Actually, no, I didn't kill her, Alesha did. But I still wanted her. We've both been trying to get this baby since the day we saw Dana at the funeral. If we hadn't been there laying flowers for our daughter, we would never have thought to follow them home. I delivered that support group flyer to her mum and dad's house, and everything would have worked out perfectly. But then you just had to swoop in and make it a competition, didn't you?' she said angrily. 'Make Dana fall in love with you. Did you succeed? Does she love you? More importantly, do you love her?' She paused, waiting for his answer. She had seen their relationship blossom and it had driven her wild with jealousy, making her act the way she had. She had been rude to him from the start, knowing that she wanted to be the one to bring Grace home, for them. Not him. She studied his face, one as familiar to her as her own.

'I was trying to help. Divide and conquer, but you were always so hostile towards me when we saw each other. It was kinda hot actually,' he said, walking across the room to her. He pulled her to him and roughly kissed her, not caring if he hurt her. It wasn't like what he felt with Dana. He finally realised what he had with his wife; it wasn't love. Trying to recapture the family they had together wasn't love.

As he kissed her his hands slid around her neck and began to squeeze. She tried to break his hold on her, her hands clawing at his, trying to free herself from his choking grasp. Tears slid down his face as his lips mashed against hers, even as he felt her struggles begin to weaken under his strength. *This* was love. Freeing someone from their pain was love. Another few seconds longer and he felt her go limp, her weight resting against his arms. It was finally over. He laid her on the bed, smoothing her hair down. 'I always loved you, Amanda. Be at peace with our daughter,' he whispered.

Jude grabbed his bag, took a final look at the woman he had loved for so long and the baby he so craved, and closed the door behind him. He slid behind the wheel of his car and turned onto the freeway, blending in with the rest of the cars. He would try again and he'd keep trying until he had his baby. Then *he* could finally be at peace.

ACKNOWLEDGMENTS

I really enjoyed the process of writing this book. It took me on a journey of self-discovery while I was working on it, something that I was not expecting at all. There's a saying... it takes a village. In this instance, I owe my thanks to my little village for listening and giving their opinions on endless plot twists, character arcs and the ending. Did they judge me for going on a murderous rampage? Nope, they never do. They know there's something wrong with me and love me anyway!

Love, loss, redemption. Three very powerful words on their own but put them together in one story, add in some imperfect characters and you have the recipe for a perfect storm that culminates in an ending that I hope you didn't see coming. If you picked the ending, well done to you, I'm impressed.

As always, my eternal gratitude to the amazing team at Boldwood Books, and a special mention to Sarah Ritherdon for her endless support and guidance. I may be on the other side of the world, but I've never felt alone.

Thank you, lovely readers, for spending some time in my world. I really hope you enjoyed your visit here. If you liked what you read here today, tell a friend, consider leaving a review, check out my other books and follow me on my socials.

As always, readers make the world go round.

Kirsty x

www.kirstyferguson.com
Twitter.com/kfergusonauthor
Instagram.com/kirstyfergusonauthor
Facebook.com/authorkirstyferguson
Bookbub.com/authors/Kirsty-ferguson

MORE FROM KIRSTY FERGUSON

We hope you enjoyed reading *Who Do You Trust*. If you did, please leave a review.

If you'd like to gift a copy, this book is also available as an ebook, digital audio download and audiobook CD.

Sign up to Kirsty Ferguson's mailing list for news, competitions and updates on future books.

https://bit.ly/KirstyFergusonNewsletter

Never Ever Tell, another gripping novel from Kirsty Ferguson, is available to order now.

ABOUT THE AUTHOR

Kirsty Ferguson is an Australian crime writer whose domestic noir stories centre around strong women and dark topical themes. Kirsty enjoys photography, visiting haunted buildings and spending time with her son.

Visit Kirsty's website: https://www.kirstyferguson.com

Follow Kirsty on social media:

twitter.com/kfergusonauthor

instagram.com/kirstyfergusonauthor

facebook.com/authorkirstyferguson

bookbub.com/authors/kirsty-ferguson

ABOUT BOLDWOOD BOOKS

Boldwood Books is a fiction publishing company seeking out the best stories from around the world.

Find out more at www.boldwoodbooks.com

Sign up to the Book and Tonic newsletter for news, offers and competitions from Boldwood Books!

http://www.bit.ly/bookandtonic

We'd love to hear from you, follow us on social media:

facebook.com/BookandTonic

twitter.com/BoldwoodBooks

instagram.com/BookandTonic